The Cult of the Gaal-El

Project Orpheus, Book 2

Frank J. Cavill

COMMUNITY:

All my books: relinks.me/FrankJCavill
Web: frankjcavill.com
X: @FrankJCavill
Facebook: facebook.com/frankjcavill
Threads: @frankjcavill
Instagram: @frankjcavill
Tiktok: @frankjcavill
Bluesky: @frankjcavill

Mail: frankjcavill@gmail.com

Copyright ©2024 Frank J. Cavill
All rights reserved.

Cover by:
Pilar García (pilargarcia.net)

Translation by:
Christy Cox

Edited by:
Peter Gauld

1
Quarantine

May 8, year 0
Asimov Space Station

Emily sat down on the bed and took a deep breath, as if this were the first time. It was a relief to be able to take off the exosuit after almost twenty hours of imprisonment. Despite this, she could not be happy. Private Parrish was dead and she was the one in charge of the team. She had promised Deputy Director Green that they would all come back safe and sound, and she had not been able to keep her word. The morale of the team was not what it might have been. They had barely spoken a single word during the whole return journey to the space station.

When they arrived they had to go through decontamination, then (still in their exosuits) make their way to one of the infirmaries in the Centrifuge which had been set up to accommodate quarantined patients. There, in the glass cells waiting for them, they would have to spend several days under observation. All of them resignedly accepted the rules which had been established; the risk of contaminating the whole station was high, since they had been in contact with a molecule of unknown origin.

The cubicles in the quarantine sector were individual, separated by walls of a transparent polymer, which meant that they could see their colleagues. Each had a small individual toilet made of an opaque material, to guarantee privacy. The room was very well-equipped, reminiscent of the intensive care unit of a hospital. It was obvious that it was ready for situations far more critical than this. It was not the Ritz, but at least they would be reasonably comfortable.

"How do you feel?" came the voice of Ada, the AI.
"Terrible."
"Can I do anything to help you?"
"No, Ada. Thanks, but I'm afraid there's nothing you can do."
A few moments later two people came into the area. They were

wearing hazmat suits, which allowed them to move through the quarantine area without risk of contagion.

"Good evening, everyone," came a woman's voice. "If you'd be so kind as to listen for a moment." All the occupants of the cells turned their attention to the newcomer. "I'm Dr. Sabine Schmidt, the Health Director of the project. I'm going to be in charge of coordinating the quarantine process. And this is Nurse Evelyn Brown."

Emily knew Evelyn well. She was the nurse who had put her in her cryogenization pod, and also the one who had attended to her battered ribs after the encounter with the black hole.

"During the next few days you'll be staying inside your cubicles, where you'll be under constant observation." She pointed to the cameras and sensors inside the cubicles. "I'll have to be very insistent about this and remind you not to leave your rooms, not even to help your colleague in the next cubicle. Even if it's a case of life or death. The station medical team will be there to take care of any event as quickly as we possibly can.

"You've been exposed to an alien entity, which means that we have to be meticulous. It could be that one of you is infected and the others aren't. Which means that whatever may happen in the next cubicle, don't try to leave your own."

After a brief pause, and making sure that her message had been understood, she went on:

"That said, and though some of you may be familiar with it, I'll explain the quarantine protocol. You'll be staying in this facility for a minimum of seven days." There were a few loud snorts of resignation when Dr. Schmidt revealed the figure. "You'll be fed in your cubicles," she went on. "Either Nurse Brown herself or one of her colleagues on duty will bring you your daily rations.

"Every morning we'll take blood samples, and also urine samples before breakfast. This means that you must avoid ingesting anything after midnight. You'll be given a small cup every day to use for the sample. There's no need for me to explain how, as you've had to do it innumerable times so that you could join the project. According to the results of the analysis for each case, we'll decide in a week's time whether or not you can leave quarantine. Any questions?"

None of them seemed much in the mood for talking, so Dr. Schmidt went on:

"Excellent. Now we're going to carry out a small preliminary check. The nurse will take your blood and then bring you something to eat so that you can go to bed. I'd imagine you'll all be very tired."

The doctor began to carry out the checks on one side, while on the other Evelyn began to take blood samples.

Emily was the third on the list for these, and when the nurse came into her cubicle the glass walls changed color, providing some privacy. She was pushing a small trolley with the equipment for taking the blood samples. Evelyn greeted her shyly.

"Hi there, Emily. How are you feeling?"

"Hi, Evelyn," she said sadly from the edge of her bed. "Actually, we're all pretty shaken. We've lost a comrade."

Emily was unable to hold back all the rage and grief she had been suppressing all day, and at that moment she collapsed. Tears began to well up in her eyes. Evelyn sat down beside her and put her arm round her shoulders in an attempt to comfort her.

"There, there," she whispered. "It's all over now."

"There was nothing we could do…."

"I don't even want to imagine what you've been through," Evelyn said gently. "And nothing I say can express the gratitude and the courage the rest of the ship's sending you. But you can be sure we're all with you."

The nurse's words soothed Emily, who was comforted by this show of gratitude. She wiped away the tears that were running down her cheeks

"Thanks Evelyn, I think I'm feeling better now. I'd been keeping it all inside me for hours."

"I'm here for anything you need. It's the least I can do for the first settler of the planet."

The trace of a smile appeared on Emily's face. She was still not fully aware of the repercussions these last three days were going to have on the history of humanity. No-one was. Unfortunately, though, there was no way she could enjoy the moment.

"I'm going to take your blood sample now," the nurse said. "Take off your sweatshirt and sit down in that chair in the corner."

Emily did as she was told and sat in the chair, which had an armrest. The nurse took a small rubber band from her cart and tied it tightly around her right arm, above the elbow. She took out a cotton swab, soaked it in alcohol and wiped the median vein in Emily's arm.

Then she took the small extractor syringe from the trolley and attached a small empty vial to it. She put the tip to the vein and pressed the small trigger. Emily felt a tiny prick, and when the device gave a light whistle the nurse removed it from the vein.

"There you are, that's it." She detached the half-milliliter vial which was now filled with blood. "The doctor'll come now to give you a checkup."

"Thanks, Evelyn."

"You're very welcome. And remember, we're all in this together. If you need me, you know where to find me."

"Yeah, many thanks. I mean that."

"I'll bring your dinner presently. I guess you'll be hungry." She opened the door to go on with the remaining blood tests.

Emily stayed in her cubicle for a few minutes, waiting for the doctor. To judge by the opacity of the one opposite hers, she was still occupied with Sergeant Cameron. On her right she saw Taro's cubicle darkening as the nurse went into it.

"How d'you feel?" Gorka asked from the wall which divided her own cubicle from the one on her left.

"Quite well, I suppose," she said, not entirely truthfully. "What about you? And Paula?"

"I'm fine, but Paula's rather depressed." He looked in the direction of the cubicle on his other side. "What we've all been through today… I don't suppose we'll ever forget it. But she… she lived through it at first hand."

Emily held back her tears as she imagined what her comrade must be going through, alone knowing that the moment she shut her eyes her memories would turn into the worst of her nightmares.

When he saw the look on her face, he did his best to comfort her. "Don't worry, even though we've got this glass panel between us I'm with her here."

The two nurses went on with their round of visits until Emily saw the doctor coming out of Taro's cubicle and heading to hers. Once again the walls of her own cubicle darkened the moment she came in.

"Hello, Dr. Rhodes," she said.

"Hello, Doctor."

"I think we met years ago, didn't we? When we gave you a check before you joined the project."

"That's right, I remember that day. Deputy Director Green was with me."

"That's right," the doctor said with a nod. "Well, I know you're all a bit emotionally upset. I don't need an academic degree to see that."

Emily forced a smile. "Yeah, I guess it's not our best day."

"That's understandable, and I can't do anything to change it, except to tell you that time heals all wounds." She paused and went on with her examination. "Physically, how do you feel?"

"I'm very tired."

"And apart from tired, which considering you've spent many hours without sleep could be normal, do you feel anything out of the ordinary? Any pain? Dizziness?"

"No, I think I'm okay."

"Right. Take off your shirt and stand over here with your back to me."

Emily did as she was told and went to stand in front of the doctor, who took her wireless stethoscope from her pocket and listened to her breathing through her implant.

"Take a deep breath." She listened carefully. "Now breathe out."

She repeated the process several times.

"Now turn around."

The doctor carried out the same process a couple of times more, then put her stethoscope back in her pocket. She took out a pen-light and checked Emily's pupils, first the right and then the left.

"Dilation of pupils normal," she said aloud. "Follow the light." She moved this from right to left, while Emily followed it with her gaze.

"Right, now open your mouth and put out your tongue."

The doctor checked this with the help of her pen-light.

"Good," she said, sounding pleased. "Do you feel any discomfort when I touch you?"

She passed her fingers along the nape of Emily's neck, then her throat.

"No, I don't feel anything."

"Raise your arms. Do you feel any pain in your joints?"

Emily tried to raise her arms while the doctor pressed down on them. "Not there either."

The doctor went on to check her ears and sinuses. When she had finished, she looked pleased.

"Okay, I think that'll be enough for now. Ada'll monitor you all tonight and let us know about any change in your sensations. But if you need anything, a sedative to help you sleep, or whatever, just ask us."

"At the moment I think I'm fine," Emily said. "But if you could be extra-careful with Engineer Gonçalves, I'd be very grateful. She had a hard time out there, she was there when… I mean…"

"I understand," the doctor said. "Don't worry, I'll be careful."

"Thank you."

The doctor left her room and went on to examine Gorka. Emily lay down on her bed and was thoughtful.

"What relationship could there be between the two alien species we just found on the planet?" she whispered to herself.

"Ada, show me images of the two alien races we saw today."

"Here they are," came the reply, and the AI showed her two images. "I chose the ones I think best show the faces of both species. One is Taro's recording, the other is yours."

Emily looked at both images carefully and even at first glance found a number of points that were enough for her to be sure these were different species. To begin with, there was the color of their skin: pale and dead in one case, very dark with a reddish tinge in the other. But certainly the most obvious point was the absence of eye-sockets in the skulls of the Yokai. Emily felt a deep internal shudder as she looked at the image of that terrifying creature. She could perfectly understand why Taro, and above all Paula, had been in a state of shock after the fray.

The species they had seen on the other side of the river was not in the least terrifying, if anything the opposite. The figures were clothed and were carrying fishing gear. The two individuals might well have been father and son, or grandfather and grandchild, on their way to enjoy a small family moment by the river. Even Sergeant Ortiz had said that he had often done this with his own grandfather.

She looked closely at their eyes, whose entire eyeballs were dark. They did not look threatening.

"Who are you?" she asked under her breath. "Are you the ones who developed the molecule? The ones who put up the obelisks?"

The exit of both healthcare assistants from the quarantine area brought her out of her thoughts. The taking of blood samples was over, although they still had to bring them their dinner. She had not had time to think about it, but she had not eaten in hours, barely a few small mouthfuls of the insipid mash the exosuit offered. She realized that she was very hungry.

Dinner was not long in coming. Evelyn reappeared at the door with another trolley and a couple of piles of trays. Once again Emily was the third on the list. The nurse came into the room with a tray and pulled a small table out of one side of the bed so that she could eat.

"Ada, tilt the bed forward," she said.

Emily's bed folded forward, with her on top of it. In a matter of seconds the small table and the tray were in front of her. This time there were meatballs made of artificial meat with a mushroom sauce and sautéed vegetables. There was broccoli, but she did not mind this at all and dug into it.

"Enjoy your meal," Evelyn said. "I'll come back for the tray later."

"Thank you very much, Evelyn," Emily said with half a meatball in her mouth.

"I can see all of you are hungry," she said with a laugh as she went to the door, "and that's a good thing. I'll leave you in peace."

Emily finished her dinner in the blink of an eye. She was so hungry that she even mopped up the tray. She was able to digest it in peace for a while until Evelyn came back for the empty tray. She also brought the cup for the next morning's urine samples.

"You know how it works, don't you?"

"Yeah, don't worry."

"Right. If you need me for anything, tell Ada to let me know, or else call me directly."

"Yeah, thank you, Evelyn."

"We'll be turning the lights out in a moment. Try to rest, it'll do you a lot of good."

She turned the lights out five minutes later and they were left in the dark, except for some emergency lights placed strategically along corridor and ceiling. Although she knew it was going to be hard for her to get to sleep, Emily felt tired, so she closed her eyes. Despite this, she could not stop going over what had happened. Once again she looked at the images of both species.

"Chad," she called in a low voice, "are you awake?"

"Yes," came a voice through her implant. "I'm afraid it's going to be hard for me to get to sleep tonight."

"Yeah, me too. I can't stop thinking about those two alien species."

"To be honest, I can only think about one of them," the biologist said. "Every time I close my eyes I hear last night's growls. Just thinking we might have to share the planet with those devils gives me the creeps."

"Yeah, well, that too. But you think it's clear they're different species, right?"

"Absolutely clear. They have as much in common with one another as you or I do with either of them. We have four limbs, we walk upright, and not much else."

"That's how it looked to me," Emily said. "But it looks as though both species coexist in a very confined space. How can that be?"

"I don't know. I hadn't thought about that yet. But maybe the others live in cities with artificial light that keeps them away, or perhaps the Yokai can't cross the river. It looked pretty deep and full."

Maybe Chad was right, maybe they did not coexist. A simple but timely geographical accident had kept both species apart.

"Do you think the others are dangerous?" she asked.

"I wouldn't know what to say. But the fact that they were carrying fishing gear and wearing clothes makes me think they're different. Although that doesn't mean anything."

"Why haven't we seen any settlement from the station?"

"There's a lot of vegetation on the planet," Chad said. "And you saw it can be very tall. They might live in the same forests."

"I hadn't thought of that," Emily admitted. "I guess it doesn't make much sense to keep going over it. We're not going to be able to get much more information out of the images."

She decided to try and rest a little, even knowing she was going to have trouble getting to sleep. Despite this, she succeeded.

She woke up later on, startled by the sound of blows.

"Ada! Open the door, for God's sake!" Gorka was shouting in his cubicle.

Emily saw him pounding on the door, which despite his efforts stayed firmly locked shut.

"What's the matter?" she asked.

"Gorka wants to leave his room," Ada said.

"Why?"

"Paula is weeping, she's having nightmares," Gorka said as he turned toward her. "Tell Ada to let me into her room. She's having a hard time… please…"

Emily stopped for a couple of seconds to think. She was still sleepy and not sure what to do.

"Control those cubs of yours, kid!" they heard Captain Garth shout from his cell.

She ignored the captain's comment. "But we're not allowed to, Gorka. Suppose either of you gets infected with some illness? You'd infect the other one."

"I don't care, Emily. I just want to comfort her and get her calm. If one of us is infected, the other will be too. We could all be, or else none of us."

Emily weighed up the options in silence.

"Ada, let him go to Paula."

"Thanks," Gorka said. "Thanks very much."

The door opened, leaving Gorka free to get into the cubicle next to his and hug poor Paula, who had barely been able to sleep a wink because of the nightmares and the anguish of remembering what she had been through only a few hours before.

"Evelyn?" Emily called. "Are you there?"

"Yes, Emily. I saw it. As far as I'm concerned there's no problem, I won't say anything. But tomorrow morning make sure everyone's in their own cubicle, please."

"They will be. Thanks, Evelyn."

2
Mission Report

June 1, Year 0
Asimov Space Station

Emily woke up that morning without any further shocks. She went into the toilet and filled the cup with the urine sample, then enjoyed her first shower for several days. They had all slept quite a lot, almost nine hours, but in the space station it was still night and the lights were still out. Despite this, many of her colleagues were already awake.

She untangled her hair with a brush and dried it with a towel, in the absence of a dryer. She put on clean clothes, came out of the toilet and looked through the dividing glass. Gorka was back in his room by now, passing the time lying on his bed. She was hoping she would not have to give Dr. Schmidt any explanations, though deep down she knew she had made the right decision.

"What sort of a night did she have?" she asked.

Gorka straightened up on his bed.

"She had trouble getting to sleep, but afterwards she managed to rest." He glanced in the direction of Paula's cubicle. "In fact I think she's still asleep."

"That's right," Ada confirmed. "Her readings are normal. She's resting quite well, all things considered."

"Thanks, Ada," Emily said. She turned to Gorka. "And how are you?"

"All things considered, pretty well. I wanted to thank you for what happened last night," he added after a pause. "I couldn't leave her by herself."

"Don't worry. I think we'd all have done the same in your situation."

Gorka nodded and lowered his head.

"You know I wasn't enlisted on the Copernicus?" he went on.

"No, I didn't know."

"I was going to get married. We had everything ready," he told her with tears in his eyes. "She was a flight attendant with Stellar Aerospace, the same company that built a lot of the ark modules. There was a terrorist attack. It wasn't the ones who attacked the Copernicus afterwards, Global Justice. At least they ended up catching that lot. It was some sort of isolated fundamentalist group that didn't even have a name.

"They'd put the company on their target list to try and attack the project indirectly. That same morning we'd had an argument, I don't even remember what about. I left the house without saying goodbye, I thought I'd see her two days later and we'd make up. In the afternoon I found out her flight had been blown up."

"Oh my God!" Emily said, aghast. "I'm really sorry, Gorka. I had no idea."

"No-one knows about it. I don't even know why I'm telling you now. Months later came the Copernicus business and I got a letter from my old Ph.D advisor Dr Patel. I decided to enlist in the project, without much hope, quite honestly, as the ark had been destroyed. But at least I'd try and join forces as best I could against the ones who'd taken everything away from me."

He paused briefly and carefully rubbed his eyes.

"In fact I wasn't thinking about having a new life. I just wanted to help rebuild what those bastards had destroyed. But then I met her. That same day, when we came to the Asimov for the first time. Her smile, her cheerfulness, made me feel something I thought I'd never feel again."

He swallowed. The words seemed to stick in his throat.

"And to see her like that, the way I did after yesterday's attack, it breaks my heart. I don't like to see her like that, I can't allow it, not again."

Emily could not help the tears coming to her own eyes. Gorka's sad story was moving. Now she understood the way he behaved even better.

"I'm really sorry, Gorka, I really am. And I appreciate your trust. I know it's not easy to talk about things like this. But don't worry, I'm sure she'll be all right, she's stronger than she looks. And besides, she doesn't only have you, she has all of us."

"I know," Gorka said. "Thanks for listening to me."

"You're welcome. That's what friends are for."

The lights came back on in the whole area. They could hear voices on the other side of the entrance door. Doctor Schmidt came in with a male nurse, both wearing their protective suits.

Evelyn must be resting, Emily thought when she saw the doctor's new assistant.

"Good morning, everyone!" the doctor called. "Time for a new test! Get your urine samples ready to hand over to Nurse Conte."

The nurse and the doctor began their rounds, one room at a time. As with the day before, Emily's room was the third on the nurse's list.

"Good morning, Dr. Rhodes," the nurse said courteously.

"Good morning." Emily handed him the sample, which she had ready.

"Thank you. Now if you could kindly sit down and uncover the opposite arm to yesterday's."

Emily offered her left arm for him to take the sample. When he had finished, he told her that the doctor would be in shortly, and left.

"How do you feel this morning?" the doctor asked her when she was by her side.

Emily shrugged. "Fine. I don't feel anything strange, if that's what you mean. And I was able to rest a little."

"I'm glad to hear that. And in spite of that, do you feel tired?"

"No. Not more than usual, anyway."

"Strange symptoms? After dinner, maybe?"

"No, nothing at all."

"Did you go to the bathroom as usual?"

"Yeah, I guess so," she replied thoughtfully.

The doctor checked her terminal again. "I can't see anything strange in your graphics. This afternoon we'll get the results of yesterday's tests, and this morning's as well, so I'll come back for another visit with the results. That's all for now."

"Many thanks, Doctor."

She was left alone again, not really knowing what to do or how to fill her time there.

"How are you all?" she asked when the doctor and nurse had finally left the quarantine area.

"Fine, all things considered," she heard Private Ferrara's quiet answer.

"Yeah we're fine here too," Balakova said. She was in one of the corners, opposite Wilson the co-pilot.

"Fine," Paula said faintly.

An uncomfortable silence fell after the last answer. No-one felt much like talking. The loss of Private Parrish and the discovery of a dangerous alien race which might jeopardize the whole mission had taken its toll on the team's morale. Emily was not sure how to cheer them up, as it was her first experience of leading a group of settlers. What can you say when you have lost a colleague in terrible circumstances?

Nor was she given much time to think of anything to say that could improve the situation either, because two people wearing hazmat suits burst into the area. She could not see who was going into Captain Garth's room, although from his complexion she supposed it was Commander Bauer. The other opened her door to find her sitting on her bed.

"Hello there," the deputy director said.

"Hello, David."

"How do you feel?"

She bowed her head sadly. "I've been better."

"I can imagine." The deputy director sat down beside her. "But I'm glad to see you in one piece. You had me very worried."

"I couldn't bring them back all safe and sound…" Once again the tears were threatening to overflow. "I'm … I'm sorry."

"Emily," the Deputy Director said, sounding very serious, "none of this is your responsibility. Everyone who chose to enlist in this project knew what we were up against and the kind of dangers we could face. I know Private Parrish was a good lad, and at the risk of sounding a little callous, he knew the risks too. What you have to do now is get up from this bed and carry on, just as you've always done. You're a lot braver than you think, Emily."

"But all these people are expecting me to make the right decisions! I haven't even been here for three days and I've lost a comrade already!"

"Someone very intelligent and very close to you once told me: 'Great results are only obtained with great sacrifices.'"

"But that person isn't here."

"He's a lot more present than you think."

Emily said nothing and thought about her father again. It was true that he was a great leader. He had raised all this out of nothing. He had negotiated with governments, with very powerful people, and had managed to recruit the very best. But now he was not with them any longer and she would have to learn to live without him, without his advice.

"Even though you may have trouble seeing it now, I know you're going to come out of this. And you'll do that finding you're a lot stronger. All you have to do is trust yourself, and then you'll find the true leader who's there inside you."

"Thanks, David."

He changed the subject. "Now we need to talk about the mission."

"Of course, that's the only thing that matters now."

"The members of the Board of Directors are very concerned about the events of these last few days. First it was the discovery of the molecule, then that obelisk, whatever it is, and the electric storm. Finally, two encounters with different alien species. I think that's more than enough unexpected events for three days."

They heard loud shouting from Captain Garth's cubicle, whose dividing walls were not translucent now. And although Emily could not understand what the argument was about, she knew perfectly well what the conversation between the captain and his superior was about.

She nodded. "Yeah, I guess everyone'll be pretty nervous."

"I need to have a report on the mission, as complete as possible, so that I can make the right decisions."

"Yes, of course, I'll tell Ada to put together what's most relevant and help her make a summary for you."

He had noticed her concern. "What's bothering you?"

"From the point of view of environment, the third site is far and away the most acceptable of them all. The flora and fauna are far more abundant, and there's a definite increase in bio-diversity." She paused, as if the images were coming back to her mind. "But there are those creatures there, the Yokai."

"Yokai?" he asked curiously.

"Yes, that's what we've named them. It was the name they gave to a kind of demon in Japanese mythology. Poor Taro gave them the name after the fight."

"We've seen the images. They're chilling."

Emily bowed her head. Something was worrying her.

"What is it?" he asked.

"I don't know... I... I think about the Galileo... and I can't help thinking the Yokai might have destroyed them."

"I don't think that'll be what happened. I can't see any of those creatures with enough technology to bring down a space station the size of the Galileo."

She seemed to realize how baseless her fears were.

"Maybe you're right, but then what are we supposed to do now? Confront these creatures? Why have we found another alien species only a few kilometers from the site of the attack? Are there more species in other places on the planet?"

"Do you think both species have some connection with one another?"

"I was thinking about that yesterday," she admitted. "And Chad thinks the same as I do. From the biological point of view they don't seem to have anything to connect them. There are too many differences."

"But don't the Yokai attack the other species?"

"I can't answer that. Maybe they're able to keep them away, or perhaps the Yokai don't dare cross the river that separates them."

"Whatever the truth is, we'll need to keep the accident site under observation and see if we can pick up any kind of movement in that sector of the planet."

"Yeah, but we think the Yokai are vulnerable to ultraviolet rays, which means we won't find them by day."

"How do you know that?"

"By their blood," she explained. "After Taro got rid of dozens of them, the blood that had been shed nearly boiled at dawn."

"So the light of Kepler's sun kills them?"

"It looks like it, though we weren't able to recover any sample. And besides, they didn't seem to like normal light either. Paula had a light on her helmet, and they didn't even go anywhere near her."

"Well, that's very good news," the deputy director said cheerfully. "They're vulnerable."

"Yes, but we don't know their habits or where they gather. But above all, we don't know how many of them there are. In a matter of seconds dozens of them appeared, but we don't know how big their population is, or whether there are different settlements."

"We'll find out in time."

"Are you thinking about establishing a base at the third site?" Emily asked, sounding rather alarmed.

"You yourself said that from the environmental point of view it's the most suitable. If we can manage to take the Yokai out of the equation, or at least keep them at bay, it would be the most profitable one in the long run. And also it would give us the chance to study them in depth."

"And yet something tells me they're intelligent creatures," Emily said.

"Why d'you think that?"

"They seemed to have a leader."

"A leader?" he repeated in surprise.

"Yes. You need to watch the images carefully. Behind everything that happened there was a mysterious figure. My blood freezes when I think about it. It didn't take part in the whole set-to, it just seemed to be watching and giving orders."

"Okay, we'll bear that in mind. Tell me about the other species."

"They're different. Don't ask me why, but they seem to be civilized and of course they don't look half as threatening. They were wearing clothes and carrying fishing gear, so there's no doubt they're intelligent. They seemed just to be on their way to a family afternoon fishing."

"And have we given them a name?"

She smiled. "No, not yet. Although we could call them Keplerians until we have a better name."

"It seems appropriate," the deputy director said. "Do you think we should try to contact them?"

"Yes, they might be the key to understanding the Yokai."

"On the other hand they didn't seem to have a very advanced technology, right?"

"No, they hardly even had wooden tools. But we need to be very cautious. We can't make the same mistakes we made in the past. We need to be more respectful toward the inhabitants of the area than we were on Earth, historically speaking."

He indicated the other room. "True. I guess you're talking about Captain Garth,"

"He went crazy when he saw the two individuals going to the other side of the river. I don't trust him at all, quite honestly."

"We'll try not to let him get out of hand. We'll be organizing a military command to inspect the accident area and try to find out more about the Yokai."

Emily was startled by this. "Are we going back to the area?"

"We certainly are. Commander Bauer, and the rest of the Board as well, think it's vitally important to find out what we can about our new neighbors. Getting a proper view of the dangers we're facing is going to be crucial when it comes to establishing a base."

Emily was silent. He was right. Once they had seen the danger the planet offered them, it seemed logical to assume that they would have to fight it. If not, they would never have enough assurance to establish a colony. Wherever they went, they would be threatened.

"Do you think the Keplerians could be behind that alien structure you found?" he asked. "Or the molecule?"

She shook her head. "I don't know. We don't know anything about them. Although I'd say they're unlikely to have been the creators. Especially considering the level of technology that'd be necessary to create something as complex as that. Chad says the molecule is far more complex than the largest molecule created by man. And Taro is impressed by the alloy of the obelisk, so it must be something out of the ordinary. And seeing how difficult it was to get hold of a small sample, I agree. Whoever created those molecules must have been very advanced technologically, and so far we haven't found any trace of that."

"I'd imagine they'll both be anxious to begin work on their analysis."

"I should think they'll be halfway up the wall right now," Emily said with a smile.

"Let's hope this quarantine doesn't last much longer and that you can all get on with your lives."

"Yeah, that'd be ideal. Morale's a long way from what it should be, and being shut up in here doesn't do anything to improve it."

"I'll try to keep you informed. But we're already working on getting new expeditions ready."

"What's the plan?"

"The main one now is to bring the ark closer as soon as possible so that we can deploy the satellites and long-range drones. Director Patel and his team have been working on them. With eyes in the sky, everything'll be safer and easier."

Emily nodded. "That goes without saying."

"I'd like you to lead one of the three expeditions we're planning."

"Three expeditions?" she asked curiously.

"Yes. Firstly, the one on behalf of the military command we've talked about. This very day we've started bringing more soldiers out of cryostasis so that they can take part. The commander and the captain will have to decide between them what conditions it's carried out in. The second expedition will be concerned with recovering as much of the Icarus as possible. We'll also be evaluating the damage as best we can. We might not be able to rebuild it in the short term, but the idea is to do it in the mid or long term. This second expedition will be concerned with making an evaluation of the damage and getting back whatever can be reused, such as the ship's rover."

"And the third?"

"That's the one you'll be leading, under my supervision. Apart from establishing an operational base on the planet, one of the objectives of the project has always been to contact some intelligent alien species. That means your main goal will be to try to establish contact with the Keplerians. Of course you can have the team you like, including some military personnel for the protection of the rest of the team."

"I'd like to have the same ones, if possible. And if they're willing, obviously."

"Of course, there's no problem on our side," the deputy director said. "So it'll depend a hundred per cent on every one of your comrades."

"Good. In that case, you can count on me."

"Wonderful! And if you need any other profile we have available in the project, a linguist, an anthropologist or any other kind of specialist, don't hesitate to ask."

Emily smiled. "As a linguist, always assuming we can use the satellites, we can use Ada herself. I think she'd be the most suitable help. Unless she doesn't want to, obviously…"

"I'm afraid that as an artificial intelligence built to collaborate in the project I have no choice," the Ai said jokingly. "Even so, I'll have to check my busy schedule."

"I'd better go now," the deputy director said. "I'll keep you up to date with the agreements that are made."

Quite unexpectedly, when the deputy director had left the room Emily once again felt that she was looking forward enormously to setting foot on the surface of the planet again and beginning the work of establishing a permanent base.

3
The analyses

July 2, Year 0
Asimov Space Station

After seven days in the quarantine area, the twelve members of the expedition were tired and bored with staying shut up within the same glass walls. Playing virtual reality games and spending the day lying down was beginning to take its toll on all of them. They needed to get back to work and at last leave behind that routine of blood, urine tests and enforced rest.

Despite everything, they had gradually recovered motivation and a certain cheerfulness. Paula was sleeping better by now and had even got her smile back. In fact she was even able to joke every now and then. Despite this, Gorka, concerned about her emotional state, had not left her side for a moment.

The only one who did not take part in the conversations was Captain Garth. The impression they had was that his way of looking at things did not fit in with that of the rest of the group. Even Sergeant Cameron seemed rather less stiff than usual.

They were all confident that they would be released that same day, assuming Dr. Schmidt thought it convenient. No-one had revealed any worrying symptoms. With the possible exception of Chad, who had briefly gone down with a common cold which had eased a couple of days later with the appropriate medicine.

As was usual by now, Dr. Schmidt came into the area. This time, however, she was alone.

"Good morning, everyone."

They all waited expectantly, each in their cubicle.

"As you know, you've been in quarantine for a week," she began, and paused dramatically. "I'm very pleased to tell you that the results of the tests carried out over these last few days have shown no sign that would make us think any of you are infected with anything. So we've decided to end your period of isolation."

"Great!" Wilson the co-pilot exclaimed.

"At last!" Private Ferrara was heard to say, with enormous relief.

The doctor raised her arms for attention and finished her explanation.

"At the same time, and before I let you leave this place, I'd like to have a word with each of you individually."

The announcement rather dampened the general enthusiasm, although it failed to quell the badly-hidden delight. They were going to be able to pick up their lives again and go back to being some use to the project.

Emily had to wait for the doctor to see several of her colleagues before she came to her room.

"Hello, doctor," she said

"Good morning. Keen to get out?"

"Quite honestly, I'm dying to."

"Don't worry, I'm not going to take up much of your time. As you know, we've studied and compared all the analyses we've made during this time with other tests of yours we already had."

"Is everything all right?" she asked. There was a slight tremor in her voice.

"Oh yes!" The doctor smiled. "Don't worry, there's no problem. All the indicators seem correct, your health is good. However, we've detected some slightly abnormal levels of calcium in your analysis. In itself it's nothing bad. Since we began to be woken from cryonic sleep we've been introducing foods which are rich in calcium, or which facilitate its absorption. Hence, as well as including certain food supplements, we're following diets rich in leafy vegetables, like spinach or broccoli."

Emily nodded with a touch of resignation, understanding the motives which explained her diet.

"The goal is to induce strengthening of the bones to match the increase in gravity we're going to experience on the surface of the planets. In fact several of you are showing similar symptoms."

"What could that be the result of?"

"Oh, lots of things, don't worry," the doctor said reassuringly. "It might be completely normal. The mere fact of being exposed to a higher gravity could stimulate our own metabolism to start working on its own. All the same, I have to admit that this sort of thing usually takes longer, not just a matter of days. We'd like to make a test. Don't worry about it at all, it's completely harmless and painless. I'm talking about a densitometry."

"Densitometry?"

"It's to measure the bone density of your body by emitting a small quantity of radiation."

"And what are you expecting to find?"

"Well, given that the amount of calcium in your blood is rather in excess of normal, the logical thing would be to expect that your bones have started to absorb that calcium, and hence to be growing stronger."

"That doesn't sound bad."

The doctor smiled. "No, not bad at all. In fact it would be wonderful news, because it would confirm that the diets designed for the project are working."

"All right, then, no problem."

"Good. We'll do it right away."

"Great."

"Wait outside if you don't mind, while I talk to the rest of your colleagues."

Emily crossed the decontamination chamber, while the doctor went into Gorka's cell. At last she was leaving the quarantine area.

"Hi, Emily," Evelyn said. "Free again!"

She gave her a cheerful smile. "Yup."

"Come with me, your colleagues are over here waiting."

Emily followed her across a corridor. When they came to a small space with several closed doors, Evelyn opened one of them and motioned her in.

"Wait here," she said, "We'll test you all presently."

Inside the little waiting room Private Ferrara, Pilot Balakova, Chad and Lieutenant Beaufort were waiting for the doctor.

"Emily!" Chad greeted her with his usual effusiveness. "We're out of prison at last!"

She gave him a hesitant smile. "Yeah, we seem to be."

"How are you?" Robert asked her.

"I'm fine. What about all of you?"

"Very well," Private Ferrara said. She was obviously delighted to have finished the quarantine.

"Fine," the pilot said softly.

"Are they giving you a densitometry test too?" Chad asked.

"Yeah," she confirmed as she sat down. "I presume we're all here for the same reason."

"That's right. The doctor told us our calcium levels are a little higher than normal."

"But that's not a bad thing, is it?"

"Well, not up to certain levels, at least," Chad explained a little more seriously. "If the amount of calcium in the blood goes over a certain level could turn into hypocalcemia."

"That doesn't sound so good."

"Excessive calcium in the blood might turn into hyperparathyroidism, and some types of cancer show an overproduction of calcium in the blood. But don't worry, it's nothing science hasn't found a solution for. At most it means we'll be given some drug to block the overproduction."

"I'm not sure you've altogether reassured me," she admitted uneasily.

A little later, Evelyn opened the door and asked Lieutenant Beaufort to go with her. Two minutes later the same happened with Private Ferrara. They seemed to be following the order in which they had left the quarantine zone. When her turn came, Evelyn made her go through a door with the *Danger: Radiation* symbol above it. On the other side, Dr Schmidt was waiting.

"Right, Emily, take off your uniform and lie down on the table."

Emily took off her clothes and shoes, left them on a chair and was left standing there in her underwear. Luckily the room was warm. She lay down on the table, following Evelyn's instructions. Once the nurse had made sure she was in the right position, with one arm at an angle of forty-five degrees, both she and the doctor left the room by a side door.

She was able to hear the doctor through her implant.

"You'll have to stay still while the robotic arm does the scan," she explained. "It'll only be a few seconds, but we're going to do a scan of your forearm and hip."

Emily began to hear an electrical hum, and saw a robot arm stopping only a few centimeters from her own forearm. Once its work was done the arm moved down to her hip and followed the same procedure before returning to its original position.

"Now we're going to scan your spine," Evelyn said when she came back. "Turn around and put your head in this hole so that you'll be comfortable. You need to keep your neck as straight as possible."

Emily duly adjusted her position and the process was repeated, though this time all she could hear was the hum of the arm as it moved.

"That's it, you can get dressed." Evelyn said a little later.

The doctor came over to her when she was finished dressing.

"Is everything all right?" Emily asked.

"Oh yes, everything's fine," she reassured her. "As there's a higher level of calcium in the blood, we thought it'd be best to check whether that calcium was being absorbed properly. And in fact it's quite surprising."

She touched something on her terminal and showed Emily two x-rays of her forearm.

"If you look carefully, the bone seems to have a higher density in the image on the right, which is the one we've just taken.

"And is that normal?"

"Well, it's unusual to see such a positive change in such a short time, but it's wonderful news. Your bones are a lot stronger than before."

"That sounds good."

"Yes, it certainly is."

"So can I go now?"

"Yes, of course. That's all as far as we're concerned. Although we'll do a follow-up on you all during the next couple of months. We'll let you know."

"Thanks for everything," Emily said as she left.

She had not even got as far as her room when she received a notification from the deputy director, who wanted to see her in his office.

"Hi there, Emily. I'm glad to see you out of observation at last."

"So am I, quite honestly."

"How do you feel?"

"Pretty well rested. It's what I've been doing mostly all this time."

"And the rest of the team?"

"Doing well, considering what they've been through."

"Wonderful," he said with a smile. "Little by little things'll get back to normal. Remember the other day we talked about setting three operations in motion, right?"

"Of course."

"Well, I need you to start getting the expedition ready. We want to set up a small scientific base on the surface where we can study planetary conditions. For that we'll deploy a few living modules, thanks to the filters Dr Patel has been making with his engineers."

"Where have you decided to locate the base?"

"At the third site."

"What!?" she exclaimed in surprise. "And what about the Yokai? What happens if they attack the base?"

"Easy now," the deputy director pleaded. "Director Patel himself and Commander Bauer have been discussing the matter. The facilities will be robust enough to avoid an attack like the one you suffered. Even so, I understand your reluctance, so for added security there'll be ultraviolet lamps along the whole camp perimeter, together with motion detectors, radar and defense systems that are sufficiently robust."

"Robust defense systems?" she asked warily. "I thought that with the loss of the arsenal we had no weaponry on the station."

"That's not altogether true. Some of the transport vessels and vehicles in the hangar are fitted with light weapons. A few months ago I asked Director Patel to adapt some of the autonomous machine guns that are fitted to some rovers so that we could use them as defense of the bases."

She thought for a few seconds about what he was suggesting and weighed up the dangers and implications.

"All right, I suppose it'll be enough."

"That's great! This very afternoon we'll be starting maneuvers to put the station in a closer orbit. Ada's done the orbital calculations that'll keep us aligned with that site. And we're going to launch three satellites to allow us to have correct geotagging for the contingent on land. And we'll be able to start generating models of atmospheric forecasting, as well as getting real-time feed of the situation at the base."

"But the satellites don't have as much precision with infrared lenses. At night we'll still be depending on ourselves."

"True, but the satellites will let Ada monitor the sensors installed around the base at every moment. You'll be fine. Anyway, if anyone, you included, doesn't feel up to going back to the planet, that's fine. We'll look for other volunteers."

"I don't think there'll be any problem with the rest of the team. And certainly I don't intend to stay up here."

"We still have a few days left to reach that point, but we have to start organizing the expedition. In the first place we're going to set up a habitat that can hold thirty or so people. They'll also have a fully-equipped lab, a provisions store and a gym, so that they can get used to the gravity. A wide enough perimeter will be set up, and the different modules will be connected. In a few days we should have the base ready. Even so, we'll keep it uninhabited for as long as we need to as a precaution. Ada will be checking the area until we make sure it's safe." He paused for a moment, then went on. "For the moment we won't use any of the water purifiers. We'll use the station supplies to install a tank large enough to survive for months. After that, in the mid-term, we'll channel the water of the river you all saw and install a treatment plant to supply the base. Electricity will be generated using solar panels and accumulators for the nights. Although Director Patel's weighing up the possibility of installing a small fusion reactor, he doesn't trust the panels to give a good supply with the amount of light the sun gives. I'll also need you to ask your scientists what equipment they think is absolutely necessary so that it can be installed on the base."

"I'll have a word with them."

"The plan, once the satellites are deployed, is to carry out a military raid on the accident zone. Captain Garth will lead a detachment of fifty soldiers who'll try to pick up the trail the creatures left after the attack. We'll try to reach their point of origin. Once the mission's over, retrieval of the equipment from the Icarus will begin, along with setting up the base itself. You'll keep the rover you left there, for longer trips. Of course you'll also have a transport for base evacuation in case of extreme danger, or if you need to cover long distances."

"Will we have a pilot?"

"Yes, I've spoken with Captain Mei, and she's offered Balakova for this mission. Both Wilson and Balakova will take part in the scouting mission."

"Great," Emily said enthusiastically. "Sounds like a good plan."

"I think it is."

"What are the main objectives of our mission?"

"To go on with the work of exploration, including analysis of samples, studying the geography of the place, working out a plan to connect the water supply to the base, and the most important thing: gathering information about the species on the planet which seems to be more… let's say friendly."

"And establish contact with them?"

"In the last resort, yes."

Emily could not help feeling a small shiver when she thought of herself making conversation with an alien, however civilized those aliens might appear. This would be a historic milestone, and once again she was going to be the one responsible for it. It was difficult to keep up with circumstances.

"I'll have to go over the protocol for contact with an alien species."

The Deputy Director smiled. "I fear you will. Though I'm sure between you and Ada you'll know how to manage the situation wonderfully."

"Mathematics is the only universal language," Ada put in. "I'll be delighted to be able to use all my knowledge to communicate with the new species."

"I think I'm going to need a lot of that knowledge," Emily admitted.

"That's enough for now," the deputy director said. "But I suggest you have a word with the rest of the team. We need to plan the jobs that need to be done from now to the start of the mission."

"I understand."

"And I hope to have you here tomorrow. The deployment of the satellites will represent an important stage in the success of the project."

"Which will also allow us to get a better idea of the area for the future base," Emily said in conclusion.

"That's the idea."

"All right then, see you tomorrow." She got up to leave the office.

Once outside, she went to her room. She needed to put her thoughts in order before confronting her next objectives. The first of these would be to gather the team together to share the news with them.

"Ada, send a message to all the civilians in the team. I want them to join me in the mess hall at lunchtime."

"Done."

She spent the morning going over the images of the location which Ada had selected. The lie of the land was familiar, as they had been evacuated from the planet from that same spot. It was an enclave with vegetation that was not too dense and a clear space wide enough for the installation of the base.

The river ran close by, little more than a kilometer away, which meant that channeling the water to the base camp did not seem an impossible mission. They would have to install suction pumps to carry the water from the nearest point. Perhaps in the future they would be able to channel it from a point further up the river, but that would require more work.

A few minutes before lunch she left her room to go to the mess hall. She was struck by the number of people she saw. A lot of soldiers had been awakened. Most of them had just joined the crew and would form part of the military expedition which was to track the Yokai from the site of the attack. She could not see any of the ones she knew.

She had trouble finding the table where Gorka and Paula were waiting.

"Hi!" she called. "How are you both feeling?"

Paula got up, smiling as usual. "Pretty well. I'm much better, calmer."

They embraced warmly.

"Thanks for everything, Emily," she said. "Gorka told me what you did for me."

"There's no need. I'm just glad you're feeling better. And I can't believe I'm not the last one. I got here before Chad and Taro!"

Gorka laughed. "Those two are sure to be wrapped up in their test tubes and microscopes and haven't realized what time it is."

He had hardly finished saying this when both of them appeared in the hall. They too were surprised by the number of soldiers who were there, but they did not find it hard to locate their friends waiting at the table.

"Sorry to be late," Chad apologized, "we were busy with some analysis and completely forgot the time."

Their three friends burst out laughing as they found that Gorka had been right.

"What is it?" Chad asked, not understanding the reason for their laughter.

"I think that answer was exactly what they were expecting," Taro said.

They went to the menu machine, and each took their own. To Emily's surprise, this time there was no broccoli in hers. As it was rich in calcium, her tests had caused a slight change in her menu. This time she had rice, sautéed vegetables and wild mushrooms, plus a small steak and yoghurt for dessert.

She waited until they had finished eating before she broached the subject.

"I wanted to speak to all of you," she began, "though in fact I'm not very sure how to do it. Deputy Director Green has asked me to lead a group to establish the first of the permanent bases on the surface of the planet."

There was a heavy silence.

"I'd very much like you to come with me," she went on after the pause. "But I'll understand if you don't want to, in the circumstances. You can be sure there won't be any trouble if you refuse, it would be perfectly understandable."

They looked at one another.

"I'd already taken it for granted that we'd be going back," Taro said. "And as long as the project lets me, I'll follow you wherever you go."

"So will I," Chad said.

Paula cleared her throat, with Gorka's eyes fixed on her.

"I … well, actually Gorka and I have talked about it," she began, "and we decided that in spite of everything, we still want to be part of this."

"Bravo, Paula!" Chad said.

"I'm sure I'll find it a bit difficult to get over the fear at first, but if I'm with all of you I'm sure I will."

Gorka held her hand under the table to convey his support.

"And I'll go wherever she goes," he added.

"You've just made me the happiest woman on the planet," Emily said. "Well, on the station," she corrected herself.

"When do we go back?" Chad asked.

"I don't know for sure yet. The station is going to move to a closer orbit this afternoon, and that'll allow us to deploy the satellites tomorrow. At least this time we won't be going in blind. All the military personnel you can see here today"—she waved her hand around her— "are going to follow the trail of the Yokai and retrieve all the equipment possible from the Icarus. After them, it'll be our turn."

"So is that why there are so many soldiers?" Paula asked.

"That's right."

"Do we have to prepare anything?" Taro wanted to know.

"More or less," Emily said. "A group of technicians and engineers will install the base, led by Director Patel. The modules are prefabricated, so they just need to be assembled. And apart from having the satellites at our disposal, they're going to install some extra security systems."

"What do you mean?" Chad asked curiously.

"Motion sensors, ultraviolet lamps and an autonomous machine-gun."

"Wow! That sounds like big stuff."

"Yes, though we'd better hope none of it will be needed."

"What can you tell me about the goals of the mission?" Paula asked.

"To analyze the environment," Emily said, "to work out how to channel the water from the river to the base, and to try to make contact with the alien species we saw on the shore."

Everyone at the table looked taken aback when they heard this last point.

4
Eyes in the sky

July 3, year 0
Asimov Space Station

She got out of bed feeling well-rested. Knowing she was free from quarantine had allowed her to sleep far more relaxedly, though her back ached after nearly ten hours in the same posture. Since they had gone out in their first mission, the station high command had decided to adopt the Keplerian day of twenty-nine hours. This meant that they would all have to stay awake longer than usual, but also that they would rest for longer. Even though this might seem trivial, getting the body accustomed to these new hourly cycles was not as easy as might have been hoped. Emily had been noticing something like jet lag, but every day now she was resting a little better.

She got ready to attend the satellite launch from the station bridge. When she arrived there were already a lot of people with Deputy Director Green: a small group of assistants, Commander Bauer, Captain Mei and several of their second officers. She could not see Director Patel anywhere, so she supposed he would be directing the operation from the hangar.

"Morning," she said as she sat down beside the deputy director in one of the chairs that were free.

"Hi, Emily," he whispered back.

"Has it started?"

"No, but we're almost ready."

On the radio they could hear the different voices of technicians and mission control making the final checks prior to the launch. In the multitude of images projected on the wall they could see the different views from each of the active cameras. Some were directed at the hangar door, others at the space outside and several at the planet, which could now be seen from very close.

"Have we finished the process of changing orbit?" she asked.

The deputy director nodded. "Everything's gone as expected. We're in a geostationary orbit at a little over fifty-two thousand kilometers from the surface."

"Great!"

Through the radio they began to hear the countdown which announced the launch of the first of the satellites.

"Hangar door open," a male voice announced. "Beginning deployment in 10…9…8…"

Everyone on the bridge saw the small ship carrying the satellites preparing to leave the station.

"3…2…1… Starting lift-off."

The unmanned vehicle, specifically designed for this purpose, appeared in the hangar door. On it was the first of the satellites, its wings still folded. As the vehicle moved away from the door, the cameras turned to follow its path from different angles. The ship was moving cautiously during this first exit maneuver.

Once it was a safe distance from the station it speeded up. Soon it was far enough away for all the cameras along the station hull to have a very similar point of view.

"Transport reaching thirty-two thousand kilometers from the surface," the off-screen voice announced. "Beginning deceleration."

The vehicle began to turn ninety degrees forward. It was now showing its underside to the station cameras.

"Destination position reached. Beginning deployment of satellite."

Through the camera of the vehicle itself they could see the satellite separating and beginning to carry out the deployment maneuver. Its photovoltaic plates were gathered accordion-like on four of the six sides of the cubical satellite. After deploying completely, the satellite began to receive the light of the star of the solar system and was able to generate the necessary electricity to start working.

Two powerful ion propulsors drove it forward. A few minutes later, the off-screen voice confirmed what they were all expecting to hear.

"Satellite in position."

They heard applause through the radio, supported by those on the bridge. The process had taken so long that by the time the satellite finally reached its final position, the unmanned vehicle had returned to the station and was already in position to take off carrying the second satellite.

The process was repeated twice more with as many satellites, though the tension was now considerably less. By the time the morning was over, all three satellites were operative and sending a constant stream of information to the station.

"Well, that's the first step," the deputy director said with relief. "Congratulations to all, Director Patel."

"Thank you, Deputy Director," the chief engineer replied by radio. "This is a small success for all of us involved."

"Remember, the ceremony will start in twenty minutes," the AI reminded her.

Emily gave a start. She had thought she had more time left. She checked her wrist to see the time superimposed on it. She was late. She was at Ada's control center, and time had flown by while she was checking the correct flow of information from the satellites. She had taken too long checking the real-time images of the site for the future base. Especially considering that she had not seen any activity other than that of some small, curious herbivore.

"I'm running late!" she exclaimed as she hurried out of the hall. She had to go to her room first to put on formal clothes.

There was going to be a memorial service for Private Parrish, killed in action after the accident to the Icarus. Neither she nor the rest of the team had fully gotten over that fateful night, or the outbreak of violence they had been through. It was going to be a very emotional ceremony.

Twelve minutes, she thought as she went into her cabin.

She got ready as fast as she could and put on the most elegant civilian clothes she had: dark trousers and jacket over a white blouse. She put on a dash of perfume and fixed her hair in a bun, without fussing too much about the final result. Then she ran to the atrium, where the ceremony was due to take place.

When she reached it, it was packed. Including the final additions, the station army had now reached a total of seventy-five. Together with the rest of the non-military crew which had come to the atrium, this meant some three hundred and fifty people. All the military personnel were wearing dress uniform, which made it harder to recognize anyone familiar.

Those she could locate were the remainder of her civilian comrades, Taro, Chad, Paula and Gorka, who were also looking better.

"Hi," she said. "Have I missed anything?"

"Wow," Chad exclaimed. "How elegant you look!"

"The occasion deserves it."

"You haven't missed anything," Paula said, sounding moved. Tears had come to her eyes even before the ceremony had begun.

"The military staff hasn't arrived yet," Gorka said.

"But there are more people out of the pods all the time," Taro pointed out. "That explains why we're finding it harder and harder to find any room in the mess hall."

"The army's getting ready for the mission," Emily pointed out. "It's logical for there to be more. Facing up to the threat from the Yokai is one of the major priorities of the project."

Chad was standing on tiptoe. "We still haven't seen any of our own people. Mind you, it wouldn't surprise me if they'd passed in front of our noses without our noticing. They're pretty elegantly turned out, but as they're all in the same uniform you can't recognize any familiar faces."

"Who are you calling elegant?" came a voice behind them.

They turned and saw Private Ferrara and Sergeant Ortiz in their dress uniform, which consisted of a dark blue jacket with a lapel collar and silver buttons, paired with straight-cut trousers in the same shade with a yellow stripe down the sides. Their shirts were white, with the addition of a tie the same blue as their suits. The uniform also included a dress cap bearing the symbol of the Orpheus Project.

"Wow!" Chad said. "It's hard to recognize you all dressed up like that!"

"You're looking very elegant," Emily said. "I'm very pleased to see you."

"Yeah, except that I'd rather be dressed up for other reasons," Ferrara said.

"How are you doing?" Paula asked them.

"I guess we have our moments," Ferrara admitted. "It's not easy to get over a thing like that."

Paula put her hand on her shoulder and gave her a hug. The soldier hesitated, but ended by sharing her grief for the loss of the young soldier. Emily was moved by the gesture. She knew that the ceremony was going to be very emotional, but it had not even started yet and she was feeling very moved.

"Commander on deck!" came a voice.

The soldiers ran to stand in line so that they could salute Commander Bauer, who was coming into at the atrium with a largish entourage. Beside him were several officers and NCOs, all in dress uniform, showing their stripes and a range of decorations.

They could make out Sergeant Cameron, Lieutenant Beaufort and Captain Garth. There were also three other soldiers Emily did not recognize. After the top commanders came another seven soldiers carrying an ancient ceremonial rifle. The procession crossed the empty space at the front and stopped in the exact center of the hall.

A bugle began to sound. The notes of *Taps*, the classic tune the New United States Army had spent centuries playing in ceremonies like this, and which the International Army had adopted for the project, filled the hall.

Emily watched Sergeant Cameron and Lieutenant Beaufort moving with slow, synchronized steps to a mast carrying the Project Orpheus flag in one corner. While the bugle went on sounding, both of them tugged at the strings to bring the flag down gradually.

Once it was in their gloved hands they took it to the center of the hall, where Captain Garth was waiting with three other officers. Between the six of them they spread the flag out completely, then in a very ceremonious manner proceeded to fold it.

They did this six times until it had been transformed into a blue triangle bearing the Project Orpheus symbol in the center. Captain Garth, who was standing at the final stage of the process, held the flag while everyone there gave a military salute with surprising coordination.

The commander accepted the flag, walked to the dais and laid it gently on the lectern. All the soldiers stood to attention before him in a perfect choreographic movement

The commander took a deep breath and began in a firm voice:

"Dear friends and colleagues, comrades in arms. Today we are gathered here to pay homage to a hero, a brave soldier, who gave his life in defense of the project, and of humanity. A man who, despite his youth, possessed great courage and indomitable strength. A man who will inspire us all with his bravery and sacrifice.

"There are no words to express the sadness we all feel at the loss of one of our own. But despite this pain, we should remember that this project is stronger thanks to the service of Private Brian Parrish. His sacrifice will never be forgotten, and will always be a reminder of how complicated the page of history is which humanity is writing here, on Kepler-442b."

He paused, looked at the crowd and went on firmly:

"But we can't simply stay here lamenting his loss and weeping over his absence. We need to go on fighting for the freedom and justice he always defended. We need to keep going, but always remembering his sacrifice and his example. We need to honor his memory by working for a better society, for a society where the ideals this young man fought for may become reality for all of us, and for future generations.

"At this moment we need to unite as a single people, a single voice, to honor our fallen comrade and offer comfort to those who loved him and who will certainly miss him. Their pain is our pain. We will strive to keep his memory alive and go on fighting for those very convictions for which he sacrificed himself."

The crowd showed its approval of the commander's words as he went on to finish his speech:

"In the name of the Project Orpheus army, I would like to thank Private Parrish for his service and sacrifice. Rest in peace, comrade. Your legacy will forever be remembered. May your spirit guide us and inspire us in our struggle for survival and justice. We will always remember you with respect, gratitude and admiration."

The commander left the lectern with the folded flag under his right arm and joined the remainder of the officers who were still in the middle of the hall. At that moment a group of seven soldiers armed with rifles raised their weapons, aimed at the ceiling and shot three volleys each: twenty-one salvoes, as military tradition required.

The soldiers saluted during these fusillades, and with this the high command of the project brought the ceremony to an end.

Next Captain Garth stood to attention before all the army personnel and shouted:

"Break ranks!"

Immediately everyone relaxed and began to disperse and mingle with everyone else. Soon Private Ferrara and Sergeant Ortiz went back to their friends.

"That was really nice," Paula said. She sounded very moved.

Taro nodded. "Yes, it was."

"Had you known him very long?" Paula asked Ferrara and Ortiz.

"Actually, not really," Ferrara said. "Just since we were woken up from cryo. But when you're thousands of light years away from your family, the people around you end up being your new family. He was someone very special, without a trace of anything bad in him. I'm going to miss him a lot."

"We'll all miss him," Taro said. "He was a good man."

Lieutenant Beaufort and Sergeant Cameron soon joined the small group of explorers. Emily was impressed by the lieutenant's bearing, his dress uniform and all his decorations.

"How are you all holding up?" he asked.

"Pretty well," Chad said. "Although it's hard to think we'll never see him again."

They were all silent for a few moments in memory of their dead comrade.

"It was a very emotional ceremony," Emily admitted.

"It certainly was," the sergeant agreed. "But I really hope we don't have to see another," she added with rage in her voice.

"We'll find them and get rid of the lot of them," Ferrara said firmly.

"When's the operation planned for?" Emily asked.

"The captain wants to find the Yokai and deal with them as soon as possible," Sergeant Cameron said.

"I have a proposal," Emily said. "I hope it won't upset you. It might not be the most suitable moment, but everything's going so fast I don't know when that would be. As you know, we're going to be the first settlers on the planet. Our main mission is to establish the first of the permanent bases on the planet. The idea is that it'll be a scientific camp, but we need a military presence to guarantee our safety when we're moving across the planet."

She paused for a moment before putting what was on her mind into words.

"I think I'm speaking for everyone if I say we'd love to have the four of you as part of our mission. We make a good team. So would you like to come with us? Of course you're under no obligation," she added hastily, "if you don't want to or if you'd rather be assigned to other kinds of missions, we'll understand."

"Are you kidding?" Private Ferrara said. "You can count on me for whatever you need."

"I'm in too," said Sergeant Ortiz. "I've had quite enough of being locked up here."

Cameron and Beaufort exchanged a glance, then the lieutenant spoke for both of them.

"Of course, Emily. Always assuming the commander gives his approval."

She smiled. "I'm pretty sure that won't be a problem."

5
Counterattack

July 4, year 0
Asimov Space Station

The programmed alarm woke Robert at half past five in the morning. He roused himself and did a series of arm- and back-stretches. That morning he decided not to go to the gym. After a week in quarantine, and even though he had carried out a program of calisthenics daily, he intended to save his energies for the long day ahead of them. He wanted some peace and quiet before they set out, so he had breakfast by himself. The two transport vehicles of the operation against the Yokai were due to leave at half past seven, just when the sun was beginning to emit ultraviolet radiation in that zone of the planet. This made any chance of meeting them face to face remote, or at least so they hoped.

Captain Garth had outlined the strategy of the operation. Their goals were clear: to find the creatures' lair and reduce it to ashes. For this he was going to count on the help of fifty soldiers and some of the arsenal which had not been lost in the black hole

There aren't many of us, Robert had thought, *but there aren't many more exosuits available.*

After doing full justice to his breakfast, he went to the hangar where the transports which were to take them to the accident site were waiting. He decided to take one of the pods closest to the mess hall. He waited a few minutes for the pod to come back from the other end, but as he was waiting, someone came out of the one on the other side of the corridor, the one which led to the Engineering zone.

"Emily!" he said in surprise. "Good morning!"

"Morning, Robert!" She too had not been expecting to find anyone as early as that.

"Isn't it a little early to be up?"

She gave him a nervous smile. "Yes, I suppose so."

"Couldn't you sleep?"

"It's just that I woke up early and I've been puzzling over something I wanted to try with Ada. Well, you know… one of those things that tend to occur to you when you're in bed."

He smiled. "And couldn't it wait?"

"No," she answered shyly, "I'd be sure to forget all about it later on."

"I hope you come up with a lot more interesting things in bed." She bowed her head, blushing. "I mean… about work," he hastened to clarify, and his pale cheeks immediately turned red.

"Are you leaving for the planet now?" she asked, to change the subject,

"Um… yes." He was still a little nervous. "At half past seven."

She checked her watch. "Looks as though you have plenty of time."

"I couldn't sleep either."

"That doesn't surprise me, my blood freezes when I think about coming across those creatures again."

"As long as we move during the day, I don't think we'll have too much of a problem."

Her deep eyes were looking at him with concern. "Even so, be careful, okay?"

"Don't worry," he said reassuringly. "I'm trained for this type of mission. And besides, I won't be alone."

"I know, but I can't help worrying,"

"Everything'll be fine." he reassured her.

"And look after the others too."

"We'll be looking after each other."

"Then please do everything you can to come back in one piece, please."

"We will."

Finally he was able to enter his pod, and the moment he lost sight of Emily he hit his forehead hard with his hand.

You idiot! Couldn't you think of anything else to say? 'I hope you come up with a lot more interesting things in bed.' Honestly! How stupid can you get!

He made an effort to erase that unfortunate episode from his mind. This was not the best day for having his mind on other things, nor on any task apart from that of surviving. He left the pod and went, without holding on to anything, to the hangar the shuttles would be leaving from.

It was far larger than the hangar for the Icarus. In it dozens of transport ships of different sizes were fastened to the floor. He crossed part of the platform and floated down the ladder, holding on to the many bars set along the blocks. Once below, he crossed the runway and reached two of the ships. There a small team of technicians were finishing the process of tuning. He could see the pilots, Wilson and Balakova, who would be piloting one of the transports carrying twenty-five soldiers.

Captain Garth gave a grunt when he became aware of his presence in the hangar.

"At ease, Lieutenant. I hope you had a good rest, because we've got a busy day ahead."

"Yes, sir. I feel rested and perfectly ready."

Garth came close to him. "I hope this time you'll be able to follow my orders, Lieutenant."

"Yes, sir," Beaufort answered briefly. This was not the moment for arguments.

Neither of them had gone back to the subject of what had happened near the river that afternoon, before they were evacuated from the planet. Robert thought that as the captain felt that he had been the winner of the dispute between them, there was no reason why the commander needed to know what had happened. The captain knew, almost without a doubt, that their superior would not share that opinion, which was why he had let the matter rest. However, the tension between the two of them had not decreased in the slightest. Garth did not seem to be one of those people who would forget things just like that.

"I hope so, Lieutenant," he said by way of warning. "You'll be on this transport, I'll be in the other one. Take care of all the preparations. I'd advise you to start putting on your exosuit."

"Yes, Captain."

Both of them went to the side of the hangar where the exosuits for the entire crew were anchored. Robert got into his and secured himself to the metal floor by means of the suit's magnetic system. He went over to his transport, on the left. Balakova, the pilot, seemed to be checking the maintenance the technicians had just carried out on the ship.

"Morning, Balakova. Anything I ought to know?"

"Morning, Lieutenant. No, nothing so far. The transport's in perfect condition."

"Is it the one we were evacuated in?"

"No, but it's one of its twins. The one that evacuated us last week was the other one,"

"Right, so we keep to the initial plan, right?"

"That's right, Lieutenant."

"Oaky. I'll do a quick visual inspection, if you don't mind."

"Not at all, go ahead."

Robert went up the access ramp and crossed the small room which allowed the crew to go through the process of decontamination before they went into the cabin, and which kept the interior of the ship free from external pathogens.

He checked the two rows of seats, on either side of the fuselage.

Between both was enough space for a light armored vehicle. However, almost all of them, at least those which had weapons of any kind, had been lost along with the rest of the arsenal. High Command had decided not to risk the few armored vehicles which had been put in the hangar. At that moment they were very valuable resources in the circumstances. What they did have were a couple of transport mules which could be seen fixed to the floor of the ship, laden to the brim. Some light weaponry, but mostly riot shields.

"Let's hope we won't miss having some kind of land vehicle," he murmured as he checked that the load on the mules was correctly stowed.

He also went over the seat fixtures until he was satisfied, then came back out of the transport. Outside he could see the slow build-up of soldiers getting into the exosuits on the side of the hangar and then joining the team. It was a little worrying that apart from having lost all the arsenal in the black hole, the military command could count on not much more than fifty exosuits for the entire military crew of a little over a thousand soldiers. Even with that they were going to have to ration their use, or else start using the technicians' exosuits, which were less advanced, to carry out specialist military tasks.

By a little before half past seven in the morning all the soldiers who were to make up the two platoons taking part in the mission were there. Sergeant Cameron was with Captain Garth. Robert went over to receive his orders.

"Sergeant, order both platoons to line up, each in front of its own transport."

"Yes, Captain."

"Your attention!" the sergeant shouted in her unmistakable tone of voice. "Each platoon, line up in front of your transport! Captain Garth's on this side! Lieutenant Beaufort's in front of this other one!"

The groups broke up and the conversations were replaced by hurried footsteps. Captain Garth began to pace in front of both groups, while Robert and the pilots stayed behind him. The tension was palpable.

"Pay attention," Garth began, "because I'm not going to say this again. Today we're embarking on a mission of vital importance for our species. We're going back to that damn planet to finish what we started a few days ago: to colonize and conquer. But make no mistake, our task's going to be a very difficult one, because the threat is very real. Many of you knew Private Parrish before you embarked on the project, some even shared a few months in this very station. Those damn monsters took him from us. But this time we're not going to show any mercy, we're going to take revenge for our comrade's life. There'll be no pity for those who sow terror. I won't tolerate weakness or hesitation during the operation."

It seemed to Robert that some of those words were addressed to him.

"But above all, remember this: you're fighting for something greater than yourselves. You're fighting for the future of humanity. You're fighting for glory and victory. And what I'm saying to you, soldiers, is that victory will be ours!" He held up his clenched fist. "We're going to fight like warriors, like soldiers, like human beings. And we're going to win!"

There was a chorus of cheers and shouts of encouragement. Robert located Private Ferrara and Sergeant Ortiz among the members of his platoon. They were the only ones who were unmoved in the face of Captain Garth's words.

They know what we're up against. They know we're going to need more than inspiring words and empty war cries, he thought.

The captain made a sign to Sergeant Cameron, who once again addressed both platoons.

"Move on, you useless bunch of slackers!" she shouted. "To the transports!"

The soldiers went to their own vehicles in an orderly manner. While he was still waiting outside, Robert went over the files of every soldier who was boarding the ship. They were all very young, none of them even twenty-five.

They've selected the youngest and most malleable, he thought. *But what'll happen when they come face to face with death? Will they be ready?*

He turned to watch the other platoon. The situation here was very different, with men and women who were mostly over thirty boarding the second vehicle. Some of the profiles Ada was showing him in his exosuit helmet were impressive. There were elite commanders among them. Captain Garth was taking the most experienced ones, while Robert himself was left with the newest products of the military academies.

Finally he boarded the transport, where all the crew members were waiting in their seats. The pilot was checking the anchoring. He found a free seat at the far end of the room, next to the cockpit. Private Ferrara had saved a seat for him

"What do you think of the troop?" the private asked him as soon as he had sat down.

"Very young."

"Yeah, I noticed that too as they were arriving. They're all newly-graduated."

"Looks like it."

"All the same, the captain's brought all the bullies from his old commando group."

Robert nodded resignedly. "Yeah, I noticed that too."

"Is this his way of getting his revenge for not defending him the other day?"

"I'm afraid so."

"Fucking son of a bitch!" Ferrara whispered.

The pilot started the engines and the hangar, as on other occasions, was left without oxygen. The alarms had already been ringing for a while, but the absence of any means of letting the sound expand meant that they were inaudible. The hangar door opened after a few moments. Inside the transport they heard the sound of the ship's moorings as they were released under their feet. The captain's ship was the first to make its exit maneuver. Once it was outside, it was the turn of Robert's. Once both ships were out of the station they began to travel the slightly more than fifty thousand kilometers which separated the Asimov from the planet.

Minutes later, the transports began to cross the outer layers of the planet's atmosphere. The noise was now deafening. By the time they had passed through that area, no-one seemed to be in the mood for talking in the cabin. The tension in the air was palpable.

The two vehicles landed in a clearing close to the site of the accident to the Icarus, almost a kilometer away.

"You're good to go," Robert heard the pilot say as a green light came on in the crew cabin.

He got up from his seat and went to the rear door, which by now was beginning to open.

"Right, we'll go out one by one, in order. You two"—he pointed to the two soldiers closest to the door— "cover your comrades as they leave. Stay vigilant at all times. As of now we're in hostile territory."

The soldiers obediently left the transport, perfectly coordinated, their weapons aimed to either side. Once they had set foot on land, the others followed.

Robert left the vehicle after them, escorted by Private Ferrara and the medical sergeant Ortiz. Those from the other transport were in position by now. The day was considerably sunnier than the last time they had been there, with only the occasional cloud in the sky. Even so, he could not quite get used to the faint light of this sun.

"Private Ferrara," he called. "Take three men with beacons and set up a safety perimeter of a hundred meters around the transport."

"Yessir!"

"Captain, can you hear me?" Robert asked.

"Loud and clear," came Garth's voice.

"We're in position, waiting for orders."

"Form an advance line. We're going back to the site of the impact."

"Message received."

As soon as Private Ferrara and the three soldiers had come back to the group, Robert began to give the platoon their orders.

"Listen carefully, everyone! We're moving in a wedge formation toward the northeast. Stay in formation and be alert to your surroundings at all times. Remember, we're in hostile territory, so stop looking at the landscape and focus on the goal of the mission."

The soldiers of the platoon separated into two oblique lines, forming an arrowhead pointing in the direction of their advance. Both platoons, one after the other, went into the small patch of forest which separated the landing spot from the accident site.

The soldiers who were accompanying Robert looked nervous. More than one of them tripped on the undergrowth and fell, making more noise than would have been desirable.

"Control your platoon, Lieutenant," came Captain Garth's warning via the radio. "They're giving our position away to the four winds!"

"Yes, sir." Robert made no protest, despite the fact that both of them knew very well what the true reason for this was.

He's enjoying the situation, he thought.

Despite everything, he did not tell his soldiers off. Nor did they have much time to manage things better, because almost immediately they reached the clearing they had camped in a week before. The Icarus was still there, or rather what was left of it.

"Right!" the captain yelled. "Lieutenant, I want you to set up a defensive perimeter here. Sergeant Cameron, get the drones and the sensors on the perimeter ready."

"Yes sir!" both of them called.

Robert gave the appropriate indications, and the soldiers of his platoon unloaded the riot shields and two light machine-guns from the mules. With the equipment they had at their disposal they set up a couple of triangular defensive posts, twenty meters or so from one another. In the center of each protected spot they set up the two machine-guns.

"Leave five of your soldiers behind each shield," the captain ordered Robert and the sergeant. "They'll be defending the rearguard."

"Private Ferrara," Beaufort said. "Choose four soldiers and get the rear defense ready."

"With all due respect, Lieutenant," Private Ferrara said once she was sure they could not be heard, "if you think I'm going to miss the dance and stay behind to babysit, think again."

"All right." A faint smile appeared on his face. "In that case, pick the smartest you can find and make him a knight if it so pleases you."

"Yes, milord," she replied, satisfied.

"But leave the ones who tripped over on the bench," he added.

Once everything was ready, the captain ordered the two platoons to form again.

"Lieutenant!" he barked. "Tell the rest of your soldiers to re-form. We're going to march through the forest as far as the point where we lost the trail. Comb the area for recent signs of the creatures. We'll keep a distance of thirty meters between the two platoons."

"Yessir!"

"Sergeant Cameron! Deploy the small drones. Have them follow us through the trees."

Once again Robert formed his soldiers into a wedge. He, Ortiz and Ferrara went to stand at the head of the platoon. Sergeant Cameron deployed the drones as the captain had told her to. These were miniature versions of those they had used before for the scouting trip. Their size made them more maneuverable and hence better suited to covered terrain, such as a forest or a cave.

"Move in silence," he ordered them. "Leave five meters on either side. Use the radio only if strictly necessary. And above all, watch where you step. I don't want to have to stop to pick up the stragglers."

The two platoons set off through the forest in the same direction the Yokai had taken to ambush them. The vegetation was dense, which meant that progress was going to be heavy and difficult. Even so, at least so far, Robert's platoon seemed to be responding well. They all moved on in relative silence, very alert.

"Lieutenant," Private Ferrara whispered, "don't you have the feeling there's more life in the forest?"

"Yeah, there are more animals."

Everything felt more alive. There was the noise of insects, songs of tree-dwelling creatures hidden from the soldiers' eyes. Robert passed a kind of giant slug which was climbing up the huge roots of a tree. A little further ahead, a kind of insect which reminded him of a giant dragonfly passed in front of the platoon, leaving them all frozen to the spot when they heard the sound of its beating wings.

"What the hell was that?" he heard one of the soldiers ask.

"It looked like a fucking chopper," another said.

The distraction meant that Captain Garth's platoon gained an advantage over Robert's.

"We need to get a move on," he ordered via the open channel.

The platoon speeded up until it had caught up with the others. However, Robert stopped suddenly. He raised his right fist so that the others would stop too.

"Captain," he said. "I just found Parrish's remains."

"Right. Check the area for any trail we could follow."

"Yes, sir. Though I'm afraid the area isn't as trampled as it was a week ago."

He made a careful check of the area around the remains. There were still signs of the small army that had passed that way a few days before.

"There are no traces of blood or other fluids," he reported, "but the trail seems to go on to the east."

"Understood. We'll go on."

Both platoons went on in the direction marked by the trail. Robert used Ada to detect trampled vegetation, broken branches on the ground or any other sign that might tell them which direction to follow. Despite this, they could only find slight traces of the small army which had passed that way.

After two hours of tense travelling and with a few kilometers behind them, the trail seemed to go on toward the southeast.

The attack came from behind.

Robert's suit showed a pair of red squares aiming toward his right. Immediately there came the shouts of at least two of his soldiers. They all turned toward the attack, and he ran at once to the right flank, keeping his gun aimed all the time.

"We're under attack!" he yelled via the radio to warn the other platoon.

The shots began, mingled with the soldiers' screams of pain. Amid all the confusion Robert heard guttural growls which did not sound familiar. They were just as bloodcurdling, but these were definitely different.

The dense vegetation got in the way of eye-contact with his soldiers. Desperate to reach them, he made his way through a group of gigantic ferns until he was able to see the attackers. Two enormous quadrupeds with long, jet-black fur rose before him. Their dark, unsettling eyes were scrutinizing their surroundings above their fearsome jaws. Their long muzzles were divided into three jaws, two on the upper part and one, slightly larger, on the lower part. They were clutching their two victims tightly.

The poor soldiers were screaming and writhing in pain as the two creatures tried to bite off their limbs, shaking them violently at the same time.

Robert aimed at the nearest creature's chest to avoid the shot going astray and hitting the unfortunate soldier. The creature took three bullets but stayed on its feet, though he had managed to make it drop its prey. But now its attention was focused on him. He heard more shots to his left; the other creature too was being attacked by the rest of his platoon. He aimed again, this time at the head, and did not miss. The creature rolled on the ground, stunned, but far from being dead, it got to its feet again. Three other soldiers reached him and helped him to finish the job. There was still the second specimen left.

"Medic!" he shouted into the radio. He turned to the soldiers. "Stay with the wounded man and defend the position!"

He ran to the place where he could hear the rest of the shots coming from. By the time he reached the area, Private Ferrara was already having a look at the other creature's dead body.

"Are you all okay?"

"Two wounded!" Ferrara said. At the same time she turned around quickly to check the state of one of her comrades.

Sergeant Ortiz examined the wounded men, who looked bad. One had both left limbs severed from his body and his vital signs were very weak. His suit was tattered and no longer airtight, and his oxygen supply was beginning to fail. The other had been attacked while trying to intercept the creature as it tried to escape, and the front of his suit had been torn by a tremendous swipe with a claw which had reached as far as the ribs. His breathing was labored, but he was still conscious.

The sergeant medic had to act quickly. He applied disinfectant foam that could stop hemorrhages very rapidly. He waited a few seconds for it to take effect, then injected a compound through the rips in the exosuit to try to stop hypoxia from lack of oxygen in the air. When his condition had been stabilized, he examined the other soldier. His vital signs were very weak, and he had lost a lot of blood through the femoral artery. Ortiz turned to Robert and shook his head very slightly.

"There's nothing I can do for him."

"Go and help the other one," Robert said. His voice was heavy.

Sergeant Ortiz ran to the first position. Meanwhile Ferrara, who was beside the unfortunate soldier, certified his death.

"He didn't make it," she said faintly.

"It's not your fault, private," Robert said in an attempt to comfort her.

She gave the fallen creature a kick. "Isn't there anything that doesn't want to kill us on this damn planet?"

"I'm afraid those two are just wild animals."

Robert went over the body of the dead alien. It seemed to be smaller than the one he had killed a few meters back. He pointed to its belly.

"I think this is a female."

"Was it pregnant?"

"Looks like it. It was just feeding itself."

Captain Garth's platoon arrived to help their comrades

"Report, Lieutenant."

"We have a casualty," Robert explained. "And two more wounded. We need to evacuate immediately."

Garth pointed to the creature. "What the hell is that?"

"I'd say a female predator, Captain,"

"And the other specimen?"

"It's been killed too."

He turned to the sergeant. "Sergeant Cameron, why didn't the drones detect them in time?"

"I don't know, Captain," she said. "The readings are correct. Everything seems to be in order."

"I have the impression they didn't attack from the ground," Robert put in. He was looking up at the huge, densely leafy trees which surrounded them.

"How can you be so sure?" the captain asked.

"You said it yourself, the drones didn't detect them. But the drones only keep watch on the ground." He pointed to the body. "And look at the claws of those animals. They're prehensile, ideal for climbing into trees."

6
The lair

July 4, year 0
Location 3, Kepler-442b

Robert ordered a couple of soldiers to go back to the camp with the two wounded and the body of the dead soldier on one of the mules they had brought with them.

"Balakova, are you receiving me?"

"Loud and clear, Lieutenant."

"Get one of the ships ready for immediate evacuation. We've lost a man. And you'll be getting two wounded who need urgent medical attention. Warn the station so that they can get the operating theater ready. Ada will send the diagnostics."

"Copy that."

"Once you've left the wounded at the station, go back to your position and wait for new orders."

Captain Garth had accepted Robert's theory that the creatures might have attacked from the trees, so he had ordered all the soldiers to keep a lookout above their heads as well.

"How are you doing?" Robert asked Private Ferrara and Sergeant Ortiz.

"Ready to go on," Ferrara said.

"Ready," said the sergeant.

"We have to go on. Let's hope we don't come across any more surprises from now on."

The officers reorganized their troops. Two soldiers from the captain's platoon joined Robert's to make up for the casualties and both groups set off again, this time looking in all possible directions as they went.

After a few kilometers of relative quiet, they came to a small depression in the terrain. The forest went on, but they had to cross an embankment to be able to go on down. Thanks to the exosuits they were able to cross it without trouble, though at one point they were forced to make a detour to the south because of the steepness of the terrain.

"How far are we thinking of going?" Sergeant Ortiz asked when they had covered almost thirty kilometers.

"Until we lose the trail or have to go back because our oxygen's running out," Robert said. "And it may be weak, but for the moment we still have a trail."

"How's that possible, after all this time?"

"The vegetation takes days to regain its original shape," the lieutenant explained. "Rain usually helps the process, but it hasn't rained these last few days."

"Don't you find it strange that the Yokai should go so far to get to our camp?"

"I've been asking myself that same question since we reached fifteen kilometers," Robert said. "But something tells me we're getting close to something."

"Why do you think that?" Ferrara asked.

"Because we've been walking almost half a day, and even if they moved faster, it would take them half the night to reach our camp. If the ultraviolet rays affect them, they can't go too far from their lair. That, and the fact that we've been walking a couple of kilometers where the vegetation's getting more trampled all the time. And recently, I'd guess."

"Recent?" the sergeant asked uneasily. Ortiz was a great doctor, but not outstanding as a fighter. The moment he knew they were coming close to the enemy base, his voice had sounded much more nervous.

"Yeah. I guess they must have come out from wherever they are to hunt these last few days, which is why there's been more activity in this area."

No sooner had he finished speaking than they saw in the distance, behind all the vegetation, a small clearing. When they reached it they were taken aback by the macabre spectacle thirty meters away. A huge outcrop of almost vertical rock blocked their way, so that they could only go on to the north or south. To the north the small clearing came to an end and the forest continued, skirting the cliff. But to the south, the clearing allowed them to see a small mountain of rubble, dozens of meters high.

"What's all that?" Sergeant Ortiz whispered.

"It can't be…" Private Ferrara said, horrified.

"Jesus Christ!" muttered one of the soldiers of the platoon.

"Zoom," Robert snapped.

What he saw in that artificial mound left him petrified. Piled on the rocky slope were thousands of bones, skulls and remains of all kinds of horrible creatures. All along the slope, vertically, the rock wall was stained with dark patches as a result of the activity which had caused this gigantic ossuary which was piled up on the ground. Sixty meters or so above them they could make out the entrance to a cave.

"Captain" Robert called on the radio. "I think we've found them."

Captain Garth's platoon arrived a couple of minutes later.

"What the hell is that?" the captain barked.

"Bone remains, sir. And a little further up you can see what looks like the entrance to their lair."

The captain tilted his head back to see the dark opening in the rock-face, which would surely turn out to be infested with Yokais.

"Hell!" he exclaimed. "That looks totally unreachable."

"I'm afraid so, captain. It looks as though they're good climbers."

"Sergeant Cameron!" he called. "You and your platoon, comb the surroundings. Find some way of reaching that cave, if possible."

"Yessir!"

"Lieutenant, come with me."

Robert went with the captain to the gigantic and macabre mound of bones a few meters away.

"If this is what it seems to be," the captain began, "we might find the remains of Parrish's exosuit here."

"Yeah, that makes sense."

"I don't want to make any of these weak-kneed soldiers scrabble among the remains," the captain went on condescendingly, "so let's go."

Both of them began to climb the enormous ossuary, which must have been at least thirty-five meters high and with a base of about the same in diameter.

"How many creatures and how much time could they have needed to produce this amount of remains?" the captain asked.

"Too many."

"And I don't even want to imagine the stench that must be coming from all this." The captain waved away some insect from his sight.

"I'm certainly thankful for the exosuit."

The remains seemed to be from different animals and creatures, as they were of all sizes and shapes. Robert was no specialist in biology, but from that distance most of the bones looked like any animal remains on Earth. There were some that were very different, darker or lighter in color, and shapes that were rather varied and curious.

"Have you ever seen anything like this on earth, Captain?" Robert asked.

"Not even remotely," Garth admitted "This would turn the blood of even the bravest into ice."

Robert could feel that the captain was annoyed. All this had taken him by surprise, and not pleasantly. All those past disputes had ceased to make sense. The enemy was ruthless.

They went up carefully until they reached the highest part of the pile. The terrain was very irregular and they could easily end up putting a foot into one of the nooks and crannies that were left uncovered. After a few minutes of fruitless searching, Robert caught a glimpse of something shining a couple of meters ahead. He had to go back down a couple of meters to reach what was clearly some other material.

"Captain!"

"Have you found something?"

"Yes. I think this was the suit's oxygen tank." He held up a metal plate thirty centimeters or so across, bent and bearing stains of dried blood. "And this one here looks like a chest plate."

The captain waved his hand around. "There are plenty of remains."

"And going by their position on the pile, they look to be the most recent."

"Fucking bastards!" the Captain snorted. He began to turn around, as if he were searching for something.

"What is it, sir?"

"Have you found … well…. Parrish?"

"No, sir. Although I don't even know if I want to."

"At least we ought to gather his remains together. He deserves a decent burial."

"You're right, sir."

Searching for something that might look like human remains among millions of bones of alien creatures was neither an easy nor a pleasant task. But Robert had a sudden idea.

He pointed to the remains, most of which had an indigo shade. "Bearing in mind that the blood of these creatures, and I understand a lot of the creatures on this planet, looks bluish, maybe we ought to concentrate on anything with a different color."

"That makes sense," the captain admitted.

Both of them searched the area carefully, but it turned out to be too complicated, not to mention macabre.

"Ada," Robert asked, "could you separate out those of the remains with a different shade of color that could belong to a human body?"

"I'll try."

After a few seconds, both the captain and Robert saw a couple of spots on their helmets which might fit the parameters. They found what looked like a human shin-bone and femur. Every time they changed their angle of vision, Ada would tell them of another. Until the captain himself hit on the definite proof that Private Parrish was one of the unfortunate victims.

"Found him," he said succinctly.

Robert spun round and came over to see what the captain had picked up. It might have been better, he thought, not to have found anything. The captain was holding a jaw and the lower part of a human skull.

"Visual analysis of the dentures leaves no room for doubt," Ada said. "It's Private Parrish, I'm very sorry."

"I think that's enough," the captain said. "Let's go back to the others."

They went back to the rest of Robert's platoon

"Fetch a blanket from the mule," the captain said to Private Ferrara.

Then he wrapped Parrish's remains in it.

"The slope goes on to the south for several more kilometers," Sergeant Cameron reported, "but we haven't found a more accessible way in."

"Thanks, Sergeant," the captain said. "The lieutenant and I have found Parrish's remains."

"Let's go after those filthy cowards," the sergeant muttered under her breath.

"That's not going to be possible," the captain pointed out.

"What? Why not?"

"We can't get up there. And even if we could, the cave looks so narrow we'd lose our tactical advantage. And besides it's almost midday. If we want to keep up our rearguard without moving the transports, we haven't much time to organize an attack."

"Just like that?" the sergeant asked. "Are we going to let these creatures get away like this?"

"No, sergeant." He looked at her with a gleam of hatred in his eyes. "I said we're not going after them, not that we weren't going to do anything. Get one of the drones ready. I want to see what that cave is like inside."

The sergeant's expression changed, and she hastened to prepare two of the small drones they had brought with them. A few moments later one of them began to fly toward the opening in the mountain.

"What do you want me to do with it?" Cameron asked.

"Take it in. I want to see the shape of the cave and if possible, how many of those demons there are inside."

"Copy that."

The drone went into the hollow, which was not large enough to allow an incursion, as Captain Garth had anticipated. Soon the drone activated its infrared camera so that it could see in the dark. The cave seemed to go downhill, and the drone advanced between stalactites and stalagmites, showing the horrific spectacle its camera was picking up. The bone remains on the ground could be numbered by the thousands, but the quantities inside were an order of magnitude larger.

The cave went on descending, and as it went, the drone found more and more spaces and openings.

The sergeant pointed. "Through that huge opening there."

"This is a bloody labyrinth," Robert said.

"How far has it gone?" the captain asked.

"Nine hundred meters," came Ada's voice.

"It's too large," the captain said, sounding disappointed. "We'd need a whole army to be able to attack this place."

"So what are we going to do?" Private Ferrara asked.

"The art of war," the captain said. "Know thy enemy."

"The art of war?" Sergeant Ortiz asked. "What's that?"

"The Art of War is a book written in China in the fifth century before Christ. It's mostly about how you need to know your enemy as well as you know yourself if you want to defeat them. And what do we know about them?"

"They can't stand the sunlight," Ortiz said.

"Exactly. We know that as long as there's sunlight they won't attack us. But now we have the exact location of their lair, we also know that if we lead them away from their base they'll lose the advantage of the terrain. And also they'll be more tired."

"And we'll have a better defensive position," Robert added.

"All we have to do is knock politely on the door and see who wants to come out to play," the captain added with a twisted smile.

The drone went on with its progress through the multitude of openings and nooks of the cave. There were so many possible paths to take that it had to turn around several times after it had entered galleries which came to a dead end.

In one of those changes of direction, without warning, several figures approached the drone very fast. Something appeared just in front of its camera at the moment the signal was lost.

"Right," the captain said. "Now we know they're at home. Sergeant Cameron, let's send them our respects."

"Yessir!" the sergeant hastened to reply.

The second drone, carrying a small load of explosives fastened to its belly, took off and headed to the opening.

"Lieutenant, just in case, I want you to deploy the two platoons on either side of the opening. Shoot at anything that pokes its head out."

Robert passed on the orders, and the platoons assembled on both sides of the hollow. All available forces were now aiming their guns at the entrance. Even the most experienced soldiers were nervous. Everything was ready to show whether the captain's stratagem was right.

By now the drone did not need any kind of direction, it knew perfectly well where the first one had gone. All it had to do was locate the creatures. After a few endless minutes and before it reached the same spot, it sent images in which they could see dozens of creatures, hundreds of them, perhaps even more, moving toward the little device.

When the signal was lost, they heard a deafening explosion which echoed throughout the valley. After a few more moments they saw a cloud of dust billowing out through the opening, making it hard to see anything. The tension among Robert's soldiers was nerve-racking. No-one was entirely sure whether the creatures would come out of their hiding-place to deal with the threat which had just reached the very door of their abode. They waited tensely while the dust cloud cleared. No-one said a word as they waited without taking their eyes off the cave-entrance. Robert feared that at any moment a stream of creatures would come out of it. The silence was so intense that they could hear their own heartbeats.

"Hear that?" someone asked.

"Yeah," another replied.

"They're coming," said another. "Sounds like a lot of them."

"Quiet!" Robert ordered.

That slight sound in the distance soon became something more definite, and very soon they heard hundreds of terrifying growls. A couple of soldiers took a step back. Suddenly the sounds stopped completely.

A figure emerged from the darkness and seemed to be watching them from above. Its head turned compulsively in all directions. Its body, thin and athletic, was a pale shade of blue. Robert could see its skin in every detail, covered with capillary vessels of an intense blue. However, its skin soon began to darken and he saw a trace of steam coming from its arms and head. The sunlight was affecting it. But if it was painful, the creature was bearing it very well.

One of the newly-enlisted soldiers began to tremble, and the clatter of his suit and weapon made the creature turn its head immediately. It had located him. The soldier, suddenly panicking, began to run in the direction of the forest.

The creature, which was still unmoving, threw its body slightly back. It showed its threatening rows of teeth and gave a terrifying scream. Without a word, several soldiers opened fire.

"Hold your fire!" Robert ordered unsuccessfully. "Hold your positions!"

The creature fell inside the cave, brought down by the dozens of bullets which had hit it.

"Hold your fire!" he repeated.

This time the soldiers obeyed. From the cave there came hundreds more growls. Spurred on by their fellow-creature's fall, they seemed to be calling for revenge. Another figure, far larger and more threatening than the one before, leant over the edge of the cliff. Its limbs were far more powerful, while the lower lip of its enormous mouth was split in half. On its chin a long scar went down the neck as far as its pectoral muscles. It seemed to be a war wound. It gave a kind of guttural grunt, which it accompanied with the movement of its lips. In a strange way it seemed to be speaking.

The other creature's cry might have frozen their blood, but this specimen's would have been capable of freezing hell itself. Robert felt a supernatural terror run down his body. He was beginning to think that maybe the plan had not been a good idea after all, bearing in mind the lack of manpower, ammunition and weaponry.

A few seconds later the creature went back into the cave, and gradually the murmur from inside became fainter and fainter.

7
The trap

July 4, year 0
Near location 3, Kepler-442b

"That was horrific," Private Ferrara said as she remembered the terrifying figure they had seen at the cave mouth.

"I nearly shat myself," Sergeant Ortiz admitted.

"That doesn't surprise me. I'd have loved to put a bullet in the middle of its head."

"I don't even want to imagine what Parrish went through."

Ferrara nodded. "Or the fucking nightmares Taro and Paula have been having."

"I think we ought to get out of here as soon as possible," the sergeant said.

Robert was talking to the captain, Sergeant Cameron and Sergeant Reynolds, one of Captain Garth's old commandos who had rejoined the service for this mission.

"We're not going to be able to do much more here," Reynolds was saying. "Without a good supply of explosives and drones it's going to be impossible to reduce that cave to rubble."

"And suppose we blow up the entrance?" Cameron asked.

"A cave as deep and wide as that might have different exits." The sergeant pointed to several small hollows along the rock wall. "The slope itself seems to have one or two smaller ways in."

The captain nodded. "Yeah, they might not use this opening except for other than throwing out their garbage. We can't afford to waste what little explosive we have."

"We ought to divide them," Robert suggested.

"Divide them?" the captain repeated.

"Yes, you said so yourself earlier. There are too many of them here, and they're very close to their refuge. If we can get them to come closer to the accident site, we might be able to decimate them with the machine-guns. And I very much doubt whether they'd come with all their forces. They'll have to leave a garrison."

"Do you think they'll follow us?" Cameron asked.

"No doubt of it," the captain said, supporting Robert's idea. "You saw the one that looked like their leader. I'd say we've pissed them off so much they're going to take it as something personal."

"It's been personal ever since they attacked our campsite," Sergeant Cameron pointed out.

"Right then, that's decided, we'll do it like that. Lieutenant, get the two platoons organized. We'll make faster progress if we go together this time. We've got to reach base camp before dusk."

"Yes, sir."

Robert went over to where the rest of the soldiers were waiting nervously for the order to leave that place and never come back.

"Ferrara," he called. "Get everybody organized, we're off. We're about forty kilometers from the camp, and we have to get back before nightfall."

"Are we leaving everything like this?" Private Ferrara said, sounding disappointed.

"No, we're going to get a welcome committee ready for them."

"At last, some action!"

"I want you to leave a beacon right here, then another every ten kilometers. That way we'll know when they come close."

"Copy that."

"Sergeant Ortiz, find that soldier of ours with nerves of steel. Try to calm him down so that it doesn't happen again."

"Yes, sir."

Robert also gave orders to the remaining soldiers to go back to camp, where they would prepare a good defense. The march began quickly and calmly. Perhaps it was the calm that precedes the storm, but Robert, knowing what they were up against, felt a certain reassurance, even though the appalling creatures made his hair stand on end. He thought about the viability of the scientific base Emily had to set up a few kilometers from there. With the Yokai so near it was going to be a risky business.

"Ada, bearing in mind the distance between the cave and the accident site, could you calculate the creatures' approximate speed and tell me whether they'd reach the site where the first of the bases is supposed to be set up in a single night?"

"Sure, Lieutenant," the AI replied at once. "They'd certainly reach it if they decided to, or if they had a reason for doing so."

"Why wouldn't they have reasons?" he asked in surprise. "We've just bombed their shelter."

"Correct, but the base is going to be built twenty kilometers or so to the northwest of the accident site. The creatures don't know anything about our plans to set up a base, they have no reason to go to that area. Being intelligent, as they seem to be, I understand that for them the accident site represents something like the lair of their enemies. Hence it's possible that the proposed plan won't have any consequences for the base camp."

"I understand the point of view, but in that case do you think it would be safe to set up a scientific base at the third site?"

"I'm afraid that on this planet we can't take anything for granted. But considering that there's another intelligent species on the planet and that both of them coexist separated only by a river, I think the distance might be enough to avoid any confrontation with the Yokai. Even so, take these precautions with an element of caution. I can't anticipate much, seeing how little we know about them."

"Aren't there any safer locations? Why's this one so important?"

"I'm only an artificial intelligence, and though I don't share that human curiosity about establishing contact with other intelligent species, I have to admit that even for me it's very motivating to be able to meet a new civilization after so many years and learn new things. It's fascinating. And besides, if you'll allow me, Lieutenant, one of the main motives is to trace the footsteps the Galileo expedition might have taken. That particular site is the most promising of all those we've studied. If the Galileo was ever on the planet, I'm sure it was here."

"I get you."

"But if you want to feel more at ease, the idea in the mid-term is to increase the human population on the planet by setting up other bases. Let's hope we don't have these problems in future neighborhoods."

"Or something worse," Robert concluded.

This time he placed himself at the rear of the platoon, together with Private Ferrara and Sergeant Cameron. They had barely travelled half of the forty kilometers which separated cave from base camp.

"Considering what we've seen, this is going to be complicated," Ferrara said. "Travelling to the other end of the universe and then ending up being wiped out like this doesn't look like a very promising future."

"We've certainly started on the wrong foot," the sergeant agreed. "Losing the arsenal and the terraformation module was a massive setback. Then the accident to the Icarus, and now coming across these damn demons… it looks as if someone's put the evil eye on us."

"We all knew when we enlisted in the project that it wasn't going to be easy, Sergeant," Robert pointed out. "For me, just walking on this planet now is a massive achievement for humanity."

Ferrara nodded. "If you look at it that way…it's true, we're not doing so badly. In fact the people on the Galileo didn't even get to make it."

"And how," Sergeant Cameron agreed. "I had colleagues from the same intake on it."

"What we have to do is find our place on this planet and try to live as comfortable and simple a life as possible," Robert said. "We have to make sure the scientific teams on the ship can do their job. It's the only way humanity might have another chance."

They reached the spot where that same morning they had been attacked by the two wild animals. The bodies were still lying in the same place. Everything looked relatively calm.

"How many beacons have you set up so far, Private Ferrara?" Robert asked.

"Three, with this one I'm setting up now and the one we left at the foot of the cave."

"Right. Ada? What activity is there near the beacons behind us?"

"No movement so far. However, it has to be said that the second one isn't altogether working properly."

"What's wrong with it?"

"I'm getting images from both normal and infrared cameras, and the motion sensor is working too, but I'm not getting any sign from the radar. It doesn't seem to be operational."

"But as it is right now, could you detect them when they come closer?"

"Yes, I don't think I'll have any trouble, though without the radar working they'll have to pass in front of the motion sensor or the cameras."

"Okay. Any sign of suspicious movement, let me know."

"Sure, Lieutenant."

The entire platoon, including the soldier who had run away, reached the site of the accident to the Icarus without further trouble. Here the ten soldiers who had been on watch duty all day were waiting. Robert also had the two who had accompanied the casualties on the way back to the ship.

He asked about them immediately.

"Dr. Schmidt took them in at the hangar, and then they were taken to the operating theatre," the soldier told him.

"What was the situation?"

"Critical, I'm afraid, but stable."

"Okay, well done, private."

Captain Garth gave the order to all the soldiers to dig holes in the terrain, not to stop the enemy but at least to slow their advance. They did what they could with what few tools and resources they had at their disposal.

Robert analyzed the situation together with Private Ferrara. The small defensive posts they had prepared were a few meters from one another, allowing the defense to be focused on them. But even so, they had too much forest perimeter to defend.

"It's not the best possible position," Ferrara admitted.

"No, but I think this is the best we're going to manage. We don't have elevated positions either, and nor do we have enough time and tools to dig a decent set of trenches."

"If they got it into their heads to surround us, we might not get out of this."

"I've been thinking about that all day," Robert admitted. "I'm also worried they might attack the transports first and cut off our retreat."

"But to do that they'd have to take a detour to get to them."

"Yeah, but the fact is we don't know how intelligent they are. Certainly it's what I'd do in their place if I had enough information at my disposal."

He walked around the terrain and made a careful study of the layout of the forests, the clearing they were in and even the remains of the Icarus. There were still a couple of hours left before the light vanished completely. After that they would have at least two more hours before the creatures reached them.

"We need light," he said.

"Light?"

"Yes, as a last resort. Come with me, Ferrara."

He and Ferrara went back to the Icarus. They went into it through the emergency door, which was still just as they had left it a few days before. When they reached the cargo hold, they found what he had come in search of.

"Do you want to move the rover from here?"

"Yup. If we find ourselves surrounded, we could turn on the front lights."

"That would puzzle them," she said.

"Seventy thousand lumens of puzzling artificial light. It'll be just like day. If it's true the Yokai fear the light, we'll give them an inferno of it."

Private Ferrara smiled as she sat down in the pilot's seat. "I have to admit, you have some pretty good ideas."

"First, let's make sure this thing works."

Ferrara pressed the *on* button and the inside of the vehicle was flooded with light. A faint electrical buzz echoed through the half-ruined hold of the Icarus. The engine seemed to be in perfect condition.

"Turn on the front lights," he said.

The front lights of the armored vehicle, designed to carry out missions of exploration in very adverse conditions, consisted of three full rows of spotlights: two on the lower part of the nose and another on the top, immediately above the armored windshield. In addition this provided illumination at an angle of more than a hundred and eighty degrees, as the spotlights at the corners were directed toward the vehicle's sides.

Private Ferrara turned on the lights, and Robert checked that the strong light illuminated the exit from the hold.

"We have light!" Ferrara exclaimed.

"There are a couple of broken spotlights, but yeah, it'll be more than enough."

"D'you want me to take it out of here, Lieutenant?"

"Yes, let's take it as far as the clearing. But let me get in first."

He got in through the other side of the vehicle. The exit from the hold had not been entirely unblocked, but this was nothing the powerful engine could not overcome. Ferrara deactivated the anchoring which kept the rover fixed to the floor of the Icarus and stepped on the throttle. The vehicle began to move, and they soon noticed that it was tilting toward the left. They had to overcome a couple of piles of rubble and tangles of metal before they could reach the exit ramp.

It was no trouble at all for Private Ferrara, and very soon they went out of the exit. The ramp was not in the best condition, but it withstood their weight with barely a few slight metallic creaks. Ferrara maneuvered skillfully to guide the vehicle through the same spot where they had taken out the survival unit days before. The terrain, which was very irregular and full of remains of trees and metal plates from what had been the ship's fuselage, made it difficult to move forward. Even so, it took them barely five minutes to appear behind the Icarus. The soldiers who were getting the terrain ready for the confrontation began to cheer and shout when they saw that they had an armored vehicle at their disposal.

Ferrara stopped between the two defensive posts, with the front pointing in the direction they expected the Yokai to appear from. Then they got out of the vehicle as the captain came over to them.

"Good idea, Lieutenant," he said with a nod. "This is certainly a magnificent plan B."

"Thank you, sir."

"It's a real shame we don't have the vehicles from the arsenal. Although in that case the battle wouldn't last very long. This is going to let us enjoy the taste of victory even more."

"Yes, sir."

"Come with me, Lieutenant. We need to discuss strategy. The way we're placed, we don't have any tactical advantage, the opposite, if anything. If those bastards had long-range weapons we'd be completely fucked."

"Luckily it doesn't look as though they do."

"Right, we'll distribute the soldiers between the two defensive posts. You'll be in charge of the one on the south and I'll take the one on the north. Make sure this time no-one opens fire before time. We need to let them come close enough to start feeling confident. Once they reach the middle of the clearing we'll open fire, not before. Put your best shot on the machine-gun."

"Copy that, sir."

"It's not a great plan, but we're dealing with savage creatures, and I'm confident they'll fall into the trap."

"Let's hope so, for what it's worth."

At last night fell, and utter darkness took possession of the clearing they were in. Among the soldiers, nervous conversations gave way to a sepulchral silence. Robert deployed his soldiers in the space allowed them by the counter-insurgency defenses. Ferrara took charge of the machine-gun. Sergeant Ortiz, who was not notable for his skills on the battlefield, would act as operator to keep the machine-gun continuously supplied with ammunition. He posted a couple of soldiers at the rear so that they could keep an eye out for a possible encircling attack, and the rest he placed close to the riot shields, armed with their own assault rifles.

"Ada?" he called impatiently.

"There's still no activity in the cave," she reported.

"Lieutenant Balakova, do you read me?"

"Loud and clear, Lieutenant Beaufort."

"I want you to keep the transports with their engines running, ready to take off. If this goes wrong we'll have to get out of here fast. Keep your ears open for the radio and keep watch on the perimeter."

"Copy that."

"Lieutenant Beaufort," Ada interrupted him, "a figure has appeared at the cave entrance."

"Show me on the screen."

Through the first beacon's infrared camera he saw a figure shaking its head compulsively. It seemed to be its way of scrutinizing its surroundings in the darkness. It was searching for something, and Robert knew very well what it was: it was searching for them.

After a few moments the figure vanished into the cave once again. Then an endless stream of creatures began to pour out of the opening. They dug their claws into the rock so that they could climb down without falling to the ground. They were hundreds of them by now, and more and more of them were following. It was an army of demons. It did not take them long to reach the ground, and in the blink of an eye one of them approached the beacon and they lost the signal.

"What happened?" Robert asked.

"We've lost the beacon, Lieutenant," Ada confirmed. "I think they've destroyed it."

"How did they know there was a beacon there?"

"I don't know, Lieutenant. Perhaps they know their environment and detected that there was something there that didn't belong."

Robert thought for a moment. He was not too convinced by Ada's explanation.

"Okay, it's not important for the moment. Time them. I want to know how long it takes them to travel the ten kilometers to the next beacon."

"Copy that."

Almost thirty minutes later, the AI warned him again.

"Lieutenant, I'm detecting movement at the second beacon."

"How long did it take?"

"Twenty-eight and a half minutes."

"That gives us less than an hour and a half till they get here. How fast are they going? Twenty kilometers an hour?"

"Twenty-one, Lieutenant."

"Have we lost the second beacon?"

"No," she replied. "This time they didn't touch it."

"And can we get some idea of how many of them they are?"

"It's hard to tell, the camera's covered, so that I can't see how many individuals are coming. But I can be clear that it's over a thousand."

"A thousand!"

"Yes, and I fear it might be more."

"Okay. Let me know when they reach the next beacon."

Robert contacted the captain privately to inform him of the number of individuals they might be about to face. The captain could not hide his surprise, but at no moment did he seem to show any fear, if anything the opposite.

"We're going to have an epic battle, Lieutenant," he said with great satisfaction. "Start prepping your men."

The tension among the waiting soldiers was already noticeable. There was not even a whisper to be heard. They were all very focused, very expectant. They had to wait another half hour before Ada reported to Robert again.

"They've just reached the halfway point, Lieutenant. And I'm afraid we've lost this beacon too."

"How long do we have left?"

"They seem to have slowed their pace a little. But I calculate that they'll be at the clearing in an hour."

Robert noticed that he too was beginning to feel the tension growing. The long wait was doing nothing to calm his nerves. It was turning into an eternity.

"Turn out all the lights, we're going on to infrared," he ordered via the radio. "And avoid using the radio unless it's strictly necessary."

They all obeyed, and total darkness fell on the place.

"Lieutenant Balakova?"

"Yes, Lieutenant Beaufort?"

"We're going over to total radio silence. But stay alert for whatever might happen."

"Copy, Lieutenant. Good luck."

"Thanks, we're going to need it."

Another thirty minutes went by before Ada gave her report.

"Lieutenant, they've just reached the fourth beacon. They're barely thirty minutes from your position."

Robert took a deep breath and tried to stay calm. The Yokai were not simply neighborhood bullies from his native Marseilles. The moment of truth had come. The future of the colony depended on whatever happened during the next few minutes. If they won, perhaps the Yokai would cease to be a threat. If not, not only would the project lose a significant number of irreplaceable personnel and equipment, they would find themselves doomed to survive amid the uncertainty and constant threat from a highly aggressive alien species. He began to wonder whether all this had been a good idea. Perhaps choosing another, quieter location would have been more suitable. But now there was no going back, they were betting everything on a single card.

"Ten minutes," Ada reported.

"Ten minutes," Robert repeated through the radio. "Remember, don't open fire until I give the order. And most important, everyone stay calm."

Those were the longest minutes of his life. No-one made the slightest sound, but the tension was unbearable. Soon they began to hear growls in the distance. They were here.

He watched the nearest trees closely. It was impossible to see clearly what was between the trunks. Suddenly he detected movement. First dozens, moving fast through the underbrush, then hundreds. There were too many of them.

"They're here," he whispered. "Keep calm. Hold fast."

And yet the creatures suddenly stopped dead. He could see them in the distance, within the forest, behind three or four rows of trees. There was a deeply disturbing silence, interrupted only by a few guttural sounds which were even more disturbing than the silence itself. One of those demons came forward to the edge of the forest.

The creature was considerably smaller than the one they had seen in the middle of the day. But even so, it was obvious that it could tear a human being apart in the blink of an eye. It emerged into the clearing and then moved forward a few meters, turning its head rapidly in every direction as it did so. It was looking for them. Its growls indicated that it was succeeding. It stopped dead some forty meters from the two defensive positions and reared up on its hindquarters, showing its pale abdomen in full. And without doing anything more, it turned and went back into the forest.

The rest of its companions waited a few moments, barely making a sound.

"What are they waiting for?" he heard Captain Garth say on the radio.

"I've no idea."

"Why don't they attack us?" Garth asked uneasily. "We're here, in the open."

"I think they've found the trap."

"In that case, why are they staying still there on the edge of the forest?"

"No idea."

A single growl began to be clearly audible within the forest. It was still horrible, but it was not threatening, not like those they had heard until that moment. It was something Robert would never have believed these creatures capable of. They were laughing.

"Lieutenant Balakova!" Robert shouted. "Take off! Take off at once!"

"Copy that!" he heard on the radio.

He went through a few moments of sheer panic. If they destroyed the transports they would be lost. If the Yokai failed to kill them the lack of oxygen could do it instead, if another transport was not sent to pick them up. The Yokai had set a trap for them.

"Jesus Christ!" Robert heard the pilot say. "There are hundreds... thousands... maybe even more..." She sounded terrified.

"Are you in the air now?"

"Yes, Lieutenant. We're safe. But without your warning we wouldn't have had time to react. They came from nowhere and they've got rid of all the perimeter beacons. I'm afraid you're surrounded. Be very careful."

"Make for our position. If this gets difficult, we'll need you to shine the spotlights on us."   "Copy that."

"Captain?" Robert called.

"I heard, Lieutenant. Reorganize the defenses, get ready to counter a pincer movement. They'll be coming from every direction."

Robert reorganized his soldiers so that they faced the different fronts offered them by the riot shields. He left Private Ferrara with Sergeant Ortiz on the main flank and a couple of soldiers to cover the machine-gun. The remainder he posted on the other two flanks. Above all, he was worried about what might be on its way from the south. All the creatures coming back from where the transports were waiting were going to hurl themselves on them.

The two transports arrived first and stayed flying over the area. As they were unarmed, there was not much they could do except wait for events to unfold. The attack was swift and coordinated. Thousands of the creatures appeared in the clearing and surrounded them completely. The captain's plans had collapsed even before they had begun the fight. There were too many of the Yokai, and they were attacking from every direction.

"Fire at will!" Robert shouted. "Defend the position!"

The soldiers began to shoot. The creatures were still a long way from the defensive posts, but if they went on appearing by the hundreds, they would soon have trouble keeping them at bay.

The soldiers, though they were not very experienced, were responding well. Robert took charge of those areas that were least well-manned. He shot small volleys to left and right to deal with those creatures the remainder of the platoon had not eliminated. Even so it was not enough, there were too many of them, and little by little they were gaining ground.

Private Ferrara tore down the forward part of the defensive post. The machine-gun, with a greater caliber and a far higher rate of fire than the guns, was wreaking havoc among the hosts of the Yokai. But it was not as maneuverable as a gun, so that in very little time the soldiers who were guarding it began to have trouble keeping those flanks which were not covered by the machine-gun free.

"We need help over here!" Private Ferrara yelled desperately.

Robert, even seeing that the southern flank was far from being under control, decided to move to the front to give what help he could. Two creatures which had dodged the machine-gun bursts had very nearly reached the defensive position. They gathered momentum and with their powerful hind quarters rose more than two meters from the ground. He reacted in time and brought them down, although they fell on one of the soldiers on Ferrara's right. The soldier fell on his face with both bodies on top of him and began to scream in panic.

Robert took up his post at once as new creatures went on making their way across the stretch of open ground. There was no time to help the young soldier. He got ready to repel them, but soon found himself without ammunition. He had been so concerned with the other soldiers that he had forgotten to check his own charge. An unforgivable mistake for someone of his rank. Hastily he took another magazine from the side of his suit and readied his gun as fast as he could. But by now it was too late. Three other creatures had leapt through the breach and were heading toward him at great speed. He aimed at the first and fired twice. Success. At the same time the other two were barely two meters from him. He was lost.

While he was getting ready for the impact, a powerful volley flew over the area and the two creatures fell to the ground, hurled several meters away by the power of the machine-gun.

"I think you'll need to be more alert next time, sir!" Private Ferrara shouted, while at the same time she swiveled the machine-gun in the opposite direction and went on defending the front line.

"That was close!" he said in some puzzlement. "I owe you one, private!"

"I'll settle for getting out of here!" she said without taking her finger off the trigger. "Although I won't refuse a good jug of cold beer."

"Consider it done!" He had no time to get his breath back, because the Yokai were pressing on every flank.

"How's the situation there, Lieutenant?" Captain Garth asked.

"I don't think we can hold out much longer, Captain." he admitted. "We don't have that much ammo, and they're getting closer and closer. We've already had a couple of scares."

"I get you. I think it's time to move on to plan B."

"Lieutenant Balakova!" Robert called. "Lights on, now!"

"Yessir!"

In unison, the pilots switched on the ships' powerful spotlights. Instantly many of the creatures stopped dead, surprised by this sudden source of light.

"Lieutenant, aim your spotlights at the rover!" Robert called. "I need you to clear a way for me!"

"Copy that!" the pilot replied as she steered the ship toward the armored vehicle.

Just as Robert had intended, the creatures began to leave the area around the vehicle. But even with the light, they were still coming forward via the blind spots which the spotlights of the transport did not illuminate so strongly.

He ran out of the defensive perimeter and jumped over the piled-up bodies he found on his way. He was only ten meters away from the vehicle, and hurried toward it. But when it was almost within reach, and even though the pilot was illuminating the area intensely, a huge figure leapt on to the roof of the rover. Its lower lip was crossed by a huge scar. It was the leader of the Yokai, and it did not seem to be in a very good mood.

Robert stopped. The creature gave a powerful roar and its face, even though it had no eyes, seemed to stare straight at him. In some way it knew where he was. He took his gun, but before he could even aim at the creature it hurled itself on him. He dropped the gun from the force of the impact and fell backward to the ground. The creature, which perhaps was expecting a stronger rival, rolled over his head.

Both of them got up quickly, but they had changed positions and now it was Robert who was closer to the rover. He decided to make the attempt. He ran to the co-pilot's door, but his enemy was far faster and more agile than he was. With an almost feline movement it hit him from behind and threw him head-first against the side of the vehicle. The blow was so violent that it took him several precious moments to recover. He rolled over several times and managed to turn so that he was on his back. But the creature was still there above him. It was getting ready to finish the job it had started.

When he realized that he was beside the underside of the vehicle he clicked on the suit thrusters and the creature ended up driving its claws into the ground. At the same time the thrust enabled him to move toward the other side of the vehicle. Now was his chance to get inside and switch on the front spotlights. He had to take advantage of the enemy leader's puzzlement. He got up and opened the door as fast as he could, climbed into the pilot's seat and slammed the armored door shut behind him.

The creature appeared beside him on the other side and gave a leap. It seemed rather puzzled by how its prey could have escaped. Robert took advantage of the confusion to start the engine of the rover, then turned on the lights.

"Here's some light for you, you bastard!" he roared.

The creature gave a start beside him as it took the power of the lateral spotlights almost directly, and gave a desperate growl. It ran toward the forest, as did the remainder of the creatures which had still lingered there.

Robert gave a long, loud sigh when he realized that the danger was over.

"At last!" he heard Ferrara on the radio. "They're going!"

"Flee, you bastards!" the captain yelled euphorically.

Cautiously, Robert came out of the vehicle. Seeing that everything was clear, he picked up his gun and made his way to the defensive post.

"Report on the situation, Private Ferrara."

"We have two casualties, sir. Just before the lights on the rover went on there was a wave that was too big for us."

"Hell!"

"But this time I don't think they managed to carry away all their casualties." She indicated the piles of enemy bodies on the battlefield.

The captain came over from the other defensive post.

"Great work, Lieutenant!"

Robert could not share his superior officer's enthusiasm. "We had two casualties, Captain."

"Well, that's war for you," he said coldly. "Sometimes there are casualties. What matters is that we won this battle even though we were completely outnumbered."

Robert did not add anything to the captain's words. He could not bring himself to rejoice over what had happened. That same morning they had lost one man; tonight, two more. Three good soldiers who would never know what it would mean to start over again. He could not be happy. Nor did he want to be.

8
The waiting

July 5, Year 0
Asimov Space Station

Emily spent part of the night watching the progress of the military team in the distance. She was one of the few people in the station with enough privileges to do so. As a result it was hardly surprising that at this hour in the morning she was yawning as if she had not slept for a week, in spite of the very strong coffee she had drunk.

Even after the confrontation had come to an end, she had found it hard to get to sleep. She had followed events with her nerves on edge, especially when the leader of the Yokai had got in Robert's way as he made for the land scouting vehicle.

"What happened yesterday is making me think we might need to postpone preparations for the first base," Director Patel was saying at that very moment.

Emily was not paying too much attention. There seem to be voices opposing the setting up of the first of the bases at the site near the accident, even though according to Ada it was the most promising of them.

"We can't put this off any more, Suresh," the deputy director said.

"Let's use one of the sites on the other continent," the engineering director insisted.

Emily was still going over yesterday's attack in her mind. She was quite clear now that the Yokai, in addition to being savages, were intelligent creatures.

"But here we have the chance to make contact with a new civilization," Deputy Director Green pointed out.

From the images caught by the cameras of the surviving beacon, Ada had calculated that over four thousand Yokai had taken part in the skirmish. And though their casualties ran into the hundreds, many had fled back to the cave.

"The other sites aren't as promising," Janice Jones put in. She was a member of the board who was unable to keep her opinion to herself.

Many dead Yokai had been left in that clearing, even though some of the survivors had risked trying to recover the bodies of their fallen mates. There seemed to be some kind of cultural tradition, or something of the sort, which was compelling them to do this.

"But we'd be safer there while we get a better idea of how dangerous those damn creatures are," Director Patel insisted once again.

"At one of those sites there's an alien device that's emitting a molecule we still don't know very much about, Suresh," the deputy director reminded him.

The military team had got back from the site well into the night. They had left the vehicle, the barricades and also some of the beacons on the ground. They wanted to find out whether the Yokai would return the following night. It seemed a good idea. In addition they still had one beacon left, which they had placed ten kilometers or so from the cave entrance. For some reason the Yokai had not destroyed this.

"I don't know why," Director Patel protested uneasily, "but it looks as though I'm the only one here who's aware of the danger we're in. Call me crazy, but I wouldn't like to risk any more human lives just for the sake of playing cowboys in the old Wild West."

"No-one wants to risk lives, Suresh," the deputy director said. "And believe me, I understand your objections perfectly well. But there's nothing to lead us to think the Yokai are going to get as far as that site."

The next few nights were going to be deeply important for the colony's future. Depending on the reaction of the Yokai, the guarantees of success would be greater or lesser. They had lost many of their number, but nobody yet knew how large their community was.

"Commander Bauer, what do you think?" the deputy director asked.

"I think it's too soon to make a definite decision. It's been a very long day and night for everyone. But there's still too much we don't know about the behavior of the Yokai. My men have assured me that the blow we've given them is a significant one. On the other hand, caution prevents me recommending the installation of any kind of base at this particular site. In the same way I can't guarantee safety anywhere else. There are too many unknowns."

In fact there was no indication that the Yokai might travel beyond the accident site. But nor was there anything to assure them that they would be safe from an attack anywhere else on the planet, whether from the Yokai colony or any other that might exist.

"What do you think, Emily?" the deputy director asked.

Emily was lost in her own thoughts. She had to replay those last exchanges in her memory so that she could give her opinion.

"We're never going to have a full guarantee of safety. Neither now nor in ten years' time. But Ada thinks that's the site the Galileo would most probably have chosen. And besides, we could find other threats anywhere else on the planet. Now I'm not the one who has to make a decision on this scale. I understand that we can't put human lives at risk, nor the station's valuable equipment. But I think we could go ahead with setting up the base by day while we keep an eye on the behavior of the Yokai during the night, then decide in a few days' time whether or not it's safe for a small group to move in."

"Do you approve of Dr. Rhodes' suggestion, Director Patel?" the deputy director asked.

Patel thought about what had been said.

"All right then, I think it could be a midway point between both positions. If by doing that we can manage to avoid risking human lives, that's good enough for me."

"Perfect!" the deputy director said. "It looks as though we're agreed. Tomorrow we'll start to take equipment and supplies so that we can begin preparations. The engineering teams will travel to the area every morning and come back before nightfall. Can we find some way of guaranteeing safety during the day, Commander?"

"No problem. I'll assign a detachment to protect the engineers."

"Well then, I think that's all for now," the deputy director said, satisfied with the result of the meeting. "We all have things to do, and once again we're on the threshold of making history."

Around noon Emily went to the mess hall, where her colleagues were waiting. They had been informed of the previous day's events, but they did not know what had happened during the night.

"How did everything go last night, Emily?" Paula asked nervously.

"Fine. Well, not entirely. I guess it's hard to answer that question with just one word."

"What happened?" Taro insisted.

"The soldiers repelled the attack. But those creatures showed that they're very intelligent. We had a really bad time. They're terrifying, and there were thousands of them."

"Thousands?" Paula repeated in horror.

"Yeah." She lowered her voice. "Ada counted at least four thousand of them. And that's taking into account that the sensors can't detect what's in the dense foliage with any degree of precision, so there might be many more of them."

"How horrible!"

"And what about the soldiers?" Gorka asked.

"We had two more casualties."

There was a small silence at the table. The mere thought of what their friends must have gone through after losing two more comrades in the fight made their hearts sink.

"And what are we supposed to do?" Chad asked. "Are we going to be safe at the base?"

"I'd be lying to you if I told you everything's safe," Emily admitted. "I wish I could give you some sort of guarantee."

"We'll be fine," Taro said confidently.

During lunch they chose trivial topics of conversation, consciously avoiding any mention of what had happened. Despite this the atmosphere was heavy and somber, especially among the soldiers.

Emily looked around to see if Robert was there, but could not see any of his comrades. When she turned round, she came abruptly face to face with the three soldiers.

"Hi there," Paula said softly. "How are you?"

Private Ferrara was looking resigned. "Alive, at least."

"We've been brought up to date," said Chad. "We're really sorry about your loss. If there's anything we can do for you…"

"We're really grateful," Lieutenant Beaufort said, sounding rather taciturn, "but we just need to rest and get over it as soon as possible."

"Even so, anything you need, we're here," Paula insisted.

Emily did not want to add anything. Robert looked defeated. She would have liked to cheer him up, put her arms around him and help him get over the situation, but this was clearly not the right moment.

She spent the whole afternoon at her terminal reviewing reports and data about the planet. It was a boring job, but she preferred it to the previous day's tension.

"Emily," Ada told her, "you have a message from Lieutenant Beaufort."

She looked up nervously. "What?"

She stopped what she was doing at once and read the message aloud under her breath.

Hi, Emily. Perhaps I seemed a little distant before. In fact I was having trouble getting used to everything that's happened. I just wanted to say I'm sorry if I seemed rude. This whole situation, the constant risk, the loss of comrades, is getting hard for me to bear. I hope things will be better from now on.

Robert.

She was thoughtful for a while. She read the note a couple of times more while she thought about the right reply. Then she began to write:

    Hi Robert. No apology needed. It's understandable that you're rattled, as we all are more or less. The important thing is that we're all in this together….

But the last sentence did not seem right, so she re-wrote it:

    …The important thing is that we're all united. So if you need to talk about it, I'm here.
    Emily.

After reading it over a couple of times, she sent it.
But by now she could no longer concentrate on the task at hand. Every two minutes, again and again, she checked her inbox for any new messages. And though it took quite a while, she received an answer.

    Thanks, Emily. It means a lot to me that you, that all of you, should be worrying like that. And maybe I'll take you at your word; it would be a good idea if I talked to someone. Thanks again.
    Robert

Emily replied again.
    Not at all. Whenever you need to. You know where I am.
    Emily

    This time she did not expect an answer, and though once again she checked her messages from time to time she managed to make some progress with what she was doing. There was no news during the day from the surface of the planet, as was to be expected. But she was very curious to know whether the Yokai would go back to the site of the confrontation. She spoke to Ada so that the AI would keep her informed.
    "Ada, set up an alert, I want to monitor the Yokai situation as soon as it gets dark. Let me know a few minutes before that."
    Ada's warning came as she was coming back to her cabin after a fairly light dinner.
    "You have another message from Lieutenant Beaufort, Emily," she said with a touch of humor.
    Emily smiled. "You're enjoying all this, aren't you?"
    "I must admit that as a rule I get a little bored. And human interactions seem very interesting to me. So yes, I think I'm quite enjoying myself."
    "What a gossip you're turning into!"

She went into the bathroom and brushed her teeth while she read the message on her terminal.

Hi, Emily. I guess you'd like to know what happens on the surface around dusk too. I thought we could watch together, if you feel like it. Unless you have something else to do or have a meeting with the board. Let me know.
Robert.

Emily's heart skipped a beat and she smiled broadly. She wrote back:

Of course! If you like, we could see it from one of the multipurpose halls near the mess. Sunset will be more or less around eight, so shall we meet at seven forty-five in the area?
Emily

A few seconds later came the reply.

Perfect. See you there.
Robert

She was only five minutes late this time. Luckily the last rays of light still lingered in that zone of the planet.

They greeted one another. "How are you feeling?" she asked.

"Better. Although I guess there's still a lot I have to take in."

"As time goes on you'll start to see it differently," she said encouragingly.

They went into one of the halls which had a projector good enough to be able to show the images from the satellite and from the beacons themselves.

"Ada, connect all available cameras and sensors to the screen," Emily said as soon as they had sat down.

Ada showed them a huge map via satellite, with the important locations marked on the screen. On each location data and images were superimposed as they arrived from the sensors: images of the beacon ten kilometers from the Yokai cave and images and data from the radars of the three beacons still intact in the accident area, where the fight had taken place.

"Has anything significant happened during the day?" Robert asked.

"No, Lieutenant," said Ada. "Except for one or two small, rather strange animals, I haven't registered anything out of the ordinary."

"How long is it before it's completely dark?" Emily asked.

"Seventeen minutes."

"We have a while to wait," said Robert.

Both of them were silent, searching for a topic of conversation. Emily broke the uncomfortable silence at last.

"Well? How do you really feel?"

Robert lowered his gaze and gave a gentle sigh.

"I don't really know. I couldn't sleep a wink last night. I've spent the whole day going over and over everything that's happened since we got here. I've lost four men in less than two weeks. And all of it in my first two missions." He paused, and it was obvious that he was suffering. "They were barely more than kids, Emily," he went on while a tear slid down his cheek. "The eldest was the same age as my little brother. The thought that something like that could happen to either of my two brothers makes my heart sink."

"It's perfectly normal for you to feel like that, Robert." She took his hands in her own. "I can't even begin to imagine what you must be going through at the moment."

"There was nothing I could do. I… I suppose I feel powerless."

"You couldn't have done anything, Robert. There were too many of them, I saw that myself. It was eighty to one. In fact it seems a miracle to me that so many of you made it back. Seen in perspective, I have the feeling it was a suicide mission."

"It probably was."

"In that case stop blaming yourself. You did everything you possibly could to bring them back, but the situation was a lot more critical than you could have imagined. In fact if it hadn't occurred to you to use the rover, I'm practically sure a lot more would've died. As far as I'm concerned, you're a hero."

Robert seemed to become a little calmer.

"Thanks, Emily. I suppose I'm not used to situations like this."

"No-one has ever been in this situation before," she pointed out pragmatically. "We all have to get used to the new situation."

"I think I'm feeling better now. I don't know why, but with you I find it very easy to loosen up."

Before they could even exchange a glance, Ada interrupted them.

"Night has fallen now. At this same time yesterday the Yokai left their cave in the direction of the base camp."

Emily let go of Robert's hands, startled. "Can you see anything via the satellite?"

"No, it's dark by now and the satellite's optics aren't able to detect infrared radiation so far away. And the lasers are no use for detecting moving objects."

"Does that mean we have to wait until they reach the first beacon?" Robert asked.

"I'm afraid so, yes."

"What's the reach of the beacon radar?" Emily asked.

"In open land it might be tens of kilometers," Ada said, "but as it's in a forest the range will depend a lot on the obstacles it finds. In any case, we have no radar on that first beacon."

"Why? What happened to it?" Emily asked.

Robert shrugged. "When Private Ferrara set it up it was already broken."

"Already broken?"

"Yeah. Why, what is it?"

"No, it's nothing. It's rather odd, but it might not mean anything."

"How long would we have to wait for them to cover that distance to the beacon?"

"Yesterday it took them twenty-eight and a half minutes," Ada said.

"It's going to make it a long wait," Emily said resignedly.

She did not want to mention the matter of the fight to avoid depressing Robert, who was now looking more cheerful.

"May I ask you a personal question?" she asked.

"Sure, fire away." he said in surprise.

"It was a few days ago, when we had that argument with Captain Garth by the river. The captain accused you of always siding with the aggressors. What did he mean by that?"

Robert bowed his head. He knew perfectly well what she was referring to. There was a pause.

"Actually… I'm not authorized to tell you anything about that. But I think that… in a way you deserve to know."

"Oh, no! Sorry, I didn't mean to put you in an awkward spot."

"Don't worry, it's okay. I don't think it matters much by now if the truth comes out, except that I'm going to ask you to make sure it doesn't leave this room." He was looking up, hoping for a sympathetic reaction from Ada.

"I'll be a tomb," the AI said.

Emily smiled and raised her right hand. "So will I, I swear it."

"Let's just say the two dead workers on the Copernicus weren't exactly workers."

"How am I supposed to take that?"

"They were two of the terrorists."

"What!" she exclaimed, much more loudly than she had intended. "What?" she repeated more quietly.

Robert gave her a summary of what had happened that day, and how at the moment of truth Captain Garth had ended up executing the two men with no chance of a fair trial, or even any opportunity to give their own version of the facts.

Emily covered her mouth. "That's terrible."

"Yes, it certainly is."

"Now I understand a lot of things."

He turned to her very seriously. "You must promise me that whatever might happen from now on with the captain, you won't mention anything."

"Yes, don't worry, I promise."

"The high command decided to keep it from public opinion so that the prestige of the project wouldn't suffer. I don't even know whether Deputy Director Green knows what happened. I think only Captain Garth and I know what happened that day. And now so do you."

Ada cleared her throat. "Ahem."

He smiled. "Yes, and you too, Ada."

"If those creatures have been keeping up the same pace as yesterday, they should appear shortly in front of the beacon," the AI informed them.

"Show us the images on the big screen," Emily said.

Ada did so, but the infrared camera was not showing anything. They spent a long time staring at the image, almost without blinking, but it was not much more than a static shot. As the minutes went by they began to lose any hope of detecting movement. But then suddenly something moved in the distance.

Robert pointed to the screen. "What was that?"

Emily leapt up from her chair. "I think it's them."

There were a lot of them, several hundreds. And they were making the same journey. It took some time for all of them to pass the beacon.

"Ada," Emily asked, "based on the time it's taken them and the number of individuals you estimated yesterday, how many do you think there are?"

"Rather fewer, but not much. About three thousand individuals."

"My God, that's still a horde," Robert murmured.

They sat down in their chairs again, feeling defeated. Deep down, they had been hoping yesterday's defeat would have somehow undermined the creatures' morale. Seeing them coming back tirelessly in search of confrontation meant a massive setback for the project.

"And now what do we do?" Emily asked.

"We'll have to reduce that lair of theirs to rubble," he said resignedly.

They were both silent. The situation was not exactly ideal for making long-term plans. They spent the next hour arguing over the different possibilities for the project, almost repeating each of the different opinions Emily had heard in the meeting that same morning. There were other alternatives, but none as promising as the third of the sites. They were so close, and yet so far away, that they could not help feeling frustrated. But at least the discussion lasted long enough for Ada to have to interrupt them.

"They should be about to appear within range of the accident site radars."

They almost jumped when they realized that almost an hour had gone by.

"Show us information about all three beacons on the screen," Emily said.

Ada superimposed the images and the radar representation on a static image of the area by day. At the moment they could see nothing. But then, just as it had happened before, the radar began to mark small red dots in the forest. They were coming very fast. The location of the dots was confirmed by the infrared images of the beacons.

"They've got there," Robert said.

The sequence seemed to follow the same script as the previous night. The creatures stopped dead. One of them moved forward to the edge of the forest and looked out into the clearing. After a few minutes it went back into the vegetation again.

But this time, instead of waiting for things to happen, three of the creatures ran out of the forest. Each took a different direction, straight to the beacons. In a matter of seconds, one after the other, the signals were lost. The last images they picked up were those of the creatures about to destroy them.

"What did we just see?" Emily asked in amazement.

"We've been blinded."

"Yes, I know, but why did they destroy the beacons? Why haven't they destroyed everything that's left of the Icarus? Why have they left the rover intact?"

"They might know we're watching them."

"Yeah, maybe, but it might be something simpler than that. Did they set up beacons at the landing-spot?"

"You mean where we landed? A few kilometers from the accident?"

"Yes."

He thought for a moment. "I'd swear I gave the order, it's the usual procedure."

"Yes," Ada added, "four beacons were set up."

"And what happened to them?" Emily asked.

"They destroyed them when they came and saw that the transports had taken off," Ada said.

"And how many were set up at the site of the accident?"

"Four."

"But we've only seen three here, so where's the fourth?"

"Destroyed."

"Where exactly was it?"

Ada superimposed the location of the fourth beacon on the satellite image.

"Just as I thought." Emily said. "It's in the area closest to the forest where the main mass of Yokai came out."

Robert looked at her in puzzlement. "I don't quite follow you."

"The radar!" she cried triumphantly. "They're only after the radar."

"What?" he asked, even more confused. "Now I'm really lost."

"Think about it. The first beacon's still intact. Why? Because the radar isn't working." When she saw that he was still frowning, she went on: "Ada, can you tell us what radar is?"

"Radar is a system that uses radio waves to detect, locate and track objects in space," came the obedient response.

"Right, radio waves. And we could also talk in terms of radio frequencies. On Earth the radars work with certain frequencies, which depend on the purpose of the radar and the place where it's going to be used. D'you follow me now?"

"Yeah, I think so."

"One of the things to consider when you use a radar is the impact it might have on the animal life of the area. On Earth we've always tried to make sure radar doesn't interfere with animals like bats or dolphins, with their communication or geolocation. That's why they're set up to operate at frequencies that don't affect animal habitats."

He stared at her, wide-eyed. "We were disturbing them!"

"Exactly!" she said euphorically. "If you think about it, it makes all the sense in the world. Their way of locating us, their lack of eyes. I'd even say we were the ones who attracted them to our position after the accident."

Robert put his hands to his head. It all made sense. It had to be that.

"You're a genius!" he said.

"I have to warn the deputy director," said Emily. "Ada, d'you know whether he's awake?"

"Yes, he and Commander Bauer are doing exactly the same as you two."

"Put me through to him."

"What is it, Emily?" she heard the deputy director's voice at the other end.

"Have you just been watching what we have?"

"Yeah, that we've been left blind."

"But I know why," she said exultantly. "It's because of the radar."

9
The first base

July 8, Year 0
Asimov Space Station

The preparations for setting up the first base on the planet had begun days before. After the discovery that radar had been the reason why the Yokai had attacked them, there was general agreement to begin on the colonization of the planet. Emily and her colleagues used a transport to go and see what progress was being made.

"I'm looking forward to seeing our new home," Chad said excitedly.

"You mean the lab at our new home," Gorka joked. "We all know you're going to be sleeping beside the atomic microscope."

"What can I do about it if I enjoy my work?"

"You ought to find yourself a hobby."

"Well, I'm looking forward to seeing the views," said Paula. "The dawns must be beautiful."

"They certainly are," Emily said.

"How do you know?" Paula asked in surprise.

"I…. well… one of the days I got the last watch duty," she said nervously.

Paula giggled at Emily's reaction. Even inside her suit, she was as red as a ripe tomato.

"I'm nervous about everything," one of the newbies admitted.

Emily smiled. "Don't worry, Kostas. You'll soon see it's a really peaceful ecosystem."

"Well, it's not exactly the fauna and flora that are worrying me most."

"We'll be all right, honestly. We haven't heard anything more of the Yokai since they destroyed the radars. And they've installed beacons with motion detectors all around the base which don't use any kind of radar. And they've been installed at different points between the cave and the base. If they come the slightest bit close, we'll be able to act before they get to our position."

"And we'll be protected by the defense systems," Chad added.

"And we'll have military support," Paula said.

"Oh, I know all that," Kostas admitted. "But after hearing the things you've all been through… well, I'm not exactly reassured. I get the impression this planet attracts bad luck."

Kostas Angelopoulos was the new member of the team. Emily had met him a few months back, when she had ventured into the greenhouse area. He was one of the technicians in charge of managing the ship's hydroponic crops. Both Director Patel and Emily had thought it would be interesting to include an agricultural engineer in the planet's first settlement. It was vitally important for the colony to start assessing how to develop Earth's crops in Kepler-442b conditions.

The other newbie of the expedition was silent in one of the corners of the shuttle which was taking them to the base. This was Jonathan Wiśniewski, the self-confessed perpetrator of the sabotage attack on the Asimov Ark. Only Emily knew this, and for the moment she had preferred not to share the information with her comrades. She and the deputy director had agreed to begin with his reinsertion in the colony, and as a welding technician he had been assigned the post of manager in charge of general maintenance.

"Are you all right, Jonathan?" Emily asked. "You haven't said a word since we sat down."

"Yeah, yeah."

"You're not nervous?" Chad asked. "I remember my first day on the planet, and I was so nervous I almost threw up inside my suit."

"I … I guess I'm fine," Jonathan replied hesitantly.

"Don't worry," Gorka said, "Chad could throw up even if he was taking an aerocab."

The shuttle went through the planet's atmosphere and readied itself for its landing maneuver. In the blink of an eye they had arrived at the site, where the work of assembling the modules of the base were almost finished. When they got out of the vehicle a fine rain welcomed them. The sky was dark, and the threat of a storm could not be ruled out. They were going to find out at firsthand what it was going to be like, the place chosen to house the building which would serve as both residence and workplace.

The engineers had decided to set up the structures in a wide, treeless area surrounded by bushes and vegetation which would act as natural defenses. Somehow they had managed to hide it, and the modules were only visible to anyone coming from the west. The vegetation itself hid the buildings almost completely from other angles. The overall space was some fifty meters wide by the same in length.

A number of the engineers were still adding the final touches to the roof of the structure, where they were installing solar panels. The heavy machinery which had been used to dig and level the terrain was still visible. A rather squat figure, wearing an exosuit with the orange Engineering stripe, waved at them from the access zone.

"Hello, everyone!" Director Patel called cheerfully. "Welcome!"

"Hello there, Director!" Paula said as she gave him a metallic but heartfelt hug.

The director of the engineering sector was much liked by everyone for his kindness. There was not a soul in the expedition who did not have good things to say about him.

Emily too greeted the director. "Everything looks so nice!" she exclaimed.

"It's beginning to look good," Patel admitted. "In fact I'm beginning to feel envious."

"Stay with us, director," Paula said.

"Ufff! I'd like that very much." He laughed, then put his hands to his stomach. "But before that I'm afraid I'd have to get back to my exercises if I don't want the planet's gravity to take its toll on me. But let's forget about my excess fat. Come with me and I'll show you the facilities. We've just sealed it and checked it for habitability. You're going to be the first ones to see it."

The facilities consisted of two distributor areas linked by a corridor and five modules with different uses. The only entrance was in the first of the distributor areas, a square structure which served as a decontamination module. Patel went to the entrance, where they could hear sounds of decompression coming from inside.

"The wait is because the decontamination chamber's being emptied," he explained. "It's entirely automatic, it detects who comes in, who goes out, and manages the whole process of changing between halls safely. You couldn't go out without a suit, even if you tried."

The two huge doors of the facilities opened on both sides, showing the interior of the first distributor area, a hall some ten meters across and almost four in height. Once they were all inside, the doors closed, and after they heard the familiar sounds of a decontamination system, the blinking red lights gave way to a more reassuring green light.

"Now it's safe to take off your suits," the director announced as he took off his helmet.

They all followed his example.

Chad sniffed the atmosphere. "It smells half-musty, half new."

The director nodded. "Yes, the first few days it might smell rather strange when you come in from outside, but you'll soon get used to it. The whole facility uses air from outside as raw material. Filters have been installed, and under the floor we're standing on now generators of breathable air fed with the air outside have been installed as well. Which means that even though for safety reasons you all have a small oxygen tank, the facility's self-sufficient."

"And what about the rest of the life-support systems?" Gorka asked.

"We have solar panels and accumulators on the roofs of all the halls to generate the electricity we need, as well as a small fusion reactor to complement them. As far as the energy system's concerned, I'm afraid we're going to have to make one or two improvements with an eye on the future to make everything more efficient. We don't yet know for sure what kind of performance we're going to get from the sun, and as for water, at the moment we have the water tanks on top of the other distributor area. We'll go and have a look at that afterwards."

"I see," Gorka said, satisfied with the explanations.

"On either side we have two halls. On the left, as we came in, is the lab."

The director went to the laboratory doors, which opened as he approached. They saw a brightly-lit space of some two hundred square meters, which still lacked the necessary equipment to make it into a functioning laboratory.

"All the halls are the same size," the director went on. "This is where we're going to install all those toys Drs. Williams and Murakami have decided are necessary. And there'll also be space for one or other small office, work areas and meeting rooms."

"It's impressive," Taro murmured.

"It's fantastic!" Chad said enthusiastically.

"I'm glad you like it. Here in the other hall," he went on as he went into the room on the right of the entrance, "we'll have the storeroom."

The door opened in the same way, revealing the equipment and tools which the engineers were using in their installation work.

The director pointed up to the storeroom ceiling. "I haven't mentioned it, but if you look closely you'll see we have skylights in all the halls, which will mean you'll have some natural light. As is logical, they've been given ultraviolet treatment to prevent the sun's radiation affecting you. Although we're going to have to complement it with artificial light, as unfortunately here there's rather less light than on our dear Earth."

"Hey, I thought it was just me," Kostas joked.

The director turned to Gorka and Jonathan. "The idea is to install a polymer and alloy printer so that you can print everything you need in the future."

"Sounds good," Gorka said.

The director came out of the storeroom and went through the door opposite the entrance. This opened on to another corridor with innumerable closets on one side and terminals with connections for exosuits on the other.

"As you can all see, here you have your lockers and enough storage space for the twenty-five people this station can house. We haven't yet connected the supplies to the charging sockets for the suits, but if you like we can leave them here, even if it's only to taste real gravity a little, without assistance."

He and the rest of the team each went to one of the terminals and left their suits there. They went through the door at the end of the corridor and reached an open distributor area like that at the entrance, this time with no decontamination system.

"Right. In front we have the bedrooms. On the left are the common spaces: kitchen, mess hall and leisure room. On the right, toilets, showers and infirmary, and also a small gym so that your bodies can start to get used to the planet's gravity"

"It's certainly quite a lot better than my house on earth," Kostas said in surprise.

"Yeah, pity there isn't a good burger place nearby…" Chad muttered.

"You're going to have a traditional kitchen," the director said, "so that you'll be able to prepare the food the way you like, Chad. Let's take a look at the mess area. I'd imagine my boys are still in there."

He crossed the door to the shared area of the facility, and just as he had announced, three people were in it busy with finishing the installation of a food printer.

"Hi there!" the director called. The three technicians greeted them with a timid wave, and he went on with his explanation. "You'll have the kitchen here, at the beginning of the hall, the dining area in the middle and a small common hall at the end."

"I feel as if I were being given the keys to a new home," Paula said jokingly.

The director smiled. "That's understandable. In a way, that's what it is. Let's take a look at the bedrooms."

They went back to the second distributor area and crossed the door opposite the corridor. This particular hall was divided into two by a screen. At the moment they could not see any beds anywhere.

"We thought it would be interesting to divide it into two living spaces because of the classic segregation by birth sex, but you can use them any way you want."

"It's great," Emily said.

"Right, and last, but no less important because of that, we'll have a look at the area which includes toilets, infirmary and entertainment area."

They went on to the last of the halls.

"Here you have a couple of dressing-rooms, and further along we're going to prepare a functional gym so that you can stay in shape and start exercising your bodies and get them used to planetary conditions. You'll be checked and monitored constantly as long as you're here. And though she's not here at the moment, Nurse Brown has volunteered to form part of this colony and she'll join you once the remaining work is over. So we'll also be setting up a small infirmary here. We'll bring all the equipment from the station, starting the day after tomorrow."

Emily, who had just found out this particular detail, was delighted to know that Evelyn was to be the resident healthcare worker.

"They've done a great job," Gorka said. "Everything looks fantastic."

The director nodded. "Thank you. Oh, I was forgetting." He went back to the distributor area. "Under here we have the main reactor."

He pulled a ring on one of the tiles, and they saw a flight of stairs which went vertically down to the underground level.

"The spare reactor is under the storeroom. Although we'll be able to talk about all these details at some specific meeting before the move. Today all I wanted to do was show you how the work's coming on, which is always more interesting than a mere boring meeting."

"What happens if there is a storm like the one we had a few weeks ago?" Chad asked.

"We've installed an enormous lightning rod outside. You might not have noticed when you came in, because it's set a little apart from the facilities. In theory it can withstand the tremendous electrical power of the storm you all had to cross a few days ago. Perhaps in the future we may be able to use that electricity the way people used to on Earth. For the moment we haven't wanted to overcharge the base circuit until we've carried out some tests. We'll study the possibilities once the sensors of the lightning rod give us more information."

Gorka nodded in agreement.

"And of course, and although there's no access from inside," he added, "just above here is a small tank with five thousand liters of drinking water, and another one like it to gather and filter the rainwater and use it for other purposes."

"For irrigation?" Kostas asked.

The director nodded. "For example. Or to clean utensils."

He paused, suggesting that the visit had ended.

"When do we start?" Chad asked.

"At the end of this week we'll have everything ready for you to move in. The commander is going to have the defenses installed tomorrow, so you'll be able to count on guarantees that any kind of threat will be repelled."

"Thank you, Director," Emily said. "We really appreciate the enormous effort your team has made to get all this done in record time. And besides, it's looking really cozy and welcoming. It's all going to be very exciting."

"It certainly is," Paula agreed. "Thank you very much, Director. It makes you want to stay the night here."

"I'm glad you like it. And of course if you have any suggestions or improvements, or anything you'd like installed, we'll try to manage it."

Emily smiled. "We'll keep that in mind, Director."

They got into their suits once again and left the facilities. From outside they could get a view of everything the director had explained: the solar panels, the water tanks. Chad was even able to locate the huge lightning rod in a gap between two of the rooms. The rain had stopped, but it gave the impression that at any moment a storm might break out. Kostas walked forward a few meters and stopped to observe the area of land in front of the entrance.

"What are you doing, Kostas?" Emily asked. "Thinking about where you're going to put your greenhouses?"

"Actually, yes. This looks like a good place for my experiments."

She was intrigued. "What do you have in mind?"

"Well, I want to try the principal crops on the planet: wheat, oatmeal and barley. But also all kinds of vegetables and greens: spinach, peas, tomatoes, potatoes…"

"That's a lot."

"Yes, but it's necessary. And I aim to cultivate them in triplicate."

"In triplicate?"

"Yes. My idea is to have a small vegetable garden outside and two greenhouses. One of them'll have extra artificial light to complement what it gets from the sun."

"I get you. You want to try different conditions to see how Earth vegetables behave in each of them."

"That's right. All the same, we won't be able to eat any of what we cultivate yet."

"I can imagine, until we know how the existence of the alien molecule affects the development of the plants."

"Among other things, yes. But we also have to study the composition of the soil. Depending on what we find, the vegetables might even turn out toxic."

"Oh dear, that doesn't sound too good."

"No. But still, we'll find solutions. That'll make up a good part of our work here. Once we've checked that conditions are acceptable enough, getting Earth agriculture to work here will only be a matter of time."

Suddenly a flash of light raced throughout the sky in the distance, startling the group. The clap of thunder which followed came accompanied by another flash. Memories of the previous storm went through their minds, and they feared one or other of those bolts of lightning might hit the still-unfinished facilities.

"Looks as though we're going to give the lightning rod its first outing," Gorka said.

"We'd better leave," Chad said. He sounded frightened. "I don't want to be here when that storm gets close to the base."

10
The settlers

August 4, Year 0
Magellan Base, Kepler-442b

"Home, sweet home!" said Chad the moment he had taken off his helmet.

Several days had gone by since their previous visit, and by now the first of the project's scientific bases was fully functional and well-stocked. Thirteen people were going to form part of the first human colony on Kepler-422b. Thirteen settlers in hostile territory.

"Time to unpack!" said Kostas enthusiastically.

"We've been assigned lockers in the corridor," Paula said when they had been through the first door.

They left their own exosuits in front of their own lockers.

"This is my place," Gorka pointed out. "Yours is this one here."

"Oh, right," Taro said apologetically. "Sorry, I hadn't realized it was yours."

They all seemed to be thrilled with the new base. They hastened to stow the contents of their suitcases in the lockers and went to check the final state of the facilities.

"I'm going to change," Emily said enthusiastically.

Private Ferrara nodded. "Yeah, that's not a bad idea. You have to admit this wretched tightsuit is comfortable, but it gets to be a drag when you've worn it for a while."

Emily went into the dressing-room of the right-hand wing. Everything smelled newly-installed. It was not particularly pleasant, but she supposed they would get used to it. She put on her usual engineering uniform and went back to the locker to stow away her tightsuit.

By now her colleagues were scattered around the base, all thrilled by some new discovery they had come across in the various halls. She decided to go into the dorms, where Sergeant Ortiz and Private Ferrara were talking about how to get things organized.

"There are fifteen beds in each room," Ortiz was saying. "How are we going to sleep?"

"I don't particularly mind," Ferrara said.

Emily sat down on one of the beds to test the mattress. They looked comfortable, and not surprisingly they were like the ones on the ark.

"I was thinking we could all stay in the same place," she said. "You know, thinking about solidarity."

Ortiz smiled. "Do you realize, some of the people who're going to sleep here might snore like troopers?"

"Well, Ada could cancel the noise so that no-one hears the snoring."

The soldiers looked at one another in surprise.

"Can Ada do that?" they asked.

"Sure." She looked at them, smiling. "Didn't you know that?"

"I can do that and lots of other things," Ada said boastfully. "White noise, relaxing music, sounds of the sea, anything you need to help you sleep peacefully."

"Are you telling me we've spent months putting up with other people's snoring and you haven't done a thing?" Private Ferrara complained.

"I don't usually interfere in human affairs, but if you ask me, I'll do it with pleasure."

Sergeant Ortiz shrugged. "Well, at least I'll be able to forget about earplugs."

Emily left them arguing about which of the rooms was the best. When she came out she crossed paths with Sergeant Cameron in the distributor area.

"I wanted to speak to you, Dr. Rhodes," the sergeant said. Her voice was businesslike, even abrupt.

"Sure, fire away."

The sergeant made sure there was no-one else around.

"What the hell is he doing here?" she asked roughly.

"Who?"

"You know perfectly well who I mean."

"He's done his time," Emily said when she understood that the sergeant was talking about Jonathan Wiśniewski. "He's repented. I don't see why he—"

"He nearly killed us all!" Cameron interrupted her in a harsh whisper. "He ought to be rotting in a cell for the rest of his life."

"In the first place: a judge determined his sentence and he's already served it," Emily said. She was annoyed by the sergeant's manner. "Secondly: Jonathan Wiśniewski might be a great help for the project; and thirdly: if you don't like the decisions I make, you can go back to the

Asimov whenever you like. Understood, Sergeant?"

The sergeant left in a huff toward the dressing-rooms without even attempting to respond to this. Still, though she felt she had won that particular confrontation, Emily had to calm down a little before she was able to go on reviewing the facilities. She had not liked the sergeant's tone at all. Jonathan Wiśniewski was a repentant man, and if when they were all making a new start they did not believe in second chances, when was humanity ever going to do it? Either way, the sergeant had managed to ruin the day for her.

She took the corridor toward the exit and once again put on first her tightsuit, then the exosuit.

"Are you going out?" Robert asked her. He was on his way back from the storeroom.

"Yeah, I need to clear my head," she said grumpily.

"Fine." He did not want to ask the reason for her obvious anger. "But don't go too far, we haven't secured the perimeter completely yet."

Outside, a faint sunlight bathed the area. She had not yet grown accustomed to that orange tint of the sky and the light itself. That day there were plenty of clouds as well, some of them even threatening rain.

A few meters from the entrance to the base, the shuttle which had brought them over was parked. Balakova was busy carrying out maintenance tasks on it, bent over the electrical outlet which allowed her to keep it charged in case of whatever might happen. Beside her was the Rover from the Icarus which the commander's team had recovered from the accident site.

When they had established that the radar had been the real problem with the Yokai, a small group of soldiers and engineers had gone back to the fateful place. They were surprised to find that the Yokai had taken away their dead. Emily was sure this must be in compliance with some kind of ritual or habit. In fact the expedition had been given the job of recovering the equipment that might still be useful, and at the same time had dismantled part of the Icarus. Some day the deputy director intended to put it together again.

She decided to take a short stroll while her anger subsided. She turned toward the northeast, to the right as she came out of the base. She wanted to see how far away the river was in that direction. If she looked toward the northwest she could see an extensive mountain range on the horizon. It looked fairly steep and dangerous. On the highest peaks the unmistakable whiteness of snow could be made out.

"How high are those mountains, Ada?" she asked.

"Four thousand seven hundred meters, according to the satellite's laser measurements."

"Wow," said Emily. "That's high."

"Yes, there's a range that stretches for hundreds of kilometers and crosses the area from east to west. Although it's interesting that this same range seems to follow a closed circle, as if it were a crater. It's certainly an extremely curious formation."

Emily nearly stopped dead. "A crater? Didn't you say there was no volcanic activity in the area?"

"And there isn't, so don't worry, I didn't say it was volcanic. It might be a crater formed millions of years ago by a meteorite impact. And though anything can happen in geology, it gives the impression that it was formed a very long time ago. I can't give you more data without studying the composition and age of the terrain."

She was startled by this. "A meteorite?"

"Yes. I can understand that it's scary, but it's quite normal in astronomy," the AI said reassuringly. "The chances of the same thing happening here as on Earth are practically nil."

She sighed. "Let's hope you're right. How far is the range from here?"

"The base and the foothills are about thirty kilometers away."

"That's quite a long way for a first excursion."

"Yes, especially if you go by yourself, like now. Can I advise you not to go too far from the base?"

"How obsessed you all are with safety," she said resignedly. "It's daytime, and all I want to do is get to the river."

"I'll mark the shortest route on your helmet visor."

Emily followed the path, free of vegetation and geographical features, which Ada had marked for her. A few minutes later she began to hear the unmistakable sound of water. She had to find a comfortable way of getting to the particular stretch of the valley which led down to the riverbed. And there, on a large boulder she sat down to watch the force of the water.

The area sloped slightly, and the riverbed was made up of large boulders which obliged the water to make its way on with a great deal of noise. Along this stretch the river was still too wide, and the strength of the current did not encourage wading.

"How far to the other side?"

"Sixty-five meters from where you are."

"Is there any spot along it that might be easier to cross?"

"I can see one or two stretches where some kind of bridge could be set up. There's machinery at the Asimov that can install one up to a hundred meters long in a matter of minutes. But if you mean on foot, I'm afraid the river's too wide for the whole length of its course to be crossed on foot. On the other hand you might be able to cross the quieter stretches with the suit."

"Not even at the source?"

"I'd say the source of the river is a huge waterfall thirty-five kilometers or so from the base, high up in the mountains. And from that same point the volume of water is large enough to make any attempt to cross inadvisable."

Emily relaxed for a long time, looking out at the water. The sound of the rapids camouflaged any other sound from the abundant trees that protected the area, but the place breathed peace on all sides. Very soon she managed to forget all her problems, forget Sergeant Cameron, forget the goals of the expedition. Here there were only herself and the river, nothing else.

Suddenly a bird flapped its wings in a tree on the other side of the river, rose and glided above the stream. It seemed to be searching for prey, and was a creature of some size. Apparently it did not find what it was looking for, so it landed on the rock beside her. She stared at it in fascination. It was the size of a seagull, but its body was covered with a fine dark gray fluff instead of feathers. Nor did it have a beak, only a sharp muzzle and two huge black eyes which were staring at her curiously. What attracted her attention most were two protuberances, like antennae, which came out of its head and which the animal kept erect until they reached the same length as its tail. Both tail and protuberances were a striking blue.

The creature watched her attentively, apparently trying to decide whether this metal figure watching it was dangerous, or whether it could eat it. Suddenly it opened its mouth and began to crow. It was a curious sound, almost amusing. As it did so Emily saw its small sharp teeth. A bite from them would be dangerous, she thought, but luckily she was wearing her exosuit. And without more ado, the bird began to preen itself. It raised one of its enormous wings and began to pass its muzzle along them. To Emily this was a very familiar gesture. After all, many animals had similar rituals on Earth. Perhaps it was searching for some kind of parasite, or simply cleaning that coating of fluff all over its body, as cats did.

After spending some time on the rock nearby, the bird seem to tire of being there and with a swift, graceful movement it took off. It flew over the rapids to make sure there was nothing interesting there, and after skimming back and forth a couple of times it vanished downriver in search of somewhere it could look for something to eat.

Emily, much calmer and more relaxed now, got up from the rock and decided to make her way back slowly to the facilities.

"Ada take me back along another path, even if it's a bit longer."

The AI indicated a route which followed the riverside for a couple of kilometers, then went back into the vegetation to end up skirting the base, then approaching it from the south. Emily walked on for a few minutes, dodging vegetation and the odd huge boulder. She ended up reaching a place of quiet water where the river widened even further. A few meters below, something caught her attention. The river seemed to be dammed at this point.

"Ada, that arrangement of the rocks isn't natural, is it?"

"No, from the similarity of the rocks and their arrangement, I'd say they were put there deliberately."

Emily looked carefully around, as if she suspected that someone were watching her, but saw nothing except reddish trees, water and those enormous rocks. They were all rectangular, almost perfectly so. They were set to form a line with a slight curve in the center. With the widest part of the rocks parallel to the flow of the river itself, it looked as though it had once been some kind of walkway, or perhaps a dam had been made to slow down the flow on this stretch of the river. It was three meters or so between one rock and the next: a manageable distance.

"This looks like one of the tests in the exosuit training course," she whispered.

"If you're thinking of crossing over, allow me to dissuade you," came Ada's warning. "Crossing to the far side seems feasible, but we don't know what there could be over there. And don't forget, you're alone and unarmed."

"Ada, sometimes you need to learn to run before you know how to walk."

And in one leap, assisted by her suit thrusters, she landed on the first of the rocks. It seemed stable. The surface was covered with dried remains of some reddish moss or algae.

I'm pretty sure when the range to the north melts it causes floods, she thought, *then these rocks'll be submerged for part of the year.*

She readied herself and jumped to the next rock with no further problem. And then to the third, the fourth and the fifth. She looked back to see how much she had moved on and immediately regretted it. Seeing what she had left behind gave her a slight feeling of vertigo, but even so, she decided to go on. She miscalculated her next leap and landed with the tips of her boots on the edge of the rock. If she had not thrown her arms back and used her thrusters she would have ended up in the water. Luckily she had been able to react in time.

She was a little more careful with the remaining stones, which she could now see were exactly the same size. After a few more jumps she reached the other side, feeling proud of herself for having done it. Ahead, the scrub had reclaimed what looked like an old path which crossed the dense forest of huge red-tinged trees.

"It's been ages since anyone came this way," she said aloud.

She went on with some effort, zigzagging and making her way through the abundant vegetation. Then she saw something that caught her attention: ahead of her was a wooden house, or rather what was left of it. It was almost completely ruined, and decay seemed to have finished off what little was left standing. It looked as though it had been abandoned for years, though perhaps here materials decayed at a different rate. It had been put up around the thick trunk of a tree, using the lower branches to add a second story, though barely a single length of wood was left of this.

She looked around, toward the remaining trees. In the next one was another structure, if anything in a worse state than the first. It looked much smaller, and had only a single floor. It might have been a small shed or a barn. If this was the work of the Keplerians, it would certainly explain why the satellite images had shown no kind of settlement in the area. It seemed that they lived in the forests, under cover of the trees.

"Ada, memorize this location. There might be more structures nearby."

"Copy that," she heard her say. "And please be very careful."

She went on very warily. Any animal sound made her tense, stiff as a reed. More than once she stopped dead in an attempt to locate the source of the sound, especially when she heard some animal moving through the bushes.

"Can you detect anything, Ada?" she asked to calm her nerves.

"No, or at least nothing out of the ordinary. There seem to be a lot of birds and small animals round here."

Emily crossed a clearing, feeling unsafe because she had no weapon with her. She was beginning to think it had been a bad idea to come so far, at least by herself. What would happen if she were attacked by the Keplerians? In fact they knew very little about them. Or suppose some other kind of creature were to appear, like those that had attacked the soldiers?

She tried to eliminate those thoughts from her mind, and a surprising self-control came from her inner depths to help her stay calm. She went back between the trees. Something had caught her attention. From the clearing she detected an area where the forest seemed to have less underbrush. More than that, the trees were perfectly lined up, forming a straight, artificial avenue.

This can't be just chance, she thought as she went deeper into the trees.

The area, though covered by a blanket of leaves, did not have the same wild, chaotic look that nature always offers. The trees were rather younger here, and someone seemed to have taken the time to set them at regular intervals. Almost without meaning to, she had now gone a couple of kilometers from the river.

As she was watching the curious spacing of the trees, she came face to face with a creature. It stood erect on its two legs, with skin that was jet-black tinged with red, a meter and forty centimeters tall.

Both of them were frozen, watching one another from barely ten meters apart. Its large dark eyes seemed about to pop out of their sockets.

Its large mouth, which was wide open, revealed a long row of what looked like teeth, though she could only see two long strips which ran across its mouth from side to side with a very small gap in the middle. It had something inside this, but the shock caused it to fall out. She saw that it was carrying something in its small left claw which looked like food. Whatever it might be, a piece of it had fallen from the creature's mouth. She was looking at a young Keplerian: a teenager, or perhaps no more than a boy.

He was barefooted, but wore a worn-out doublet in an attractive though discolored blue and dark, rather threadbare pants. She was sure it was not one of the two they had seen from the other side of the river when they had been on their way to the pickup point.

As fast as she could, she tried to remember the protocol for the first contact with extraterrestrials. But her mind was blank. So she opted for using common sense, raised both hands with the palms toward the creature to try to show she meant it no harm, and said:

"Hi! My name is Emily."

The creature, who had given a start when she had raised her hands, waited for the sentence to end but then ran away in terror in the opposite direction.

Wünisht! he shouted, *Wünisht!* he repeated as he fled as though the devil were after him.

Emily was dumbstruck by the youngster's reaction, though in all honesty it was rather comical. She reacted when she realized the kid had dropped what he had been carrying in his hand. She bent down and picked it up from the ground.

It's bread! she cried inwardly. *Whole wheat bread, to be more precise.*

She decided that it was time to get back to base. She did not want to be there when that Keplerian youngster came back with a group of ill-tempered adults because she had scared one of their young. She put away the piece of bread to analyze it. The possible implications of this discovery were enormous. She forced herself not to run as she retraced her steps and crossed the river again, this time without any more frights.

11
First contact

August 4, Year 0
Magellan Base, Kepler-442b

Nervous and sweaty, Emily went into the facilities. It had been three hours since she had gone out to try to relax. She could not stop thinking of the implications of what had just happened. She took off her helmet and went into the laboratory. There, as was to be expected, Taro and Chad were going over all the material they had at their disposal there.

"Guys!" she cried enthusiastically, "I've brought you something I want you to analyze."

They were both surprised by her sudden excitement.

"What's happened?" Taro asked curiously.

Emily told them where she had been and what she had found there.

"You shouldn't have gone alone," Taro pointed out.

She tried to dodge the criticism "All right, yes. But it's done now, so that doesn't matter anymore."

"Something might have happened to you," Chad said. "We can't go around on our own here. You've seen the kind of creatures there are on this planet."

She did her best to close the subject. "You're both right, I get the point."

"Okay," Taro said. "What have you brought us?"

"Bread."

Both of them made a face. "Bread?"

"Yes, the creature I met was eating it and dropped it when he ran off."

"Leave it here, quick," Chad said. He pushed a small white container over to her. "You need to be very careful with these things. We could contaminate the whole base."

"I've been through decontamination."

"Yeah, but the process is only superficial," Chad explained. "Anything of non-human origin has to be put into the appropriate airtight container."

"I understand." She put the small piece of bread in the container.

"It certainly looks like bread," Taro said. "And if this is Keplerian bread, that means they know about agriculture."

"Can you analyze it to find out what it's made from, or what cereal it was made from?"

Chad nodded. "Of course. Although I can tell you straight away, they'll be different cereals from ours. The interesting thing about this bread would be to study the kind of yeast that was used in the process. But unfortunately yeasts die in the process of baking, so we won't be able to get much out of it."

Emily sighed in disappointment. "Oh, well…"

"But don't be disappointed, the implications of what you've found are huge. In the first place, we can assume they know about agriculture. It's true that on Earth cereals grew wild as well, but the amount of grain needed to make bread tells us they're capable of growing their own cereal. Secondly, we know they have mastery of fire and they have ovens. And lastly, they know what yeast is, or some type of micro-organism that does the same thing."

"Is yeast a micro-organism?" Emily asked in surprise. "Biology isn't one of my strong points."

"Yes, and when you mix it with water and flour it feeds on the natural sugars of the cereal and produces alcohol and carbon dioxide. Then the carbon dioxide that's generated forms small bubbles, and that's what makes the dough expand, then gives that spongy texture to the bread."

"I see. But in that case analyzing this piece of bread isn't going to tell us much."

"Oh yes it is!" Chad exclaimed. "If we're lucky we might be able to extract enough genetic material from the cereal that was used. In spite of the high temperatures the dough almost certainly went through while it was baked, it's possible there still might be something left we could use to reconstruct the DNA of the cereal. The DNA begins to become denatured at around a hundred and thirty degrees Celsius. Depending on the internal temperature the bread reached, we might be able to map its DNA."

"Well, at least that's something."

"Actually, it's a lot," Chad said. "And I'm sure Kostas will be really interested. If the crops he sows don't manage to germinate, we might modify Earth cereals genetically to adapt them to planetary conditions. It might mean a huge milestone in the survival of the colony. Above all bearing in mind that cereals grown using hydroponic technology give a very poor yield."

"Well, I'm glad this can be some help."

"But you can't take risks like that, Emily," Taro insisted.

"Yeah, that's been made very clear," she admitted as she left.

Just as she was taking off her exosuit, Robert and Private Ferrara appeared from the corridor. They were both on their way to make an inventory of the military equipment in the storeroom.

"Have you been outside until now?" Robert asked her in surprise.

"That's right."

"Where were you for so long?"

"Well, I guess you'll find out sooner or later, so I can see I'm going to get told off again…"

She told them what she had just told Taro and Chad a few moments before. The river, the stepping stones, the cabin, the forest and finally the young Keplerian with the loaf of bread.

"Have you gone completely insane?" Robert exclaimed.

"Something might have happened to you," Private Ferrara added.

"You can't go around on your own, Emily," Robert said angrily.

"This isn't Orlando, Emily," Ferrara pointed out.

Emily did her best to joke about it. "Don't scold me anymore. I'm grounded."

"This is no laughing matter," Robert said very seriously. "If we agreed to come here it was to work as a team, not so that every one of us could do whatever takes our fancy. And anything might have happened! Do I have to show you the images of how those two creatures left Private Anderson?" This was the soldier who had died in the attack.

Emily regretted her attempt at humor. "Sorry. You're right, I did something stupid. I promise I won't do it again."

"Of course you'll never do it again," Robert said, and strode off angrily toward the storeroom.

"Don't worry, he'll get over it," Private Ferrara said. "But you've got to understand that we've only just arrived, and this damn planet has already killed three people. We can't allow ourselves the luxury of losing anyone else, least of all someone as important as you, Emily."

She felt terrible all of a sudden. She was just beginning to be aware of the tremendous stupidity of what she had just done, particularly considering Robert's state of mind, not to mention that of the other soldiers. It had been reckless, and what was worse, it began to look like an absurd act of rebellion on the part of a spoiled child who had not thought much about the consequences her acts could have.

"Take a good shower and you'll feel better," Ferrara encouraged her before she went through the door into the corridor.

She decided to take her advice and went to the dressing-rooms, which luckily were deserted at that moment, and took a long shower to help herself relax. She could not stop thinking about what had just happened. But Ferrara was right, she felt a little better when she had finished her shower.

She dried her hair and dressed again. Ada informed her that the deputy director had tried to talk to her while she was in the shower.

Wonderful, as if I hadn't been told off enough as it is… she thought. Despite this, she agreed to call him back in twenty minutes' time.

She decided that things had to get back to normal, so she set off for the entrance area. She went through the storeroom door, where the two soldiers were carrying on with the inventory.

"Ferrara, would you mind leaving us alone for a moment?" she asked, her hair still damp.

The soldier turned to her lieutenant, who nodded.

"Sure, no problem," she said. "I'll be back in five minutes, Lieutenant."

"Thanks, Private."

Emily thanked Ferrara's gesture with a hesitant smile.

"I … wanted to apologize," she began. "What I've done wasn't good. I was reckless and I not only put my own life in danger, but the mission too. But what hurts most is that even knowing everything that's happened to you since we reached the planet, I never stopped to think about what you… and what all the rest of you might suffer if anything happened to me. I'm truly sorry, Robert. I've behaved like a selfish child who only ever thinks of herself. And I suppose I have to work harder at getting it into my head that I'm part of a team now and I can't make decisions lightly."

Robert was silent.

"Please say something," she pleaded. His silence was making her feel even worse.

"What do you want me to say?" he said at last. "I've confided things to you I haven't told anyone. I thought that coming here we might be able to form… not just a group of people with common aims, but a family. And then it turns out that you don't seem to take others into account, or that you'd rather do whatever takes your fancy. In fact I was very worried about what might have happened to you. Although actually I think the worst thing is that I'm a bit disappointed. I thought we had enough trust between us to be able to rely on each other. Now I don't know what to think."

"You can trust me," Emily said with tears in her eyes

"Really? What you did today doesn't seem to say the same thing."

Emily was silent. She did not really know what to say. When she had imagined the conversation she had not expected Robert to be so disappointed.

"Emily, I'm going to be honest with you. At this moment the trust I had in you is not what it was. I'll get over it, but right now I don't feel like talking any more. The only thing I want to hear you say is that you'll never stray from the base like that again. And I'm not asking as the person responsible for the safety for these facilities, I'm asking you as Robert."

She nodded. "Yes, of course. It won't happen again, I promise."

She left the storeroom downhearted. What hurt most was knowing that they were right, that her attitude had left a lot to be wished for. Someone who was supposed to be leading a team could not act in this individualistic way. She knew she would have to do a lot better in that aspect, but at that moment all her efforts were focused on preventing herself from bursting into tears in the middle of the public area.

She took a deep breath, tried to put her thoughts in order and decided to go into the lab. Here she went into one of the small rooms and got ready to call the deputy director, but before she did this she made sure her nerves were rather calmer.

"Hello, Emily!" she heard him at the other end of the line.

She did her best to pretend everything was normal. "Hi, David."

"How's the bungalow?"

"Good, very good. Actually, it's really great. Director Patel and his boys have done a wonderful job."

"So I've been told. I'm looking forward to dropping by one of these days."

"That would be great," she said enthusiastically. "It's high time you came out of that metal box."

"Yup, I'm looking forward to getting a live view of what the planet's like. And what better excuse than to make an official visit to the first human base on Kepler-442b."

"You know we'll welcome you with open arms."

"I know, I know. But tell me, how's the day going?"

Emily bowed her head but even with everything she had just been through, she decided she had to tell him the truth.

"The thing is, I'd like to tell you something," she began. "But before I do that, I'd just like to say I'm very disappointed with myself and that it'll never happen again."

"Hey, that doesn't sound too good." She could see him frowning. "Is everything in order down there?"

"Yes, yes, everything's fine. Let's just say I've done something really stupid."

She explained for the third time what she had already told her comrades. She told Green

about the little spat she had had with Sergeant Cameron, her annoyance, her short stroll and how she had found out how to cross to the far side of the river. And of course she also told him about her encounter with the young Keplerian. The deputy director listened attentively, while she was aware that with every word his facial expression was turning more and more serious. So when she had finished the story, she added:

"And before you say anything and tell me off"—she tried to soften the blow in advance— "everyone here has made me see just how reckless I've been, so I'm not exactly having my best moment."

The deputy director relaxed his anger a little as he became aware of the situation.

"Emily," he said gently but firmly, "I'm not setting out to give you lectures on anything at this stage in life. And besides, I know you yourself will draw the right conclusions about everything that happened. But you'll have to learn to make decisions with a cool head, to analyze things more critically. There'll come a day, in all certainty, when you'll have to make decisions that might mean life or death for someone. And I'm absolutely sure you'll make the right ones, I can guarantee you that. So I'm just going to tell you to think of this as a lesson."

She listened carefully to the deputy director's words. David had always given her very good advice, but in this case he had managed to make the hair on the back of her neck stand on end. His faith in her was absolute, and despite her own bad decisions he seemed to go on having blind faith in her. This certainly comforted her, but hearing him talk about decisions of life and death made her even more aware of what it meant to have a responsibility like the one she had at that moment: toward the colony, toward her comrades, but most of all toward her friends.

"Thanks, David. You've no idea how much it comforts me to hear you say that." "Be very careful, oaky? There's no reason to be over-hasty. We have all our life ahead of us to make contact with the other civilizations of the planet, but we only have one Emily Rhodes and I wouldn't like to lose her."

"I get you."

"That said," he added, turning pragmatic, "what are you going to do now you've made the first contact?"

"I'm not really sure. I suppose several of us appearing in the Keplerian village armed to the teeth wouldn't exactly be seen as a gesture of peace and concord. So I can understand that the most logical thing would be to send a drone to try and investigate a little more."

"That sounds pretty intelligent."

"We'll make decisions according to what we see, but right now we need to know more about them."

"Just in case, have Ada take maximum care. We don't yet know whether the Keplerians are friendly. If they've survived sharing space with the Yokai, they might not be what they seem."

Emily nodded "True. We'll have to keep our eyes open."

"Keep me informed about anything that happens, however irrelevant. These first nights will be crucial."`

"I'll do that, David."

"We'll talk again tomorrow."

She ended the call and felt a lot better. But the deputy director was right, she needed to learn to be more cautious, to consider the team, and most of all to think like a leader. Feeling calmer, she reviewed the satellite images of the area where she had met her little friend. Ada showed her images of the area in real time. The weather had changed a little and there was a fair amount of cloud-cover, which prevented them from getting a proper view of it.

"Do you have any images of this morning without clouds?" she asked.

"Sure. Do you want video, or just a static image?"

"A static image would be fine."

Ada showed her some clearer photos taken that same morning, and Emily took a careful look at the vast area of red forest in the area. She went on moving the image slowly as she reviewed the various sectors of terrain to the north of the river. She located the clearing she had crossed, and with Ada's help she checked the area she had visited after crossing that strange avenue inside the forest, where she had met the creature. A little further north she could distinguish several other clearings. They followed no definite pattern, but there was something strange about them.

"Zoom in on one of those clearings."

When Ada had done this, Emily nearly fell off her chair at the sight of what was there.

"Ada, please call Lieutenant Beaufort, tell him to come here at once. And when he's here, call the deputy director."

"Copy that."

She sat down in her chair once again and stared hard at the image. It was certainly what it looked as though it was. There was no other possible interpretation.

Robert arrived a couple of minutes later, and soon they heard the deputy director's voice.

"What is it, Emily?"

"I've been reviewing the satellite images of the area I visited during my little excursion this morning. And leaving my own stupidity to one side, I've found something I wanted to show you both."

"Okay, I'm all ears," the deputy director said.

"Ada, show them the images."

The AI showed both of them the same static image Emily had reviewed. And the deputy director could not restrain a small cry.

"Dear God! Is that what I think it is?"

"They're crops!" Robert exclaimed.

"That's right!" she said excitedly. "We've just found the Keplerians' vegetable gardens."

"That's an amazing piece of news!" the deputy director admitted.

"Yes, it is," Robert agreed. "And I'd go so far as to say the settlement shouldn't be too far away."

Emily pointed to the wooded areas around the dozens of small clearings they could see in that particular sector. "That's right, logic tells me the settlements should be around these clearings."

"What do they grow?" Green asked.

"It's hard to tell," she said. "But each one looks different. This one here, judging by the way it's laid out, makes me think of cereal. And in this other one here, if you look closely, there are furrows and some small red plants."

Robert nodded. "Of course, seeing that everything else on this planet is red."

"Perhaps we ought to send a drone to the area to see if we can see anything else," the deputy director suggested.

"We need to think carefully about that," Emily said thoughtfully. "If we're found out, they might take it as an act of aggression. We need to be cautious about that."

"Right," Green said, sounding pleased. "I'll leave it in your hands, both of you. I trust your good judgment."

"Thank you, director."

"Keep me informed. Oh, and good work, both of you," he added before he cut off communication.

Emily and Robert were left in an awkward silence, which he was the first to break.

"I…. I'm sorry if I was too hard on you before."

"No, you were right," Emily said, feeling an unfamiliar self-confidence. "You've all made me realize what it really means to lead a team. I shouldn't make decisions lightly and I have to learn to think more coolly about what I do. I've been selfish, and I didn't think at all about the consequences my acts might have for the rest of you. I can only ask you to forgive me and I can assure you it'll never happen again."

"Well, as far as I'm concerned I have nothing to forgive. I think I can understand what led you to go on beyond the river, and I admit that the taste for adventure takes its toll on all of us."

"Yes, but I shouldn't have done it. I think I've learned my lesson."

"Ada, did you record that?" he joked.

"I record everything, Lieutenant Beaufort."

They spent the afternoon inside the facilities because it was raining non-stop outside. The rain on the planet always seemed to be much finer that on Earth; the high pressure of the atmosphere ensured that the raindrops were tiny. Even so, what was falling was a real deluge which had already made puddles here and there on the ground. Ada said it had been generated in just a few hours and that it was a summer storm. Luckily for all, there were only a few flashes of lightning in the distance.

That same evening, Chad had promised everyone that he would make hamburgers for dinner. He had carefully set up the food printer to get the perfect ingredients. Then he had baked bread from the dough he had printed He had a substitute for Cheddar cheese, and of course pickled gherkins and lettuces brought from the station itself.

"Hey, Chad," Ferrara said when she smelled the bread. "This smells fantastic!"

"Well, just wait until you try everything together."

"Mine without cheese, please," Evelyn said. "I'm not a great fan."

"No?" He looked at her as if she were an alien. "I thought everyone liked cheese."

She shrugged. "It doesn't appeal to me."

"Okay then, one with no cheese, noted!"

He heated the small griddle he had asked to be installed and added a little butter, which melted quickly. He took a couple of nearly perfect balls of artificial meat he had lovingly arranged on the kitchen counter and pressed them against the griddle, then left the thin circle of meat cooking against the hot metal.

He repeated the process with the rest of the meat until the griddle was full. And when he thought they were sufficiently done, he turned them over one by one to cook on the other side. Then he added a couple of slices of cheese, except on Evelyn's.

The rest of the team arrived in dribs and drabs and were duly impressed by the aroma that now filled kitchen and mess hall.

"Wow! That smells really good!" Lieutenant Beaufort said appreciatively.

"I think I'm going to start drooling," Sergeant Ortiz admitted when he came to the kitchen   to see how the hamburgers were going.

Chad put the newly-baked bread on the griddle for a few seconds so that it would pick up the flavor of the meat. As soon as everything was ready he set about preparing the hamburgers: bread, double hamburger, double cheese, pickled gherkins, lettuce and a special sauce he himself had made.

"My goodness, Chad!" Kostas exclaimed. "I didn't know this chef side of you. You look like a real professional!"

"He certainly does!" Emily agreed. "You had us all fooled, you're not a biologist at all!"

He smiled. "Let's say it's one of my frustrated professions."

Ceremoniously, he handed all his comrades a plate with their burger, then sat down at the table with them.

"I hope you like them."

"They certainly look wonderful," said Paula. "It's as if we were back on Earth."

Emily got up from her chair before Gorka could dig his teeth into his hamburger. "I'd like to propose a toast."

"Good idea!" Robert said.

"I know we all had our own lives on Earth," she began. "We might have belonged to different communities, even different countries. Maybe our worlds were separate there. Maybe we had problems, maybe in other circumstances we wouldn't have been able to live together, wouldn't even have met. We might have had our differences, might even have argued, but now all that's pointless, only the present matters, but most of all, the future matters. What we're doing here is going to make history. And I can't think of better company to spend the rest of my life with than each one of you. I'd like to propose a toast for family, that word which has such a wide and personal meaning, but which at the same time unites all of us around this table."

"Family!" they all called.

At last they were able to taste the wonderful hamburgers dear old Chad had made with so much affection for his comrades. During that dinner, which they would all remember for the rest of their lives, they were happy, once again enjoying the warmth which feeling part of a group of people was giving them: a group of people for whom many of them would be capable of giving up their own lives.

They dined as a family.

12
The visit

August 5, Year 0
Magellan Base, Kepler-442b

Ada's alarm woke them all up. They had decided to share the room and also the schedules, so that they all began to stretch and yawn in their beds at almost the same time.

"Gorka and Evelyn snore like troopers," Chad joked. "Thank goodness we told Ada to cancel the noise, or I wouldn't have been able to sleep a wink."

Emily smiled at the biologist's comment. The snoring of both of them had been remarkable once Ada had stopped making it easier to sleep. She saw that Robert was not there.

He'll have got up earlier to do some exercise, or maybe something's happened? she wondered.

The previous night they had decided not to set a watch. The quantity and general distribution of sensors and beacons was such that they felt it would be enough to allow them to rest in peace. Apart from that, Ada would let them know at once if she detected anything strange, whether around the base or at the remaining beacon near the cave of the Yokai.

"Morning, team!" Paula said. "Did you all sleep well?"

"Like a log," said Kostas. "Didn't hear a thing."

Emily came out of the dorm. "Where's the lieutenant?" she asked Ada.

"He's in one of the lab rooms. A couple of hours ago I detected movement near one of the sensors, and when that happens I have to call the most senior officer. It turned out to be a false alarm, but he decided to stay awake to monitor everything."

Hearing this, she felt much easier. "I see."

She crossed the corridor which separated the two general areas and went into the lab. Robert was in the room they had seen the crops from the day before. When she went in she saw him concentrating on the scattered clearings amid the immensity of the forests.

"Couldn't you sleep?" she asked him from the doorway.

"Morning. No, Ada alerted me to possible movement at one of the southwest beacons, and as I wasn't particularly sleepy by then I decided to stay here."

"False alarm?"

"Yeah, just some underground animal that was very taken with our beacon and couldn't get away from it."

"A mole?"

"Something like that, but with a more disturbing look about it."

"Wow. And what are you looking at now?"

"I asked Ada to look in the surrounding areas for any kind of distribution of clearings like the one you found yesterday."

"And?"

"She's found two other areas like it, one of them a lot bigger than the others. With different crops, but looking much like the ones we saw yesterday."

"D'you think there could be more settlements?"

"Yes, at least two more. And one of them's very large."

"But where?"

He moved further out of the image he was looking at and showed her a couple of points several kilometers to the east of the crops they had found the previous day.

"How far are they from the first settlement?"

"This one, which is further south, about twenty-five kilometers. The one to the north a little more, thirty-five or so."

"Hey, that's incredible. Yesterday we had nothing, and today it turns out we've located three Keplerian settlements."

"We're taking it for granted that they're the ones who are doing the cultivating," he objected.

"It's got to be them, I'm sure of that."

"I've been thinking about how we're going to make a proper investigation of all these areas. And I think you were right yesterday, we can't do it just like that. We don't know these creatures at all. Maybe sending drones would be interpreted as an act of aggression. We'll have to think of some way of getting close to them without provoking a confrontation."

She nodded. "Yeah, we have to be cautious about that."

"That's going to be our first task here."

"Maybe we ought to take a trip out there to see if we bump into my new friend."

"We could, but I wouldn't like to fall into an ambush. I'd rather have some more information about the place, and if possible about the Keplerians themselves."

"Without any satellite view through the treetops that's going to be difficult."

"I know. That's the challenge. Have you all had breakfast?"

"Not yet."

"Well, come on then. I need something to eat," Robert said. "I'm beginning to feel tired because of the extra gravity."

While some were taking showers and getting ready to face the new day, others were having breakfast in the mess hall. The menu was much like that at the station. The food printer, which could imitate a great variety of flavors, dealt with everything. All they needed to do was replenish the supplies of the different raw materials it needed.

In the mess hall they found Sergeant Cameron, Paula, Gorka and Balakova the pilot. Jonathan, still a little drowsy, took his breakfast from the machine and went to sit in a corner of the hall apart from the others. Emily was unhappy about seeing the welder isolating himself, so when she sat down herself she urged him to come over.

"Come sit with us, we don't bite."

The welder hesitated for a few seconds, but on second thoughts he left his corner and came to sit with the others. At the same moment Sergeant Cameron got up in something of a huff.

"I seem to have lost my appetite for breakfast," she snorted, throwing her breakfast into the trash bin at the same time. Then she left the mess hall.

"What's gotten into her?" Gorka asked.

"No idea," said Paula. "But ever since we arrived she seems to have a broomstick up her bum. No offense, Lieutenant," she added when she realized that her superior officer was present.

He was equally puzzled. "I've no idea what's up with her. I'll have a word with her."

"I'll help you with that," said Emily who knew all too well was happening.

Jonathan finished his breakfast in silence, without looking up. And in spite of Emily's efforts to get him into the conversation, he would only speak in monosyllables. Integrating him into the team was going to be a hard and tedious task. Although she could understand the welder perfectly well; he felt guilty about what he had done, and that was a feeling which was hard to get rid of if you had to share your days with the people you had tried to kill.

When she had finished her breakfast, she decided to open up to

Robert.

"Do you have a second?"

"Yeah, sure."

"Better keep this private."

Once again they went into the multipurpose hall to find some privacy.

"Tell me," he said, intrigued.

"Well... you see... it's about Sergeant Cameron."

"Yeah, I plan to have a word with her. I've no idea what's got into her."

"You see, I know what the matter with her is."

He looked at her in amazement. "Really?"

"A little while ago you told me a secret about what had happened on the Copernicus," she began. "So I think it's fair if I tell you something in confidence too."

He looked at her in some surprise, but in some way he was pleased by the mutual trust implied by this exchange of information.

"You remember the black hole event I told you about the first time we landed on the planet?" she asked.

"Sure, how could I forget that? We all came close to dying, and we were left without a lot of equipment for the project."

"I didn't tell you the whole story. In fact it was sabotage."

His eyes opened wide at this.

"Sabotage? Who?"

"Apparently, the terrorist group Global Justice. The same ones who attacked the Copernicus."

"But how did they manage to infiltrate the station?" he asked in disbelief. "It was supposed to be totally secret."

"That's something we're not at all clear about, all we know is that they infiltrated a pawn into the system. He carried out the sabotage thanks to the very precise instructions he was given. But in fact even he didn't know who the terrorists were."

She told him everything that had really happened during those intense days a few months before. Even so, she left out the name of the saboteur until he was very clear about what had happened at the trial.

"And now you have the information, all I have left to tell you is the saboteur's name."

"Wiśniewski," he guessed.

Emily nodded, without adding another word. Robert was now aware of why Sergeant Cameron was acting in that way. And she could also imagine what this might mean for that little community of settlers if they were to be able to work like a well-oiled machine.

"What are you thinking about?" she asked nervously when he said nothing.

"About how to bring up the situation with the sergeant."

"Doesn't it worry you that the saboteur's here with us?"

"Well, you yourself said that he's done his time. And besides, I understand the reasons why the judge made that decision. He'll be very useful to us down here. So I also understand clearly why you and the deputy director should have decided to include him in the team."

She gave a sigh of relief, realizing that they were both on the same page.

"I should've told you when we made the decision. Or better still, you should've been part of the discussion. Forgive me."

"Don't worry," Robert said. "The fewer people who know, at least for now, the better. Who else knows about this?"

"Sergeant Cameron, Evelyn, who also testified at the trial. And the two of us."

"Right. I'll try to ease things with the sergeant."

"Thanks, Robert. I think it's the right thing to do."

After taking a good shower, Emily gathered them all together in the inner area of the facilities to plan the daily work to be carried out at the base. The previous day's storm had moved away and the sun was shining with its usual orange tinge in a clear sky. Hence they were going to be able to start work outside.

"We'll have to get used to getting together for fifteen minutes every day to organize the work," she began. "Each one of us will explain briefly what he or she is going to do during the day and whether we have any urgent problem we need to solve with the help of the rest of the team. If that's all right, I'll start and we'll go on in order, as we're standing in a circle."

"Why are we doing it standing?" Chad asked.

"Because then we won't spend two hours talking. It has to be dynamic, and it has to let everyone know what's happening in the base, okay?"

They all nodded.

"Right, then I'll begin. Yesterday, thanks to the satellite, we found a few cultivated areas. We think they're the Keplerians', as they're in a wooded area near where I bumped into one of them. We need to draw up a strategy so that we can establish contact and get hold of more information. So that's what I'm putting down as my objective for today."

Kostas was immediately interested. "Have we really detected alien crops?"

"Yes, if you're curious I can show you later, and anyone else who's interested." She beckoned to Taro, who was next.

"I'll be going on with what we started yesterday. I'm analyzing some of the samples we got from our first visit to the planet."

"I'm going to start tracing models of the artificial molecule we found on the planet," Chad said.

"Sergeant Cameron and I," Sergeant Ortiz began, "will take the first watch outside so that Kostas, or anybody else, will be free to work outside in peace."

"Private Ferrara and I are going to check one of the beacons which has stopped working properly," Robert said. "It's possible the rain may have affected it, maybe its sealing was defective. In the afternoon we'll take over from Ortiz and Cameron."

"I'll be organizing the infirmary," said Evelyn. "I have plenty of equipment, but it's all still packed."

Next came Paula's turn. "As for me, I'm going to check the telecoms module on the roof. I want to see how it's been installed."

"Well, I'm going to start ploughing the three areas where I intend to grow different plants," said Kostas. "So if anyone's bored, I have work to spare."

Balakova was going to check both the rover and the ship to make sure they were all in perfect working order, and she offered to help anyone once she had finished. Finally, Wiśniewski and Gorka would go on with a general check of all facilities.

"I guess it'll take us all day," Gorka said in conclusion, "but as of tomorrow, if nothing breaks down, we can help other people too."

"Good," Emily said, satisfied to see how quickly they had all grasped the dynamic of those morning meetings. "If there's any problem, or if anyone needs urgent help to get any of their jobs done, just say. Now let's get down to work!"

They all dispersed to begin their chores. But Kostas stayed there with Emily.

"Will you show me what you found?" he said.

"Sure. I think you'll find it very interesting."

Kostas followed her into the lab.

"Ada, show us the satellite images."

Ada reproduced the images in real time, and Kostas went over them attentively. He pointed to one of the clearings.

"There seems to be someone there."

"That's true. What's he doing?"

"He seems to be carrying a utensil of some kind. I think he's ploughing an area of the clearing."

"Ada," Emily asked, "can you monitor all the areas in real time and let us know if you see any activity in the clearings?"

"Sure," the AI said. "In fact that's not the only clearing where there's activity right now."

Ada switched images and took them to one of the clearings of the settlement further to the east. Here a Keplerian seemed to be leading two bulky draft animals which were helping him to work the soil. It was clear that he had just started his day, as only a single furrow was visible across the clearing.

"There seems to be similar activity in several places," Ada said. "I can see at least twelve individuals doing different jobs."

"Wow…" Kostas said, impressed. "This is rather overwhelming."

Emily nodded. "It certainly is. We're looking at a society of peasants. It's like traveling back in time."

"The implications of what we're seeing are enormous. I'd very much like to talk with them about their agricultural methods. It would be very helpful for us to have access to their crops, we could try to graft them on ours. Maybe that could be the key to cultivating something edible on this planet."

"Certainly. I'm keen to establish contact with them too."

"Doesn't it frighten you?" he asked. "Suppose they're not friendly?"

"I guess curiosity about getting to know an alien society overcomes any fear I might have of them," Emily said. "It certainly gives the impression that they're a civilized society. It's clear they have nothing to do with the Yokai."

After this aerial check of the individuals who were working the land, Kostas decided to get down to work. But this new discovery added more interest, if that were possible, in speeding up operations to establish contact with the Keplerians.

So that while some of the team had gone outside by now, either to go on a small patrol, to replace the faulty beacon or prepare the land chosen for cultivation, Emily walked around the base wondering how to broach the subject.

She had rejected the idea of sending drones, but suppose they did it by night? The drones were silent enough to pass unnoticed.

We don't know what kind of technology they have, she thought. *Even though they use draft animals to plough, that doesn't mean they stay in the dark at night. More than that, their eyes may somehow be adapted to night vision and they can see just as well as we do with the help of our technology.*

She walked around for a long time, puzzling over all this. She had been intending to speak to the deputy director some time during the morning, and as she could not come up with a simple way of getting close to them she decided to make the call earlier, at least to inform him about everything they had found out during the last few hours.

She was on her way to the hall when Kostas interrupted her on the radio

"Emily?"

"Yes, Kostas what is it?"

"You're not going to believe this," he said. "But I'm afraid you have a visitor."

"What?" she said in surprise. "Is the deputy director here?"

"No, not even remotely. I think it's your little friend. I've no idea how he found us, but he's standing there a few meters from where I am now, waiting for someone to approach him."

13
The new friend

August 5, Year 0
Magellan Base, Kepler-442b

Emily ran to the mess hall, operated the food printer and selected a chocolate cake. In a very short time the machine prepared a juicy slice which she wrapped in a couple of paper napkins.

"If I could eat it, I'd print two of them," she murmured to herself when she saw how good it looked.

She ran to the terminal for her exosuit, put the cake very carefully on the floor so that it would not collapse and put on all her equipment, even the helmet. She came out of the complex and looked in the direction where Kostas and the four soldiers were looking. They were all waiting expectantly for some movement from the small Keplerian figure which had stopped a few meters from them.

"Has he done anything else?" she asked.

"Nope," Kostas said. "Ever since he arrived he's stayed there, sitting on the ground. He seems to be waiting for us to do something."

Emily noticed how tense the four soldiers were. "I think you can all lower your weapons. He looks harmless."

"Okay," Robert said, "but if you're going to go near him, at least I'd like to have someone in hiding to cover you from a distance. He's come here without triggering any of the sensors. We'll have to check the perimeter, but it looks as though he's a very elusive creature. And there might be more of them hidden."

"Okay, but try not to frighten him. Making contact might help us answer a lot of the questions we still have unsolved."

"Ferrara," the Lieutenant said, "find an elevated position and try to stay out of sight."

"Right away, sir," she said, and went quickly away toward the complex.

Robert turned to Emily. "Wait till Ferrara's in position before you approach him."

"Understood."

"What's that you have there?" Kostas asked

"A piece of chocolate cake. I think he's just a kid, and if he likes it half as much as a human child, success is guaranteed. And we know they have bread, so this should be familiar."

"Good idea. You'd already have won me over, but let's hope the Keplerians don't teach their young all that stuff about not accepting food from strangers."

"Yeah, keep your fingers crossed."

"In position," came Ferrara's voice on the radio.

"Cut off communications," Emily said nervously. "Wish me luck."

Cautiously, she covered the distance that separated them. At the same time, as she came closer to the young Keplerian she deliberately slowed down. More than anything, she did not want to scare him off. The creature meanwhile was waiting, sitting there with his legs crossed. If it were not for that unmistakably alien look, she would have said that this posture was that of a typically human kid.

She thought carefully about what to say, how to act. She thought about what might be going through the mind of a young human if an alien in a metallic suit were to approach him like this. The boy was watching her closely. When she had crossed more than half the distance, he got up. Emily stopped at once, not wanting to frighten him, so she held the piece of cake in her open hand and raised the other to communicate calm. The boy seemed to hesitate.

"I'd hesitate too if I were in your position," she murmured to herself. "Now it's your turn to come a bit closer."

His clothes were plain, quite like those which humanity had worn several centuries back. From his general appearance it could be guessed that he belonged to a family of peasants. The same rough doublet of gray material with hints of blue he had been wearing the day before and roughly-stitched breeches which came to his knees and which were obviously not his size. A narrow cord acted as a belt. He was carrying a small, battered satchel of black leather over his shoulder and across his chest.

Emily walked on a few meters more, this time much more slowly. She wanted to assess his level of distrust. She kept her hand raised so that he could see it all the time. When she had judged that they were near enough to have a conversation and yet not enough to scare him away, she stopped. She picked up a large flat rock she had seen beside her feet and put it on the grass between them. They were still separated by twenty meters or so. She left the piece of cake on the rock, took a few steps back with her palms visible all the time and sat down on the ground in the same posture he had been sitting in.

"Come closer," she said, beckoning with both hands as the same time.

The boy stared at her with awe and admiration, giving the impression that inside him curiosity was winning the battle over caution. Very slowly, he began to come closer. First one step, then another, and then one more. When the cake was more or less at the same distance from both of them, he stopped again. He looked at the cake, dark and with a layer of white cream on top, then once again at Emily. He seemed to be waiting for instructions.

With simple gestures, she tried to communicate her intention of sharing the gift with him. She pointed to the piece of cake, then to her own mouth, trying to establish a connection between the need to eat and the delicacy in front of them. Then she pointed to him and waited for him to do the same.

The young alien followed her gestures closely, then as she had expected, began to imitate her. He pointed to the cake and then, shyly, at his own mouth.

Jitov am, he said, almost in a whisper.

"What did he say, Ada?" Emily asked under her breath.

"I would imagine he's naming what he believes the cake to be, or the act of eating itself. I've made a note of it as something referring to food. Although it's not ideal, and in the absence of a Keplerian-Human translator, I'm going to try to note down everything according to context. I need him to speak as much as possible so that we can add to our dictionary. I'd advise you to use gestures and simple sentences."

Emily repeated the same gesture, but this time she also drew a circle on her own stomach. She knew nothing about Keplerian anatomy, but to judge by outward appearance and knowing that they would have to convert food into energy somewhere in their bodies, she wagered on the similarity of the two species.

Wii vi jitov am, the young Keplerian said as he repeated, one by one and in the same order, the three gestures she had just made.

"It sounds like a more complex sentence, but he's still referring to food," Ada said.

Once again Emily beckoned to him to come closer, pointing to the cake, then to him.

"Yeah, it's for you."

Come on, kid, you'll love it, she thought.

The young one moved a little closer to the food, and when he was level with the rock, in a swift movement that surprised even Emily, he stretched out his hand and took the piece of cake. Even so, he moved back a few steps at once so that he could examine it undisturbed. He looked at it, clasping it in his claws, which were small but sharp. He seemed to sniff at it through the two small holes which could be guessed at above his long lips.

Emily could not help a giggle when her new friend realized that the white cream had smeared his hand. The Keplerian stared at the underside of his claw in annoyance and began to sniff it, still holding the piece of cake in his other hand, though this time more carefully. When he realized that the smell was not unpleasant, he licked his hand delicately. Almost at once, his eyes opened wide.

Vi wii difotshya! he exclaimed, narrowing his huge dark eyes in a sign of approval. Emily even thought she saw a smile appearing on his face.

Difotshya, she repeated as best she could to try to get a conversation under way.

Biif, difotshya, he repeated, waving his arms triumphantly.

Emily breathed out heavily, feeling more relaxed. Despite the fact that he seemed to be young, his limbs looked a lot more developed than those of humans. And with those sharp claws he could cause real damage to her if he were to get angry.

Well, he seems to like it, she thought, feeling relieved.

Now that they seemed to be getting along well, she took a better look at the creature. His height was less than a meter and a half, so that compared to a person he was short. All the same, his muscles were a lot more solid than those of an average human adult. More than that, they were well-defined, and he looked quite strong. His skin seemed to be very thick and hard. Relatively speaking it reminded her of an elephant's, although his was darker and had a curious touch of red.

His eyes were very large and dark, but in spite of that darkness Emily was able to see something moving inside them when he stopped to look at something. They had lids, and she could almost have sworn that they were double, like those of some species of lizards or amphibians on Earth. But the feature which caught her attention most was the bony protuberance on his head, which meant that his skull was not completely round. It started at the forehead and spread toward both sides of the head, more or less above the tiny, slightly ridiculous ears. It was not too farfetched to think that perhaps those bulges grew over the years, and might even indicate some kind of social status among his people.

The young Keplerian, spurred by the taste of the cream, decided to try the rest of the cake. First he sniffed it carefully, then immediately opened his mouth and took a good bite from it. Emily was surprised by the size of his mouth and the oddness of his teeth; they seemed to consist of only four pieces, so long that they covered the entire width of his mouth. But the one who was really surprised was the Keplerian himself, whose eyes widened again. He did not hesitate for a single moment before he took another bite out of the now-shrunken cake.

Vi wii laaj waii! he said again, smiling.

Laaj waii, she repeated.

The boy narrowed his eyes in a sign of confirmation and went on with his feast. Emily let him finish it without interruption. It was a treat to see him eat. Then he licked his claws so as not to miss a crumb.

When he seemed to be satisfied, she gestured to him to come and sit with her. The youngster, much more trusting after filling his stomach, obeyed and came to sit a little closer. At that distance she could even have smelled him, if her suit had not got in the way.

She touched the chest of her suit with both hands. "Emily," she said.

After this she directed both her hands toward him, waiting for a reply. When there was none, she repeated the gesture.

"Emily," she said again

The youngster was thoughtful for a while, but then suddenly his eyes opened wider than normal.

"Shildii," he said, pointing at himself.

Okay, Shildii, pleased to meet you, she thought.

And to make sure she had understood correctly, she repeated the gesture one last time.

She pointed to herself. "Emily." She pointed to him. "Shildi."

"Now we only need to know whether he means himself or his species," Ada pointed out.

Oops, she's right, she thought, *He might think the whole human race is called Emily.*

"Shildii," he replied pointing to himself. "Emily," he said in his strange accent, pointing at her.

Next the young Keplerian narrowed his eyes as if he were pleased and twined the four claws of his hands together in a gesture which must surely have some meaning for him. Emily decided to imitate the gesture, which to judge by the look on his face Shildii seemed to appreciate.

Right, once the introductions are over, let's get down to the basics, she thought.

"One," she said showing him her right index finger. "Two." She raised her middle finger. "Three." She went on with her ring finger.

One by one, she spread all the fingers of both hands and counted to ten. Once she had come to the end of the count, she gestured to him to do the same. The youngster slanted his eyes at once in a sign of approval. He seemed to have understood what she was asking.

"*Wu,*" he began, *shish,* he went on, *shu, shov, ziid, la, shyaaw, woj*

The young Keplerian seemed to be enjoying the game. Once again he narrowed his eyes, showing that curious smile.

He's only counted up to eight, she thought, *but of course he only has eight fingers, so that makes all the sense in the world. I suppose they must use a numeric system based on eight instead of ten, like us.*

She spread out two fingers on her right hand and one on her left.

Shish, wu, she said as she put both hands together to indicate that she was going to add them. *Shu!* She raised her voice a little and showed him three fingers of her right hand, keeping her left closed.

The youngster reacted quite excitedly and once again made the gesture of twining his claws while he narrowed his eyes again. Emily was not clear whether he had understood what she had tried to do, so she did it again. This time she held up three fingers in her right hand and one in her left.

Shu, wu, she said while she joined her hands again in the same gesture. But this time, instead of saying the result herself, she pointed to him so that he would finish the operation.

Shyov! he said excitedly.

That's four. Right, you obviously know simple mathematical operations, she thought. *That's very exciting, maybe they have some kind of basic educational system.*

She did the same exercise, but subtracting. This time she showed four fingers on her right hand.

Shyov, he said obligingly.

Straight away she separated both hands, clenching the right and showing him only two fingers of her left. She pointed to him with her fist and waited to see whether he understood what this was meant to imply.

Shish! he cried delightedly.

Two, that's right, she thought. *The other mathematical operations are too complicated to do with my hands and the few words we know, so let's go on to concepts and objects.*

She operated the terminal of her suit from her left arm, and it projected a hologram which showed a tree with red leaves, much like the ones all over the planet.

The young Keplerian made a brief but intense sound of admiration, and his eyes opened wide when he saw the hologram seemingly appear from nowhere.

She gestured for him to speak. "Tree."

Chon! he exclaimed, in spite of his obvious expression of surprise. Although he soon intertwined his claws again.

Looks as though that gesture shows we're understanding one another.

She repeated the gesture and showed him another image on the visor. "Rock," she said.

Lirkjj, he answered.

The rock was followed by grass, plants, the river, the bird she had seen by the river, the mountain to the north, the sky, the stars, the rain, a flash of lightning and endless other things. One by one the Keplerian put a name to all the images she was showing him. There was only one she did not get a reply to, so she presumed Shildii had never seen the sea.

This rules out the possibility that they might have a technology that lets them visualize images or show them concepts the way we do with our terminals, she thought.

She showed him the image of the star that illuminated the planet. But seeing that it brought no recognition, she looked for the sun above their heads and pointed to it.

"Sun," she said.

U! Shildii exclaimed.

Now we've gone through all the commonest things in his day-to-day life, let's see if we can come up with something more interesting, she thought.

She showed him a hologram of a human soldier and a civilian, each wearing their exosuits of different colors.

"Humans," she said.

"Hu-mans," Shildii said, trying to imitate her. He had no word for them.

Emily clicked on the terminal and the armor of the exosuits vanished from the image, revealing the man and woman inside.

"Humans," she said again.

"Hu-mans *am,* Shildii repeated. He did not sound very convinced.

Either he doesn't understand that the suits are only external armor, or else he finds it difficult to believe there's a soft person inside that armor, Emily thought, seeing the doubtful look on the Keplerian's face.

She decided to show him a photo of herself.

"Emily," she said.

The youngster seemed to hesitate for a few moments, but in the end he pointed to the photo and said, but without much conviction:

"Emily *am.*"

"What can it be, that tagline he says at times, *am?*"

"It might mean doubt, or it might be his way of asking," Ada said. "If you listen carefully, he's barely modified his intonation, he's only raised his voice when he wants to indicate he's comfortable, or agrees with what you're saying."

"I think I need to know what words mean yes and no in his language," Emily said. "If I can know that, asking and replying will be a lot easier."

She showed him an enlarged image of the two Keplerians they had met at the riverside a few weeks before. She decided to ask him whether he was one of them. The chances were slim, so at least she would find out what sound meant *no*.

"Shildii *am*" said Emily, waiting expectantly for the Keplerian's reaction.

The creature stared thoughtfully at the image.

Ju. He frowned, which was something he had not done so far.

Well, we seem to have a no for an answer, Emily thought. *And also that means his name is Shildii, not his species.*

The next thing was to get an affirmative answer. She showed him an image of himself from a few moments before.

"Shildii *am,*" she said again.

Biif! he replied excitedly.

Well now, this seems to be working well, so let's try some anatomy, she thought as she clicked on her terminal.

She showed him parts of the human body and the Keplerian body at the same time. One by one Shildii named the words they used for head, eyes, mouth, teeth, hands, arms and many more. It was interesting to see him react at the sight of human hair, which when paralleled with his bony swelling caused a most curious reaction in him, which Emily catalogued as amusement. Even so, the youngster did not hesitate to tell her what they called that part of the body.

Loaa, he said.

Now we have the basics, so we'll see whether you can sort out some of the doubts we have.

She showed him the image of the alien obelisk they had found on the other continent. But this time she had no luck, and the little Keplerian made a gesture which she interpreted as a shrug.

Lu a pi liik tumbi li wid, he said.

Okay, let's move on to something more disturbing, Emily thought, knowing she was taking something of a risk. She showed him an image of the Yokai attacking the camp.

Suddenly Shildii's eyes opened wide. Without waiting for Emily to ask her question he got up from the ground and ran away in a panic.

Wiijof jikhaashyush! Wiijof jikhaashyush! he shouted as he ran as if the devil were after him.

"Subject on the run!" she heard Ferrara on the radio. "Do I shoot?"

Emily leapt to her feet and spun round. "No, Ferrara. I think I just scared him."

She picked up the napkins the cake had been wrapped in and went back to where Kostas and the other soldiers had been waiting observantly.

"What happened at the end?" Robert asked. "Everything seemed to be going well."

"Yeah, I think I was a tad reckless," she admitted. "I showed him an image of the Yokai and he was frightened. I hope that doesn't stop him coming again. Just in this short time we've been able to get some very valuable information for future contacts."

"Let's hope he comes back tomorrow for more cake," said Sergeant Ortiz.

"Ada," Robert said, "try to follow his route to see where he got through our perimeter without being detected."

"Copy that, Lieutenant."

"Let's go inside," Emily said. "I've got a lot to think about, and we've almost missed lunchtime."

"That's true, and I know I'm pretty hungry," Kostas admitted as they all followed her into the facilities.

Just before they went in, Ada interrupted Emily.

"The creature's climbed up a tree," she said.

"What?" Emily said in surprise. "Show me the images."

Just as the AI had said, the young Keplerian had climbed one of the trees around the perimeter. From there he seemed to be watching them from a distance. His expression did not look friendly, nor scared, but forbidding and not very friendly. The shadow of doubt crossed Emily's mind. She began to wonder whether this had been a good idea.

14
Dark secrets

August 7, Year 0
Magellan Base, Kepler-442b

She was still going back over her moment of carelessness a couple of days before. Showing the Keplerian a picture of the Yokai had been a bad idea. Everyone agreed that as a first contact everything had gone very well, especially considering how different it had been with the Yokai.

Still, Shildii had not come back the following day and Emily was very worried. She had been reckless again because of failing to think about the consequences of her actions. She needed to work more on that aspect if she wanted to become a good leader.

That same morning they were to receive the first official visit to the base, and though she was excited about showing it to the deputy director, her mind was more concerned with the young Keplerian than with anything else. In addition to that she had to travel to the space station that very afternoon to attend an important meeting with the project board, a meeting the deputy director himself had called. It must be something crucial if he wanted to get her off the planet for a few hours.

"What are you thinking about?" Paula interrupted her. "You look as if you're somewhere else."

"Sorry, I don't feel very communicative today. I can't stop thinking about what happened the day before yesterday."

"I thought you'd be nervous about today's visit."

"I ought to be, but to be honest I haven't even thought much about it." She took a sip of her coffee.

Evelyn was in the mess hall as well. "And then you're going back to the station, right?" she asked.

"Yeah, looks as though there's something important to discuss."

"At least the trip doesn't take too long," Paula pointed out.

"No, but I might have to spend the night there if the meeting goes on for too long."

Evelyn sighed. "What a drag. Although at least you'll be sleeping in a room by yourself."

"And what do we do if your new friend appears?" Gorka asked.

"Well, I don't know, quite honestly," Emily said. "Ada could modulate my voice so that any one of you could take my place, but I've got a nasty feeling he'd notice the change and turn distrustful. I'd rather he came when I'm there, but in fact any of you could win his trust too."

"Let's hope he doesn't come quite so soon," said Evelyn. "I'm sure I'd be tongue-tied, not knowing what to say."

"And if we send Chad, he might get bored with everything he says when he gets nervous," Gorka joked.

"Hey!" the biologist protested. "I haven't said anything this time."

Emily finished her breakfast and got ready to wait for the deputy director's arrival. It would be the first time David Green had set foot on Kepler-442b, and she presumed that for him it would mean something special. Not so much because it involved setting foot on another planet, as he and her father had been to the Moon and Mars, but rather because it meant the culmination of countless years of effort and sacrifice to turn the project into reality.

She went outside to wait for him. The day had dawned rather cloudy, which prevented her from seeing the approach of the shuttle which was bringing him. She went down the path which separated the base entrance from the work Kostas had been doing during the last few days. It seemed to her that everything was making real progress. He had ploughed the soil in three different areas and installed automatic irrigation systems. In one corner were stacked the frames of two greenhouses he would use to cover two-thirds of the cultivable surface.

"Let's see what comes up here," she murmured, feeling curious.

They were expecting the deputy director around nine in the morning. By now it was fifteen minutes past and the only ones who had appeared were Kostas, to go on with his work, and Jonathan, who was going to help him erect the structures for the greenhouses. The soldiers were getting ready to do their usual morning rounds.

She amused herself by watching a curious insect which was walking near one of the gardens. It had four long legs and a thin body which thickened a little in the middle. At that moment she heard the unmistakable sound of engines in the distance. She looked up at the sky and tried to locate the source of the sound. It took her a while to do this, as the clouds prevented her from seeing anything beyond a few meters up.

The deputy director's shuttle approached the base and landed near Balakova's ship. Emily went across to it and waited for the rear door to open completely. Two people came out, one of them dragging a suitcase.

Behind them came an autonomous mule carrying something so bulky she could not make out what it was.

"Emily!" the deputy director called.

"Hello, David!"

He was looking around. "Wow! This is a lot more impressive live."

"Yes, it is," she admitted. "I still haven't got used to the new landscape."

"Allow me to introduce you to Doctor Rakesh Kumar." The deputy director indicated the person dragging the suitcase beside him, who was too impressed by his surroundings to react to the introduction the deputy director had just made.

"We know each other," Emily said.

"You do?" he asked in amazement.

"Yes," the doctor said, "we met at the station mess a few months ago. We had a more than pleasant chat." He was unable to take his eyes off the planet.

"In that case I guess there's no need for introductions. The doctor's going to join your little detachment. I think it'll be useful to have an anthropologist in the group, now that it looks as though we've established contact with the alien race. In addition he's a theologian, and that'll be useful when it comes to studying the beliefs of the Keplerians."

"Of course," Emily said warmly. "Your knowledge will come in very handy here."

But the doctor was still fascinated by the reddish aspect of the planet.

"I think this is certainly the strangest place I've ever been in," he said.

The deputy director laughed. "Yeah, me too."

"And so far you still hold the record for number of planets visited," Emily said jokingly.

He smiled. "True." He pointed to the dark plastic sheet which covered what the mule was carrying on its back. "I've brought you all a gift."

"Oh! And what is it?"

"All in due course. But first let's go inside. I'm looking forward to seeing the facilities."

The three went into the base, while Emily called her comrades to ask them to come back. Once there, they took off their exosuits and although they stayed in their tightsuits, at least they removed their hoods. She gave them a quick tour of the base and introduced everyone they met on the way to the new member of the team.

Finally they came to the mess hall, where the rest of the team was already sitting waiting in the common area at the end.

"Good morning, everyone," the deputy director said. "How are you all?"

"Fine," they chorused.

"Wonderful. As you know, this is the first official visit to the planet. I hope there'll be many more. In fact this place is very welcoming. I can't help saying I'm a little envious. It reminds me of my younger years on space missions."

"You could stay for a couple of days," Emily suggested.

He laughed. "Don't rule it out! But at the moment this very important mission rests on your shoulders. It wouldn't be right for an old curmudgeon like me to come and bother you with tales of ancient battles from the Pleistocene."

Everyone smiled at the deputy director's sincerity and closeness. Many of them only knew his more institutional side, which in a way could be overwhelming. For most of them this was the first time they had met with him in a relaxed setting.

"Although I'm afraid that today I haven't come to deliver the typical encouraging speech for your mission, repeating the clichés that humanity trusts you and all that kind of empty talk. I'd like this to be a more informal visit. I just want to spend a pleasant time with all of you. Ah yes! And though Emily's already introduced him to some of you, this is Doctor Rakesh Kumar. He's an anthropologist and a theologian, which means he'll be a great help when it comes to studying the Keplerians and their customs. Anything you'd like to add, Rakesh?"

"Only that I realize I'm going to be the oldest person on the base, so I suppose my job will be to tell you tales of ancient battles from the Pleistocene."

The comment made everyone laugh.

"Joking aside, I'm delighted to be part of all this," he went on. "And if you'll allow me, I'd like to emphasize the point that we're making history and that humanity has put its trust in what you're doing and what's going to be created here. And I'm anxious to start working with all of you."

"Thank you, Dr. Kumar," the deputy director said. "I think this is the moment to reveal what, as you'll have noticed, we've brought from the ark."

Carefully, he removed the plastic sheet which covered the load on the mule.

"It can't be!" Ferrara exclaimed.

"Is that what it looks like?" Gorka asked in disbelief.

"How much is there?" Chad asked.

"Two barrels of twenty-five liters each, of the best Earth beer," the deputy director announced while everyone made enthusiastic noises. "It's been brought from Earth at a temperature of absolute zero so than none of its qualities would be lost. And for those who don't like beer, we've brought six bottles of wine and the same of champagne and Earth water, so you have a choice."

"I think I must be the happiest man on the face of Kepler-442b," Gorka joked.

"But don't just stand there like dummies. Here's the spigot, and although it's still early, I'd like to taste that beer."

Private Ferrara and Gorka, the two most enthusiastic of the group, got up quickly and unloaded the heavy barrels from the mule. In no time at all they had the refrigerated spigot installed on the barrel. One by one they poured out the beer in glasses which were handed around among the group. Taro, Chad, Evelyn and the newly-joined Dr. Kumar opted for a glass of wine.

The deputy director waited until everyone was holding a glass so that he could propose a toast.

"To the hope that everything we set our minds to do in life may be a success for humanity."

"To success!" they called.

"This is wonderful," Private Ferrara sighed after the first sip.

"I think I'm going to burst into tears," Chad said with his glass of wine in his hand.

Although Emily was not particularly keen on beer she had to admit that, cold as it was, it tasted heavenly. After finishing their glasses and going on to a second round, everyone went back to their tasks.

In one of the meeting rooms Emily, Dr. Kumar and the deputy director went over every detail of the encounter with the young Keplerian. Both of them commented, to her relief, that they would have done the same thing in that situation.

"It was perfectly relevant to show him the Yokai," the deputy director said.

"And the terror in his face is clear," Dr. Kumar added. "I have no doubt that both species know one another and that there've been interactions between them."

Emily was looking unsure. "But now I'm wondering whether he'll come again, or whether we've lost that opportunity to get closer to them."

"He'll come back," the doctor said.

"How can you be so sure?"

"He risked his life coming here without knowing whether we were dangerous. The fear he felt was more than obvious the first time he came across you. But even so, his curiosity was strong enough to make him come in search of you."

"You could be right," she admitted.

"What's more, he might have shared his encounter with someone and they didn't believe him. On Earth, for centuries there were all sorts of cases where people thought they'd had encounters with extraterrestrials, or even claimed they'd been abducted by them. It wouldn't be surprising to find similar behavior in other intelligent civilizations."

Emily thought about what Dr. Kumar had said. The situation was very much like that of an alien race visiting Earth in the Middle Ages. The associations an event like that might have had would be very interesting from the social and anthropological point of view. The parallels between the two cases were undeniable.

After an interesting conversation, they had lunch with the rest of the team. Without being a banquet, they were able to savor the director's gifts once again and relax for a while. Later, Emily packed a small backpack of clothes, thinking she might be spending another night in her old cabin on the Asimov Ark.

The sensation first of weightlessness, then of lighter artificial gravity made her dizzy, but she recovered soon enough. The meeting with the full staff was to begin soon after, so all she had time to do was leave her backpack in her cabin and go straight on to the bridge.

There, as usual, some of the usual crowd were chatting as they waited. She greeted Director Patel and the commander. Captain Garth gave her no more than a brief, disdainful glance when she came into the hall. This time she was not the last; the deputy director had not arrived yet.

"How's everything going down there?" Patel asked with interest.

"Very well, thanks. The facilities are working like a dream."

"I'm glad to hear that."

"Quite honestly, you've all done an amazing job," she said gratefully.

Deputy Director Green walked in, looking sterner than usual. Emily had noticed an obvious change in his behavior as soon as they had finished eating. Something was troubling him, and it was clear that this meeting had something to do with it.

"Good afternoon, all of you," he said. "I'm sorry I've kept you waiting. We've only just got back from the planet and I had something urgent to attend to."

They returned the greeting politely, but it was obvious from the atmosphere that this meeting was not a mere matter of routine.

"What we're going to be dealing with in this meeting, as so often before, is strictly confidential," he began. "Hence there won't be a record of anything that's said here. As you'll all know, this project was conceived as an alternative way out for humanity after the disaster caused by the asteroid Belial. And I say 'alternative', because humanity's main asset is still Project Atlas."

The deputy director paused. Emily had never seen him so worried.

"Project Orpheus was financed directly or indirectly, and to a greater or lesser degree, by most of the governments of the planet. Nevertheless, Project Atlas, being the most important plan, soon took up the majority of those funds. I won't enter into discussion on that matter, I'm simply explaining the facts."

He paused, this time for much longer, before he went on.

"The commitment between the governments to collaborate went as far as the construction of the Copernicus Ark. Needless to say the cost of the project exceeded anything humanity had built to date, with the exception of the Atlas Project itself, obviously. This fact meant a challenge of immense proportions, and that's why Director Rhodes and I began to look elsewhere for the financing required for the construction of the Asimov Ark."

A slight murmur began to be heard in the hall. The audience seemed to have plenty of questions about this.

"But in that case who financed all this?" the second officer asked.

"Private patrons, technology companies, foundations…" the deputy director explained. "People with a lot of money who were very interested in financing the project."

"And why would they be interested in something that wasn't intended to save their lives?" Barrios asked. He was the officer in charge of security.

"That's the real reason for this meeting. What they received in exchange for the financing was a passage on the Ark."

"What?" several people exclaimed.

"Are you saying," Captain Garth shouted, beside himself with anger, "that a group of plutocrats have paid to come as part of an expedition which was supposedly conceived as fair and egalitarian?"

"No, I'm saying that all of us here, scientists, health workers, technicians, those in charge of equipment and military teams"—he emphasized this last part without changing his facial expression at all— "are in that position thanks to a group of private patrons who financed all this."

"Spare me the underhand tricks and cheap populism!" Captain Garth replied rudely.

"The fact that the financing may be private doesn't diminish the value of the project one jot," the deputy director said firmly, "nor does it take away the slightest trace of rigor in the process of selecting the personnel of this station. Quite simply, there were fewer places available on the ark."

"How many places are we talking about?" came the voice of one of the assistant directors.

"Half the ark, about ten thousand people."

Captain Garth banged the table hard, surprising everyone.

"This is inadmissible!" he shouted. "How the hell are we expected to trust the project if it was created on a basis of lies and deceit right from the start?"

"This project's intention was to take fifty thousand people of different ethnicities and social strata in order to give humanity a second chance. I sincerely believe that ten thousand additional passengers was an acceptable price in order to maximize the chances of survival of the species."

"And what we now have are ten thousand snobs we're going to have to feed and wipe the shit off their delicate asses," the captain shot back. "Don't count on me for anything of the sort," he added as he stormed out of the hall.

"Captain Garth!" the commander shouted, without much conviction.

"Let it be, Commander," the deputy director said. "In a way he's right. I know things haven't come out as we were expecting, to put it mildly. First we lost the Copernicus, then the Galileo, and now I'm revealing all this. I think the captain's anger, or that of any of you, is perfectly legitimate. We haven't been honest, we haven't played fair and we might have harmed the project's good name. Bu I swear to all of you, on my life, that we did it to have more chance of success. And luckily, seeing what's happened, if we hadn't taken the decision to build a third ark, at the moment humanity's hopes would be limited to Planet Earth and the Atlas Project."

"I always believed I was working for a fairer world, a better one," said Second Officer Kuijpers sadly.

"And we can achieve that. This doesn't change the fundamental purpose of the project one little bit. This is about the survival of the human being."

"But this project was based on justice, on mutual trust, on concord between different peoples," the security officer added disappointedly. "And now it turns out that in the end we're going to have to build this new civilization on the mistakes and injustices of the previous one."

"I understand all your reservations perfectly, I really do. And I'm not asking you to share the methods that have brought us here, or even excuse me. I'm only asking that you understand the motives."

"And what about you, Captain Mei," Officer Barrios asked. "Were you aware of the existence of those passengers?"

"A good captain needs to be aware of every single one of the passengers on her ship," she replied.

"And what are they supposed to do here?" one of the assistant directors asked. "There are brilliant minds on this ship, experts in their fields. We even had a Nobel prizewinner on the Galileo. Most of these are going to be businessmen and -women who are used to a life of luxury and easy incomes."

"Ada has the records of all the passengers and is going to carry out a study of the skills of each of them. They'll be assigned a team and a purpose."

"But it's going to be a major job getting them to cooperate," the second officer pointed out. "I don't think the managing director of a successful company is going to take orders willingly from any of us here."

"I don't think they'll have any choice," said Emily, trying to help the deputy director.

"No? And why won't they have any choice?" the second officer asked.

"Because here they have nothing, all their money's done is allowed them to buy a passage, nothing else. At the moment we have neither money nor trade, so they have nothing themselves."

"You knew, didn't you? And you must have agreed to all of this."

"No, I had no idea of any of this," she retorted. "And I don't agree with those methods. But as the deputy director said, I can certainly understand the motives that led them to make that decision. You might not like the situation at all, not even remotely, but you can be sure that if it hadn't been for that decision none of us would be here now. And unfortunately, maybe humanity wouldn't be either.

"And I'd also point out that we have two options now," she added, "Fighting among ourselves and making the same mistakes as in the past, or accepting reality and all of us trying to row in the same direction."

They were silent, aware of the truth in those words.

"And can we know why it's being made public now?" the security officer asked.

"We intend to enlarge the Magellan base with another module like the one already there," the deputy director explained. "And of course in the mid-term we also have the idea of creating a second base, presumably to the north of the current one."

"Are you suggesting you're going to start waking those passengers up?" Second Officer Kuijpers asked.

"Yes, that's what's going to happen. They'll be assigned tasks according to their skills, and they'll try to join the life of the project with the same rights and obligations as any other crew member."

The meeting ended up moving on to other matters, but both Emily and the deputy director noticed a permanent resistance when the other points on the agenda came up. What in normal circumstances might have been a quiet meeting turned into a constant battle of opinions and complaints.

He went up to Emily before she went to have something for dinner and rest.

"Thanks," he said. "I know it must have been very difficult for you to find out about this."

"I'd be lying if I said it was easy for me. But I trust your good judgment completely. I know it must've been a very difficult decision to make and that you'd made it for the good of the project. So I have no more objections."

"That's right. It wasn't an easy decision. And I can assure you, there won't be any more surprises."

"I'm very glad to hear that. Although we'll have to think about how to incorporate all those people who aren't prepared for the scientific life."

15
The pioneer

August 8, Year 0
Magellan Base, Kepler 442b

That morning she got up earlier than usual. She wanted to get back to the base as soon as possible to see whether Shildii would make an appearance again. The shuttle pilot went back to the station as soon as he had left her on land. The day was beginning and the ground looked wet even though it was summer, thanks to the dew. She saw that the greenhouse structures were nearly finished, with only the translucent coverings to be added which would let in the sunlight and allow them to be kept at a constant optimum temperature so that the plants could grow and develop.

She went into the base, where she felt the usual morning buzz, greeted everyone and asked about the previous afternoon. Nothing worthy of mention had happened. A quiet afternoon, though Chad said he had found several species of extremely curious insects.

"This time I came on a species of small dragonfly with a surprising tail which… I bet you won't guess what it does. It emits small electrical discharges to stun its prey."

Emily frowned. "That sounds rather sinister."

"Yeah, but it turns out to be really interesting. On Earth I'd only catalogued a few marine species with that kind of physiological adaptation. It's the first time anything like this has been found out of water."

"What you need to think about is finding another name for that bug," Kostas joked.

"What did you call it?" Emily asked.

"Sparkbug," Chad said, sounding proud of his idea and unaware of his colleagues' giggling.

Emily was smiling broadly. "Doesn't sound very scientific."

She was grateful for these relaxed moments, as the previous evening had been rather difficult. She had slept in fits and starts, waking up suddenly for no apparent reason. She had never had any trouble getting to sleep before, but since they had come to that planet she was finding it hard to fall asleep in the normal way. And she still had to find some way of telling her comrades the reason for that meeting the previous evening.

It was a few minutes later, during the coordination meeting, that she decided to speak when the others had finished listing their plans.

"Before you all go back to your tasks," she began, "I'd like to tell you about what was discussed at yesterday's board meeting."

Here she paused. She had the deputy director's approval to make it public, but even so, she was not at all sure how to begin, nor how they would take what she was about to tell them.

"As you know, the Copernicus was destroyed by a terrorist group, and if it hadn't been for the third ark's existence none of us would be here today. And if we add the disappearance of the Galileo to that, if it hadn't been for the Asimov perhaps the human race would have been doomed to extinction."

"You're beginning to scare us," said Chad.

"Don't worry, it's not that there's anything wrong," she hastened to say. "It's just that yesterday we found out that because public funding ended with the construction of the second ark, the third was financed by private capital."

"And how does that affect us?" Paula asked.

"Not too much, I hope. But that private finance came in exchange for giving passages on the ark for those people who gave money."

"What?" Paula exclaimed. "That's terrible!"

"And it goes against the essence of the project itself," Sergeant Cameron said angrily.

"I know that, I know it's against the principles of equality and freedom the project itself proclaimed to the four winds."

"And do you agree with all this?" Taro asked.

"No," she replied bluntly. "I don't agree. But I'm also aware of the fact that if it weren't for it, we wouldn't be here at this moment having this conversation. I'm absolutely sure it was a decision that was taken very carefully, and also that it was a difficult one. But both the director and the deputy director wanted to bring the largest number of qualified people possible into the project. And this was the only way to get a lot of other scientists and very valuable people to be with us here to create a new civilization."

"Do you trust the deputy director's explanations?" Gorka asked.

"Yes, a hundred per cent."

"Well, then, as far as I'm concerned there's nothing more to say," he said decisively. "We're with you to the end."

"Exactly," Chad said. "Well said."

"We're with you, Emily," said Taro.

"As far as we're concerned there's nothing else to add," said Robert.

Emily was relieved to see all the members of the expedition rallying behind her, all except one. Sergeant Cameron's stern expression did not change in the least. Clearly she did not feel the same way as the others. And perhaps because Robert had already had a word with her about her hostility toward Jonathan, or perhaps because she knew she was in the minority, she did not want to go against them publicly.

Meanwhile they all went back to their tasks and Emily spent most of her time waiting for news of Shildii, the young Keplerian. But a few minutes later, she heard Ada's voice:

"Emily, I think your little friend is on his way."

The AI showed her the images taken from one of the new beacons which had been set up in the area he had come through the time before. It looked as though this time they had the perimeter under better control. Emily gave a sigh of relief when she saw that Shildii was coming back to see her again. But once again a sense of urgency took hold of her.

I've got to get everything ready so that I don't keep him waiting.

She got up hastily and ran to the mess hall.

This time, apart from producing a piece of cake like the one before, she prepared a croissant. She wanted to show him that they had a wide variety of food. By the time she had got into her exosuit Shildii was waiting for her, sitting beside the rock she had put there a couple of days before.

"Ada, I'm going to need you to begin translating what he says in his own language, at least with the words we already know, and vice versa."

"Copy that, Emily," the AI said obligingly. "Consider it done."

Emily walked over warily, not wanting to scare him away again. Once she was a reasonable distance away she sat down on the ground in front of him. She had wrapped the two delicacies carefully in napkins, and when she was about to put them on top of the rock as she had done the previous time, she saw that Shildii himself had got there ahead of her. On top of the rock was a small, grayish loaf of bread which at first glance looked appetizing. Emily put her own two items on the rock, beside the loaf of bread, and made a sign that they were for him.

She pointed at the two pastries. "Cake and croissant."

His attention was focused on the first of them. "Ca-ake…?"

"It's for Shildii," Emily went on without Ada being able to translate anything.

Then she translated back some of what the young Keplerian had said: "Is this *thü yü?*"

"Yes, it's for Shildii." She pointed to him

"This is for Emily," said Shildii, making the same gesture.

She narrowed her eyes as she had seen him do when he was pleased and took the bread, while Shildii began to eat the cake with relish. He seemed to enjoy eating it, because from time to time he made a soft sound of pleasure. Also, he had learned his lesson this time and did not get his hands messy when he picked it up.

When he had finished the cake he realized that she had not tried the bread. She had only examined it and checked its shape and weight. The young boy put his hand to his mouth, then to his stomach.

"Emily *thiivaak* no *yob?*"

She interpreted this as asking why she was not eating the bread, so she showed him images on her screen to explain that humans could not eat inside their suits. She emphasized the images by hitting her bread against her suit helmet and shrugging. Shildii was a little disappointed by this, but seemed to understand. In any case, he forgot the problem the moment he saw the croissant in top of the rock.

"The croissant is for Shildii too," she said.

"Croi-ssant?" the Keplerian repeated with difficulty.

"Yes, croissant."

Once again he picked it up carefully to avoid getting some kind of cream smeared on his hands. He looked at it and sniffed at it thoroughly. After it had passed some kind of acceptance test, he took a bite. His eyes showed Emily that though he found it to his taste, it had not reached the level of the cake.

Noted, she thought.

"Cake or croissant?"

"I *wuch* ca-ke *wod.*"

She twined her fingers together in the sign of mutual understanding, and the young Keplerian seemed to support it completely and repeated it, narrowing his eyes eagerly at the same time.

We're going to start our learning today with one or two simple things, she thought. *Let's see how well you do with colors.*

She showed him different colors, one after the other, on her screen.

"*Pashy, lab, azeii, wik, g'rii, nou, thatmi,*" Shildii said happily as he called out the colors he was seeing.

There came a moment when the young Keplerian could not distinguish between different hues, so that all he could do was repeat the same colors, something which was also common in human individuals. But he had certainly shown that he was capable of differentiating between the primary colors. Emily was left wondering whether they were able to see other wavelengths beyond the range of human beings, like infrareds or ultraviolets, but her suit terminal was not prepared to show colors of the spectrum that were not visible to the human eye.

We're going to need to get to know other words that'll give us more information.

Adjectives, pronouns, prepositions, adverbs…

She showed him a stone on the screen.

"Stone," Shildii said but with a rather odd look on his face, aware that he had already answered this question a couple of days before.

All the same, she showed him the same stone repeated a hundred times.

"*Lamrishy* stones," he said doubtfully.

Next she showed him an infographic with a 3-D model of a Keplerian.

"Keplerian," Shildii said, this time without hesitation.

A tree appeared in the infographic, much taller than the Keplerian himself.

"Tree," he said.

Then another tree appeared, much larger than the first, so that it made him look tiny. His expression changed as he began to see the nature of the game.

"*Wod chaz tree,*" he replied.

She repeated the exercise, but this time the tree was smaller.

"*Ghak* tree," he said without hesitation.

She did the same again, but this time she moved the tree away from him.

"Tree is *jaw chii.*"

Shildii smiled when he saw he had been right and that the next test consisted of bringing the tree closer.

"Tree is *thaakhi.*" He twined his fingers together. "Like *khoshy,*" he added.

Now she showed him a large rock, but he seemed to be waiting for something else to appear:

"Rock," he said.

The virtual Keplerian appeared again, but this time he was on top of the rock.

"Keplerian *ghij* rock," he said. And when the rock changed to being on top of the Keplerian, he added: "Keplerian *tab* rock."

Little by little, and with simple related exercises, Emily began to learn the words the Keplerians used to refer to less tangible concepts. In fact it was turning into a most productive morning. Once she had enough words she decided to change the topic. She showed him a black circle on a white background.

"*Laazaav,*" he replied.

Then came a triangle.

"*Laash.*"

Wonderful, you know geometry, she thought. *This is getting interesting.*

After defining different simple geometric figures, she tried showing him a piece of writing. On the screen of her suit several words appeared being written little by little, as in a writing class for small children.

"That is *fid*," he said unsurely.

"Shildii knows how to write?" she asked.

"Yes. But no *jaa* that."

She guessed that he meant that their way of writing did not look at all like the human kind they were seeing, but it seemed that the Keplerians knew writing. Emily wrote a couple of words with her own finger on the holographic screen and urged Shildii to do the same in his own language.

"Can Shildii show Emily?"

The boy hesitated for a moment, but got up and came over to her. They had never been so close to one another. Without realizing, the young Keplerian had sat down beside her arm and was already touching the screen with his fingers. She could feel his breathing, his chest rising and falling in a continuous loop.

They have lungs, or something like what we have to breathe with, she thought in fascination.

Seeing that things happened when he interacted with the holographic terminal, Shildii gave a sound of surprise and satisfaction. He was enjoying this. Nor did it take him long to get used to the interface, so that he was not very different from a human child in that way. Soon he was writing something in his own language. It was clear that although the sounds he made could be reproduced and were audible to humans, his written language was very different. As a rule their shapes were much straighter, as if they were made only with lines that crossed one another. They reminded her of the *kanji* characters of Japanese, but these were considerably simpler and did not represent concepts but sounds. She was convinced they had an alphabet of their own.

The fact that the Keplerians have a system of writing is very important, obviously, but the fact that an ordinary person, as Shildii seems to be, knows it, is a clear sign that education's a basic part of his society. It means anyone can have access to it, even the least privileged.

Shildii spent some time writing, but then realized how close he was to Emily and gave a start. But far from returning to his original place, he began to take a close look at her exosuit. He felt the arm with the tips of his fingers, so that his sharp claws made their characteristic sound as they struck the metal. Then his attention was drawn by the torso of the suit, the legs and finally the helmet. He peered inquisitively through the opening of this. Emily remained composed, but this was so exciting that her heart seemed ready to jump out of her chest.

"Everything okay, Emily?" came Private Ferrara's voice through the radio.

"Yeah, fine," she whispered. She supposed that as had happened the other day, they had not lost sight of Shildii from the moment he had arrived in the base clearing.

Now she was able to watch him too while they both looked at one another's eyes. Once his curiosity was satisfied, the Keplerian got up from the ground and walked behind her as she went on sitting there. He was looking with great interest at every one of the tiny details of the suit.

"I'd give a lot to know what he's thinking right now," she murmured.

After a while he seemed to lose interest and sat down again in the same place. He was expecting his private games session to continue. Emily played up to this, and they began a new round. This time they worked on possessives, pronouns and adverbs. It was quite hard work, but she was able to elicit some useful information for the budding Keplerian dictionary.

Let's see what a Keplerian family's like, she decided when she had had enough.

For this she had prepared some infographics with human figures. They did not yet know whether the Keplerians had two sexes like humans, still less what their reproductive cycles were. Hence it seemed to her that the best way to find the words denoting kinship would be via images of the human being.

So she showed him pictures of men side by side with women, then pregnant women, then babies and children. She did not go into details about reproduction on Earth; that particular subject had been taboo in many societies for a very long time, and the last thing she wanted was for Shildii to run away again as he had last time.

She was surprised that the youngster seemed to grasp what this new game was about perfectly.

"*Shaz!*" he exclaimed with narrowed eyes when she showed him the father of a baby. "*Wij!*" he said when she pointed to the mother.

Great, their social structures are like ours in many ways, she thought to herself. *This should be a great help when it comes to mutual understanding and empathy.*

Thanks to this exercise, she got most of the nouns that described family ties. But then something changed in Shildii's expression. He pointed up at the sun with a certain regret. In fact almost the entire morning had gone by, and the sun was at its zenith.

"I *zaan* go back," he said.

He had to leave. She supposed that either he was expected for lunch, or else he should not have been here and had slipped away from his duties.

I hope you don't get into trouble, she thought. *But I enjoy talking to him.*

The only drawback was that she did not know how to ask him whether he was going to come back. So she tried using other words. She pointed up to the sun's position in the morning.

"Shildii wants to play with Emily when the sun is there?"

"Yes," he said with the usual delight in his eyes, making the familiar gesture with his fingers.

"Goodbye!"

"*Shyaap!*"

She watched him walking away as she went over all the progress they had made that morning. She was very happy. Not only had they managed to add a lot to Ada's dictionary, but she knew he would be back tomorrow. She saw Ferrara getting up from her hiding-place on the roof of the main building.

"Seems to have gone better than last time, eh?" she said.

Emily smiled. "To be honest, yes. I'm very pleased, and besides, he said he'd be back tomorrow."

Everyone outside the base decided to have a break and go for lunch. But just before she went into the building Emily remembered the grayish bread Shildii had left on the rock and went back for it. She remembered the protocol for introducing external agents into the base, which Chad had reminded her of a few days earlier.

"I'm afraid you're going to have to suit up for a moment and come out to pack a sample for analysis," she said.

"What is it?" the biologist asked.

"A kind of loaf of grayish bread. And I must admit that apart from the odd color it doesn't look at all bad."

"Okay, I'm coming out. In fact I'd like to talk to you later. We've been making some progress."

After the lunch break Emily went to the lab, where as usual she found Taro and Chad, who normally spent the whole day locked up there, only leaving to make short excursions and find new varieties of animals and minerals.

"What have you found out?" she asked.

"That the alien molecule is quite simply the most fascinating thing we've ever seen," Taro said.

"In fact," Chad added, "it turns out there isn't only one type of molecule. We've isolated at least four different types. And though it's still a bit early in the day to reach conclusions, each of them seems to have more than one purpose."

"More than one purpose?"

He nodded. "Yes, they seem to be real molecular Swiss Army knives. We tried exposing them to different compounds and micro-organisms, and it caused some sort of change, or reaction, in nearly all of them."

"I presume that's not usual."

"No, it isn't." said Taro. "But that's not the weirdest part."

"No?"

Chad shook his head. "No, what really scares us is that the molecules themselves are able to control these changes, or even stop them completely, without causing the destruction of the cells. I've never seen anything like it"

"Does that mean they're dangerous?"

"We're not sure," he admitted, looking concerned. "But somehow they seem to encourage cellular mutation."

"That sounds dangerous."

"Yeah, without control it would be, but these molecules are able to stop those changes before anything really dangerous happens. We'll go on working on them, but so far I wouldn't think of taking off your exosuit outside the base."

16
The fog

September 1, Year 0
Magellan Base, Kepler-442b

"Rakesh," Emily asked the anthropologist over breakfast, "would you like to come with me this morning and meet the Keplerian?"

He was delighted. "Of course. It'll be a pleasure to come with you. I've had a look at the images of your encounters with that creature, what's his name?"

"Shildii."

"That's right, Shildii. I'm looking forward to having the opportunity to meet him."

"I think it might be interesting for him to have contact with someone else from our group, even if he can barely tell us apart in our exosuits. And he'll be able to see the differences between men and women and also that within the human race there's a lot of ethnic diversity."

"All I know is that the mere thought of meeting an alien makes my skin crawl, look!" He showed her the hair on his forearm.

"I know. I still can't really take in everything it means."

"What have you got planned?"

"I'd be lying if I told you I've prepared for the encounters," she admitted. "In fact I improvise as I go, depending on the situation. If you can think of some subject to talk about, that would be very welcome."

"No, though according to the protocols we ought to try to contact the leaders of the alien communities."

"That's true. I hope Shildii can help us with that somehow."

"But before that, I understand we need to improve our Keplerian dictionary."

"That's the idea, and he's very important for that. Which reminds me, I have to prepare something for him to eat, because I should think he'll arrive any moment."

As was to be expected, soon after this Ada detected movement outside. After a few minutes Shildii appeared amid the vegetation, following the same route as before. This time it was Emily who was sitting waiting for him, and also she was not alone.

Shildii approached absent-mindedly, but when he saw the second figure he stopped in his tracks. He hesitated for a few moments, but in the end he came warily over to the rock.

"Hello, Shildii," Emily said.

"Hello, Emily." His eyes were fixed on Rakesh.

"This is Rakesh," she said. "Rakesh, this is Shildii."

The anthropologist greeted him with a slight nod. "Hello, Shildii."

Shildii seemed surprised by Rakesh's voice, perhaps because it sounded very different even though they were wearing the same kind of suit.

Emily showed him a couple of images of herself and Rakesh without their exosuits, and after pointing to each one she repeated the names. Shildii gave a small cry of what sounded like surprise.

"You very *now*," Shildii said. He was studying the photographs in surprise.

Apparently they did not worry him much, because he soon realized that Emily had brought him two pieces of cake that morning. One was her favorite, which was carrot, and the other the one he liked most, which was chocolate. She wanted to show him that in human society there was diversity in many aspects. The youngster took the carrot cake, and as before, sniffed it before tasting it.

Apparently he liked the carrot cake better than the previous day's croissant, and he let Emily know.

"This very good *iw*," he said, narrowing his eyes as he ate it.

"Emily is happy."

But there was no comparison with the look on his face while he was eating the chocolate cake. Emily was fascinated by his way of eating; he seemed to enjoy food immensely.

I hope I'm not spoiling him, she thought. *I suppose somewhere there are a couple of Keplerian parents wondering why their son isn't eating his lunchtime broccoli.*

Once he had finished the second piece of cake, he seemed to feel so good that he even let out a light burp. The sound he made was so amusing that all three of them began to laugh. It was the first time Emily had seen him laugh heartily, and in fact his laughter was not very different from that of a human.

"Rakesh is a human friend," Emily told him as soon as they had calmed down.

"Ra-kesh friend," Shildii repeated in agreement.

"Has Shildii friends?" Rakesh asked.

"Yes, Shildii have many friends in *fiihtiw*."

"And family?" Emily asked.

"Yes, father, mother and two siblings *shyish*."

"How many Keplerians live in *fiihtiw*?" she asked.

"Shildii not know," he said. "Shildii not know all. *Wuw* are many."

"Is there a father of all?" Rakesh asked, meaning their leaders.

Shildii did not seem to understand the question very well, so Emily decided to show him the image of an old coronation on Earth. When he saw it, his expression changed slightly.

"You talk of the *chach*?" he asked.

"Do the *chach* wear anything on their heads? Or perhaps they carry a long sick?"

"Yes, they carry a long stick. And they are old."

"Could we get along with the *chach*?" Emily suggested as she made the twining gesture with her fingers.

He shrugged. "Shildii not know. But Shildii can take you to *fiihtiw*."

Emily and Rakesh looked at one another. They knew what this meant, and they could not make that decision lightly. They would have to plan it well, or they would be taking a serious risk by going into a Keplerian village alone. And apart from that, to appear out of the blue in a native settlement could easily unleash chaos among the planet's inhabitants.

"Emily and Rakesh must think about it," she said at last. "Maybe next sun, Shildii show *fiihtiw* to them."

The youngster was delighted with the idea of showing them his village, so much so that he spent a long while talking non-stop, as if he were thinking of all sorts of things at the same time about where to go or what to show them.. But unfortunately they could not understand even half of what he said, because either many of the words were proper nouns or else they had not yet had the chance to mention them in any of the didactic games they had used for learning new vocabulary.

"What is the name of your *fiihtiw*?" Emily asked, in the hope that this word would not be a proper noun.

"*Wükhaadiiz ofiz*," he replied proudly.

Learning all the possible words that might be some use to them if in the end they decided to venture into Shildii's village was the objective of the next few hours. Of course it was no easy task. Concepts like *peace*, *tranquility* or *danger* were not as simple as those they had been learning. But little by little they began to find a way of understanding one another and getting hold of enough vocabulary to enable a possible diplomatic meeting between different civilizations.

As he had the day before, Shildii left at noon. He said goodbye to both of them happily, and they agreed to meet again the following day.

"What are you going to do?" Rakesh asked when the boy had left.

"If you think it's a good idea, I'd like to meet the Keplerian leaders."

"I can't show you what the skin on my arm is like at this moment, but this is incredible. It's a dream come true. Thank you for letting me share it with you."

"We're all in the same boat, Rakesh. There's no need to thank me."

Both of them went back to the base entrance, where the soldiers were waiting for them as usual.

"Did you hear?" Emily asked Robert.

"Yes, and I think we've got a lot to get organized."

"We'll make a start after lunch. "Watching Shildii eat has made me really hungry."

"How's the Keplerian language map coming along?" Rakesh asked as he sat down in one of the chairs in the hall. "Will it be enough to let us get by in a diplomatic meeting?"

"We have about six hundred words," Ada said. "Although it's not enough for a very profound understanding, I think you'll be able to carry on simple conversations without trouble."

"If you listened to them talking among themselves," the doctor asked, "do you think you'd be able to get the meaning of words from the context?"

"In theory, yes, but I'd need to hear the same words in different conversations and contexts to be able to infer their meaning. Keplerian doesn't seem to be a very complex language. Its syntax, relatively speaking, seems reasonably like that of a human language, so I don't think it'll take us too long to master it. Another way of speeding up the learning would be through reading, if someone were to teach me how to read Keplerian, obviously."

"Don't worry, Rakesh, I think we'll be able to manage with the language," Emily said to resolve the issue. "What we really need to discuss here is how we're going to guarantee our own safety."

The anthropologist nodded. "Of course."

"We'll cross the river behind you," Robert said. "We'll try to follow you at a safe distance and keep you monitored all the time. I don't suppose for a moment they have a good enough technology to interfere with our communications, so I don't think we'll have any trouble doing that."

"But if you're following us, who'll be in charge of keeping the base safe?" Emily asked.

"Good point. I've asked the commander to send us reinforcements to keep watch on the base while we're away."

"Wonderful."

"And how will you know if things turn nasty?" Rakesh asked rather nervously.

"Apart from the fact that we'll be seeing everything you're seeing from your exosuits, Ada'll be monitoring the sensors in real time. We'll know what's happening around you all the time."

"And we'll be watching from up here too," came the voice of the deputy director, who had insisted on being present in the meeting from where he was in the station.

"Once we cross this area here"—Emily pointed to one of the clearings she had crossed before— "you'll lose satellite vision."

"True, assuming it's not a cloudy day," the deputy director agreed. "We don't yet have valid meteorological models, but there could be cloud tomorrow."

Emily nodded. "That's true."

"We'll take the drones just in case, though we won't use them unless strictly necessary. We don't want to scare the Keplerians of the village."

"What do you expect to find there, Emily?" the deputy director asked.

"I don't really know, we don't know very much about them as yet. Except that the village is large enough for Shildii not to know everyone, that they have family structures that resemble our own, and also some kind of leader, or group of leaders, who seem to have an element of power or responsibility over the others."

"We'll need to be very careful," Rakesh pointed out. "This morning I had a close-up view of those very sharp claws the young Keplerian has. If those of his fellow-villagers are half as threatening, I don't think the suits would stand up to a major assault."

The lieutenant hastened to reassure him. "These suits are made of a special alloy, highly resistant. It can take quite a lot more than you think, Dr. Kumar. Even so, we hope it won't be necessary to reach that point."

"No, I don't really think so either. As a rule, at least on Earth, agricultural peoples have always had a much more pronounced tendency to pacifism than nomadic ones. But even though Shildii seems a very quiet Keplerian, I couldn't help noticing those enormous claws and wondering why evolution has caused them to develop."

"We'll be fine," Emily insisted. "We'll be going with one of them."

"Do you trust him?" the deputy director asked.

"Yes, but I'm afraid he's only a teenager, and I don't know about his fellow-villagers. Let's hope they welcome foreigners just as warmly."

"Have you thought about carrying weapons?" the deputy director asked her.

"Yes, I've thought about it, David. But I don't think it's the right thing to do. We might make them feel threatened and ruin the whole thing. And also in a situation of extreme danger, surrounded by hundreds of Keplerians, I doubt very much whether a couple of firearms would get us out of a tight spot."

"Especially considering I've never used a weapon in my life," Rakesh added. "I'm pretty sure I'd end up shooting myself in the foot."

"The ideal thing in a case like this would be to take a combat drone," Robert pointed out. "But we don't have any."

"I think we're being very cautious about this," Emily said. "I don't think anything's going to happen. It's more than likely they'll be a quiet, peaceful people. At least Shildii seems very calm to me."

"And the first time he saw you he ran off in terror," Rakesh reminded her. "The fact that he didn't look for confrontation when he was faced with the unknown is a good sign."

"Anyway, we need to be cautious," Robert said, "especially if we could cause fear or distrust in the Keplerians. A frightened creature could end up turning very dangerous if cornered or threatened. And the fact that there are hundreds or thousands like Shildii is something to take into consideration."

Emily sensed his unease. "Maybe we should avoid going through very busy areas as far as possible."

"That would certainly be a good idea."

"And why don't we try to set up a meeting with their leaders at some midway point?" the deputy director asked. "I don't really think it's such a good idea to show ourselves in public at the drop…" His signal was lost for a few seconds. "…and cause panic among…" The video began to blink. "a good idea…" After several gaps in both image and audio, the connection cut out completely.

"Deputy Director?" Emily called.

There was no reply from the space station. The image had frozen and an intermittent red signal was blinking in one of the corners.

"Ada what's happening?"

"I can't connect with the station. We have no connection,"

"No connection?" Doctor Kumar repeated. "How can Ada be without connection?"

"Ada's main core is in the ark," Emily explained. "What we're hearing now is a reduced copy of Ada which is carried out on the main base computer."

"Are there two Adas?" he asked in surprise.

Emily smiled. "There are a lot more than two. In our exosuits, on some ships and of course in the ark. All of them communicate among themselves to share information and make decisions."

"So do they make decisions together?"

"As a rule the main version does that, the one on the ark, because she's the one that collects the information from the others and has more capacity for it. When they can't communicate between themselves, that's when the copies take control, like now."

Rakesh looked satisfied. "I think I understand now."

"Ada, what's happened?"

"I'm not sure," came the reply. "I lost connection with the ark without warning. The only strange thing I can see is that outside everything's covered by thick fog."

"Fog?" Robert asked. "Can fog interfere with communications?"

"It shouldn't," Emily said, puzzled. "At least it wasn't usual on Earth. But we don't know what atmospheric phenomena on this planet are like, and maybe the fog's thick enough to do that."

"And can't we do anything?" Robert asked.

"We'll ask Paula to check the antenna," Emily said, thinking aloud. "It may be that the laser's power can be regulated to strengthen the signal."

At that very moment Paula appeared in the lab hall.

"Sorry," she said, "but I think we've lost the connection. Something's wrong with the transmitter."

"Yeah, Ada says it might be the fog."

"Fog?" she asked blankly. "I'd never heard that the kind of equipment we have here would stop working because of the fog."

"Doesn't fog affect communications?"

"Yes, it certainly can. I said I'd never heard of it affecting them, but that would be on Earth. Having lived through an electrical storm like the one a few days ago, I'm beginning to realize that this planet has very extreme atmospheric phenomena."

"Can you fix it?" Emily asked.

"I hope so. If it's because of the fog, increasing power might be enough. Although we'll be using more electricity."

"Okay, please check it. If you manage to, we'll see whether Ada can manage it by herself in the future."

"Perfect," Paula said, and left the hall.

"Ada, show us the images of the outer cameras of the base," Emily said.

When the AI showed the images on the screen, all they could see was absolute and total nothingness. All the images were a very dense dark gray. There was nothing visible except fog.

"For goodness' sake!" Robert exclaimed. "This certainly looks like one hundred per cent fog."

Emily did some checking. "The relative humidity outside is off the chart."

"I think it's worth taking a look at it," Robert said. He got up.

The three left the hall and put on their exosuits. When they opened the exit door they had a strange feeling of unease. There was so little light that it might have been nighttime, and they could barely see the ground beneath their feet. If they walked a few steps away, they risked getting lost.

Beside the door, flat against the wall of the base, were Kostas, Sergeant Cameron and Private Ferrara, still amazed by that strange meteorological phenomenon.

"Don't go too far," Ferrara called in warning.

"What's happened?" Emily asked. "This doesn't look exactly normal."

"It came all of a sudden," Kostas said. "In less than five minutes I almost lost vision completely. Luckily we were able to reach the wall of the base, because staying out there doesn't seem very pleasant."

"It's scary," Rakesh agreed.

"And it's also affecting communications," the lieutenant added.

"I can't say that surprises me," Kostas said.

They watched the terrifying beauty the planet offered them. It was like watching emptiness. Even in the safety of the doorway, the sensation produced by looking in any direction and seeing only that dark gray cloak was the most disturbing one Emily remembered ever feeling.

"We'd better get back inside," the corporal suggested after a couple of minutes. "This looks as if it's here to stay."

"And what are we going to do tomorrow if the fog doesn't go away?" Rakesh asked. "Or if Paula can't manage to fix the coms?"

"If the fog goes on I very much doubt whether we'll be able to go anywhere," said Emily. "I hope Paula can get communications back, but if the fog goes on I'm afraid we'll have to postpone our little excursion."

17
Diplomacy

September 2, Year 0
Magellan Base, Kepler-442b

Emily woke that morning feeling sleepier than usual. However much she tried, she could not stop thinking about her little excursion to the Keplerian village. Rakesh and she were going to be the first human beings ever to visit an alien settlement. She was nervous. There were too many things that might go wrong, and they had so little information about the Keplerians she was beginning to wonder whether it had all been such a good idea after all.

She went to the bathroom as the rest of her colleagues began to stir. The previous night she had drunk too much water and now her bladder was pressing. Then she took care of other matters.

"Good morning, Ada, are we connected to the space station?"

"Yes, Emily. We're connected."

She sighed. "Thank goodness."

Paula had told her shortly before going to bed that to increase the power of the antenna she would have to go up on to the flat roof of the base and work on the laser transmitter. It seemed that not everything was ready for Ada to modify the power to fit external conditions. But considering the visibility and the fact that nightfall was almost on them, Emily had told her only to do it once the fog was gone. And luckily it seemed that there was no trace left of it that morning.

After showering and having a reasonably full breakfast in case of what might happen, all she had left to do was sit down to wait for Shildii to appear. She used the time to speak to the deputy director and finish the conversation that had been broken off. Although in fact there was not much more to add. She would try to get the Keplerians to meet with them somewhere away from the village. Robert had prepared everything, and the replacement must be on its way by now.

"Today it's your turn to be very careful," he told her when they met in one of the distributor areas.

"We will be," she said, even though she did not seem very sure of it.

"Anyway, we'll be keeping an eye on you," he said reassuringly. "Nothing's going to happen to you."

"Thanks. I feel a lot better knowing you'll be just a few meters away from where we are."

"I'd much rather we could all go together, but I understand the reasons why we shouldn't."

"Everything's going to be fine," she said firmly. "It's only a diplomatic mission."

"Maybe that's what's making me even more nervous."

She smiled. "Hey, the warrior is frightened of diplomacy and politicians."

"Let's just say I've never trusted them entirely."

"I'm sure they're a peaceful people."

"If they've been living only a few kilometers away from the Yokai they must have defenses," he reasoned. "And if they do, we'll have to be very careful they don't feel threatened."

The shuttle bringing the small group of soldiers who were coming to help with surveillance at the base arrived at eight forty-five that morning. Outside, everyone was ready to leave by now. The only one who was missing was Shildii. Leading the group was Sergeant Reynolds, one of the experienced officers who had been with Captain Garth on his missions on Earth. He was a tough man, with an unfriendly face and a mass of tattoos on his arms and legs. He looked as though he had been made in the image of the captain, so that it was obvious he had grown under his tutelage.

The sergeant, along with nine other soldiers, stood to attention in front of Lieutenant Beaufort.

"At ease," Robert said after returning their salute. "Reynolds, you and four of your soldiers will come with me. The others will stay with Sergeant Cameron at the base camp."

"Excuse me, sir," the sergeant interrupted, "but I have orders from the captain to be on guard at the camp myself."

The lieutenant looked at the sergeant and weighed up Garth's orders.

"Very well, then," he said resignedly. "Choose four soldiers. The others will come with me."

"Any additional guidelines, sir?" the sergeant asked.

"No, none. Pay attention to the radio and how the mission's getting on. I don't expect we'll need air support, but make sure the pilot's awake and alert, just in case."

"Understood, sir."

The sergeant chose his four soldiers, and the other five were now under the direct orders of Lieutenant Beaufort, who organized them and gave them a brief summary of the nature and parameters of the mission.

A few minutes later Ada reported that Shildii was approaching the base. As usual Emily had remembered the piece of chocolate cake for him. But unlike those other days, this time she had prepared many more. You should never go to someone else's house without bringing some kind of gift, or at least so her grandmother Karen had taught her.

When Shildii reached her she offered him a piece of cake, which of course he took and celebrated with various eloquent gestures.

"Emily and Rakesh come with Shildii to village?" he asked eagerly.

"Yes," Emily replied, "But there's a problem."

"Problem?" he asked blankly.

"Shildii ran fast when he saw Emily seven suns ago."

"Yes, I *ghayi* a little," he admitted, embarrassed.

"Emily and Rakesh don't want *ghayi* the village."

Shildii was thoughtful for a while. He had understood the problem, but it did not look as though he had a solution.

Rakesh anticipated the Keplerian's answer. "Could the leaders of the village come halfway?" he asked.

"Shildii not know. Mother of Shildii is *popfa* in house of leaders. Shildii can speak with his mother."

"That would be very good," Emily said, sounding more cheerful.

Shildii smiled in his own way to celebrate the understanding they had just reached.

"Shildii *chan* you the way," he added cheerfully.

Emily and Rakesh followed him back to his village. She was carrying a box with several pieces of cake inside. The soldiers meanwhile followed her every move attentively.

"Robert," she said, "we're on our way."

"Message understood. We're ready to go for a stroll at this end."

"We'd better shut off coms until further notice."

"Message understood. Good luck."

Shildii led them through underbrush and vegetation along the winding path he had been using over those last few days. Once they reached the area with the huge rectangular stones, he picked up a huge board from the shore. It was five meters or so long.

So this is how he's been crossing the river, Emily thought. *Very clever.*

Shildii placed the board between the first two stones and crossed as far as the second. Once he was there he gestured to Emily and Rakesh to follow him. Both of them hesitated for a moment. The wood of the plank looked very solid and heavy, but it was one thing for a young Keplerian to walk on it, a very different one for two humans clad in metal armor.

"Ada, how much do we weigh with the exosuits on?" Emily asked.

"You, about a hundred and fifteen kilos, Dr. Kumar about a hundred and forty."

"Do you think the plank will hold?"

"Based on its thickness, I'd say yes. And considering how difficult it was to cut off that branch the day you first set foot on the planet, I could infer that the wood of this planet is tougher and more compact than that of Earth. I don't think you'll have any trouble, but even so, I'd recommend that you go one at a time."

Shildii went on gesturing to them to cross, unaware that an artificial intelligence was making the appropriate calculations. He must have thought that they did not dare, and he was not entirely wrong. Emily crossed first. The hard wood of the plank barely yielded a couple of centimeters. It suffered a little more with Rakesh's extra weight, but nothing to make him think he could end up falling into the water.

Once all three of them were on the narrow space afforded by the second stone, Shildii seized the end of the plank and dragged it toward the third. Emily and Rakesh were impressed by the boy's physical ability; a plank as large and hard as that must have been extremely heavy.

One by one they left behind each of the stepping stones until they were on the other side. Shildii hid the plank in a clump of bushes under a tree with huge red leaves. They followed more or less the same route Emily had taken a few days before, and in the distance they could even see the old wooden house she had found.

"Is that an old Keplerian house, Shildii?" she asked out of curiosity.

He shrugged. "I suppose so, Shildii never see anyone around here."

In a few minutes they had reached the clearing where Emily had stumbled on Shildii the first time. They decided that this was the most suitable site for their first encounter with the Keplerian leaders.

"Shildii," she called. "Can you bring the leaders here?"

He smiled. "Yes, I think so. But before, Shildii must speak to his mother," he added, sounding rather less pleased.

"Be careful, Emily doesn't want Shildii to be in trouble."

"Yes. Emily and Rakesh wait here for Shildii."

The youngster set off at a run along the strange avenue formed by the forest trees.

"Now all we have to do is wait," Rakesh murmured.

"Robert?" Emily called. "We've stopped in the clearing, waiting for the Keplerian committee."

"Copy that," she heard on the radio. "We have a visual. We'll stay at a safe distance without losing sight of the situation."

"Okay, thanks. Shutting off coms."

Twenty minutes or so must have gone by when at last she saw signs of movement within the forest. Two figures seemed to be moving forward shyly toward the clearing. When they saw them, the taller figure stopped dead. With a gesture of her arm she held the other one back. The figure behind, of course, was Shildii, and the one in front must be his mother.

She was the first female Keplerian they had seen, and the difference was obvious. With barely any bulges on her skull, her figure was much more slender. Her eyes looked smaller and her face much longer and finer. But it was her clothes which particularly caught their attention, as she was wearing a kind of long, threadbare apron which reached nearly to her ankles, which they assumed meant that she belonged to a working family.

The look on her face was one of great worry. And to judge by her son's attitude Emily supposed that like any mother or father in that situation she had been very disturbed to find that her son had established contact with some unknown visitors. She seemed to be addressing him in a way that reminded Emily of a scolding, which made her feel very bad. She had grown fond of the young Keplerian.

Shildii's mother pointed inside the forest, and after another look at Emily and Rakesh, both of them vanished from sight.

"I think Shildii's mother must have given him a good scolding," Emily said.

"They seemed to be in quite a hurry to get out of here," Dr Kumar said. "I don't know whether that looks hopeful, or whether it's going to end up with Shildii being punished for keeping bad company."

"They might have gone in search of their leaders."

"Yes, what worries me now is that instead of coming themselves they might send their army, that is if they have one."

"Robert," Emily called, "are you still there?"

"We're here," came his voice. "We're still in position. We have the drones covering the area, and there's good visibility."

Emily looked up at the sky, but she could not see any of the drones until Ada marked them in a square on her helmet screen.

"At the slightest sign of trouble, get out of there as fast as you can," Robert said. "We'll cover you."

"Let's all stay calm," she said, trying to sound reassuring. "Probably nothing'll happen and she'll just have gone to warn their leaders."

The wait was a long, tense one, but after some interminable minutes of doubt and anxiety they saw movement in the forest again. This time there were more Keplerians, a small committee appearing from amid the trees. In the lead were several soldiers riding beasts like those they had seen beside the river the first time they had set foot on the planet. She could count at least four huge hairy mounts, each of them jet-black.

Not far behind, two other animals were pulling a huge wooden carriage, simply painted and decorated. It was led by an elegantly-dressed Keplerian with an impassive expression. Behind the carriage a small group of infantry accompanied the rest of the group at a brisk trot. They were wearing a green uniform with blazons on the front which Emily was unable to see in detail because of the dense vegetation. They were carrying spears, as well as some kind of sharp weapon sheathed at their belts. She could not help thinking of *The knight of the lagoon*, the medieval novel she had brought with her from Earth and which was one of her all-time favorites. If the procession was a reflection of Keplerian society, this reminded her very much of the human medieval epoch.

The small diplomatic group halted at the point where the avenue opened into the clearing where Emily and Rakesh were standing. The animals emitted a thunderous sound of relief. Moments later, one of the doors of the carriage opened wide. Out of it came five Keplerians. The first to come out was a female wearing what seemed to be a turquoise-blue ceremonial dress. She wore a kind of long stole around her neck which fell to either side and reached below her waist. In her hand she carried a large wooden staff which was also dyed in faded shades of blue. She certainly had the poise of a leader, and although Emily could not tell the age of a Keplerian, the difficulties she was faced with when she got down from the carriage led her to think that she was old.

Behind her came another female and two males, all wearing elegant tunics, but without reaching the level of the apparent leader of the retinue. In addition, none of them carried a staff. There could be no doubt that she was the leader of Shildii's village. Suddenly Emily felt very nervous, so much so that her leg began to twitch with that nervous restlessness that came over her at significant moments. Finally, after the four individuals, she saw a familiar face getting down from the carriage: Shildii.

"Robert," she said into the radio, "Shildii's with them. I don't think there's going to be a problem. It looks like a formal welcome."

"Copy that. Anyway, we'll keep our eyes open. Our drones will stay in the area to prevent any ambush.

"Copy that, shutting off coms."

One of the riders, who had now alighted from his animal, seemed to be talking heatedly with the leader of the group and gesturing wildly in the direction of Emily and Rakesh. She seemed to be reproaching him and ordering him to withdraw with a wave of her hand. Then she turned and seemed to say something to Shildii, who nodded in delight. This was probably the thing which most reassured Emily, when she saw him narrowing his eyes as she had seen him do so many times by now when he was feeling relaxed and happy.

The presumed leader grabbed Shildii's arm and with the other three Keplerians began to come closer to where they were waiting in the clearing. There was no doubt now that she was really old; her slow walk and bent posture made it more than evident.

The retinue reached the clearing, and the old woman looked up at the sky as if she were evaluating the weather. That morning there were one or two clouds, but the planet's sun was bright with its thin orange light. The group covered the distance which separated them and stopped five meters or so from Rakesh and Emily, who had not moved an inch from their spot.

The leader waved her hand after she had let go of Shildii's arm. *"Yirnu, khol."*

"They don't speak well," Shildii said. He had seen Emily's passivity. "I *jüv* them, they are *thaamfii,* but soon be *oppi."*

The leader gave a nod of approval, then repeated the gesture with her hand. "Hello, humans," she said.

Emily imitated the greeting. "Hello, Keplerians."

She was so nervous that she could not think of anything else to say, apart from imitating her hostess, whom she was now able to closer look at. The bulges on her head were finer and more subtle than Shildii's, allowing them to distinguish clearly between females and males. Numerous wrinkles ran down the skin of her face, revealing the relentless passage of time. Her deep eyes were full of wisdom, and her keen gaze had certainly analyzed the threat posed by the foreigners standing in front of her. She had the air of a respected leader. The stole she wore around her neck was a vivid blue, decorated with glyphs sewn on to it with fine golden thread, which gave her an air of nobility. From her neck also hung a medallion of stone with a faded rune carved in the center. But what most caught Emily's attention was the staff in her right hand. Of dark wood, without any carved designs, it was shaped like the branch of a tree and was a light, faded blue. It was almost as tall as she was herself. The upper part was decorated with rough metal filigree, and this, like an improvised cage, held something like an egg crudely painted with Keplerian landscapes and motifs. It was more reminiscent of the staff of a wizard or a druid out of some fantastic tale that a mere staff of authority.

"My name is Khikhya," she said. "I am the leader of the *Wiikhaadiiz ofiz*. Shildii has told us about *ghaa* you."

"Yes, Shildii is a very intelligent boy," Emily said. "We are Rakesh and Emily, of the Human people. Oh yes, and we've brought food for Khikhya and those with her."

She took the cardboard box from the cloth bag she was carrying and offered it to the leader. Seeing that she was unable to take it without letting go of her staff, she handed it to Shildii.

"It's for them," she explained with a smile when he came to take the box.

He opened it, and his face lit up at the sight of a dozen pieces of cake, six carrot and six chocolate. He was soon a little disappointed to realize that this time they were not for him.   He showed her the contents. "This is delicious food, Ma'am."

The moment he pronounced the word *food*, the other female of the group hastened to Khikhya and whispered something in her ear. Thanks to the amplifier in her suit Emily was able to hear but not understand what she had said. Ada could only translate the words *food* and *danger*.

The leader raised her hand with some authority and ordered her counselor to stop speaking. Khikhya held out the arm which was holding the staff, and one of the Keplerians who was standing impassively behind her hastened to take it. Once both her hands were free, the leader turned to Shildii.

"Which is the most delicious?" she asked.

He pointed to one of the chocolate ones. "This one."

"Good." With enormous care she took two pieces of cake. "Give *iki* to Shyilru."

Shildii turned to another of the group and gave him the box containing the rest of the cakes, after which Khikhya gave him one of the two pieces. Shildii, ignoring the decorum the situation required, and despite the fact that he had already eaten one piece that morning, began to eat the cake. Khikhya, on the other hand, bit off a corner with great delicacy. However, this did not prevent Emily noticing a look of satisfaction on the old woman's face as her eyes widened, subtly but quite clearly.

She looked at Emily, narrowing her eyes. "This is delicious." She turned to her three companions. "Eat one."

The two males in her retinue took a piece without hesitation. Even the female, who seemed more reluctant to try the foreign food, gave way to temptation in the end. What followed was a rather comical scene. Watching five Keplerians enjoying the food she had given them made her think that she could not have started on a better footing. Although one of the followers gave them a slight scare, as his eagerness to try the treat made him choke slightly. Luckily he took only a moment to recover.

"Humans have given food to Keplerians," the leader said when they had all finished their cake. "In gratitude, Keplerians give *wiijiib thiipiar* to humans."

The companion who was holding Khikhya's staff gave his leader a kind of rope very reminiscent of the ancient handcrafted ropes of esparto grass which had once been made on Earth. It was made up in turn by three other, thinner ropes of three different colors: gold, silver and the same turquoise blue as Khikhya's robe.

The old woman took the rope and went up to Emily. She passed the rope over the helmet of the exosuit, then after tying a simple knot she joined both the ends at the front, leaving both of them hanging. When she had finished, Emily twined the fingers of both hands together to show that she understood what the gesture meant. Then the old woman did the same with Rakesh, who responded to the gesture in the same way.

"With these *wiijiib thiipiar* you can enter our village as guests of the *Wükhaadiiz ofiz*," said Khikhya, twining her hands as she spoke. "Keplerians want to share *diij* and *jad* with humans."

Although they had not understood the key words of the sentence, both Emily and Rakesh returned the gesture politely.

"The human people are grateful," Emily assured her.

"The Keplerians feel honored by it. We will show you the village now."

18
The guardians of hope

September 3, Year 0
Near the Keplerian village, Kepler-442b

Emily, Rakesh and Shildii politely declined Khihkhya's offer to take them into her carriage for the distance between the clearing and the Keplerian settlement. Instead they walked while she went ahead with her retinue. But this time they were the ones the soldiers were escorting. Perhaps this was to prevent the Keplerian citizens from feeling threatened by their presence, or perhaps to protect the humans themselves from the Keplerians. There was no way of knowing the real reason.

"Robert," Emily said in a low voice, "we're beginning to move toward the village. We have an escort of eight Keplerian soldiers."

"It's going to be difficult to follow your trail into the village," he said uneasily.

"Don't worry, I think we're fine."

"I'll send drones so that at least we'll have images. We'll wait on the outskirts of whatever the Keplerians may mean by a village."

The clothes the eight lancers wore were much coarser than those of the village leaders and were different colors. All of them wore thick greenish breastplates of something which resembled leather. At last Emily was able to get a clear view of the crest depicted on the front of the breastplate: a mythological creature—at least she hoped there was no such animal in reality—with three heads, standing on its hindquarters and holding some kind of snake on a shield whose background was turquoise blue. On both sides of the shield rose two trees with red leaves whose branches hid the top of the shield. On the lower part was a small inset with something written in an unintelligible script, much like what Shildii had written on the screen of her suit a couple of days before.

The soldiers looked distinctly intimidating, and all seemed to be cut from the same pattern: none of them was taller than an average human, but their limbs were much more developed. Bulky torso, unfriendly faces and huge bulges of bone on their heads. Thanks to the protection of the exosuit she felt reasonably safe, but she had not the slightest desire to test the soldiers' training or the effectiveness of their weapons. Everything on this planet seemed rougher, harder, which meant that its weapons must be the same.

Soon they saw small, simple wooden huts built around the trunks of the trees. Small and rather strange domestic animals wandered at will along the perfect avenue formed by the artificially-ordered lines of trees. Astonished Keplerians paused in their daily tasks and stared at them, barely blinking, as they passed in front of their houses. Some took hold of their children and led them into the safety of their homes, away from the strange foreigners.

"I can see these people's reaction, and I can't help thinking about what would have happened on Earth," Rakesh said. "If a human from some other time were to see a scene like this at their doors, I'm pretty sure their reaction would be very much like this."

Emily nodded. "Yes, they seem to be curious, but most of all cautious."

What she was seeing was not too far from the idea they had of human societies in other epochs. Humble people on the outskirts of urban centers, living off what the earth provided them with. There was no doubt that they were unaware of the supreme importance of the moment they were living through.

The boy pointed happily. "That is Shildii's home."

"It is very nice," Emily said, more politely than realistically.

"Emily and Rakesh come with Shildii. Shildii show you."

Around the huge trunk of the tree which supported Shildii's house were three other small, rather tumbledown huts. With only one floor and made of solid though well-worn, wood, it was more functional than anything else. The roofs were made of large dried leaves from the same trees. Going by their color and appearance, Emily supposed that they must change them now and then to avoid leaks.

Shildii crossed the little porch and pushed the door open, then turned toward them and invited them inside. The soldiers escorting them stopped, but made no move to interfere. It seemed that the *wüjüb thüpiar* they wore gave them certain privileges. Emily and Rakesh crossed the threshold. The interior was dark, with only a few rays of light coming in through the two front windows. In the main room the small stone hearth was still smoking. On a small table beside it there were still the remains of breakfast. The room was cozy, in spite of being very small and humble. It was obvious to Emily that Shildii's family was not one of the wealthiest in the village, if indeed there was such a thing as money in Keplerian society.

"Come, I show you where Shildii sleeps."

He led them through a door covered by a cloth, beyond which were two small bedrooms. When he went into one of them they saw three irregular-looking cloth mattresses stuffed with some kind of dried grass on wooden ledges. One window let in a bare minimum of light, but they almost needed to activate their infrared vision to see anything inside.

He indicated the first bed. "Shildii sleep here."

"And the others?" Rakesh asked.

"That one is my older sister's, but she does not live here anymore. She has her house in another place. And this one is my little brother's."

As they left the hut, he took a piece of bread from a shelf and nibbled at it as they went into the heart of the Keplerian village. Emily checked that the soldiers were still where they had left them. The neighborhood looked very humble, very quiet and with hardly any activity apart from one or other small street animal. Behind the huts they could see in the first row of the avenue were more huts in the rows behind. A fair number of them urgently needed repairing.

As they moved on, turning to right and left, the huts began to be larger, and they could even see different materials, such as a kind of adobe, or even limestone here and there. There were also many more animals: some for riding, in the form of small groups running hither and thither, one or two pens containing animals which looked like huge balls of fur. Emily could almost hear Rakesh's grimaces every time one of those curious animals crossed their path.

But what most surprised her were the constructions which were now beginning to appear more frequently above their heads. In the case of some of them, which by now were beginning to be made of alternate layers of stone and wood, those more than a single story high blended in and climbed waywardly up the trees. Sometimes the builders had made use of the branches themselves to create genuine mansions and incredibly complex, chaotic architectural structures. And the further they went on, the more common it became to find wooden walkways, which in the manner of bridges and floating sidewalks connected the structures of one tree with those around it.

What had not changed in the least was the reaction of the Keplerians as they passed, whether at ground level or walking along the wooden structures above their heads. Everyone gaped at them open-mouthed. There were a fair number of cries of surprise and fear, mingled with the banging of doors and shutters to avoid the sight. Although the majority could not help peering out at the varied scene.

By now they had been walking for some time, and as they went on the trees around were looking more and more densely-inhabited. And if they looked in the direction of the other avenues, they could see that both activity and density of population were increasing as they came closer to the center. Nothing strange if it were compared with what would be a normal contemporary human city.

"Now we are near," Shildii said. "There are only two *pathi* left."

In the centermost area the trees were enormously tall, many of them over a hundred meters. It seemed to be an unmistakable sign that this part of the settlement was the oldest. The activity here was little short of frenetic, with carts and draft animals everywhere crossing the various streets and avenues, hundreds of Keplerians going here and there, busy with their routines. The most curious thing was that all of them seemed to be more concerned with their own business than with these two foreigners being escorted by a group of soldiers.

Most of the buildings in this area were of stone, but wood was still prominent, especially in the three or four levels of complex walkways and bridges which joined the trees with no apparent order or design.

"Wow!" Emily exclaimed. She was looking from one side to the other, wide-eyed. She felt that she was inside a science-fiction movie, surrounded by strange constructions she could never even have imagined.

"This is really impressive," Rakesh murmured. By now he was in a trance as deep as her own.

"Unbelievable," she whispered.

"Emily and Rakesh like Wiikhaadiiz ofiz?" Shildii asked, amused and pleased at the same time by the reactions of his friends.

"Wiikhaadiiz ofiz is very pretty," Emily said. "It's impressive, do you understand the word?"

"I think so," Shildii said, making a show of narrowing his eyes.

The boy led them through a market. Hundreds of Keplerians were crowding around the dozens of small wooden stalls, set in several rows. There was a vibrant buzz of activity. The stalls were very close to one another and the passageways between them for the customers very narrow, and the vendors were shouting the quality of their wares at the tops of their voices. Emily could now see from close at hand a great variety of what looked like fruits, of very different shapes and colors, which at least at first glance looked very appetizing. Nor was there any lack of vegetable stalls. The produce here was mostly red, though there were green, blue and white ones too. The variety of products on sale there was overwhelming.

Rakesh elbowed Emily in the ribs and pointed to a stall where some kind of bird was being sold, together with something that looked very familiar to them both.

"Eggs!" she exclaimed. "Those are eggs over there!"

"You like *shüp?*" Shildii asked, intrigued by the sudden outburst of excitement.

"Animals give those?" Emily asked.

"Some, yes." He shrugged, not attaching any particular importance to mere eggs.

"They know about coins too," Rakesh said excitedly.

Emily paid attention to the small transactions being carried out between the vendors and their customers, who seemed to be handing over some kind of metal piece in exchange for the goods they were handed. At the same time they also saw one or two cases in which customer and vendor exchanged other goods. Emily knew the use of physical coins from history books, but she had never seen an economic transaction which was not digital, as physical coins had fallen out of use on Earth more than a century before.

"How can we buy things?" she asked.

Shildii looked at her with a curious expression.

"Emily *shyu thiiniz* for *wamovid*," he said with the air of someone explaining the obvious.

Ada translated the sentence: "Emily pays for products with coins." The activity in that market was turning out to be very useful to the AI, enabling her to listen to everyday conversations, detecting facial expressions or studying the social behavior of the Keplerians. In the barely five minutes they had been in the market she had been able to collect and analyze more useful information than during those three previous days with Shildii put together. She was also able to learn that many of them were whispering words of surprise or even fear as they watched them passing. In addition, as the Keplerians were some ten or fifteen centimeters shorter on average than the humans, locating them in the crowd was very easy.

When they reached the other end of the market they made their way to a quieter area with buildings that were more elegant and carefully-maintained than they had seen so far. Here, at the doors of a building decorated with banners which fluttered in the wind, Khikhya's retinue was waiting for them.

"Let us go inside," the Keplerian leader said. "We will be quieter away from *jinaa shov*."

Emily and Rakesh followed her into this two-story building with a huge shield carved on the façade. Emily recognized that strange animal with three heads as the one on the soldiers' clothes.

"Shildii will accompany us in case we need some *po*," she added when they had crossed the small line of guards who were guarding the enormous door of dark wood.

Emily was fascinated by the quality and the detail of the engravings. On one of the panes was a tree carved in intricate detail, and on the other the shield they had seen on the façade of the building and Khikhya's staff.

"It is the *thiinur jiiw khi* of Wiikhaadiiz ofiz," the leader said.

"I think she's referring to the city's coat of arms," Ada translated almost simultaneously.

"And this," she added, pointing to her staff, "is the *puf fajlan,* which the *uw jo* carried before Khikhya"

"Was *Uw jo* Khikhya's family? Emily asked.

"No, no. The *uw jo* are not allowed to have family. Khikhya and the *uw jo* are chosen by the Keplerians of the village when the previous *uw jo* dies."

How interesting, they seem to be a democratic people, Emily thought. *But it must be hard to hold a post of that kind of responsibility without being able to have a family of your own.* At the same time she twined her fingers together to show that she had understood what the old leader was telling them.

"Come this way," she called as she went forward with slow steps toward the right of the entrance door.

In the center of the hall inside, a huge flight of stone steps led to the upper floor. Sumptuous tapestries showing sylvan landscapes and all manner of portraits of illustrious Keplerians decorated the walls. The surface, which was of limestone, looked well-tended, and led on to beautiful wooden floors treated with some kind of varnish which made the whole place look welcoming and luxurious.

Khikhya invited them into what seemed to be her official office, with a small wooden table and several finely-ornamented chairs on either side. On the floor was a large carpet, and the four walls were covered with shelves of books.

Books! Emily said to herself. *Hundreds of them.*

"Do the humans have *tozuk?*" Khikhya asked when she saw her staring at the shelves.

"Yes, we have books," Emily said excitedly. Ada was translating simultaneously and more fluently every time as she incorporated new words and expressions into her vocabulary.

"Humans and Keplerians have many things in common," Khikhya said, narrowing her eyes.

Emily smiled. "So it seems."

"Please sit down." Khikhya indicated two chairs on one side of the table. "And you, Shildii, bring that chair over here and sit beside me."

Shildii did as he was told, and all four sat down around the table, humans on one side and Keplerians on the other.

"Your city is very beautiful," Rakesh said to break the ice.

"Thank you. What are human villages like?"

"They're big," said Rakesh, "much more so than this, and there's very little wood left. They're made of metal, and sometimes they're very noisy."

"They must be very beautiful too," the old woman conceded. Then she paused and changed the tone of her speech. "Forgive me if I am so *poz,* but as humans can see, my age does not allow me to waste time. Humans are *jongha* here, but I want to know what they seek from the

Keplerians."

Emily swallowed at the sudden twist of the conversation.

"We have made a long voyage in order to get here," she began. "The only thing we want is to find a place where we can settle and live in peace. Of course we don't want to interfere in the life of the Keplerians, but we would very much like to learn about your Keplerian customs and culture."

The old woman meditated for a few moments.

"Our people are peaceful," she said at last, "something which other peoples can certainly not say. If the humans want to make war, they will not find it here. What is more, I would ask them to look for somewhere else, far from here."

"We don't wish for war," Emily hastened to explain. "We're a community of scientists."   "The soldiers who have been watching us until we reached the entrance of the village and those *laak* gadgets that have been seen in the village do not say the same as the female human in front of me."

Emily felt ashamed, but did not feel in the least that she had been anything other than truthful.

"We have soldiers, just as Khikhya does. They were worried about our safety, in the same way your soldiers were about yours. I hope you can understand that."

"I understand," she admitted, narrowing her eyes and twining her shriveled fingers together. "But Emily might have been *taai* with Khikhya. There was no need to hide anything."

"I'm sorry. It won't happen again."

"No, it will not. Khikhya will tell you what we are going to do. Only Emily and Rakesh can come into the village, without restrictions. One of my *khaakho* will answer all the *iighraachiiz* they want to know about the Keplerians. If there is trouble in the village, Emily and Rakesh will not return *tiin*, do you understand that word?"

"Yes," Emily replied, "I think we do."

"Everything is perfect then," the old woman said in conclusion, in a softer voice. "Khikhya will speak with the others."

"Excuse me," Rakesh interrupted her, "but who are these others you mention?"

"The Keplerian people has been traditionally been made up of four great *chakii*," she explained. "Each one of them is *yäk* to decide the fate of the Keplerians who form it. We are the Wiikhaadiiz ofiz, but there are also the Khapabir, the Gaal-El, and of course the Khaavahki." Her tone of voice indicated a certain disdain at the mention of this last name. "The Keplerians have inhabited these lands since very ancient times, and though many have not survived until today, we still continue to use the same *chiw* our ancestors used before us."

"I understand." Rakesh supported his words with the appropriate gesture.

"Khikhya would like to offer you something in gratitude for your delicious food," she added, "but Shildii say that Emily and Rakesh cannot eat our food."

"We can't breathe this air," Emily explained.

"Is that why the metal clothes?" the old woman asked curiously.

"That's right. We have air and food inside the metal clothing."

The old woman looked incredulously at the exosuits her two guests were wearing. "There doesn't seem to be room for much food and air in there."

Emily did her best to explain with gestures. "Everything is packed very close together."

"The Wiikhaadiiz ofiz do not understand metal gadgets," the old woman apologized, waving away the explanation, "That is a task for the Khapabir."

"Does each village have a different duty?" Rakesh asked.

"Yes. Do all humans know about everything?"

"No," Rakesh said thoughtfully, "I suppose they don't. Every human knows something different."

"In that case humans and Keplerians have many things in common," Khikhya repeated as she narrowed her eyes again, looking amused.

"Humans have *thiishyaph ghip* in their metal clothes," Shildii put in, pointing to the terminal in Emily's right arm.

"I would like to see that," the old leader said.

Emily operated her terminal, and the holographic projector showed images of a real human being, as well as photographs of Emily and Rakesh.

Khikhya laughed. "Humans are very strange inside those metal clothes. Even so, you have things in common with the Keplerians. Two hands, two feet, two eyes…"

Emily wondered whether to talk about the Yokai with the old lady when she paused, but then remembered Shildii's reaction when she had brought up the subject and dismissed the idea. She did not want to ruin everything they had achieved so far, and nor was it a suitable subject for a first diplomatic contact like this.

"Shildii, do you know who Yisht is?" the old woman asked.

Shildii narrowed his eyes. "Yes, ma'am."

"Go and fetch her. I want Emily and Rakesh to meet her."

Shildii slipped out of the room, happy about the task he had been given.

"Yisht is a young Keplerian, very *chuw*," Khikhya explained. "She will show you everything humans need. But Emily and Rakesh need to remember: you must not cause trouble here."

"We understand," both of them promised.

"The others will have had news of the humans," she added thoughtfully. "We must be cautious. Khikhya must go to speak to the Gaal-El. They are wise. Many suns ago they were the only leaders of the Keplerians. They know the history of our people, they will understand what it means, the arrival of humans."

Shildii came back with a young, slender Keplerian. Her clothes were simpler than Shildii's, but still elegant, and her manner was more intellectual, but at the same time the girl looked very nervous.

"Yisht," the old woman called. "These are Emily and Rakesh. They are foreigners who come from very far away. They don't speak our language, but *duz* in your intelligence to help them with whatever they may need."

"Hello, Yisht," Emily said. "Pleased to meet you."

The girl returned the greeting with a shy nod, but did not say a word.

"Our *noshvi* have complete freedom to ask questions or consult any of our books," Khikhya went on. "Treat them as if they were your own leader."

She narrowed her eyes and gave them a shy smile. "I understand."

The old woman turned back to Emily and Rakesh. "Now, if you will excuse me, Khikhya has a journey to prepare. Come back tomorrow to get all the information you want. The soldiers will wait for you from the first ray of light at the place where we met."

"Thank you, Khikhya," Emily said. "You've been very kind."

Both of them stood up and left the building, accompanied by Shildii. At that hour of the day the market was no longer as busy as before, and some vendors had even closed their stalls. Shildii went with them as far as his home, where he said goodbye to them, not without asking Emily before they left him whether she would bring some chocolate cake for him the next day. She said yes. She was beginning to think that she was spoiling him.

Back at the base, just as Rakesh and Emily were getting ready to go into the decontamination area, all the alarms went off. The whole entrance hall was lit up by a stroboscopic red light, and a shrill sound flooded the base. Something was wrong.

"An unwanted organism has been detected inside the base," Ada said. "Doctor Kumar, you must go outside and eliminate the organism which is stuck to the back of your exosuit."

Startled, Emily took a look at his back. When she saw what was there she took a couple of steps back

"Rakesh, we'd better go outside."

"What is it?" he asked nervously. "Get it off me."

"You can see for yourself through my camera. But I'm not sure you're going to want to."

"Ada, open the exit door!" he shouted in alarm.

Once again they went back outside.

"Get it off me!"

"I don't know, Rakesh. What happens if it turns out to be dangerous and attacks us?"

"I don't care!"

"Wait. Chad's sure to know what to do."

She called him through her suit. "Can you come out for a moment?" she begged when he had answered.

"What is it? Is it something to do with the alarm we just heard?"

"Yeah. But please hurry, we've got a small emergency out here."

On Rakesh's back, an animal whose thorax was protected by several segmented shells was moving slowly, using its dozens of pairs of small pincer-tipped legs. The four antennae on its head moved quickly all the time, as if assessing threats from outside. But the most disturbing thing about it was the dozen tiny dark eyes which seemed to be looking at her curiously.

It took Chad an eternal five minutes to get there. By then Rakesh was on the verge of a panic attack.

"Wow!" Chad cried excitedly when he saw the specimen. It was ten centimeters or so long and eight across. "It's some kind of alien land trilobite."

With no trace of fear, he grasped the creature by its shell and detached it from Rakesh's back. When he did so the arthropod began to move its dozens of tiny legs, annoyed at having lost its grip. It tried to free itself from his grasp by twisting its abdomen in every direction.

"Fascinating! Our trilobites were mostly sea creatures which went extinct in the Permian-Triassic period. Even so, they've been studied in depth thanks to plentiful fossil deposits. And here they are, look at them, taking a stroll in the countryside without a care in the world."

Rakesh turned around to take a look at the animal. He could not help a shiver running down his spine.

"So what are you going to do with that bug?" he asked.

"Study it. What else?"

"I hope you wash your hands very carefully before your next meal," Emily pointed out.

Later on, once the problem with the prehistoric animal had been sorted out and after dinner, Emily was doing her best to make sense of everything that had happened that morning.

"But how did they manage to detect us?" Robert wondered. "We took all the care in the world."

The deputy director was following things carefully, as he always did at these meetings. "We've obviously underestimated them," he pointed out.

"The fact that they know money indicates a certain degree of financial and commercial development," Rakesh said. It's more than likely that they have commercial treaties with neighboring settlements, or maybe even ones further afield."

"I suppose you'll have to find out that sort of thing from the leader's assistant," the deputy director said. "Do you think they have religious beliefs?"

"We haven't seen anything that would make us think so."

"But they seem a very odd community. Is there any record of a similar order on earth?"

"Their technological development is like that of the European Middle Ages," Rakesh explained, "though in a society which as far as we've been able to deduce is a democratic one. We'll have to get to know the other three settlements and their leaders to see whether they're really a kind of feudal society, or just communities with different purposes who cooperate among themselves to form something bigger. But of course they seem to have a pretty advanced society. Being surrounded by trees seems to have allowed them to develop paper, and hence writing. I'd even go so far as to say they probably have an educational system. But the point about the whole visit that really caught my attention is their visual ability. The rooms we went into were poorly lit, to the point that we needed the infrared vision of our suits to see properly. And yet despite this I didn't see a single lamp, not even a small oil one with a wick."

"Are you suggesting they have natural infrared vision?" Lieutenant Beaufort asked.

"It's a possibility. I just wanted to share it with you all."

"Emily," the deputy director asked, "you're very thoughtful, what's worrying you??"

"Nothing… Well, really everything, I guess."

"Well, that doesn't sound like nothing."

"It's just that… you see… I've been thinking about all this ever since we saw the first Keplerians on the other side of the river. We were supposed to come to this planet to find a home, but as it is, the atmosphere of the planet stops us living on it without the help of the exosuits."

She paused briefly to put her ideas in order, then went on.

"Without going into the small detail that we don't yet have the means to modify the atmosphere, what moral right do we have to modify the conditions on this planet to make them compatible with human life if by doing that we could drive another intelligent species to extinction? What I mean is, they were here before. The planet, more or less, belongs to them. I suppose seeing such a lively and advanced society, that idea I've been uneasy about for some time has got stronger."

They were all silent. Emily had posed the question they had all been avoiding. And it seemed to make the point that this was going to be the key to the whole mission.

19
Keplerian society

September 4, Year 0
Wiikhaadiiz ofiz village, Kepler-442b

Just as Khikhya had told Rakesh and Emily in advance, the soldiers were waiting for them when they reached the clearing. Without saying a word they began following them a few meters behind. They made a brief stop when they reached Shildii's home, and the young Keplerian appeared on one side of the cabin.

"Hello, Emily and Rakesh," he greeted them in his usual cheerful way.

Emily smiled. "Hello, Shildii. Good morning!"

He joined the group, and they went on to the village. But she could tell that he was a little more nervous than usual. He looked at her out of the corner of his eye, first unobtrusively but then openly.

"I've brought you a piece of cake," she said. She had guessed the reason for his nervousness. "But you have to wait till we see Yisht, all right?"

"All right."

The strangely-assorted group of walkers followed the same route as the previous day to the building which housed the village government. This morning the bustle at the market was even greater. Perhaps because of the hour, which was rather earlier, or perhaps because it was a date marked in the Keplerian calendar. Whichever way, it meant that it took them some time to cross the market, which was bursting with activity.

When at last they managed to get there, they found Yisht waiting for them. She accompanied them to a room on the top floor of the building.

"The leader Khikhya is getting on in years," she told them shyly. "Many suns ago she asked for her *afeek* to be on the *thiiw* below, so that she would not have to go up and down *yöv*." Suddenly she realized that her guests did not know the language. 'Oh, forgive me, I don't know if you're understanding me," she added nervously.

"We understood you," Emily translated, counting on Ada's invisible help. "You were saying Khikhya has asked for her office to be downstairs so that she doesn't have to go up and down stairs. There's no need to worry, we'll ask you if there's something we don't understand."

"Oh! Good, good," she said, sounding relieved. "This is an office we use for other, less *aacho*, matters which don't need Khikhya's presence."

She opened a door and invited them in. It was much like the office they had been in the previous day, with shelves full of books, carpets with fine decoration on the floor and portraits of illustrious Keplerians hanging on the walls.

"Take a seat if you want," Yisht said.

At that moment Emily was able to gratify Shildii, and she offered each of them a piece of cake. In fact she had brought enough and to spare once again, since she knew there would be more Keplerians in these little learning sessions. As it looked as though no-one else was going to join them, she decided to give the rest of the box to Shildii when they went back at noon so that he could share the cake with his family.

Shildii very nearly lunged at his piece of cake, and as usual, devoured it with that look of satisfaction Emily was delighted to see. Yisht, on the other hand, showing off her good manners and the maturity appropriate to her age, thanked them for the cake and savored it with small bites. The cake, though it was not Emily's own favorite, was very good, and it resulted in satisfied expressions among the Keplerians, even those better brought up in terms of etiquette.

"Where shall we start?" Yisht asked once she had finished her piece of cake. "Excuse the lack of preparation, but I wasn't sure what would interest you most. Would you like me to bring you some books?"

"That would be good," Rakesh said, "but actually we can't yet read your language."

"Oh dear!" she said, sounding rather worried. "That might be a problem."

"But perhaps it would be a good way to start, Yisht," Emily said. "Can you bring us a book so we can learn to read?"

Emily knew Ada would be able to learn just by looking at a children's book, so it seemed a good idea to her if they wanted some independence. In fact, given Ada's processing speed, by doing no more than idly turning a couple of pages she could assimilate the information far faster than any human.

"Learn to read?" Yisht repeated, sounding rather surprised. "Like the ones the children use at the *shyaa*?"

Emily smiled. "Yes, those. And also a book of words."

"Book of words?" Yisht asked, not understanding. "All books have words… do you mean a *yü-tozuk*?"

"Is a *yü-tozuk* used for learning the meaning of words?"

"Yes."

"Then we want a *yü-tozuk* too."

The girl nodded disbelievingly, but obeyed without a word. She left the office and came back five minutes later with two volumes of soft leather, one reasonably thin and manageable, the other a great deal heavier and more voluminous.

"This is all I could find. It's not something you can find easily in this building."

"It's perfect," Emily assured her. "Thank you."

She began to leaf through the book for Keplerian children, which included illustrations of some of the animals they had seen on their way to the village center. There were also a few drawings of the wild creatures which had attacked the soldiers in the forest. She went on turning the pages in a way that would allow the camera in her suit to get a full view of each of them.

"Ada, do you think that'll be enough?"

"Yes, I think so. As long as you keep turning the pages at a steady rate it's okay, you needn't stop at any of them."

"I beg your pardon?" said Yisht, "I didn't understand you."

"Oh, I'm sorry," Emily said. "I wasn't speaking to you."

"So who were you talking to?" the girl asked in puzzlement, with a nod in the direction of Rakesh who had gotten up and was looking inquisitively at the paintings and books.

Emily tried to choose her words carefully so that the young Keplerian would understand what Ada was.

"I've seen you have carts," she began as she went on turning over the pages of the book. "Without them you'd have to carry everything, making more trips and making more of an effort, right?"

"Yes."

"Well, we humans have created mechanical minds that can think and learn more quickly, just as the Keplerians have created carts to carry things more quickly."

Yisht was lost in thought for a while.

"And can you speak to that mechanical mind as if it were another human being?"

"Yes." She was intrigued by Yisht's reaction. "Would you like to speak to her?"

She opened her already enormous eyes wide. "Yes, please."

"Hello, Yisht," Ada said through Emily's suit in her own synthetic voice. "My name is Ada, I'm delighted to be able to speak to you."

Shildii, who had never heard Ada until that moment, gave a start in his chair. This made both Emily and Yisht laugh, and also made Rakesh emerge from his long reverie for a moment.

"Hello, Ada," Yisht replied courteously.

"Your village is very interesting," the artificial intelligence said. "You have a very busy market."

"Yes, we certainly do."

"You can ask whatever you like," Emily said encouragingly.

Yisht glanced timidly at her, and she nodded so that the girl would feel free to ask whatever was on her mind at that moment.

"Where are you?" she asked.

"A very long way from where you are, I'm afraid" said Ada. "In space."

"Wow!" Khikhya's assistant exclaimed, obviously impressed. "And what does it feel like to be a mechanical mind?"

"I was created to be the closest thing possible to a human being, so I feel fine, although sometimes I spend a lot of time alone."

"Alone?" Yisht asked, interested. "Wow, I think I understand you perfectly. I spend a lot of time alone too."

"Do you live on your own?" Emily asked.

"Yes. My parents died years ago, and since I came to *Wiikhaadiiz ofiz* I haven't... well, met anyone."

Emily noticed what seemed to be a blush on Yisht's cheeks. "Sorry, I didn't mean to make you uncomfortable."

"Don't worry, it's nothing. It seems incredible to me that you have mechanical minds. And Ada sounds very nice."

"Thank you," said Ada.

"You'll have plenty of opportunities to talk to one another," Emily said. "I'm quite sure of that."

Yisht smiled. "I'm sure we will. What else can I offer you?"

"Tell us how Wiikhaadiiz ofiz works," Rakesh said. "Who governs the city? What's the life of a Keplerian like, from birth to death?"

"All right." Yisht nodded slowly. "It seems logical to start at the beginning."

She cleared her throat shyly, while Emily put aside the teaching book and began to leaf through the thickest, most dilapidated, and in some pages even most thoroughly-nibbled, dictionary so that Ada could learn all the possible vocabulary.

"The Keplerian females are in charge of *daj* and *thiiva jaa* to the babies," she began. "The children are looked after during their first suns in *wiidaap jiamovid* by Keplerians who work for the village. Afterwards, the females themselves are the ones who look after their children and feed them. Later on, when they're fifteen years old, the children start to go to school."

"Wait a moment," Rakesh interrupted. "Did you say fifteen?"

"Yes."

"Keplerian years are shorter than human ones," Emily reminded him. "Fifteen years of theirs are equivalent to just under five of ours."

'That's true," said Rakesh, a little confused. "I still can't get used to these differences."

"But it's all right, now we can ask Yisht. How many years does a Keplerian live?"

"About two hundred, more or less. Though there are cases where they've reached three hundred, or even more. The leader Khikhya, for instance, is two hundred and thirty-four years old now."

"Hmm, that sounds like quite an age, all things considered," Rakesh murmured. He had calculated that the leader must be around eighty human years old.

"Yes," Yisht said, "she's one of the oldest and most respected Keplerians in our community."

"Go on, please, and forgive the interruption," said Rakesh.

"But now it turns out that Yisht has a question for humans…"

"Ah! Of course," Emily said encouragingly. "Ask whatever you like."

"How long do humans live?"

"Translated into your age, about two hundred and sixty, though we have many cases of humans who lived to over three hundred and fifty."

Yisht and Shildii, who was also listening attentively, gave a little whistle of admiration and surprise.

"Right, I'll go on with the explanation," Yisht said after the brief interlude. "Children have the duty to learn to read and write, to learn *iima* and also Keplerian history and laws."

Emily had barely begun to turn a couple of dozen pages of the huge Keplerian dictionary, so it was not surprising that Ada was not yet able to translate some of the concepts, but she presumed it was some important subject, on a level with reading, history or law. *Mathematics, maybe?* she thought.

"Once we reach the age of forty-two," the girl went on, "the Keplerians reach adulthood and have to choose which activity they're going to follow in the community. And to continue with this…" She paused for a moment. "…I think I'd better explain how Keplerian society works.

"We're divided into four large communities. In the first place are the Gaal-El, who used to be responsible for the government and bureaucracy of all Keplerians. Nowadays they're only in charge of preserving historical memory and keeping alive the ancient cults, which are more and more forgotten. Their village is in the *lan*, at a few *chiij yii* from here. It's the smallest of all."

Emily saw Rakesh making as if to interrupt the assistant. It was obvious that this part interested him deeply, but he restrained himself. She supposed he did not want to appear rude.

"Then there are the Khaavahki. They are in charge of the security of all the communities. The soldiers who came with you this morning or the small detachment that protects this building belong to the Khaavahki people. Their village is toward the *thiilan wiivoshy,* and you could say it's comparable to ours in size.

"The Khapabir are the people of erudites and *niilnf* of the Keplerians. They construct buildings and create those very strange *taaf.* They're to the *voshy* of where we are and their village is by far the largest of all. For many it's the most important and powerful of the Keplerian villages. There have often been conflicts between the Khaavahki and the Khapabir over the course of history."

Emily and Rakesh were listening attentively to Yisht's explanations. She was making it clear that disputes between different villages were something which unfortunately seemed to be an endemic and universal evil.

"And finally there's us, the Wiikhaadiiz ofiz. Our duty is to look after the villages and keep them in perfect condition. From childhood we're taught to respect the environment, to look after our elders, to heal the different *zaabu* using knowledge that goes back many generations. We're the ones who keep the Keplerian villages habitable and good places to live."

"That's very nice," Emily said enthusiastically, seeing Yisht's passion when she talked about her people.

"Thank you." Yisht narrowed her eyes, pleased.

Emily felt that she was much more at ease now. She seemed to have shed most of the tension of those first few moments.

"As I was saying at the beginning," she went on, "Keplerian society is made up of these four main communities, but many years ago different groups left the cities and went to other points of the territory. Some live alone in houses far from the large villages, others created new villages a very long way from here. Although in fact we rarely have news of those other places.

"And as I was saying before this brief explanation about the Keplerian communities, when we turn forty-two we have to decide what our role in society is going to be. It's a very *othuc* decision, and anyone, wherever they might have been born, can ask for a change of village and hence of profession. Every year every village welcomes new pupils from other places and teaches them, without restrictions, all the knowledge they have at their disposal, as well as the responsibilities and tasks that go with their different trades.

"In Shildii's case, for instance, his family is from here, they're in charge of making sure the buildings of the Wiikhaadiiz ofiz are kept in perfect condition. It's a humble job, but a very important and respected one. Because of his age, he'll very soon have to choose what his responsibility will be. And if he wanted to he could go and live with the Khapabir, the Khaavahki or even the Gaal-El, if he so wished. Whatever he may decide, he'll become part of the community he chooses.

"In my own case I was born in Khapabir and grew up there. But from an early age I knew I wanted to devote my life to the service of the community. Also, I was lucky to be selected by Khikhya herself to work with her. Even so, they need caretakers, soldiers and all kinds of other jobs, so it's normal for young people to end up working in the same community they grew up in."

Emily felt that she understood why Yisht was feeling lonely. She supposed she must only have been there for a few years, and leaving everything you have behind is never an easy thing to do. Khikhya had chosen her as her pupil, and to judge by the way she spoke about her she seemed to have a very high regard for her. But a job as assistant to someone with so much power, at least on Earth, could be exhausting and might leave little free time to get to know other people.

"Most of the trades receive a small *tipu*, which lets us eat or *thuk* clothes. Mostly the jobs are controlled and managed by the community itself, but there are free trades, especially those that involve goods or *iighraapiiz*."

"What we saw in the market," Shildii added. He was following the explanation almost without blinking.

"That's it, you're quite correct, Shildii," Yisht said. "The prices of food and basic goods are controlled by the authorities so that no-one makes too much money. And we also pay a series of *chiik* so that we can have education, *wiithadho thiiliil* and other *iighraapiiz*."

"What was that you said?" Rakesh asked.

"*Wiithadho thiiliil?*"

"That's right."

"They're the places where Keplerians recover when they have an accident."

"Oh, I see. Thank you."

"I think that's all, in broad terms," Yisht concluded.

Rakesh was intrigued by the sudden end of the explanation. "Do Keplerians work for their whole lives?" he asked.

She shrugged. "Yes, the trade is for your whole life. Don't humans work forever?"

"No. Or… well, perhaps now they do," he added as he realized that the situation in the colony might not be the same as the one they had left behind on Earth.

"What happens when Keplerians die?" Emily asked.

"The *wiichipaap dosh* are taken to devices built by the Khapabir and burnt," the girl explained.

"I understand."

"Excuse me, Yisht," said Rakesh. "Before, you said that the Gaal-El, I think you called them, are responsible for keeping the ancient cults going. What kind of cults are we talking about?"

"Very old ones, although in fact I don't know a lot about it," she said apologetically. "It's been a very long time since the Keplerians stopped believing in those things. But perhaps I could find you a book about the Gaal-El and their cult." She pointed to the dictionary Emily was still leafing through, almost without paying any attention. "All I know is that they talked about the origin of the Keplerians and the coming of some *diil* or other who would take us to the promised land and free us from the Kholghishbik."

"*Diil?*" Rakesh asked. He was unable to wait for Emily and Ada to get as far as that page in the dictionary.

Aware that they had not understood her meaning, Yisht thought for a moment about how to explain it.

"A *diil* is a Keplerian who can do things others can't. They have more power, more strength, they can fly with the birds. For the vast majority they're just fantasies we tell little children so that they can fall asleep."

Emily nodded, intrigued by this. "I see, and who or what are the Kholghishbik?" Perhaps, she wondered, Yisht meant the Yokai.

A slight shadow appeared on the faces of both Keplerians. The mere mention of the name almost made them tremble with fear.

"The Kholghishbik are the creatures who are masters of this planet," Yisht explained in a much lower, fainter tone of voice. "Once every *shaab* they come back here with their huge *chusy* metal fliers to fetch the minerals and rocks we Keplerians have kept in store for them and destroy everything they come across. It's what we know as the Levy."

A sudden shiver ran down Emily's back when she heard these words. Unconsciously she stopped turning over the pages of the dictionary, thinking hard about the implications this revelation might have on the project and the colony.

"That's… terrible," she said almost inaudibly.

"Yes, it certainly is," Yisht said sadly.

"You said they come back, but where from?" Rakesh asked.

"No-one knows exactly, but from very far away. From the sky, from far beyond the sun and the stars."

Emily and Rakesh looked at one another nervously as they realized that as they had suspected from the beginning, there was a third intelligent alien race, and this one sounded far more advanced and dangerous than the other two.

"How long is it since they last came?" Emily asked, much more tensely than usual.

"A long time ago. I wasn't even born then."

"Excuse me, Yisht, but I have to ask you this as soon as possible." Emily was so serious that Yisht herself tensed even more. "Do you know whether Keplerians and humans have ever met before?"

Yisht stared at her, apparently not entirely understanding the question.

"No, I'd never seen humans until yesterday," she said at last.

"What Emily wants to know," Rakesh interrupted, seeing how tense she now was, "is whether in your history books there's any mention of people like us. Whether many suns ago other Keplerians met humans like Emily and Rakesh."

"Oh!" the girl exclaimed, and her expression relaxed. "No, I don't think so. As children we study the history of the Keplerian people and they've never told us about you… well, about humans. I suppose something like that would be an important enough event to be studied." She was realizing that she herself was living through events that in all certainty would go on to be written about in the history books. "What I mean is that naughty children are threatened with Kholghishbik coming to take them away. But we've never known anything about humans. Perhaps it's something Khikhya the leader might be able to tell you more about. I'm sure someone like her will know more about these things."

Emily's thoughts were going so fast that she was aware that the learning session had finished for the day. By now she could think of nothing else. These Kholghishbik might be the key to the fate of the Galileo, of her father and of so many other people.

"Excuse us, Yisht," Rakesh said once he had realized that Emily was no longer listening to anything she was saying. "We've lost some of our people and we don't know what could have happened to them."

"Oh, I'm very sorry! Do you think the Kholghishbik might be behind that?"

"Well, it's a possibility."

She put her hands to her face. "I'm deeply sorry."

"Thank you." Emily made an effort to appear normal. "I think we should leave this until tomorrow, if you don't mind."

"In fact it's time we went back to our own people," Rakesh added. "We have to eat."

"Of course," Yisht agreed. "We'll go on tomorrow."

Emily, Rakesh and Shildii left the building and retraced their steps almost without saying a word. Khikhya's soldiers accompanied them to the edge of the clearing, as was now customary.

When they got back to the base they found far more activity than usual. A number of transports were leaving supplies for where the base was to be extended, just beyond Kostas' greenhouses. The excavators were already working at full capacity to level the ground where the new buildings were to be put up.

I'd completely forgotten they were due to start work on the extension today, Emily thought, *and just at this moment I don't in the least want to have to keep an eye on all this.*

20
Rebellion

September 5, Year 0
Space Station Asimov

During the afternoon Emily went over the new information they now had at their disposal. She spent a long time thinking about the Kholghishbik, whom the young Keplerian had described as the true owners of the planet. Over and over again she had to analyze the time that had passed since their last visit to the planet. If they had had anything to do with the disappearance of the Galileo, the calculations did not fit at all.

She decided to go back to the station to speak face to face with the deputy director. A discovery like this was too important to deal with at a distance. The meetings with Yisht were now of secondary importance, but she agreed with Rakesh that he should go on with them while she was not there. She was hoping that Yisht would understand her absence. Rakesh agreed, though he was a little nervous about having to face this tremendous responsibility on his own.

Several of the engineers who had arrived the previous day and who had spent the night on the base were starting their working day at the same time as her. Which meant that that particular morning, activity on the base was more frenetic than usual.

That morning Captain Garth had requested Robert's presence at the station as well. It seemed that he wanted to organize the new military personnel who were to join the contingent which was protecting the base. For their journey back to the station both of them made use of one of the transports which were providing the necessary supplies and personnel for the work on the base.

Once at the Asimov, they went their separate ways. Robert went on to his meeting with the captain, Emily to the bridge. There, as had happened months before during those first meetings after the black hole incident, the deputy director, Commander Bauer and Captain Mei were waiting for her, and no-one else.

"Good morning," she said. She was looking slightly more serious and tired than usual. "I'm sorry to be late."

The captain of the station brushed this aside. "Don't worry. How do you feel?"

She sat down. "I guess I'm a little wound up because of everything that's going on. We're coming up against something new every day, and unfortunately it's not always a very reassuring business."

"Yes, I know what you mean."

"We're up to date with the latest discoveries both Emily and Doctor Kumar have made over these last few days," the deputy director began. "I called this meeting to assess the threat which is apparently hanging over the Keplerian people, and hence by extension over all of us."

"Is it just going to be the four of us?" Emily asked.

"Yes, I'm afraid so." The deputy director was looking very serious. "Since we made the business of private funding public, the atmosphere inside the station is a long way from being perfect and idyllic."

She sighed. "Oh dear. I'm sorry, David."

"I'd imagine everyone needs time to get used to the real situation of the project. But don't worry, everything'll fall into place in time."

"I'm sure it will."

"This situation that we still know very little about the... I'm afraid I can't pronounce the name...*Khol-ghish-bik*," he read from the screen of his terminal.

Emily could understand the deputy director's difficulties perfectly well. "I've decided to call them simply Khol, to make things easier. It means *foreigners* in Keplerian."

"Much better," he said gratefully. "We know very little about the Khol. And one of the most urgent tasks of the settlers of the Magellan base will be to gather all the information they can about this new alien race, which Emily is now going to tell us about."

"We really don't know very much," she admitted. "At this very moment Dr. Kumar is on his way to the Keplerian village, apart from going on with learning about their history and culture, to get hold of any kind of information about the Khol they might have in their leader Khikhya's libraries."

"What was your impression of this Khikhya?" Commander Bauer asked with interested.

"Actually, she impressed me positively. I was expecting more resistance towards foreigners, but they've welcomed us very hospitably. She seems to be very wise, and she's respected by her community."

"You don't think there might be some kind of ulterior motive for being so welcoming?" the captain asked doubtfully.

"I was thinking about that a lot last night, and beyond the fact that they might see us as possible allies against the Khol, I can't think of anything else."

"But now it's not her who's seeing you at her residence."

"No, she's decided to travel to discuss the new situation with some kind of ancient Keplerian wise men or clerics. One of her pupils is looking after us, Yisht. She's very helpful, and thanks to her we found out about the existence of this other species."

"Do we know anything about those clerics?" the commander asked.

Emily was aware that for the moment there were more doubts than certainties. "Not much, quite honestly. We know they've been given the duty of keeping up an ancient cult which worships a deity of some kind."

"Is it a majority cult?" Deputy Director Green asked.

"No, it seems to have fallen into oblivion. These Gaal-El, as they call them, are the custodians of those ancient beliefs. They seemed to be waiting for the coming of some messiah or god that'll help them free themselves from the yoke of the Khol."

"Actually, that sounds rather familiar to me," the captain said, "with the major difference that here evil is something very tangible which visits them every few years."

"Exactly," said Emily.

"Sorry to interrupt," they heard Ada say, "but I've lost connection with the base."

"Again?" the deputy director asked in surprise.

"Yes, I'm afraid so."

"It's a very cloudy day," Emily said thoughtfully. "Perhaps that dense fog that cuts off our coms has come back. It looks as though the improvements Dr. Gonçalves made haven't fixed the problem."

"This time it's a little different, I'm afraid," Ada went on. "I lost the signal quite suddenly. The day the fog came it happened little by little as the fog grew denser. Now it's as if they'd run out of power and the auxiliary generator hadn't come on."

Emily began to feel nervous. She hoped this was a mere blackout and that her comrades would be able to solve the problem quickly. But Ada's words had left her rather worried.

"Do we have images of the base?" the deputy director asked.

"No," Ada said. "It's very cloudy."

"It must be because of that. Let's not get worried for the moment, it might be nothing."

"But Dr. Kumar is on his own," the commander reminded them.

Emily, who had not been aware of this detail, shifted in her chair nervously. "Ada, was the translation module installed in his suit?"

"Yes, Emily. I made sure of that, anticipating some event of this kind."

"Thank goodness. At least he'll be able to communicate with them."

"He'll even be able to go on gathering information, which will be stored in the suit itself and then be added to the knowledge we already have."

"Wonderful. Thanks, Ada," the deputy director said. "Let us know if you reestablish connection, or in a couple of hours if you don't."

"Copy that."

"Right, then," he went on, "where were we?"

"We were talking about that Keplerian religion, if that's what it is," the commander pointed out.

Emily nodded. "Yes, Dr. Kumar will try to get hold of a book about the cult that might give us some relevant information. But Yisht herself told us they didn't have much literature about them, beyond what had to do with their own village and customs."

"Perhaps they'll know something about the Khol," the captain pointed out.

"That's possible. Yisht has told us that in another epoch, apart from managing the religious side of things, the Gaal-El were the leaders of the whole Keplerian society. It's possible they may have ancient writings that say something about the Khol and their origins."

"And their characteristics and weak points," the deputy director added. "Whichever way, it's important that we seek all the allies we can among the other Keplerian villages. If the threat's as crude and immediate as it seems, it looks as though we're going to need a lot of help."

"Above all bearing in mind that we don't have the arsenal any longer," the commander reminded them.

"I'm afraid we're going to have to wait for Khikhya to come back from her trip before we can even think about anything like that," said Emily. "Yisht is a wonderful hostess, but I don't want to abuse her hospitality. Which means we're going to have to go step by step, without being in too much of a hurry. And in any case, I don't think she has enough power for us to start even thinking about broadening our scope."

"If this Khikhya is as well-respected as she seems to be," the deputy director pointed out, "she herself might offer to introduce us to the other Keplerian leaders."

Emily nodded. "It's a possibility."

"But the important thing about all this," the deputy director reminded them, "and the main reason for this meeting, is the possible connection between the Khol and the disappearance of the Galileo space station."

"Do you think the Khol might have been responsible for the destruction of the Galileo?" the captain asked.

"It's one of the possibilities we've been considering ever since we got here," the deputy director admitted sadly. "Perhaps they reached the planet just at the moment when the Khol were making their visit. Or perhaps they were intercepted on their way here and never even set foot on the surface."

They were all silent. The possibilities were infinite.

"But there's something that doesn't fit, it seems to me," Emily said.

"Yes, and that's why we're here," the deputy director said. "Emily asked this assistant of Khikhya's about the last time the Khol visited the planet."

The commander turned to Emily. "And?"

"To me the calculations don't add up," she explained. "According to Yisht, the Khol were last here a few years before she was born. If she's about twenty-four human years and we add say three years more, that gives us twenty-seven human years. But the Galileo should've arrived ten years ago."

"That means they shouldn't even have coincided," the captain said.

"Unless we're trying to make a calculation we actually can't make," Emily went on.

"What do you mean?" the commander asked.

"A voyage as long as the one we made ourselves might end up experiencing all kinds of problems of different kinds and on different scales. Those problems might end up catastrophically, but on occasions they might just distort out way of seeing things."

"'I'm not sure I follow you," the captain said.

"What I'm saying is that the time that's elapsed, according to the general theory of relativity, is as its name suggests, relative. It's relative from the point of view of the observer, in this case us, with respect to the Galileo. We need to bear in mind that this is far and away the longest voyage humanity's ever taken. So it's conceivable that we may not yet have the knowledge that would be required to make a precise calculation of the time that's elapsed between two events."

"I still don't get what you're getting at," the commander said.

"I'll give you an example: Imagine two sailing-ships leaving Spain in the fifteenth century from the same port, but with a ten-day difference. When the second ship arrives, the first one hasn't yet arrived. What would the crew think?"

"I suppose they'd conclude the other ship had sunk,"

Emily nodded. "Exactly. But just suppose if the currents and the wind had made the second ship arrive first? Or made the first one veer off its course and make landfall a few hundred kilometers further south than expected?"

"Interesting."

"What I'm trying to say is that we know so little about interstellar voyages that the Galileo might not even have arrived yet, or might have got here many more years before we think and was intercepted by the Khol."

"But then how can we know which of all these possibilities is the right one?" the captain asked.

"We can't. But if we take for granted that the Galileo didn't suffer any mishap on the way to Kepler-442b, we might guess that the second possibility is the most likely." Emily's voice as she said this was rather more somber than usual.

"Why are you so sure of that?" the deputy director asked.

"Because we ourselves passed very close to one of those natural phenomena that have the capacity to alter our perception of time."

"The black hole!" the captain exclaimed.

"Exactly. The black hole's gravitational attraction must have made us lose valuable time, which might have been too long for the Galileo."

"I don't understand," the commander insisted. "Why would the black hole affect time?"

"Gravity, time and space are intimately related. Imagine a net of cloth that's perfectly taut, which we hang by its four corners. If we leave a rock or a heavy object on it, what would happen?"

The commander did his best to guess. "The cloth would sag a little?"

"Correct," Emily said. "But if I drop a marble within the radius of action that weight exerts on the net, what would happen?"

"The marble would roll toward the rock."

"Correct again. Well, this net is space-time, and the rock represents the effect gravity exerts on it. That slight funnel it forms, which attracts the marble, represents that gravity's power of attraction. And the deformation of the net makes time expand and deform, causing it to be far longer, so that it gives us the impression that time passes much more slowly.

"But in the areas furthest from the rock's radius of action, the net isn't distorted and time travels at normal speed. For an observer under the effect of the rock, those travelling along the areas at the edge of the net do so as though they're on fast forward. And to them, those inside the rock's range of action are moving in slow motion."

"So how are we going to find out whether we've lost more time on our journey than the Galileo?" the captain asked.

"We'll never find out," Emily said sadly, "unless both observers coincide in time and space and we can compare our points of view. And besides, because of the sabotage, Ada has no memory of the last five hundred years."

"Even so," the deputy director asked, "could she calculate the time we might have lost when she regained control?"

"That's complicated. The information we have about black holes is only theoretical. Even so, bearing in mind the time spent waking us from our cryostasis, preparing the escape plan and then executing it, it could be more than ten years."

"In other words," the deputy director said somberly, "Emily's theory might be correct and the Galileo could have come up against the Khol when they arrived."

The captain nodded. "That would explain why the Keplerians haven't heard of humans until now, and why there's no trace of the Galileo."

They were all silent. They did not want to admit it yet, at least not without evidence, but it seemed perfectly likely that something like this could have happened. Emily realized that the more time passed, the more information they found, the less chance there was of ever being reunited with her father.

"I'm sorry to interrupt again," came Ada's voice. "But something very strange is happening at the station."

"What is it, Ada?" the deputy director asked.

"I'm detecting a general failure in the opening gates of all the hangars."

"In all ten hangars?" Captain Mei asked in amazement.

"Yes, in all of them."

"What kind of failure'?" the captain wanted to know.

"The hydraulic systems."

"Does that mean no-one can get into the station or out of it?"

"Not while the systems aren't repaired."

"Have you regained coms with the base?" Emily asked.

"No, we're still in the dark. I myself can't, by design, locate the ship's military crew or monitor their communications, but via the security images from the station I'm seeing that Lieutenant Beaufort, even though he's sent several messages to Captain Garth, hasn't been able to find him. The lieutenant has been going from one end of the station to the other all morning, by himself."

The commander was looking worried. "Get him to come here at once."

"Anything else?" the deputy director asked.

"Yes, I'm afraid there's more to come," Ada went on. "As I was saying, I can't track the military personnel, but the civilian personnel I can, and I can't find twelve members of the station crew, among them the second officer in command of the ship."

"You can't find him?" the captain asked incredulously, "What do you mean, can't find him?"

"I don't understand it. I can detect their transponders in one of the mess halls, but according to the cameras there's no-one there."

"That can only mean one thing," the deputy director said somberly. "We have a mutiny on board."

"Ada," the captain said, "make a list of the personnel you can't find and an inventory of everything that's been taken out of storage during the last few days, as well as the ships that are missing in the hangar."

Ada showed the requested information on screen, and they saw the list was quite a long one. Ships, supplies, habitats for the expansion of the base, electronic equipment…

At that moment Robert appeared in the hall.

"At ease, Lieutenant," the commander said after they had exchanged salutes. "I'm afraid we're in the middle of a crisis. Take a seat, if you don't mind."

"We think we've just had a mutiny aboard," the deputy director said. "Do you know where Captain Garth is?"

"No, sir. He'd told me to meet him here this morning, but I couldn't find him. I've asked several of the soldiers on the station, but no-one's seen him the whole morning."

"The cowardly slug!" the captain yelled. "I was sure he'd end up causing us trouble."

The deputy director did his best to calm her. "Let's not get carried away. We don't know what's going on yet."

"The first thing we need to do is get out of here," Emily said urgently. "I think the loss of communications with the base might have something to do with this."

"You're right," the captain agreed. "Ada, please put me through to Director Patel."

She then had a brief conversation with the director, who was fully informed of the trouble in the hangars and was mobilizing the limited personnel he had at his disposal in the station to resolve the crisis as soon as possible. He also mentioned that he could not find a couple of his trusted engineers.

"Director Patel is on the job," the captain confirmed when she had finished the conversation. "He's missing two of his own people as well."

"This has been organized very carefully," the commander said. "And I too think it's Captain Garth's work. Ever since we came here he's shown his disagreement with our way of directing the expedition a number of times. He only respected Admiral O'Connell's orders. He's never seen me as a true leader," he added regretfully.

"You've done everything you had to at all times, Commander," Emily said. "He's the only one responsible for all this, I'm quite sure of that too."

They went over the list of civilians they could not manage to locate: Second Officer Kuijpers, Security Officer Barrios, a couple of engineers, Wilson the pilot, who had been co-pilot on the Icarus, and in addition up to twelve civilians with a range of duties and special expertise.

"It's a really varied list," the deputy director said. "As of this moment, essential decisions will be made in the strictest secrecy. We can't rule out the possibility that the rebels might have left someone behind within the station to learn about the decisions made here."

"Ada," the commander said, "show us a list of the military staff whose current locations we don't have."

On the screen the AI showed a list of twenty names, headed by that of Captain Garth.

"Well, well, what a surprise," the deputy director said ironically. "Looks as though all his colleagues from that special operations team have joined his private party."

"And they've left us the youngest and least experienced soldiers," the captain added.

"Ada, the transponders work by satellite too, don't they?" Emily asked.

"That's correct."

"Can you show us the exact position of the transponders of the residents and engineers who were at the base this morning?"

"Of course."

In a static image of the area from the day before, without clouds, Ada showed them the position of each of the inhabitants of the base, together with those of the engineers in charge of extending it. In the quadrangular space at the end of the base there were a total of thirteen red dots which stayed immobile. Beside each red dot Ada had placed on the screen was a photo with the name of each of them. Emily saw the transponders belonging to Gorka, Paula, Taro, Chad, Evelyn, Kostas and Balakova. They were all in the same place. Beside them were six of Director Patel's engineers. She saw that someone was missing.

"Is Rakesh still at the village?"

"Yes." Ada showed his location.

"And what about the soldiers?" the lieutenant asked.

"I can only find Private Ferrara and Sergeant Ortiz, who are in the same place as the others."

"And Sergeant Cameron?"

"I can't find her."

"Hell!" Robert cried. "I should've guessed that."

"Wait a moment," Emily said. "What about Jonathan?"

"Jonathan's outside," said Ada, showing them his red dot just in front of the entrance to

the base, apart from the rest. Emily feared the worst.

21
Traitor

September 5, Year 0
Asimov Space Station

Repairing the main hangar gates took them several hours, which in view of what had been happening seemed eternal to Emily and Robert. With them were a small group of the inexperienced soldiers who were available at the station itself who were ready to leave as soon as the team of engineers had finished changing the hydraulic systems on one of the huge opening mechanisms.

The tension of the moment, the uncertainty and gravity of what had happened made the return journey to the planet into a nightmare. With the distance growing appreciably shorter, Robert tried to calm Emily when he noticed that her legs were twitching of their own accord in the transport vehicle's austere seat.

"Don't worry, I'm sure they're all fine."

"How can they do a thing like that?" she asked, feeling useless. "We came here in search of unity and a future together, and at the first sign of trouble… and so easily, they carry out a coup to pull down what it took us so much trouble to build."

"I can't understand it either. You could only explain it from the point of view of a sick mind like Captain Garth's."

The soldiers left the ship first, guns in hands and aiming in every direction, like a well-coordinated team. They went forward a few steps and stopped a few meters from the base.

"All clear," Emily heard several of the soldiers say, including Robert.

When she got out of the ship, the first thing she saw was that there was no machinery, materials or buildings ready for the expansion of the base. They seemed to have taken everything with them, even the rover and the vehicle which was normally left there.

"They've taken everything!" Emily gasped.

"Jonathan!" Robert shouted. He ran toward a tall wooden stake which had been buried in the ground a few meters from the entrance. "Here, give me a hand!"

Emily saw something on the stake, but not even in her worst nightmare could she have imagined what she was about to find. Hanging from the stake was the lifeless body of Jonathan Wiśniewski, project welder and perpetrator of the sabotage attack on the station. The rebels had stripped him and tied him to the stake face-down by his feet, three meters up. His body was bruised and his face completely unrecognizable from the blows he had received before being placed in that macabre position. But the thing which most impressed Emily was that on his chest, covered with a clotted mess of blood, was the word TRAITOR, written in his own flesh with a sharp object.

"Bastards!" Robert growled through clenched teeth.

"What kind of monster would be capable of doing a thing like this?" Emily asked in anguish.

"Someone ruthless and unscrupulous. Now you all know what kind of a person he is."

"He's not a person, he's a monster."

"Help me get him down from there," Robert said.

Between the two of them, and with the help of a couple of the soldiers, they managed to lift him enough to untie the ropes that tied him to the stake. They laid his body gently on the ground. Robert used one of the torn nets from the greenhouse, which the rebels had made sure to reduce to rubble very effectively, then covered the body so that no-one else would be able to see him in that state.

Once they had done something to clear away the barbarity, they went into the base. After going through decontamination, which luckily was still functioning, they were able to establish that there was an electrical supply, though it seemed that only the life-support systems were working.

"I'd say it's the auxiliary generator that's working," Robert said while Emily assessed the glaring damage to the first of the distributor areas. "They must have taken the main one."

He and the soldiers went through the door which separated them from the corridor and moved forward in formation, aiming ahead with their assault rifles. When the door to the second lobby opened, Emily managed to peer between what little space was left by the soldiers in front of her and see a number of bodies scattered across the floor. Her heart skipped a beat, and she pushed her way between the soldiers to find out what was happening at first hand.

Luckily they were all alive. Garth and his followers had zip-tied them and left them there. The only one injured was Gorka, whose right eye was so swollen that he could barely see. His nose had been broken and he was breathing with difficulty, although as it was Gorka this would not be the first time. It was obvious that the captain had taken revenge for the two altercations they had had several weeks before. Beside him, Paula was trying to calm him as best she could.

"I think I'm happier to see someone that I've ever been before," Kostas said.

"Are you all right?" Emily asked.

"I think so," Paula said amid sobs. "The one in the worst state is Gorka. They gave him a real beating."

"And Taro's still unconscious," said Chad. "They shot him with a tranquilizer the moment they arrived."

Emily made a quick assessment of the damage. Her preliminary diagnosis seemed correct, the one in the worst state was Gorka, but though he looked dreadful it was not really as bad as that. His nose would have to be checked, as would his ribs, which were almost certainly fractured. The others seemed to be all right. Private Ferrara had a bruised cheek and a trace of dried blood under her nose, a sign that she too had fought back.

The others were perfectly well apart from shock, including Rakesh, who had come back after spending the morning with the Keplerians and run straight into the situation. Robert and the soldiers freed them all.

"What about Jonathan?" Kostas hastened to ask as he rubbed his maltreated wrists.

Emily shook her head without saying a word, but nothing more was needed.

"The moment they arrived he turned into the target of their attacks," Kostas told them in as voice which was barely more than a thread. "They hit him, dragged him across the floor and sneered at him all the time. He was the one who caused all the trouble at the station, wasn't he?"

Emily nodded

"Even so, he seemed like a good man. Evelyn told us what had happened during the trial. No-one deserves to go through what he had to."

Director Patel's engineers helped Emily to make an inventory of damages and losses, though in fact there was not much left to assess because all the usable supplies for the planned development had been taken. And as if that were not enough, they had taken their revenge on the current facilities.

They had taken the fusion generator, the food printer and also the printer for metal alloys, the base defenses, sensors, spare parts and equipment that was vitally important for survival. They had even taken the mattresses from the rooms and the gym equipment. The base was now all-but-useless. Some of the exosuits belonging to those who were still there were missing: those of Kostas, Evelyn and the engineers. Luckily they had been courteous enough to leave some behind, among them Gorka's He had to be taken to the ship when they found that apart from his visible injuries, his right leg was broken.

"How could they have managed to do this?" Robert asked.

"The first thing they did was to sabotage the electrical system and the coms, leaving Ada incommunicado," said Paula, who was still deeply shaken. "Then they overpowered us all. They shot Taro with a tranquilizer, then they overpowered Gorka and Ferrara, who were the ones who fought back the hardest. But the captain was especially rough with Gorka…"

"Ferrara and Ortiz did what they could," Chad said, "but that bitch Cameron took them by surprise from behind."

"That bitch is going to pay for this," said Ferrara, who was more wounded in her pride than physically.

"Then they brought us here and tied us up," Evelyn said. "They set a couple of soldiers to keep an eye on us, and the others started to dismantle the base."

"At least we're alive," Kostas said.

"I came back shortly before lunchtime," Rakesh added. "At first I didn't realize anything was wrong. And I'd noticed the lack of coms, but I thought it was a problem with my exosuit. When I came I could see more going on than usual, but I thought it was just the extension works. Then, when they'd aimed their guns at me and I saw a couple of ships taking off with some of the equipment loaded in their cargo holds, I realized what was happening."

"What direction did go in?" Robert asked.

"I'd say northwest," Rakesh admitted, "but I'm not very good at orienting myself."

"But where could they have gone?" Emily asked.

"Anywhere which isn't covered by cloud at the moment," Robert said. "I think they chose today because there was a good deal of equipment for the extension that hadn't yet been installed, and because it was cloudy and they could avoid satellite detection."

"That gives us too large an area," Emily said ruefully, remembering the ocean of cloud that covered the area in the satellite images.

"But what about the ships and the suits they took and all the equipment?" Paula asked, "Can't we track them and get it all back?"

"They've got one of the most competent military engineers of the project with them," said Emily. "Unfortunately they're sure to have taken all that into account, and they'll have disconnected the tracking systems on everything they've taken."

"I'm afraid we're going to have to evacuate the base until further notice," Robert said. "Apart from not being safe here anymore, the auxiliary generator might fail at any moment and we'd be left without oxygen."

Emily nodded, aware that the auxiliary oxygen tank had also been taken and the air inside the base might run out if the outside filter system were to fail. Even so, the idea had a few complications.

"We don't have enough suits. We won't be able to evacuate them all."

"I've asked for another transport to bring us what we need," Robert explained. "Those of you who have a suit, start going outside. The transport'll take you back to the Asimov."

"I'm staying," said Ferrara.

"No, you're not, Private. Go and have that cheek looked at, and your nose is swelling up. And besides, there's not much left to do here for the moment. We have more than enough manpower to manage the rest of the evacuation."

"Yes, sir," she said reluctantly.

He turned to Emily. "You and I will stay to coordinate everything, if you don't mind."

"Of course. In fact I'd like to take one last look around the base before we leave."

She went around checking the damage the rebel soldiers had done in the base, with a certain unease. Not only had they taken everything for the base needed to be able to function autonomously for years, they had also caused damage that was both gratuitous and meaningless. Wherever she looked she saw broken doors, lamps without bulbs, or simply massive dents in walls or floors.

The gym had been completely emptied. The dorms now had no furniture of any kind, like the mess hall and kitchen, which had been completely dismantled. Even the lockers which had contained the crew's personal effects had been destroyed. She herself had kept very little in them, but she missed some of her clothes and the two books her father had given her. Neither could she find the pendant with the dark stone her Aunt Helen had given her when she was very little. In those circumstances, these were irreplaceable objects.

They had taken everything they thought might be useful from the storeroom, though she was surprised to see they had left one of the mules, the one with the Copernicus logo on its side.

"Hey, you're a real survivor," she said as she tried unsuccessfully to turn it on. "That'll have to be repaired if it's going to work again."

Finally she went into the laboratory. There seemed to be nothing missing, but most of the instruments were broken or needed repair. She found it very hard to hold back her tears. They would have to start again from scratch. She was about to leave the lab when she thought of checking the small room where she had usually worked. It was there that she had discovered the Keplerians' cultivated strips, and for some strange reason it was intact.

How strange. The whole base looks like a battlefield except for this room, she thought.

The terminal in that room was on and someone had left a selected file on it. The title read: *To the leaders of Project Orpheus*. It was a video. When she turned it on, Captain Garth appeared in close-up. He was wearing his exosuit, but had taken off his helmet.

"The following message is addressed to the leaders of the Asimov Space Station," he began. "This is what you've pushed us to do with your lukewarm ideas and half-measures. This situation might have been averted if the high command of the project had been capable of doing their fucking job transparently and fairly. First they left us without our arsenal. Then they pardoned that useless fucking soldier, though I have to say, with a certain satisfaction, that I've thoroughly enjoyed passing a fresh sentence. And finally you've been hiding the fact that as usual, the whole project is based upon the same lies and corruption as ever.

"Admiral O'Connell wouldn't have allowed any of these disasters under his command. But for all of us"—he made a sign with both hands indicating everyone around him— "all this business of being led by weaklings and little girls doing their science experiments for school is over.

"I've just stated publicly that my group is rebelling," he announced formally, then went on to list every member of his new team. "As of now, all those I've named reject any relationship, membership or allegiance to what is known as Project Orpheus. We do not recognize the authority of any of its leaders and senior military command, and hence we intend to decide our own destiny and form of government.

"And now I'm going to tell you what's going to happen from this moment on. You are not to attempt to track us down. We've made sure you won't be able to, so save your efforts. Don't stick your noses into what we're doing. Don't try to communicate with us. If for whatever reason you find out any of our locations, we'll open fire without warning. We've been quite respectful to those we shared the battlefield with, but don't tempt your luck.

"You can go on playing with your toy civilizations, but we're going to be the ones who really colonize the planet, and if to do that we have to lay waste to the surface and finish off all the fucking species on the planet, we'll do it with a steady hand. If you fail to follow any of these simple rules, there'll be very serious consequences. We've already provided for that, so don't force us to take steps there'll be no going back from.

"Captain of the Navy of the New United States Tyson Garth. Over and out."

Emily leaned forward in her chair and put her hands to her head. Captain Garth had just blown up much of the work they had been doing ever since they had come to the planet. But even ignoring the clear reference to herself, what worried her most was the last sentence: *We've already provided for that.*

"What did he mean by that?" she murmured to herself.

Robert appeared at the door.

"Emily, we've got to go. The transport with the rest of the suits has just arrived. We can evacuate the base." When he saw that she was not responding, he asked: "What is it?"

Emily set Garth's video to play again.

"The bastard!" he spat when it was over.

"What do you think he meant when he says *we've provided for that?*"

"That we can expect to find some explosive present for us inside the station. And if he carries out his threat, it could mean the end of humankind."

The base was evacuated, but before they went back to the station all the members of the expedition wanted to pay their last respects to their murdered colleague. Kostas and Robert dug a hole in the shade of a huge tree nearby. Evelyn, Rakesh and Emily shrouded the body of the welder as best they could, using ropes and parts of the destroyed covering of the greenhouse.

It was a hard but emotional moment. Though they had not known him well, it was clear evidence of the project's failure and the fact that humanity was condemned to tripping over the same stone over and over again. There were no kind words, nor was there any eloquent, sentimental oration. Only the silence which would always accompany the father who had been forced to sacrifice everything, even his own humanity, for the life of his son.

22
Disheartened

September 6, Year 0
Asimov Space Station

As soon as they had gone back to the Asimov the deputy director summoned Emily and Robert to an emergency meeting. They needed to draw up a strategy as soon as possible. However, in case of any possible breach of information he only allowed Captain Mei, Commander Bauer, he himself, and of course the two of them, to be present. Emily told them what they had found. It was painful when they came to the horror of what Garth and his minions had done to Jonathan Wiśniewski.

"We never considered that possibility," the deputy director admitted, sounding deeply disheartened. "The project was created within parameters of humanity, respect and concord. This is inhuman, unworthy of a civilization that prides itself on being advanced."

"I don't understand why when we're even far away from earth we're not capable of forgiving and moving on," Emily added sadly.

"We wouldn't even be able to do that if we were the last humans in the universe," Captain Mei complained.

"Jonathan was deeply sorry for what he'd done, I'm absolutely sure of that," Emily said. "I'd even go as far as saying he wanted to forgive himself and become part of the project all over again."

"What did you do with the body?" Green asked.

"We buried it nearby," Lieutenant Beaufort said.

"It's the least we could do," Emily added.

"May he rest in peace," the deputy director whispered.

After a heartfelt moment of silence, Emily played Garth's video for those who had not yet seen it.

"We think he's hidden some kind of explosive device in the ship," she said when the video was over.

"Considering what that bastard is capable of, it wouldn't surprise me in the least," Captain Mei said.

"We need to find it and deactivate it," said Emily.

"We need to be very cautious," the deputy director objected. "Captain Garth is very intelligent and he's a soldier who's been decorated for carrying out a whole range of secret missions on Earth. I'm convinced he'll have foreseen all our movements, and it's more than likely that he'll have someone infiltrated here on the ship."

"Can't Ada go over the conversations of the rebels these last few days to try and find the identity of the mole?" Robert asked.

Emily shook her head. "By design, Ada isn't permitted to track or store any kind of information or conversation where a member of the armed forces is involved. I'd imagine the captain would have been very aware of that when he was conspiring to carry out his little coup."

"We could lift that limitation," Commander Bauer suggested.

"We could, but that would take autonomy away from you," she pointed out.

"I know, but by this point the expedition has nothing to do with what was planned before leaving Earth. At this moment we have more than nine hundred soldiers in cryostasis and no military gear to equip them with. I think that measure stopped making sense the moment we lost the arsenal. I'm very much afraid that the armed forces of the expedition are going to have to reinvent themselves."

"Can you take care of this, Emily?" the deputy director asked.

"I'll need to have the credentials of the two most senior officers of the project validated."

"Luckily they're sitting right here. Afterwards you can decide what you need, but even so, that'll allow us to monitor whatever happens from now on, not what's already happened. We still won't have the guarantee of being able to act with full freedom as long as we haven't found out whether there's a breach in station security."

"And what about conversations among non-military personnel?" Robert asked.

"We could explore that," the deputy director said thoughtfully.

"Maybe Ada can find something," Emily said, "but I don't suppose Garth will have shared his overall strategy with any civilians. Only the second officer and the security officer were senior enough to have played a significant part in the mutiny. And I don't suppose they've slipped up along the way."

"Even so, it's worth trying," the deputy director insisted. "It's all we have for the moment."

"Could Ada be involved in any way?" Captain Mei asked suddenly.

"No," Emily said firmly. "Unless…"

"Unless what?" the captain asked when she did not go on.

"Ada can only be modified from her terminal. And only a few people in the whole station have access to that terminal, and all of us are sitting here at this table. If we take it as read that none of us here are involved in the mutiny, there's only one possibility."

"And what's that?" the commander asked in puzzlement.

"The copy of my chip Jonathan had implanted beside his own. I suppose it would have been taken and kept by one of those involved."

"That chip has got to be destroyed," the captain said.

"But it's the evidence of a crime," the deputy director objected. "I'll have a word with Judge Meyer, because we'll have to destroy it. But for the moment we won't use Ada for anything to do with the search for the rebels, in case of what could happen."

"And we shouldn't talk about important matters outside this room," the commander added.

"If they've cut off their own coms and transponders," the captain asked, "how are they supposed to find out what we do or don't do at the station?"

"They might have agreed on some kind of protocol to communicate with someone from the ship," Emily suggested. "Or something unusual, to avoid being detected."

No-one could think of any brilliant idea for finding out how the rebels could be spying on the station.

"All right, then," the deputy director said at last, "if we don't have any new ideas to bring to the table, we'll do nothing."

"Nothing?" Emily repeated in surprise.

"I don't intend to put the mission at risk because of a bloodthirsty maniac like Captain Garth."

"But suppose they decide to detonate whatever they've left here?" Captain Mei asked.

"They won't," Robert said bluntly.

"How can you be so sure about that?"

"Because deep down, we're still their insurance policy. He'd only make the decision to destroy a guaranteed source of energy, food and technology in an extreme case."

The deputy director nodded. "The lieutenant's right. He might have left some kind of device to use in an extremity, or even blackmail us given the opportunity. But if we don't meddle in his business and they don't find themselves in a desperate situation, the captain won't use the only ace he has up his sleeve."

"So in that case does that mean we do nothing?" Emily asked, rather disappointed.

"Yes, we go on with our own calendar. We've already begun to bring a new batch of soldiers out of cryostasis. We'll strengthen the military presence on the base, just in case they decide to come back."

"The army deliberately put some light military supplies in the civil hangar," the commander added, "but we're beginning to have shortages, especially of ammunition and exosuits. But if we can't manage to secure a small area of the planet for ourselves, the rest of the expedition no longer has any meaning, so we have no choice but to put all the meat on the grill."

"I admit it's a major setback," the deputy director said, "but we'll get back to work on the planet and go on with the enlargement. Director Patel is already getting everything in place to start repairs tomorrow."

"I can't believe he's going to get away with it," Emily said angrily.

"I know it's not fair. But now more than ever we need to be pragmatic. And above all, we need to think in terms of going on with what we set out to do. We've suffered a major loss, true, but for the moment the space station has enough spares for everything they took. We have to look ahead."

"And what are we going to do about the Keplerians?" the captain asked. "That veiled threat in the video where they say they're going to eliminate the species on the planet could turn into a real problem."

The deputy director nodded. "I think Dr. Rhodes and Dr. Kumar are going to have to use diplomacy and have a word with the Keplerian leader."

"Yes, of course," Emily said immediately. "But I don't know how to introduce a matter like that, to be honest. I haven't even been able to spend time with Rakesh so that he can bring me up to date."

"Dr. Kumar has finished going over the dictionary," Ada put in. "I was able to synchronize the information in his suit with my databases."

Emily gave a sigh of relief. "At least that's one piece of good news in all this chaos. By now the language shouldn't be a problem when we're communicating with any of the Keplerians."

"Ada," the deputy director asked, "do you know whether the Keplerian leader is back from her trip?"

"Not yet. This morning Dr. Kumar asked her assistant how long the journey was, and she told him it was less than a day away, but because of the leader's age it would almost certainly take longer."

"Right, thank you," the deputy director said resignedly. "We'll have to wait for her to come back. Let's hope that for the moment the captain's rebels will be so busy setting up their own bases, they won't have time to do anything stupid."

Emily and Robert used the rest of the afternoon to talk to their colleagues. They needed to be united. Gorka had been taken to the observation area in the infirmary. Taro on the other hand had been unconscious for some time, so Dr. Schmidt had decided to keep him in at least for that night.

In the infirmary they found Paula and Chad, who wanted to stay as close as possible to their comrades.

"How are you doing?" Emily asked them.

"Counting the days left before I can get back to the planet and kick the asses of those worthless cowards," Gorka said defiantly.

Paula stared at him with her hands on her hips. "First you're going to need to get those fractures in your ribs, nose and leg better."

"This? I've been worse than this often enough."

"Who did it?" Emily asked.

"Captain Garth and his puppet Sergeant Reynolds."

"But four others had to hold him down," Chad pointed out. "And even so, he nearly took them all down."

"I should've smashed their faces in," Gorka muttered furiously.

"But they were armed and you weren't," Paula pointed out.

He raised his fists. "These two are good enough for me."

"Well, what matters now is for you to get better," Robert said. "I'm afraid we've got a lot of work ahead of us."

Emily turned toward the bed opposite. "And how are you, Taro?"

"I still feel a bit queasy," he said in barely more than a murmur. "But I guess I'm better off than some others."

"Why were you the only one they sedated?" Emily asked.

"Because he was one of the dangerous ones," Robert pointed out.

"But they didn't sedate Gorka."

"Knowing Garth, he wanted Gorka to feel every single one of the blows they gave him, because of that argument by the river. But he preferred to eliminate Taro from the equation, in view of what he was capable of doing with his katanas."

"Oh, and by the way, they took them," said Chad.

"What!" Emily exclaimed.

Paula nodded. "Yeah, they've taken a lot of valuable things from our lockers. But I don't suppose there was anything so irreplaceable, anything with such sentimental value as Taro's katanas."

"They were unique," Chad said.

"You have to be real scum to do something like that," Emily said.

Emily saw Taro looking serious, even though he was still under the effect of the powerful narcotic. There were many things within the project that were more or less unique, but a pair of Japanese ceremonial swords like the ones he had brought with him would have been irreplaceable even on Earth. The Japanese swordsmiths' traditional way of tempering steel was unrivalled. It was obvious that Taro was going through a difficult moment and that his spirits were at a low ebb.

"That's right," Paula said. "You'll probably find things missing yourself."

"They've taken my books and a pendant my Aunt Helen gave me."

"Wow, was it very valuable?" Chad asked.

"Not really, it was just a dark polished stone. It was pretty and strange, though I don't suppose it was very valuable in economic terms. But it was the only thing I had of hers left. I never saw her again."

"Did she die?" Chad asked.

"No… well, I don't really know. All I have is a vague memory of seeing her one day when I was very little. But I do remember her saying that the stone would help me to achieve great things. I guess it's the typical comment that stays in a six-year-old's mind for some reason, and maybe that's why I had a special affection for her."

"We'll find all those things and get them back," Robert said confidently.

"And we'll kick those fucking soldiers' asses," Gorka growled. "No offense," he added, turning to Robert, who nodded.

"So what's the plan?" Paula asked.

"We go back to the base as soon as Director Patel finishes reconditioning the facilities," Emily said.

"But what happens if they come back again?" Chad asked uneasily.

"This time we'll have a bigger military presence on the base," Robert said. "Recently-awakened personnel with no connection to Captain Garth or any of the rebels. I've taken on the job of drawing up a list, along with Commander Bauer."

"So does that mean the idea is to go on with the original plan as if nothing had happened?" Paula asked.

Emily looked at Robert to read his expression. She wanted to know his opinion on what she was about to do. He guessed at once what she was thinking and nodded without hesitation.

"Well, you see," she began, "Captain Garth left a video for the project leaders, and in it he threatened to take drastic measures against us if we make any attempt to locate them."

"Drastic measures?" Chad repeated. "What the hell's that supposed to mean?"

"We think he's left some kind of explosive device in the station."

"What?" they all exclaimed.

She made a calming gesture, and they lowered their voices. "No-one knows anything about this at the station, and I'd like things to stay that way."

"Yes, of course," Chad said, speaking for all of them. "We'll be as silent as the grave. We don't want to set off a panic."

"But does that mean they get away with it?" Gorka protested. "Just like that?"

"What we need at this moment is to regain control," Emily went on. "We don't even know whether Ada's under Garth's influence."

Chad looked alarmed at this. "Are you saying Ada might have joined the rebellion too?"

"No, Ada can't do that. Well, at least not under Captain Garth's influence. But the rebels have a very good engineer who's quite capable of having installed some kind of mechanism which would let them know what's happening at any time on the station without Ada even being aware of it."

"And what about your Keplerian friends?" Paula asked.

"Rakesh and I are going to go to our meetings as usual. Now we're close to a possible understanding with them, we can't afford to waste all that effort."

Paula frowned. "Are you going to tell them there are more humans on the surface of the planet now?"

"I don't know yet. The Keplerian leader isn't in the village at the moment, and I don't think it's something we ought to spring on them just like that."

"Which means we're back to where we were," Chad complained.

"Worse," Gorka corrected him.

"Yeah, I'm afraid so. But we've got to get out of this. We're not going to get another choice."

"We'll move on," Robert agreed. "All together."

23
Beginning again

September 7, Year 0
Wiikhaadiiz ofiz village, Kepler-442b

Emily and Rakesh took advantage of the fact that Director Patel and his engineers were going to start reconditioning the base to make a new start on the planet. After everything that had happened she would rather have taken the opportunity to look more deeply into the increasingly likely breach of security Captain Garth might be using to spy on everything that was going on in the station, but the deputy director had insisted that they needed to go on with their diplomatic work with the Keplerians. Deep down Emily knew he was right, but she was still not happy to have to set aside the possibility that the rebels had sabotaged the station.

But the thing she found hardest to bear was being unable to trust Ada completely. The AI herself had admitted to her the night before that she was not aware of anyone having manipulated her, or that she might even be unknowingly sending information about what was happening on the station to the rebels.

They went along the path to Khikhya's building and picked up Shildi on their way, as usual.

"Why didn't Emily come yesterday," the boy asked curiously.

She did her best to satisfy his curiosity. "Emily had something important to do in her house."

"But has she brought cake?"

With the change in routine, the haste of the moment and the tension of the last hours, she had completely forgotten to prepare a cake for him and Yisht.

It had to happen sooner or later, she thought. *I guess I have too many things on my mind to think of everything.*

"I'm sorry, Shildii. Yesterday was a complicated day for me. I'm very sorry, but I forgot to bring you a piece of cake. I promise to remember the next time."

"It doesn't matter," Shildii said understandingly, but with a certain disappointment in his eyes. It seemed that the cake was one of the boy's incentives in that situation, which was strange enough in itself.

When they arrived, Yisht was waiting for them at the door.

"Hello, Emily."

"Hello!"

"We missed you yesterday."

"Yes, unfortunately it was impossible for me to come. We had some problems in our village," she admitted, without giving any more details.

"Oh dear, I'm sorry about that," Yisht said as they went to the study on the upper floor again. "I hope you can sort it out."

"I hope so. Have you heard from the leader Khikhya? When's she coming back?"

"We have no news from her, although I'd imagine she'll be on her way by now. These trips are quite uncomfortable for her, so it takes her longer than usual."

Emily sat down. "That's understandable."

"Yesterday Yisht brought me illustrated books about the fauna and flora of the planet," Rakesh explained. "And also descriptions of the habitats of each of them. It turns out that there are creatures of all kinds, some of them a little… let's say…disturbing, from our point of view."

"Yes," Yisht said excitedly, "and Rakesh showed me what the Earth is like. Did I say that correctly?"

Rakesh nodded. "Quite correctly."

"I was surprised to see how green the fields are and how blue the skies. It looks like a beautiful place. Although rather strange for a Keplerian, I suppose."

"I also explained what a tide was," Rakesh said.

Emily looked at Yisht, who seemed to be very interested in the Earth's tides.

"Yes! That was amazing! I still have trouble understanding why you have a rock around your planet. Here we don't have any of that, the sea just grows a little more in summer."

Emily could understand this point of view. "Yes, I suppose our planets are rather different."

"What do you want to learn today?" Yisht asked with a smile.

"We'd like to learn more about the Keplerian people. Do you have a map that shows the important places, or the known areas?"

"Yes, of course," Yisht said, helpful as ever. "I'll bring them right away."

After a couple of minutes she came back carrying several large sheets of parchment, meticulously drawn by hand, under her arm.

"This is what they teach us when we go to school!" Shildii cried excitedly when she spread out one of the rolls.

"Yes. This is a map where you can see the paths that link the three main villages. This one is Wiikhaadiiz ofiz." She pointed to where they were, then to two large cities to the east and northeast. "This is Khapabir, and this one up here is Khaavahki."

Emily saw that the map represented the river separating the base from the Keplerian villages quite faithfully.

"What is there to the south of this area?" she asked. She wanted to find out as much as she could about the Yokai, but she had learned the lesson and this time she did it less directly, without even naming them.

"I don't know, I'm sorry," Yisht said apologetically. "It's a dangerous area. That's where the night-stalkers live."

"Night-stalkers?" Rakesh asked.

"Yes, they're very dangerous and intelligent creatures. They only come out to hunt at night, that's why we Keplerians never venture beyond the river, particularly at night."

"Do you know where they live, or how many are there?" Emily asked.

"No, I couldn't say, I'm afraid." She looked worried about not being able to help them. "And I don't know whether we have any books about the night-stalkers."

Emily looked back at the map again. "Don't worry, it doesn't matter. Do the paths always go under the trees?"

"Yes, always. The Keplerians have been doing this for thousands of years. I don't know whether it started for any particular reason, but it stops the Kholghishbik seeing us from their flying vessels, so I understand it's an important defense mechanism."

Emily nodded. "I see. And when are they expected to come back?"

"There's no knowing. Sometimes they take a few hundred years, others they take longer, others less. There are even records in the books where they say that now and then they've skipped a generation. Can you imagine?" There was hope in her eyes. "There were Keplerians years ago who didn't have to endure that barbarity."

"What is it they come here to do?" Rakesh asked.

"They collect minerals the Keplerians extract for them and control the population."

"Control the population?"

"Yes," she said sadly. "They eliminate the ones they regard as 'surplus population'. That way they make sure the Keplerians don't grow too numerous and rebel against them."

"That's horrible," said Emily.

"Yes, it certainly is. Although unfortunately it runs so deep in society, we're almost resigned to it."

"And why don't you all fight?" Rakesh asked.

Yisht's expression darkened. "We've tried many times in the course of history, but their weapons are devastating. Every time we've tried to stand up to the Kholghishbik, they've reduced entire cities to rubble and ashes and murdered everyone they came across."

Emily and Rakesh were silent. The Keplerians were utterly subjugated by their oppressors.

"Can you bring us all the information you have about the Kholghishbik?" Emily asked.

"Of course." Yisht left the table again.

"What do you expect to find in their writings?" Rakesh asked Emily.

"I don't know, but the more we know about them, the better we'll be prepared."

He was alarmed by this. "Do you mean to fight against them?"

"Do we have any other choice? What d'you think will happen when they see the Asimov orbiting the planet? You heard Yisht the other day: this is their planet."

He was silent, and Yisht soon came back with a couple of huge leather-bound volumes.

"These are ancient books that have survived for many generations. Unfortunately we don't have much more information from before that time, which was known as the Great Revolt."

Emily leafed through the first of the books. It was a historical account, hand-written, with the chronology of each visit by the Khol over the last few thousand years. It began some seven thousand Keplerian years before, around two thousand three hundred earth years. As she went on turning the pages the writing changed, evidence that another generation of Keplerians was in charge of updating the records.

Each entry, which covered several pages, listed the amounts of minerals and raw materials which had been delivered, the destruction caused or the casualties suffered. Her attention was drawn by the fact that instead of using numbers, they wrote the amounts using letters.

"I can't believe what I'm reading," Emily murmured. "How can they be capable of such cruelty?"

"That's the way things are," Yisht said resignedly. "We Keplerians have learned to live with it."

Emily slammed the book shut, not wanting to read any more. Millions of Keplerians mercilessly massacred, with no chance to defend themselves against the cruelty of a superior race.

"It's so horrible I find it hard to believe that with everything that you've suffered you're even prepared to talk to us."

She shrugged. "Why wouldn't we? You're not to blame for what the Kholghishbik do."

Emily began to leaf through the other book, making sure the camera in her suit had a good view of it. In this one there was more about the Khol themselves. It seemed to be a kind of compendium of all the information the Keplerians had gathered about their victimizers. Seeing that it contained illustrations of the Khol, Rakesh got up from his chair to get a clearer view of what she was leafing through.

With long, powerful limbs and over two meters tall, the Khol had four long, curved claws in each hand, which were certainly capable of ripping a human's flesh without second thoughts. Their bodies were covered with scales of a dull, matt green. Long tails seemed to help them keep their balance, perhaps even to stay upright in the same way as kangaroos on Earth.

Their heads were triangular, without snouts, with a rough, threatening appearance, crowned by two pointed knobs which formed a small rim at the front. Their eyes, which were high up in their heads, where their foreheads were almost nonexistent, were bright gold but with a thin dark area, a kind of vertical pupil. Their mouths were disproportionately large and seemed to have no teeth. On their chins was a single knob, much like those on top of their heads.

That same page included another illustration of the Khol seen from behind. In it they could see the real size of their tails and the fact that from what seemed to be their spines there grew bony knobs, the same kind and shape as those on their heads.

"They don't have ears or noses," Emily pointed out.

Rakesh was looking at the simple clothing the artist had decorated his drawing with. "And their clothing doesn't seem to fit their technological development very well either."

Emily thought about this. It was striking that an alien race with technology that allowed them to travel to other planets should dress in a mere vest of some hard organic material and something like a skirt of simple cloth, like the *shentis* of the ancient Egyptians.

"Maybe it was just something the author decided to simplify because he didn't have any more details available."

They went on turning over the pages. The next illustration was of an individual, which though it belonged to the same species was certainly of a different race, larger than the one before. It was more than two meters tall, but though its physique was very similar there were a number of clear differences between the two species. The first and most visible was the color of the skin, in this case a dull blue. The second involved the knobs on the creature's head. In the first example these were small and not very pronounced, whereas in this one they consisted of two huge horns covered in irregularities which traced a long, intricate curve and almost joined at the back of the head. In addition, below these two great horns there emerged a series of bony protuberances which ran along the sides of the creature's head and joined again at the chin, giving them an even more sinister and threatening look, if it were possible.

As for their clothing, it seemed to be much better cared-for and more refined than that of the other race. Even though the material itself was simple and functional its finish was far more detailed, decorated with metal plates adorned with filigree and glyphs of some strange alphabet.

"It says here there are two races," Rakesh pointed out "The first is called Kholvahki and the second Kholchach."

"That makes sense. It means, literally, Khol soldier and Khol leader in Keplerian."

"Emily's right," Shildii said. She was obviously delighted to be able to explain something to them. "Shildii has studied the Kholghishbik at school. They are made up of two kinds of individuals. The soldiers, who usually perform the most demanding tasks and are the ones who come here regularly. And then there are the leaders, whom we rarely see. And the times when they've been seen didn't end too well for us," she added sadly.

"I suppose the leaders only appear when things turn nasty," said Rakesh.

Emily went on turning the pages until she came to an illustration of a ship and a kind of land vehicle. As Rakesh had pointed out, the technology of those ships did not seem to match the aliens' clothing. She turned a few more pages before going back to the one which showed the ships, without having found what she was looking for.

"Those are fighters, small ships and vehicles. Don't the Kholghishbik have some kind of large ship that stays off the planet?"

Yisht shrugged. "I don't know. Everything we know is in that book."

Before they left, Emily felt the urge to ask: "Where do you live, Yisht? Is it far from here?"

"Not really, I live in the building just beside this one. Khikhya always wants to have her closest helpers near her. In fact I can get to my house directly from this very building. Why do you ask?"

"The human leaders are very pleased and excited about the Keplerian people's hospitality. So as a token of our appreciation, perhaps we'll bring some gifts for the Keplerians tomorrow. And also a gift for you."

Yisht's face lit up.

"A gift? For me?"

Emily smiled. "Yes, for you. You've been very kind to us, and besides, we've learned so many things that both Rakesh and I would like to thank you."

"There's no need," Yisht assured them humbly. "I'm just doing my job."

"Well, we humans are brought up to try and be grateful for the efforts of others. But I'd rather not attract attention, if possible. I'm sure our presence here is attracting too many indiscreet glances, and I don't want to cause any trouble, either for you or for Khikhya."

Yisht thought for a moment before coming up with a solution.

"How big are the gifts?" she asked.

Emily got up and used her own hands to show her the size of what she had thought of bringing. "Three meters long, more or less by two wide and two high," she said while Ada translated it into Keplerian measurements.

"Wow! That's a very big gift!"

Emily laughed delightedly.

"Yes, I'm afraid it is rather big."

"All right. If it's all right with you, I'll send a group of trustworthy Keplerians to go to the outskirts with a cart and bring the gift here. I'll have to think where to put it."

"It weighs a lot, but our mule will put it wherever you want. The only thing I don't want is for anyone to be scared at the sight of a mule, including the soldiers who escort us every morning."

"We don't know what a mule is."

"Oh, of course! It's a mechanical device we use to transport large heavy objects."

"I'm not sure if I understand that, but don't worry. The cart will use the back of the building, where they always bring food and supplies. No-one will take any notice of it."

"Perfect. That sounds great."

"I'll give them the order that they must wait for you at the same place a little before the soldiers arrive, so that no-one sees what you're bringing."

24
Prohibition

October 1, Year 0
Asimov Space Station

The previous night Emily had loaded one of the cargo mules with the two gifts she intended to deliver to the Keplerian government building. She had talked to the deputy director and Captain Mei beforehand to see whether the gift was feasible. Despite the limitations of the station's resources, Director Patel and his engineers had done a wonderful job with the equipment which had been recovered from the Icarus, as well as some more which could form a part of an official gift. She had also done everything possible to diagnose Ada's current state, and had at least been able to certify that her neural web was still intact. Given the complex system of verification by means of quantum digital signatures, she could be sure that there was no doubt that no-one had modified a single line of code in Ada's brain.

Still, she supposed the rebel engineers would expect this to be the first thing to be checked, so it seemed pretty clear that if anything had been inserted it would be hidden in one of the thousands of auxiliary systems Ada used and over which she herself did not have so much control. The main problem was that there were so many of them, and of so many different kinds, that there was no easy way of verifying them all.

But what was really troubling her was that the deputy director had spoken to Judge Meyer about what had happened to Jonathan Wiśniewski and his suspicions that someone might have used the fraudulent copy of Emily's chip.

"The judge told me she had ordered the chip and the rest of the evidence to be destroyed the moment the trial was over," Green had told her when he had contacted her.

All the same, custody of the evidence and the material seized had stayed with Captain Garth. If the chip had not been destroyed at the end of the trial, someone could have been coming into Ada's control hall during the previous nine months with complete freedom. And if that someone had the slightest skill, he would have been careful enough to avoid making the same mistakes which had led to Emily's unmasking of the author of the sabotage. This time it was going to be all-but-impossible to find anything.

Even so, she was going to take more time to make discreet checks on everything to do with the rebels. Now, though, she needed to concentrate on the diplomatic tasks she was carrying out with the Keplerians. She wanted to speak to Khikhya as soon as possible to warn her about the problem posed by Captain Garth's rebels.

Rakesh pointed to the logo in the center of the transport vehicle. "Why does it say *Copernicus* on that mule?"

"It's one of the survivors of the attempt on the old space station," she explained. "It's come with us ever since we landed on the planet. It's survived an attempt, an act of sabotage, an accident and a rebellion."

The anthropologist was clearly impressed. "Well, well, she's a real survivor."

"She certainly is. I'm getting quite fond of her. It helps me think that if she can survive, so can we."

When they landed, she and Rakesh checked that the reconditioning works on the base were making good progress.

"We think that in a few days' time you'll all be able to go back to the base," Director Patel announced. As usual, he was directing the work in person.

"That's great!" Emily said.

"And this time we're going to install the communications system more securely so that Ada can modulate the power and avoid those problems with the fog of the area."

They set off along the path to the Keplerian village, together with the mule and the bulky gifts, which had been wrapped in plastic to prevent anyone seeing what was inside. Over the past few days, to avoid falling into the river, they had used the same system as Shildii, a wooden walkway. However, the mule, with all the cargo it was carrying, could easily prove a problem and break the wood with its weight.

So it was a real surprise to see that in spite of the load, the mule was able to cross the three meters between one stepping stone and the next without even taking a run-up.

"Not a day passes when technology surprises me with something new," Rakesh said as they tried unsuccessfully to keep up with it on their way across the river.

Just as Yisht had promised, a four-wheeled cart was waiting for them on the riverbank. It was pulled by four animals and covered with cloth, like the ones which had been used in the old American West.

Emily and Rakesh went to the cart and greeted the two scruffy-looking Keplerians who were driving it. One of them got off using a block of wood which acted as a step. The mule climbed on to this, then up to the cart, without any assistance. Immediately the cart began to creak and screech because of the weight of the cargo. Emily was surprised by the driver's complete lack of expression.

What must this Keplerian be used to seeing, if human technology doesn't surprise him at all? she thought.

They let the cart carrying the mule make its way on while they waited for the soldiers, who, were to escort them to the village as they did every day.

"D'you think the cart will bear up with a load like that?" Rakesh asked.

"Yes. The wood of this planet's a lot tougher, and Yisht seems to know what she's doing."

Punctual as usual, the Keplerian soldiers appeared with their green uniforms and their long spears which looked as though they would have no problem skewering a bear. After picking Shildii up from his home, they went on along the path toward the village center. This time the boy did not ask Emily about his piece of cake, and she certainly did not want to mention the subject.

They found Yisht waiting for them at the door.

"Has the cart arrived?" Emily asked.

"Yes, it came a little while ago. What do we need to do with what's inside it?"

"Look for some out-of-the-way place where we can leave a box the size I told you yesterday."

"I think I have it. Beside the cellar, in the basement, there's a small room that's not in use. Years ago, other leaders used it to store their fancies. Today it's not used for anything and it's always locked."

"Will it get in through the door?"

"I hope so."

The four of them went along a corridor to the back of the building. There, in a small inner courtyard, beside the trunk of the huge, thousand-year-old tree which sheltered the building, was a small round space to enable supply carts to turn. The two drivers were waiting patiently to unload.

Emily gave the appropriate orders to the mule, which got down from the cart away from prying eyes. Both Shildii and Yisht, were impressed by the way the mechanical mule began to move and clear the various obstacles.

"What is that animal?" Shildii asked.

"It's not an animal," Emily said. "It's a mechanical mule. It's used for moving things from one place to another."

Shildii was obviously impressed. "It's as if the cart and the draft animals had had a child."

Emily laughed. "Actually, you have a point there."

They led it through various doors, rooms and corridors until they reached the basement, which Yisht opened with a huge metal key. The mule went into the room and unloaded the huge package it was carrying, with the help of Emily and Rakesh's exosuits. Once Emily had put aside two smaller packages, one the size of a backpack and the other smaller, she began to unpack the largest.

"What is this?" Shildii asked curiously.

"This," Emily explained, "is a food creator."

"A food creator?" he asked in amazement.

"I'll explain how it works. Here, in this little square, a list will appear with everything this machine can make. Ada has written it in your language so that you can understand it. All you have to do is put your finger on the option you want and the food will appear through this little door at the side. We've made you a list of foods we hope you'll like, among them the chocolate cake."

Shildii, who could not help opening his eyes wide at this, began to hop up and down in delight. Yisht was very intrigued by how the device worked.

"Shildii, would you like to do the honors?"

"Of course I would!"

The boy looked carefully at the screen and immediately identified and selected the chocolate cake. At once the machine set to work on the order, and in a few seconds an appetizing piece of chocolate cake appeared at the side door.

Yisht stared at it in astonishment. "I didn't know humans had machines for making food."

"This machine can make more than two thousand kinds of foods out of just one load of raw material," Emily explained. "Once the load runs out, we'll have to bring you more and put it inside the machine."

"I think I understand," said Yisht. "If it stops delivering food, we ask you for more,"

"That's right."

Yisht pointed to the mule. "Do you want the cart to take that… that thing back?"

"Yes, if it's not too much trouble. Have them leave it in the same spot they picked it up, and it'll make its way back to our village by itself."

"All right. It's hard to believe it can go back on its own."

Emily picked up the other package. "I don't want to pry, but could we go to your house?"

"Of course, no problem. Do I assume this is my gift?" she asked nervously.

"Yes, that's right."

All four of them went up to the upper floor of the building and turned to one side. Following a long corridor, they came at last to a small wooden door which Yisht opened with a much smaller key. Behind the door all they found was a small room with a bed and an irregular mattress. A wooden closet and a small desk with a chair completed the austere space where the girl rested from her work. It was a very simple, practical bedroom, with hardly any decoration or superfluous luxuries. Emily left the package on the bed and took off the dark plastic which covered it.

"This is a terminal," Emily explained. "It's the way we humans check information or talk among ourselves or with Ada." She turned and watched Yisht. "As you said you sometimes felt a little lonely the other day, I thought Ada could be company for you."

Yisht looked at the gift and suddenly burst into tears. The young Keplerian, deeply touched, hugged Emily in a spontaneous show of affection which caught her by surprise, but she returned the embrace without hesitating.

It looks as though hugging's something universal, she thought.

"Thank you, Emily," she said with sincere gratitude. "No-one has ever given me anything as a present."

Shildii was anxious to see it in action. "How does it work?"

"It's very much like the terminal Rakesh and I have in our suits. Yisht will learn to use it over time, but for the moment just asking Ada for things will be enough. You have access to all human history, as well as information about the different species of our planet and our solar system."

"Wow," Yisht said. She was still in a state of shock. "I don't know what to say. It's a really nice gift."

"Come on, try it," Rakesh urged her.

"Ada?" she called shyly.

"Hello, Yisht," they heard. "I'm looking forward to talking to you."

"And so am I."

"Ada, show us Earth," Emily said.

From the terminal came a hologram which showed the Earth as it had been when they had left it, so many years ago now.

"It's very beautiful," Yisht said.

"Yes, it really is," Rakesh agreed.

"And last but not least," Emily went on, "the third gift."

She handed over the last of the packages, a box less than half a meter across, to Shildii, who looked at it blankly.

"Come on, open it," she said encouragingly.

The young Keplerian used his sharp claws to strip away the plastic around his gift. Inside was a box.

"What's this?"

"You have to open the box," Emily explained. She showed him how to do it with a gesture.

Shildii managed to raise the lid of the box. Inside was a small device with a screen and some buttons.

"What's this?"

"It's a toy. To be exact, a system of holographic videogames. It's not the latest thing in human technology, but I thought virtual reality might be too much for the Keplerians. I'll show you how it works. You have to turn it on by pressing this button here."

The moment she pressed the 'on' button music sounded, and the holographic projector showed the main menu for the videogame system.

"There are thousands of games in it, except that I'm afraid none of them is in your language. I think you'll get used to it, and at least you'll be able to play plenty of the ones in it." Shildii was very touched at the sight of the huge list of games he was going to be able to play.

"To select one you have to use these buttons here. And… well, I guess you'll learn how to use it by yourself."

"Thank you, Emily," he said happily.

Back in the study, Yisht asked them what they wanted to talk about that morning. She was still so overcome that her voice was a little unsteady.

"Tell us about the other Keplerian villages," Emily said.

"What would you like to know?"

"I don't know, everything. Who are their leaders?"

"The leader of the Khaavahki is called Vaahur. He's a pretty formidable Keplerian, I suppose like most soldiers. Khikhya thinks he's too anxious for power. His predecessors were much more restrained in their politics, more ready for dialogue. He's more a Keplerian of action.

"The leader of the Khapabir, the village where I was born, is called Khaaÿ. He's a Keplerian almost as old as Khikhya. His way of doing politics is old-school, very much like Khikhya's. They get along quite well, but that's not true of Vaahur."

"Has there been any conflict between them?" Rakesh asked.

"Not yet, but everyone knows Vaahur is keen to regain sole command of the Keplerians, it's just a matter of time before he takes steps to try it."

The anthropologist was immediately interested. "Sole command?"

"Many years ago, in a very different epoch, the governance of all the Keplerian villages fell on the Gaal-El. In those times the Keplerians were more spiritual, they followed the ancient cults of worship, and of course they prayed to the gods to free us from the Khol. But time went by and the Keplerian people lost their faith. I suppose we learnt to live under a constant threat. The Gaal-El lost power and an ancient Khaavahki leader claimed power over all the Keplerian villages for himself. He rose above the others thanks to his military superiority and made all the Keplerians believe they would have to rise against their oppressors if they wanted to gain their freedom. How wrong they were.

"The Keplerian people spent years preparing for the confrontation and rose against the Khol, but they were massacred ruthlessly. From the ashes of the villages rose new leaders, but no-one wanted to be under the rule of any of the other clans, so each of them chose new leaders, four Keplerians who would represent their fellow-citizens. For many years peace and concord reigned, and we rose from the ashes.

"But history always repeats itself, and Vaahur is known to be unscrupulous. All he wants is power over everything. If it weren't for the size and technology of the Khapabir people, he'd have tried to rule over us all long ago."

"Technology?" Emily asked.

"Yes, we Khapabir… I mean the Khapabir," she corrected herself, "are a very inquisitive people, with a long scientific tradition. They don't have mules like humans, but they have carriages that move without animals. If it weren't for that technology and the charisma of their leader Khaaÿ, Vaahur would be the owner of all this now."

"Did you say carriages that move without animals?" Emily asked.

She smiled. "Yes, they're worth seeing. One day I hope to show you the village where I was born…"

Suddenly there came the sound of a growing hubbub from the street. Then muffled screams and many synchronized footsteps coming closer. Soon the sound reached them from the ground floor of the building.

"What's happening?" Yisht asked in surprise. "What's all that noise?"

"It sounds as if it's coming from downstairs," said Shildii

The footsteps were coming closer all the time. There seemed to be a lot of them, too many to mean anything good. The door of the study opened with a bang and a dozen Keplerian soldiers armed with halberds and wearing metal cuirasses came into the room in perfect coordination. They surrounded the table and pointed their spears at Emily and Rakesh.

While Shildii screamed in fear and Yisht seemed baffled by what was happening, Emily was weighing up the threat. There were ten soldiers, considerably better armed and protected than those who escorted them every morning. Their spears looked robust, but they had serious doubts about whether a spear like that would be able to pierce the tough material of the exosuits at that distance. Even so, she understood that outside the study, or even outside the building, there would be plenty of soldiers waiting, so she decided not to put them to the test.

Rakesh got up from his chair and raised his hands.

"I think there's been some mistake here," he said.

Immediately ten halberds were turned to point in his direction with their sharp tips mere centimeters from his neck, so he decided to sit down again without making any abrupt movement. At that moment they heard calm footsteps approaching the study.

Through the door came an adult Keplerian, wearing clothes that reminded them of formal military uniform. It was made very clear that there were high-ranking officers in the Keplerian army, and this was undoubtedly one of them. He was wearing a long, elegant, dark blue jacket fastened with silver buttons and an equally elegant matching threaded cord hanging from his neck, like the *wiijiib thiipiar* Khikhya had given them.

"Colonel Lajlab is addressing you," he announced, "A few days ago it came to our ears that the Wiikhaadiiz ofiz were receiving foreigners inside their quarters. At first I refused to believe it. When all's said and done, who could even imagine that one of our own people would be capable of collaborating with a foreigner? Don't we have enough of those already?" By now he was pacing the room with small steps. "But General Vaahur insisted that we should check all the possible threats which endanger our society.

"And here I am, unable to get over my astonishment at finding that Khikhya's pupil, with the obvious connivance of her leader, has not only contacted these foreigners but also invited them to her table and provided them with information about our village and our customs."

"But you see," Yisht began nervously, "I'm sure Khikhya will be able to explain everything when she comes back. I…"

The colonel raised a hand to stop her.

"It's not necessary for Khikhya to explain anything. This is certainly an offense of high treason, which is punishable in our legal system with life imprisonment."

Emily got up from her chair at once, so that the ten soldiers surrounding the table aimed their weapons at her neck. All the same, neither she nor the colonel flinched at their quick reaction.

"Colonel," she said, "we're deeply sorry if we've broken any of your laws. As you may understand, we aren't familiar with them as yet. But I would like to exonerate Khikhya and her assistant. We were the ones who asked for an audience, so we should be the ones who face that punishment, always assuming it's after a fair trial."

"Fair trial?" the colonel spat out. "Do you think you have some kind of right here, you foreigner? I could execute you on the spot and nothing would happen. Do you think I'd hesitate for a moment? One order from me and my soldiers would pierce that metal cuirass of yours as though it were a sheet of paper."

Emily did not know what to say. She did not want to test the exosuit's ability to repel the attack of ten experienced soldiers, especially in one of the most sensitive parts of the human body.

He turned to Yisht, "As for you, I'm afraid you're going to have to come with us."

"She doesn't move from here," Emily said firmly.

The colonel stared at her incredulously. "I beg your pardon? Don't tempt fate, foreigner. I wouldn't like there to be a bloodbath here today, but my advice to you would be not to try my patience too far."

"This is Khikhya's house," Shildii put in, emboldened.

"Be careful, young man. Until then you were passing unnoticed, because you're completely irrelevant. I suggest you keep quiet if you don't want to suffer the same fate as this traitor."

And with a stare of utter disdain toward Yisht, he added:

"Take her!"

The two soldiers behind Yisht moved their spears aside, seized her by her arms and raised her from the chair almost without effort. Yisht, panic-stricken, barely resisted. She would spend the rest of her life in a mine, extracting valuable minerals to deliver to the Khol

The colonel turned back to Emily and Rakesh. "As for you two, get out of here and never come back, or else…"

He stopped in mid-sentence because another disturbance could be heard downstairs. There seemed to be a problem of some sort, accompanied by a heated discussion.

"Am I not going to be able to finish a single sentence without these constant interruptions?" the colonel roared.

Footsteps, accompanied by the dull thud of wood against the floor, were approaching from the stairs.

"The cheek of it!" they heard in the distance. "Making an old woman climb stairs in my state."

Everyone in the study waited attentively for the arrival of the Keplerian voice which was voicing the complaints.

"What the hell do you think you're doing, Lajlab?" Khikhya asked the moment she came into the study.

"Enforcing the laws of our people."

The leader of the Wiikhaadiiz ofiz looked at him serenely "I see. Enlighten us, in that case. What law precisely has been broken here?"

"Your assistant was collaborating with these foreigners, revealing secrets of Keplerian society."

She turned to Yisht. "Is that true? What secrets have you revealed to them?"

"I… I was only teaching them to read."

"Well, well, well! This sounds like a very serious crime. We'll have to arrest all the teachers in every school in the city."

"Save the sarcasm," the colonel snorted. "According to our laws it's forbidden to collaborate with foreigners."

Khikhya banged the floor with her ceremonial staff. "Don't talk to me about laws! Those laws were created so that unscrupulous Keplerians like your leader wouldn't collaborate with the Khol. And they say explicitly that it's forbidden to collaborate with a Khol. Tell me, Colonel, can you see any Khol around here?"

The colonel did not answer.

"You may have won the battle," he hissed after a moment, "but sooner or later you'll end up making a mistake."

"I have no doubt your master is anxious for that to happen," Khikhya said disdainfully. "And now, if you'll allow us, you can all go and present my respects to your lord Vaahur, but my guests and I have important matters to deal with."

"Let's get out of here!" the colonel growled.

He turned toward the door, but before leaving the room he turned back toward the table and added:

"As for you two, you'd better not come anywhere near this place again. Perhaps Leader Khikhya has control in Wiikhaadiiz ofiz for the moment, but we Khaavahki rule the rest of the territory. My advice to you would be to be very careful with what you're doing."

"Thank you, Khikhya," Yisht whispered once all the soldiers had left the building.

"Don't worry, child. Under no circumstances would I have allowed those bastards to arrest you."

"Everything happened so fast…" Emily said regretfully.

Khikhya looked at her in surprise. "Well, well, it looks as though you both learn very fast, you almost speak like a Keplerian now."

"Yisht has helped us a lot," Rakesh admitted.

Khikhya sighed. "I suppose this wasn't the way I was intending to come back home after a long journey." She looked at Emily. "We have a lot to talk about."

"Yes, we want to talk to you as well."

"But I'm afraid I'm too tired for all that. My body isn't as resilient as it used to be. My joints are old and feeble, and not many days go by when they don't hurt. I think I'm going to need a good rest."

"Of course," Emily said. "We'll wait."

"Still, we can't deny what we've just seen. That vulture Vaahur is anxious to take advantage of any hint of weakness in the other villages to find an excuse to seize sole command of the Keplerians. And I'm not prepared to allow that."

She was thoughtful for a few moments, weighing up all the options which flooded into her mind all at once. There was no-one like her when it came to dealing with the intrigues of the Keplerian peoples.

"I think, she began, "that at least for the moment we need to be more cautious about these meetings. Go back to your village, both of you, if you don't mind. Someone I trust entirely will contact you in a few days' time. I need to arrange everything with the utmost care. Difficult times are coming for the Keplerian people, and we're going to have to go into the eye of the hurricane itself."

25
Reinauguration

October 6, Year 0
Magellan Base, Kepler-442b

Emily was anxious to get back to the base, but she was aware of a certain unease in the station which did not help in the least with the normal activity of the expedition. Several days had gone by since her last visit to Wiikhaadiiz ofiz and there was still no news from the Keplerians. Director Patel was going to be on the alert in case any of Khikhya's associates approached the base, but so far no-one had come near it.

To pass the time she had been checking Ada's correct functioning. Without attracting too much attention, she had taken the opportunity to look for some clue which might indicate that one or other of the ship's systems had been interfered with. But so far she had found nothing in the auxiliary systems she had been through.

The good news, and the only thing that was giving her some hope, was that she would be going back to the base that same afternoon, and this time there would be a lot more of them. No-one in the team wanted to stay on the station, and practically all of them had expressed their eagerness to get back to work. Still, she knew that morale was not at its best. They had had too many setbacks in a row.

So that after having lunch and then packing her suitcase again she decided to prepare a little surprise to raise everyone's spirits. She got in touch with the deputy director to make arrangements, then went to the cellar and had a word with several workers and gave them the appropriate orders once she had shown them the right permits. Soon she had everything she had come in search of. With the help of those in charge of the cellar, she secured everything on the surviving mule from the Copernicus. Which, it should be said, worked very well in the gravity-free environment of the ship thanks to the hydraulic system of its legs.

With the load safely packed and her suitcase in her hand, all she had left to do was go to the hangar they were to leave from. There was hardly any activity there.

With what's still at the base and what the rebels took, she thought, *the hangar doesn't look the same any more.*

As she went down the ladder to the platform she could hear far more noise than usual. As well as the team, the ten soldiers who protected the base were there. Robert had taken it upon himself to choose the soldiers who would be assigned to the base, many of whom had already served under him in the Copernicus.

"As usual, Emily's the last to arrive!" Chad announced to the four winds as soon as he saw her.

And this time he was absolutely right. She had taken more time than she had expected in the cellar loading the mule and was almost half an hour later than they had arranged. All the people there were already in their exosuits, except that they had not yet put on their helmets.

"I'm sorry. I was running some last-minute errands and I lost track of the time. Am I the last?"

Chad gave a sarcastic laugh. "Yes, and it's always the same when you ask, you're always the last to arrive."

"Except when it's a question of setting foot on planets for the first time," Ferrara pointed out.

"I know, and I'm sorry. This time, at least, it was for a good reason."

"What's that on top of the mule?" Gorka asked. He still had various aches and pains, but he would not have missed the reinauguration of the base for anything in the world.

She shooed the inquisitive intruders away from her. "You just wait and see."

"Everything all right?" Robert asked her when she passed by his side.

"Yeah, fine. I'm going to put my suit on."

She went over to the hangar wall where her exosuit was resting and put it on without bothering about her tightsuit, seeing that she was only going to need it until they landed and went into the base again.

"Start putting on your helmets!" Robert shouted to his subordinates, who obeyed without a word. "Start taking your seats in the shuttle!"

"I'm ready!" Emily said when she came to his side again.

He indicated the mule. "I see you've been very busy."

"Yeah, it's a little surprise. I thought it would be a good idea to do something about the team's battered morale."

"That was a good idea. I feel it too, that all this is taking its toll on us. Anything that distracts us for a while will be welcome."

"I hope this time things'll go better for us down there."

"I'm sure they will."

Once they were all seated and the cargo secured, Balakova the pilot began her usual ritual before the launch of the shuttle.

"How are you?" Paula asked Emily. "These days you've more or less disappeared, and we've barely had the chance to talk."

"I'm fine, thanks. I've had plenty on my mind, but now I'm looking forward to going back."

"Everything all right at the station?"

"Yeah, everything's fine. Bearing in mind what's happened, obviously. I presume you'll all have heard all kinds of rumors about it."

"Yes, no-one's talking about anything else. But it's normal enough, people need to know what's happened. Plenty of them are worried about what might happen from now on."

Emily nodded. "That's understandable. But the only thing we can do right now is get down to work together to get things going. The captain, unfortunately, chose not to see it that way."

"Yeah... that fucking rat..."

"And how are you?" Emily asked her.

"A little sad, I guess. These things affect me where it hurts. I still can't get my head around what they did to Jonathan."

Emily was silent. She too felt much the same. She was very much looking forward to getting back to work, but almost more so that she could forget what had happened than for any other reason.

The transport shuttle landed on the open area in the base. There was still heavy machinery around, together with other shuttles Director Patel's engineers had used to carry supplies and necessary equipment to the facilities.

They got off the ship with their luggage. Emily took charge of leading the mule, which followed her obediently to the base entrance. On the roof of the facilities they saw several technicians completing some last-minute repair job. This time there was no-one outside to welcome them, but they knew the way and the process of decontamination well enough by now.

Once they had all been through this, there was a general disbandment of the group. Chad and Taro went to the lab, Gorka and Kostas to the storeroom, while Private Ferrara gave the new soldiers a short introductory tour. Emily, who was with Evelyn, Rakesh and Paula, got rid of her exosuit and left her luggage in the locker bearing her name, which the engineers had repaired by now. Through the door at the end of the corridor appeared the figure of Director Patel, whose exosuit was connected to the terminal.

"Hello there!" he greeted them with his usual warmth. "Now you're all here, welcome once again." He glanced down at his wrist. "Though you're a little late."

"Hi, Director Patel," Emily said. "I'm afraid it's my fault, as usual."

"It doesn't matter, though this time I wasn't able to come out and give you a proper welcome."

"Everything looks new, Director," Paula said. "You've made a good job of it."

"Thank you, Paula." He pointed to the load on the mule. "But what's all this you've brought?"

Evelyn smiled. "We've no idea. Emily doesn't want to tell us."

"It's a little surprise," Emily explained. "To which you're invited too, by the way."

"Hey, a surprise! Well, I won't say no. Something to raise people's spirits would be very welcome. And anyway, there's not much left to do."

"Great! It's good to have you with us for a while, Director. Is the mess hall ready?"

"Yes, yes. My boys are busy making the final checks and sorting out a small leak of water they found in the dressing-rooms."

"Right," Emily said, "but I'd like to see everyone in the mess hall in an hour."

The director nodded. "Okay."

"All you others, can you lend me a hand with the preparations?"

"Of course we can," said Rakesh.

Paula indicated Evelyn. "You can count on us."

The four of them went to the mess hall. There they were able to see that everything was as it had been on the first day, as if there had been no rebellion, no dismantling of the facilities.

"Can we see what you've got hidden underneath there now?" Paula asked.

"Yes, now you can."

Paula and Rakesh, who looked restless and were smiling nervously, unwrapped the package Emily had prepared with so much love. Immediately she saw the faces of the other three light up.

"This isn't possible!" Paula exclaimed.

"Did we bring all this with us on the station?" Rakesh asked in surprise.

From the extensive list of supplies in the space station, which the deputy director had been jealously keeping secret, Emily had selected a complete set of snacks and aperitifs brought from Earth. There was everything, from popcorn and nuts to little canapés and typical dishes from the cuisines of a range of countries and cultures.

"Hey, look at that!" Evelyn exclaimed as she took a bag of fried snacks. "I used to eat these when I was little. I love them!"

"Pizza!" Paula cried. "We have pizza, all sorts of different types!"

Rakesh was staring at several airtight containers which were carefully labeled. "This one here, is it what I think it is?"

"That's right," Emily admitted. "It's chicken tikka masala."

"And there are samosas too!" the anthropologist said excitedly as he read the labels on the other containers. "But how can all this have survived a trip of almost a thousand years?" he asked incredulously.

"The refrigeration systems on the station could keep food for hundreds of thousands of years," Emily explained, "as long as they work properly, of course. The refrigeration chamber is airtight and automated, so it's impossible to break the conservation chain. It uses a process similar to that of human cryo."

"And there's beer and wine too!" Paula shouted.

"Beer?" they heard Gorka say as he came in through the door at that moment, together with Kostas, Chad and Taro. "What are we missing out on here?"

"Look at everything Emily's brought," Evelyn said.

"Wow!" Chad exclaimed. "Who's getting married? What are we celebrating?"

Emily laughed. "No-one's getting married, as far as I know." She was looking at Paula and Gorka. "I just wanted to celebrate the fact with all of you that we're getting back to work."

"Hey, look! There's even Spanish *jamón ibérico*!" Gorka shouted suddenly.

"Look, Taro, we've got sushi too!" Chad cried delightedly.

"And *dorayakis*!" Taro said, equally excited. "My mother used to buy me those when I was little. I gulped them down in school recess."

Emily felt a deep satisfaction at seeing all the products she had been able to bring to the base causing the effect she had hoped for among her colleagues. She wanted them to feel at home for a single day, but most of all she wanted them to forget the problems that were haunting them all, even if it were only for a couple of hours.

Soon they were joined by the group of soldiers. They had heard the uproar coming from the mess hall and did not hesitate to interrupt Ferrara's tour in order to join the party.

They set out all the snacks on the table, sorted out those dishes that needed warming up, put the barrel of beer in place and opened several bottles of red and white wine. The whole of Director Patel's team of engineers joined the banquet too, until very soon there was no room for anyone else.

"What are we missing?" the director asked when he arrived.

"The best sight you'll have seen since we came to this planet," Gorka said as he took a handful of nuts from the bowl he had just put on the table.

Paula, who had seen this, slapped his hand to make him put them back before he could eat them.

"We haven't started yet," she reminded him sharply.

"Yes, ma'am," he said, smiling broadly, and she had no choice but to smile back.

On the faces of both the soldiers and the engineers who had come with the director, not to mention all those Emily only knew by sight, was a look of sincere hope and enjoyment. Seeing them all, their eyes shining with emotion, was enough to make her pleased and satisfied with what she had organized. She recognized one of the engineers; it was Marko, whom she had known long before, when Director Patel himself had shown the space station to a few people.

"It's quite something, this party you've organized," Robert whispered in her ear.

"I think it was necessary. Look at them, they're having a whale of a time, like a bunch of kids."

He smiled. "They certainly are."

"This'll do us all good. It's important not to lose the sense of why we're doing all this and why we have to make an effort and give it everything we can every day."

"We've all spent months without one single moment to rest."

"Yes, it'll do us good to stop, even if it's just for one day."

"Right, so what are we waiting for?" Gorka asked in a voice which carried.

"Emily ought to say a few words, don't you think?" Robert said. "After all, she's the one who organized all this."

"Yes, Emily!" Chad shouted from the other end of the table. "Say something!"

Soon there was such a tumult that she had no choice but to improvise a short speech.

"In fact I hadn't prepared anything," she began. "This was done on the spur of the moment, actually."

"For something done on the spur of the moment it looks fantastic," Marko said.

"I just wanted to say to all of you, whether we're going to share these facilities or not," Emily began, moved by the expressions on her colleagues' faces, "that as far as I'm concerned you're my brothers and sisters, my family. And that it's a privilege to be able to share all this with every single one of you. And that I wish we could do this a lot more often. And that every single one of the members of this expedition can enjoy this sense of belonging together, regardless of personal egos and disputes, as a single family, as a single being.

"I know many of you don't know me, but thanks to my father I was able to understand at first hand, long before the first ark took off, the motives and moral principles the project was based on. And despite the fact that it's very hard to put them into words, I know they can be summarized well enough by what we're all experiencing here today.

"Different people, with different origins and different cultures, enjoying themselves together around a table. For me that's precisely what this project means, beyond even the consequences it might have for the human race. And before I go on, before we enjoy all this, I'd like to spend a few moments of silence in memory of all our fellow-travelers who've been lost, on whichever expedition and in whatever circumstance. And also for all those we left behind, on Earth."

She and the others kept a few emotional moments of silence in honor of those who could no longer enjoy moments like this one. Then unanimous applause for Emily broke out.

"Thank you!" Ferrara said. Her voice was unsteady.

"A toast to Dr. Rhodes!" Rakesh shouted, raising his glass.

Director Patel seconded this. "Yes, a toast!"

They all raised their glasses and offered her the warmth of their feelings, their affection and their gratitude.

"To Emily!"

"And now we can begin!" Chad said excitedly.

They all fell on the food, which they enjoyed avidly. By then Emily was hungry, having been so absorbed in the preparations she had not been aware of the fact till she took her first bite. There were so many things on the table, it was a complicated business deciding what to choose.

The afternoon went by very fast: too fast, unfortunately. They enjoyed all the food enormously, but above all the company. Emily exchanged one or two words with every one of them and met the new military replacements for the base, who turned out to be considerably nicer and less stiff than Captain Garth's pupils, as well as Director Patel's team of engineers. She was even able to have a chat with Marko, whom she had not spoken to in a very long time.

Exceptionally, the beer and wine flowed freely, until they had finished almost everything she had brought for the occasion. The following morning more than one young soldier would regret having drunk so much. Even Director Patel seemed very cheerful. Everyone, with the exception of the pilots for reasons of safety, drank a little too much. That day the only rule was enjoyment. However, as with everything good, things eventually came to an end.

"That was amazing, Emily," Director Patel said as he got ready to put on his exosuit. "Thank you very much for everything."

"Thank *you*. Everything's looking wonderful."

"Let us know when it's time for the next one," Marko said, laughing. "Except that there are one or two who won't be so keen tomorrow," he added, looking at the engineer in front of him, who could hardly take two steps straight.

Emily said goodbye and prepared to tackle the always unwelcome task of cleaning up the remains of a party involving more than thirty people. There were still a few soldiers and colleagues there dancing to the music from the audio system, draining the last dregs of the day. Chad, who had had one too many, was snoring placidly on the couch in the common area, while Gorka and Sergeant Ortiz were enjoying themselves at his expense.

Taro and Robert picked up the garbage and put it in bags to be recycled.

"I'll help you, guys," Emily said.

"No, you take it easy," Robert said. "Taro and I will take care of it."

Taro nodded. "Yeah, you must be tired after that busy day you've had."

"Don't worry." She began clearing the remains from the end of the table. "I've still got something left in the tank."

Robert handed her one of the bags so that she could collect the garbage. "That was amazing."

"It was, wasn't it? I think it was a good idea."

"That's true, we need to remember to enjoy life as well."

"Well, yes, we never know what'll happen tomorrow, so we have to live each moment as if it were our last."

Both of them looked into one another's eyes. Emily felt an inexplicable desire to kiss him. Her pulse began to beat faster and she could feel perspiration on her hands. Still, despite the excess of alcohol, she had to hold back. There were too many people in the mess hall to unleash everything she had spent so long repressing all this time. They both looked down shyly

Some day… sooner rather than later, I hope… she thought.

26
The visit

October 7, Year 0
Magellan Base, Kepler-442b

That morning was a little atypical for all of them. The previous night's excesses had taken their toll on many of the members of the expedition. Tiredness, hoarseness, headaches and a pill or two to soften the hangover were the norm among those who wandered the base in the early hours of the morning.

But little by little, activity began to return at the base after the hard days of reconditioning and exile on the space station. Everyone knew very well what they had to do, and in most cases it was almost a question of starting from scratch, as was made clear during the usual quick morning briefing.

Kostas began his work in the greenhouses all over again. Taro and Chad, though they had lost most of the samples they had in store, tried to get back to the exact point where they had left their studies so that they could go on with them. Paula and Gorka, who was fit enough to get back to work by now, checked the base from top to bottom to certify that all systems were functioning correctly. Evelyn and Sergeant Ortiz organized the infirmary. Robert and Ferrara set rosters to establish watch duties and make the usual tours of inspection of the surroundings. Rakesh more or less locked himself in one of the rooms to go deeply into the bibliography he had compiled from his meetings with Yisht. Ada's process of digitization was simple, but they had too much information to catalog and digest.

As for Emily, she had decided to do something she ought perhaps to have done the day before, on arrival. She put on her exosuit and went outside. Ferrara was there, wandering around with a small group of soldiers and inspecting the immediate surroundings. Kostas was taking his research material out of the storeroom so that he could restore the plantations, which had been left useless. She went a little further into one of the most densely-planted areas, never losing sight of the base.

There she looked for some striking colors amid the red sea formed by the vegetation of the area. It did not take her long to find plenty of white and violet flowers. She picked a few of them and arranged them very carefully in a bouquet. Then she went to the spot where they had buried Jonathan Wiśniewski a few days before and left them on top of the little mound of earth they had piled on the spot. Then she knelt down on the grass.

"Rest in peace, Jonathan," she whispered. "I hope that at least your son managed to survive and have a full life."

She was silent for a moment, then went back to the base, where she joined Rakesh in his analysis of the recordings and the information they had put together about the Keplerians.

"It's a pity we can't communicate with them from afar," Rakesh said sadly.

"Oh, but actually we can! Via the gift we gave Yisht."

"Well then, why don't we speak to her from here?"

"Because we've just had an insurrection. And we're still not sure whether our coms are compromised. I'm very much afraid that until things get clearer we'll need to take it for granted that someone unwanted could be monitoring everything we do or say."

"I get you," said Rakesh. "Well, it's pretty annoying. I'd like to go deeper into so many things about their society that I'm not sure how long I can put up with going over the material we have."

"Write down everything you want to discuss with Yisht or Khikhya. Although something tells me this sort of blockage could go on for quite some time."

"In all societies, politics is at the same time the source of the solutions and the focus of the problems," Rakesh said resignedly. "And as far as I can see, we're establishing that that's a universal truth."

"It certainly doesn't just seem a human problem."

Suddenly Ferrara, who was still outside with part of the detachment, interrupted them via the radio.

"Emily you have a visitor."

"Who? Shildii?"

"Yes, it's him, but this time he's not alone, there's some other Keplerian with him. "I can't see who it is, he or she is wearing a kind of hooded cloak and we can't see their face."

"Okay, we'll go right away."

"Understood. We'll take up defensive positions."

Emily and Rakesh went to the suit terminals and got ready to go outside.

"Ada, why didn't you warn us they were approaching?" she asked.

"I'm having trouble communicating on certain bandwidths," the AI explained. "That's affecting communications with the beacons and sensors across the area. Paula's checking it."

"What a coincidence that these things should happen just when visitors are coming," Emily complained as they got into their exosuits.

Once outside, they went over to Shildii and his mysterious companion. When they reached them the unknown figure pushed back its hood. Emily and Rakesh recognized Shyilru, the Keplerian counselor who had accompanied Khikhya when they had met for the first time.

"Hello, Emily and Rakesh," she greeted them, with a grimace which suggested that she was not very comfortable with the task she had been given. "Do you remember me?"

"Yes," Emily said warmly. "Hello, Shyilru."

"Khikhya would like to speak with you," she said very seriously. "All the same, because of her age we thought she shouldn't cross the river. She asked me to come over to find you and take you to her, if you think that's all right."

"Of course. Take us to her."

"These are days of upheaval," she added as she offered them two outfits like the one she herself was wearing. "The intrusion of the Khaavahki the other day has shaken up Keplerian diplomacy completely. I'm afraid from now on we'll have to be as discreet as possible."

Emily took the cloaks Khikhya's assistant was holding out to them. "Oh dear, I'm really sorry to hear that."

She and Rakesh put on the cloaks, which turned out to cover them completely.

"Right, follow me."

"Ferrara," Emily called, "we're leaving the base."

"Do you want us to follow you?"

"Negative, it's one of Khikhya's people of trust. But tell Lieutenant Beaufort."

"Copy that, we'll listen out on the radio,"

"Thanks, Ferrara."

They went back to the river to cross to the other side. However, this time, no sooner had they crossed it than they took a different path, toward the northwest and the mountain.

"Where are we going?" Emily asked.

"Nearby," Shyilru replied briefly.

Emily assumed that she was not very talkative, or perhaps she was not pleased that the humans had got on so well with Khikhya. As they went on the idea occurred to her that this might be a trap, but she tried not to think about that too much.

They had been walking for nearly four kilometers when at last they saw a small hut among the trees in the distance, in the middle of nowhere. To judge by its appearance it had not been inhabited for a very long time. There was nothing else around: no other cabins, nor the slightest trace of anything that suggested civilization. The underbrush had reclaimed its own space around the dark timber of the old hut.

Outside was a wooden carriage, but with no decoration on it at all, far more derelict than the one in which they had seen Khikhya for the first time. The driver was resting absent-mindedly in front, while the draft animals, which thanks to Yisht's previous lessons they now knew were called *fhores,* were enjoying the tender reddish shoots which poked up through grass and huge fallen leaves.

"Khikhya is waiting inside." Shyilru motioned them to enter the cabin.

Emily and Rakesh were about to go into the hut, but just before they could do so Rakesh gripped her arm.

"Wait," he said. "Let me go first, just in case."

He opened the door carefully and went into the hut. A few moments later he came out again.

"It's safe. Khikhya's inside."

Emily crossed the threshold. It was very dark inside, but that did not seem to bother those who were there. Khikhya was sitting in a rather rickety wooden armchair with her two other assistants standing behind her, one on either side.

"Hello, Emily and Rakesh," the old lady said.

"Hello," they both replied warmly.

"I hope you'll forgive this pantomime. Do you understand the word?"

Rakesh nodded. "Yes, we do."

"Good, I know Yisht has taught you well." Looking at her two bodyguards, she added: "Leave us alone."

The Keplerians left the hut obediently.

She waved at two armchairs like her own. "Please sit down, because if you don't, this poor old woman's neck is going to hurt with all this looking up."

They brought their chairs closer and sat in front of her, only a meter away.

"I have to admit that when Shildii's mother got in touch with me I had serious doubts about going anywhere near that clearing," the old woman began. "I knew meeting another intelligent species was going to involve all sorts of problems and challenges. But seeing how nervous some Keplerian leaders have started to be, I know now I was right to welcome you."

Emily and Rakesh looked at her in puzzlement, not very clear about what problems she meant.

"I'll be honest," she went on, "Keplerian politics has been fragile for some time now, and any misstep could easily shake our society to the foundations. Vaahur is keen to gain total control over the Keplerians and has spent years trying to destabilize the governments of the other villages. The moron thinks that because of my age I'm going to start acting rather less determinedly.

"We Keplerians have been a resilient people since time immemorial, we're too stubborn. We've lived for too long under the yoke of the Khol not to recognize a despot when we see one. He wants to install a dictatorship under his command, under the pretext of defending the people from our common enemy. Khaaÿ and I myself are the only obstacles which stand in his way. But I'm not stupid, I have more years on my back than I ever thought I'd have, and I know I haven't very much time left. And I fear that when Khaaÿ and I are no longer here the regional governments will fall one after the other under the power of the Khaavahki army."

"But you have soldiers too, surely?" Emily interrupted her.

"Soldiers who are trained by Vaahur's trusted subordinates. That asslicker Lajlab, whom you had the dubious honor of meeting the other day, is one of them. No, I wouldn't count on the support of the soldiers of any of the large villages. And besides, Vaahur has a better intelligence network among my very own people. As you were able to see, I can't have a meeting with any guarantee of freedom in my own house. The Khaavahki have ears and eyes everywhere, so that there are only a few Keplerians I can trust.

"I had to let a few days go by so that his spies would lower their guard and I could meet with you. Time is pressing, but we can't risk an open, public war." She paused briefly. "As you know, I visited the Gaal-El. They're the custodians of our knowledge, those who for thousands of years have been in charge of conserving our history. You could say that in times gone by they were the main pillar of our civilization. A very long time ago, many generations, long, long before the Great Revolt, they were the leaders of Keplerian society. At the time their village was the largest and most prosperous of all. Everything was decided and managed from there.

"Their cult goes back to far beyond what any book written by a Keplerian could tell us. Ever since Keplerian society has existed, we've always been under the bloodthirsty yoke of the Khol. The cult of the Gaal-El foretold the advent of savior gods from the skies and the liberation of the Keplerians. And whimsical fate has decided that your people come from the sky with those same flying ships. You can understand that in our situation that's something we can't ignore."

Emily had to interrupt once again. "But I'm afraid there must be a mistake. We're not here to save the Keplerian people. We didn't even know of your existence until a few weeks ago."

"I know that, young Emily. But the Gaal-El still believe in those ancient prophecies, and though it might not seem so, out of sheer despair many Keplerians wish to believe, need to believe. Perhaps your arrival could provoke an unprecedented union of the Keplerian people that will make us stronger, not against the Khol now, but at least against our own internal enemies."

"You see, Khikhya," Rakesh said, "I've devoted my whole life to the study of human cults and beliefs. From what little I've been able to find out about the Gaal-El, their cult meets every single one of the characteristics of any human religion. In the dawn of civilization, cults and religions emerged to provide a rational explanation for the mysteries of nature. For younger civilizations it's a widespread way of explaining meteorological phenomena or planetary physics. In the case of the Gaal-El, the existence of a superior species like the Khol could have been the detonator that allowed the ancient Keplerians to keep their hopes and their eagerness to survive.

"In many cases the cults and religions themselves became a mechanism of control through which a few might keep some order and prosperity within their own societies. However, as those societies advanced and prospered, it was the institutions of state that took over the role of providing that prosperity. That's the moment when religions lose their exclusive claim to morality, and hence gradually lose their reason for existence, and in most cases end by disappearing completely or remaining as something in the background, hardly more than a set of stories. Everything we've heard about this cult points in that direction, to the fact that someone long ago decided to invent a story which showed a divine being coming to save the Keplerians from their oppressors. The fact that we happen to be here is simply a coincidence."

The old woman had been listening carefully to the anthropologist. At last she spoke.

"Now, you see, Rakesh, I'd obviously be lying if I said I was a fervent believer in the ancient prophecies. And though I accept that lately I've been thinking about it a lot, at this moment I'm not interested in the belief itself or in its truth. I'm far more interested in the unity something like this could come to create in Keplerian society."

"But in a way that would be deceiving your fellow citizens, giving them false hopes," Rakesh objected.

"Maybe so, but you more than anyone will know that the individuals of a society need to be led, like a flock. That flock is what enables them to survive attacks by predators. More than that, it'll always be better to have a false hope than none whatever. Otherwise it could cause Keplerians like Vaahur to rise up and take control of society through populism for their own benefit.

"In a way isn't hope the reason why we're all here? You're looking to settle in a new home, and some Keplerians have the hope that they can prevent our people falling into the hands of a tyrant." Emily and Rakesh were silent. "And I would imagine that at the moment you're wondering why I'm admitting my deepest thoughts and intentions in advance."

Emily was very surprised to realize that this was just what she herself had been thinking. It was not usual for leaders like Khikhya to show their cards at the start of the game.

"I don't want to deceive you," she went on. "Ever since I saw you in that clearing I had the impression that you were people I could trust. I don't know the real reasons why you're here, but I sense that your intentions are noble and that our two peoples might be able to collaborate and grow together. Although the real reason is that I hate people trying to manipulate me, so I prefer to be direct. Above all when I need to beg for favors."

"Favors?" Emily repeated.

"Yes. I'd like to ask you to travel to the village of the Gaal-El. Knowing what you know, you can imagine the look on their leader Waafdiv's face when I told him about you. Let's say that no Gaal-El leader has ever found himself in a position like that in the last few thousand years, perhaps never. There's no need to tell you how eager he is to meet you."

Emily and Rakesh looked at one another, not understanding the nature of the favor.

"We'll be delighted to meet the Gaal-El," Emily asked, intrigued, "but what does the favor involve?"

"You're going to have to travel by ways that are dangerous and little-used," the old lady went on. "As I told you, the Khaavahki have eyes everywhere, which means you'll have to avoid busy areas and perhaps face danger, even death."

"I see," Emily said thoughtfully, "but even so, we'll need to know the exact location of the Gaal-El village."

"Their monastery is on the slopes of the northern mountains, at a great height. The usual road leads there and crosses a narrow pass which leads to the village. However, you won't be going by that way. You'll be using an ancient path which starts on the other side of the river. You'll pass the great waterfall and climb the mountain until you can go down into the little valley the village is in. The weather conditions won't be the best, of course, but it's the only route to the Gaal-El that doesn't require crossing the mountain pass. The Khaavahki have been very busy these last days and patrols and checkpoints have increased. Vaahur's trying to intimidate us so that we can't form alliances, which would ruin his plans."

"We'll need directions of some sort to get there," Emily reminded her.

"Don't worry about that, I'm not going to send you on your own. Yisht will be going with you. My dear assistant needs to see the real world, it'll do her good to get out of the bureaucratic spiral I introduced her to myself." The old lady gave them a mischievous smile. "Anyway, she doesn't know the way either, but she'll take you to someone who does."

"A guide of some sort?" Rakesh asked.

"Something like that," Khikhya said enigmatically. "Let's say he's a Keplerian who prefers to live in solitude, but who knows all the ways of the place. Very few Keplerians know of the existence of this road."

"Not even Vaahur?" Emily asked.

"Hah!" She laughed with gusto. "That bastard only worries about getting hold of the power he doesn't have. He wouldn't be able to find his own shit after he'd defecated. He's a very dangerous Keplerian, don't misunderstand me, but he hasn't come down from his imaginary throne since he was chosen leader of the Khaavahki."

"And this solitary Keplerian, will he help just like that?" Emily asked.

"Yes, don't worry about that, he'll help. He's an old curmudgeon, but he'll help you if I ask him to."

"All right, then," Emily said. "When do we leave?"

"In four days. I'll arrange everything so that Yisht goes to your village and you'll all leave from there. It'll take you a couple of days to get there and a couple more to come back." She pointed to their exosuits. "I hope those won't be an impediment in the circumstances."

"We'll have to prepare the journey, certainly," Emily said. "But there won't be any problem if we can take the supplies we'll need."

"Perfect. I'll arrange everything within four days. Thank you for everything."

"And thank you, Khikhya. Still, I'd like to pass on some important information to repay you for your honesty and trust."

"Of course. I'm all ears."

"Let's just say human politics, like religions, aren't too different from Keplerian ones," Emily began. "Our ship is outside the planet. The village we come from is only a sort of human outpost with only a few of us living there. What's happened is that a few days ago there was a rebellion in our society. A soldier, like Vaahur, by the name of Tyson Garth, stole weapons and equipment from our ship and has set himself up somewhere unknown on this planet. We have no idea where he and his followers could be, but I'd like to warn you that he's very dangerous and unpredictable."

Khikhya thought carefully about what she had just heard.

"I'm grateful for your honesty. And to judge by the tone of your voice, I'd imagine it's a very real threat."

"Yes, it certainly is."

"I am glad you've shared this with me. That does a lot to explain the rumors I've been hearing lately. They were extremely disturbing ones."

"What rumors?"

"It's come to my knowledge, through my trusted people in Khaavahki, that Vaahur has been meeting with some mysterious foreigners, I was hoping it wasn't you playing a dangerous double game. But now I think everything is beginning to fit together."

Knowing that Captain Garth had now begun to make a move on the Keplerian political board, Emily was petrified. There was no doubt that he was smarter than she had taken him to be and had realized the importance of having allies in unknown territory.

"Do you think they might have come to some sort of agreement?"

"It's more than likely," Khikhya said. "Although bearing in mind the moral worthlessness of both of them, it wouldn't surprise me if each of them had their own plans and ended up stabbing one another in the back. What really concerns me is that they might drag us all into a destructive spiral when we're on the eve of another visit from the Khol. The Keplerian people need unity to face up to the Levy. Anyway, I'll share all the information I can get hold of about these human rebels with you."

"We're very grateful, Khikhya."

"All right then. If you have nothing else to say, I think we can bring our little clandestine meeting to an end."

"Actually, I would like to ask you something."

"Of course, my dear. Ask whatever you like."

"Well, as I told you, our ship is outside the planet, in space. Still, another of our ships should have arrived here several years ago. The thing is that when we arrived, it wasn't where it should have been and we don't know what might have happened to it. When Yisht mentioned the Khol I was very worried, thinking they might have destroyed our other ship. But when I asked her whether we were the first humans the Keplerians had seen, she didn't know what to say. So I'd like to ask you, as Keplerian leader, whether during your leadership or those of your predecessors, the Keplerians have ever met other humans."

"Oh dear, I'm truly sorry you lost that ship," Khikhya said. "It must be a horrible feeling. But I'm afraid you're the first of your species to come to this planet. I'd never ever heard of humans before, either from other leaders or from my predecessor. And I'd go as far as to say he'd never heard anything from his. I'm sure something as important as that would have been worth mentioning, or at least would have been recorded in some document. Although if there's anyone who could have had knowledge of the presence of humans in the past, it would certainly be the Gaal-El."

27
The clandestine meeting

October 8, Year 0
Magellan Base, Kepler-442b

"There's a lot we need to arrange," Robert said.

"Yes, but honestly, I don't think any of you need to come," Emily insisted. "I mean, I'd love you to come with us, but I trust Khikhya. I think she herself knows she needs us more than we need her."

"It's not up for discussion," he said stubbornly. "Ferrara and I are coming with you. I'm not going to leave your safety in the hands of a bureaucrat and an aged hermit."

"Okay then." She felt a certain relief knowing that Robert would be coming with them on their trip to the Gaal-El village.

"There'll be four of us," he said, "which means we'll have to get a couple of mules ready with enough oxygen and supplies for the whole journey."

"And we'll have to go in our suits several times," Emily pointed out.

"Don't worry about that. We'll follow a strict diet during those four days and add chemicals to slow down our bowel movements."

"Hey, I didn't know you could do that."

"It's not the best solution, particularly if you abuse it, but I think in this case it's a good idea."

"Right."

"Anyway, I'll have a word with Ortiz and Evelyn so they give us a check and authorize the use of those drugs."

Both the deputy director and Commander Bauer had been very reluctant because of the nature of this little excursion, but Emily's insistence, and above all that of Rakesh, who was very much looking forward to being able to meet the Gaal-El, had managed to quell the doubts in the high command. Even so, the mission would be closely monitored by satellite.

They still had three days ahead of them before they left for the mountains, and everything pointed to the fact that this interlude was going to be rather boring for Emily, but on that planet nothing was what it seemed. In fact Shildii came back that same afternoon. As usual Emily went outside to welcome him. This time he had come closer, out of curiosity.

He pointed inside the base. "What do you keep in there?"

"What do you mean?"

"The door's very big, so you must have something very big in there."

"Very observant. The thing is that they're big so that very large objects can be brought in, like the one we took to Yisht, but also so that several humans can go in and out at the same time."

Shildii narrowed his eyes and smiled cheerfully. "You humans are rather strange."

"I thought you wouldn't want to come back after what's been happening lately."

"Yes, I was very scared when the soldiers came into Yisht's study."

"I was frightened too."

He was incredulous. "Really? Humans feel fear too?"

"Of course! In fact it's something very human. Feeling afraid is natural, it keeps us alert to danger."

She handed him a piece of chocolate cake, and though it was late by then, he accepted it and ate it in the blink of an eye.

"Thank you," he said when he had finished.

"You're welcome." She rumpled his hair affectionately.

"I wanted to show you something," he said a moment later.

"Oh, yes? What is it?"

"It's a surprise."

"Really?"

"Yes! But you'll have to come with me to see it."

"All right then, where is it?"

"Follow me."

She followed him as far as the edge of the river, but at this point she began to feel uneasy.

"Do you want me to cross the river?"

"Yes."

"I shouldn't really, there might be some Khaavahki or other keeping watch on the area."

Shildii stopped dead, realizing that she was right and that they ought not to. "But yesterday we did it…"

"Yes, but…" She almost added that yesterday's business had been important, but she did not want to hurt the boy's feelings, so she left the sentence hanging.

"I guess it'll be all right if I cross just for a moment," she said at last.

Shildii was delighted by this change of decision, and they crossed to the other side over the board he always left hidden in the bushes. Then they went on along the path they had taken the day before to meet Khikhya.

"Are you taking me to the same hut as yesterday?" Emily asked.

"Yes," Shildii said, "you see, I want you to meet some friends."

Emily slowed down almost to a stop. "Some friends?" she asked reluctantly.

"Yes, they've heard about you and they want to meet you. But don't tell them I told you. It's supposed to be a surprise."

Emily stopped dead. She did not like the idea of meeting a group of teenagers who might go bragging around the village that they had met a human and that this spiral of gossip and rumors would become untenable.

"Shildii, you have to ask me about things like this beforehand," she said very seriously.

He bowed his head and accepted the scolding.

"I thought that as we were at the hut yesterday we could go on having our meetings there…"

"And of course we can go on having them," said Emily. "Khikhya told Rakesh and me not to go near Wiikhaadiiz ofiz for safety. But she never said you couldn't come to our village. What I don't want is a lot more people finding out we're here. There are lots of Keplerians who don't like us, do you understand that?"

"Yes, I think so."

They covered the last of the distance to the hut. Shildii went in before her and looked to either side, as if looking for someone he could not see.

The moment she had crossed the threshold Emily felt a strong electric shock running through her body. She began to convulse, even inside the exosuit, which shut down immediately. With it shut off she was unable to keep her balance and fell to the ground, while the convulsions went on. She could not see what had happened. She fainted almost immediately.

Robert received an alert from Ada.

"Lieutenant Beaufort, I just lost the signal from Emily's exosuit."

"What? Where was she?"

"She'd left the base with Shildii. Her last known position was entering the hut where Dr. Kumar and she met with the Keplerian leader yesterday."

Robert gave a convulsive start, and Ada immediately showed him the exact location in his enhanced reality visor.

"How far is that place from here?"

"Almost an hour on foot. You have to cross the river."

He went for his exosuit. "Ferrara," he called, "get three soldiers ready at once. We have a Code Red."

"Copy that, Lieutenant," came her voice. "We're ready. What's happened?"

"Emily's gone missing."

"Missing?"

"Yes, there's no signal from her. I have a nasty feeling someone's done something to her."

"Understood. We'll meet you at the entrance."

"Ada," he called when he had put on his exosuit helmet, "show me the last images from Emily's cameras."

When Ada did so he saw Emily following Shildii into the hut. But as soon as she crossed the door, the signal from the suit was lost.

"Show it again."

After viewing it three times more, he gave up trying to find out what had caused the loss of the signal. There was nothing to be picked up on the video, not even whether Emily had been attacked by something or someone. It had simply stopped emitting any signal the moment she had gone through that rickety wooden door.

"Let's go, time could be crucial," he urged Ferrara once he was outside the facilities.

"Yes, sir."

"Did you see the video?" he asked as they set off.

"Yeah, and I didn't see anything odd. Could it have been just a failure in her emitter module?"

"Just at the very moment she went into the hut? I don't believe in coincidences. A suit that cost millions isn't going to fail just like that."

"What d'you think could have happened?"

"I don't know, but Garth could be behind it."

"Eh?" she said in surprise. "What would the captain gain by hurting Emily? We have more manpower than he does, and that would mean the end of this weird status quo."

"I don't know. But what I do know is that the captain and his minions are perfectly clear about the differences between an engineer's suit and a military one."

Ferrara was thoughtful. The lieutenant might be right. Only a human soldier or a skilled engineer would know how to shut down a civilian exosuit.

"An electrical discharge," she said.

Robert nodded. "That's right. A simple electrical Taser."

"The civilian suits don't have the same isolation as the military ones."

"One of the great decisions our old governments made which I never managed to understood. To lower costs, they decided the engineers' suits wouldn't have the same isolation as the military ones. As if engineers weren't exposed to electrical currents when they're working on some systems."

"And which the captain might have taken advantage of, to use against us," Ferrara said thoughtfully.

"But the worst thing of all is that the shock needed to shut down a suit like that might be lethal. They could have killed her unintentionally, even if all they'd wanted was to put her out of action."

"Best not to think about that," Ferrara said as a shiver ran down her spine.

"We have to get to her as soon as possible."

"Is air transport out?"

"Yes, the area's densely wooded and we wouldn't get there any sooner. And we can't rule out the possibility that they might be waiting for us. We need to go fast, but stealthily."

Robert, Ferrara and the other three soldiers crossed the river with their own thrusters and went on through the dense forest in the direction of the hut, following the path Ada had marked in their visors. As it was the same route Shildii and Emily had taken, it was easy enough to make out their tracks. In some places the humidity and recent rain made these easier to locate. At the same time they were also mixed up with the previous day's, which confused matters. The only thing clear to Robert was that if there were attackers, they could not have followed the same route to the hut.

He pointed up to the treetops. "Be alert to any movement, in any direction. We're going to shut off the coms channel."

He was looking carefully around at their surroundings as he tried to follow Shildii and Emily's footprints. By stages, as they neared the end of the path, he motioned the group to slow down. The five soldiers went forward as silently as they could. By now they could see the hut in the distance, sheltered by abundant foliage and underbrush. He could see that on the outside of the hut, particularly in front of the door, the footprints were more abundant, but most of them were those of Keplerians. He remembered Emily telling him the day before that Captain Garth might have made contact with the most warlike of the Keplerian factions.

He could also make out the tracks of at least one carriage going away in an easterly direction. Ferrara gave the signals for a tactical assault on the hut. Two of the soldiers went around it, while Ferrara, Robert and the third soldier got ready to enter. Ferrara gave the door a powerful kick which almost knocked it off its hinges, and in a swift, coordinated movement Robert and the other soldier slipped inside. Each of them aimed his assault rifle in one direction, so that the whole inside was covered. It was dark, with light barely coming in through the tiny windows of the old house. There was no-one there.

"All clear," the soldier reported when he had checked all the corners.

"All clear," Robert confirmed.

One of the soldiers who had gone around the hut came back to report. "Nothing here either."

Robert turned on his helmet light so that he could inspect the hut. There was no trace of struggle or fighting. When he went to stand in the precise spot where Emily's connection had been lost he saw that the floor of compacted earth in front of him was moist enough to show the footprints of a human in an exosuit falling like a tree the moment she lost her balance.

He pointed to the recent marks on the floor. "Emily fell just here."

"Fell?" the soldier repeated. "But the suits stay upright even when they're shut off, right?"

"Yes, but only if you keep still and shut it off properly. Emily was moving when she entered the hut, then she was attacked and fell over."

He looked around, checking the arrangement of what little furniture there was. The three wooden chairs were still where Emily and Rakesh had been sitting beside Khikhya the day before.

"Someone shot a Taser from this corner the moment Emily appeared in the doorway."

"How can you be so sure?" Ferrara asked.

"The door opens to the left. It's the only place you can take a clean shot from without being seen as you go in. And I'd also guess they'd have taken into account how long the suit's optics—not to mention Emily's eyes—would have taken to adjust to the darkness inside the hut. It was an easy shot. She was alone, unarmed and trusting."

"Do you think Shildii was involved?" Ferrara asked.

"Well, he's only a kid," he said thoughtfully. "He's very impressionable. I'd like to believe he was tricked too."

They came out of the hut and gathered in front of it. Robert pointed to the trail the attackers had left.

"At least four Keplerians loaded Emily on to a cart to take her away. These prints look smaller, they could be Shildii's."

"Keplerians?" Ferrara asked in surprise. "How could that be possible? As far as we know, the Keplerians don't know anything about electricity."

He realized that they knew nothing about the reports Khikhya's intelligence had got hold of.

"Yesterday Khikhya told Emily that over the last few days her spies had seen humans in contact with the leader of the Khaavahki village."

"What? Is Captain Garth making deals with the ones who want to dominate the other Keplerians?"

"Looks like it." He pointed toward the east. "We need to follow the trail of that cart."

Emily came to her senses little by little. She was in pain, as if she had been given a good beating. She could see nothing, she was in utter darkness. Nor could she hear much either, because a steady and annoying ringing was drilling into her left ear.

"Ada?" she called.

There was no answer, but she noticed a slight change of light in front of her.

"Emily *am*," she heard a voice, *"Vi li wubriik am."*

"Shildii?" she asked unable to understand what she had just heard.

"Biif lu thii. Nak taa diil, luli chow ghayi."

"I can't understand anything you're saying, Shildii," she said in the ghost of a voice.

She tried to sit up, but her suit was shut down. Without the servomotors in the joints it was going to cost her a massive effort to lift the weight of that mass of metal alloy. Her head was on the point of bursting with pain. And that damn ringing was not helping her to think about the situation. It seemed more than likely that her suit had been put out of action and her ear implant fried, hence the constant annoying ringing.

"Pi a vanma jaa am," Shildii said again.

Without Ada's help it was going to be impossible to understand anything. She knew some words, it was true, but talking to him was going to be a complicated business. All she could do was tell when he was asking a question, as all questions in Keplerian ended with *am*.

"Ju wok Koply," she said. It was one of the few sentences she had learned by heart. "I don't speak Keplerian."

Shildii sighed and was still, presumably thoughtful. She took the opportunity to go over what had happened and assess her current situation. The last thing she remembered, after making it clear to Shildii that they needed to be cautious, was going into the hut. After that, nothing except a massive shock and then waking up there.

They had fallen into a trap. Emily thought that if Shildi was there it must be because they had taken advantage of the boy's innocence to get to her. She would need to have a talk with him, but this was certainly neither the place nor the time. First she would have to think about how to get out of this mess. And she would need to have a talk with herself too. Not only had she dragged the young Keplerian into this situation, she had ended up falling into a ridiculous trap herself. She would have to change a lot of things about the way she behaved.

The suit was not working, Ada was not responding. She gave thanks for the fact that the engineers had thought about these situations so that the life support would work with no electrical supply, because otherwise she would not be alive at that moment. The battery lasted forty-eight hours, but the oxygen tank only had enough for twenty-four.

The place was pitch black. She was barely aware of Shildii's presence, even though her eyes ought to have become used to the lack of light long ago. That could only mean they had been locked up somewhere with no light, or else that it was nighttime.

Considering the suit was charged a hundred per cent when I left the base at two o'clock, she calculated mentally, *and that at this time of the year it's pitch dark by seven, I could've been unconscious for over four hours.* At the same time there was no way she could know whether they had simply been thrown into a dark dungeon.

She remembered one or two words in Keplerian, and thought about how she could ask Shildii questions and understand his answers. Luckily she could remember the word for *night*.

"*Jof am?*" she asked.

"*Ju da li jof oppi,*" he replied. Then he added: *"Lu li id. Pa chu wiivaar li. Lu iighraashii a li wiichiffpaap."*

"*Ju, ju.*" She tried to wave her hands in every possible way.

She thought she had understood a no at the beginning of the answer, but all she needed was a yes or a no by itself, because otherwise he might be wanting to tell her something completely different.

"*Biif, ju,*" she said, so that he would have to reply either yes or no. *"Jof am,"* she asked again.

"*Ju,*" came the answer.

Right, at least now I know it's not nighttime. I have to tell him I can't see or understand him.

"Emily *ju iip,*" she said, remembering the verb. "Emily *ju wok.*"

Shildii said nothing, but gave a sigh of resignation. She went back to her private assessment of the situation. If it was not nighttime she could only have been unconscious for a short time and hence still had at least twenty hours of oxygen left. Luckily she had water and mash to help her get her strength back. And she hoped they would be looking for her.

She managed to raise her arms with some effort, but the suit weighed too much for her to get up by herself. Luckily Shildii saw that she was finding it difficult and helped her to sit up. It was not the most comfortable of postures, but her body was numb from being in the same position and she was grateful for the change. She stretched her arms to both sides to see whether there was a wall she could lean against. She had the feeling that the floor was of earth, because she was able to poke a hole in it quite easily.

She asked him whether he could see. "Shildii *iip am?*"

"Bif," he replied, meaning yes.

If he could see, that could only mean two things: either she had lost her sight during the attack, or else, as she suspected, the Keplerians had a natural ability to detect the infrared spectrum and see in the dark. Which was not at all outrageous, bearing in mind that there was no moon on this planet to reflect the sunlight at night.

Certainly the situation was far from idyllic. She had no idea where she was or how long she had been there, she had no energy and she did not know how much oxygen she had left. All she could do was wait for her comrades to come and get her out of wherever she was.

Robert, Ferrara and the other three soldiers went on following the trail of the cart they suspected had been used to take Emily and Shildii away in. The trail went westward, and every few meters it crisscrossed and got mixed up with that of the old carriage Khikhya had used the previous day. This particular path did not seem to be much used, so that it was relatively easy to follow the tracks. But there were areas where the earth the wheels had gone over was much dryer, and they nearly lost the trail a couple of times.

"Do you think they were taken to the Khaavahki village?" Ferrara asked.

"It's certainly a possibility," Robert said. "But bearing in mind that the sick mind of Captain Garth is sure to be behind all this, I could expect anything."

"Let's hope we don't have to go as far as that. It won't be easy to pass unnoticed in a Keplerian village, especially if it's full of soldiers."

"I don't think they'll have risked causing a diplomatic conflict by taking one of the human representatives prisoner. But now we're here I don't care how far we have to go, just as long as we get there before Emily's oxygen runs out."

"How long has she got left, Ada?" Ferrara asked.

"About twenty hours, give or take."

"We don't have much time."

"Better get a move on, then."

The group speeded up, which thanks to the help of their suits meant no more than a slight effort, until they reached the point where the trail of the cart they thought Emily was in veered to the north. The other, the one that had brought Khikhya the day before, went on to the east.

"They seem to have veered off here," Robert pointed out.

"Ada," Ferrara asked, "do we have records of any Keplerian village to the north?"

"Yes, the Gaal-El are in precisely that direction, across a mountain pass. About forty kilometers from your position, according to the vague directions Khikhya gave Emily yesterday."

"In that case we won't get there before nightfall," Ferrara pointed out.

"Emily's in grave danger, we can't afford to think about sleep!"

"That's not what I meant. You know who loves to come out at

night..."

"There are no Yokais here," Robert pointed out.

"As far as we know, but I wouldn't like to find those damn monsters somewhere else."

Night began to fall, and following the trail became more and more difficult without artificial light. At a certain point Robert decided to turn on his helmet light. But a few minutes later he realized that the night was very dark as it was, so he changed his mind and switched to infrared vision. Though the quality of the image was slightly worse, it was still better than giving their position away.

After a little over an hour heading north, he stopped dead.

"Here it looks as though the trail veers off to the east."

"Well then, let's go that way."

"No, there's something else here."

"What's that?"

He pointed to the tracks. "Take a look. All of a sudden there are four ruts, and the two that turn east are coming from the north, not the south, like us. Look at the curve the prints make. The cart that made this turn was coming from the opposite direction to ours."

"Or else it's another one," another of the soldiers said, "or else it turned a hundred and eighty degrees further on."

Robert nodded. "That's it. We need to keep going. This is very strange."

"Perhaps they missed the exit from the highway," another soldier joked.

"Or they might be trying to fool us," Robert said.

A couple of kilometers later the tracks left by the cart turned around, so that the return trail crossed the outgoing one.

"This makes no sense at all," he said. "Let's go back."

They went back along the path more carefully, while Robert concentrated hard on the prints. Some time later he found something he had overlooked the first time and pointed to one particular area.

"There are Keplerian footprints again here."

Ferrara examined them. "Four Keplerians, and some smaller ones, most likely Shildii's."

"They're heading west."

"You were right, Lieutenant, the turn was just there as a decoy."

"They unloaded the cart before they turned east, to try and fool us," said one of the soldiers.

"That means they must be very near here," Robert said.

Hold on, Emily. We're coming, he thought.

28
The Rescue

November 1, Year 0
Unknown location, Kepler-442b

Emily went on sitting there in the dark. At least she had managed to reach a wall she was able to lean against to give her back a rest. And although the wall seemed rather strange to her, as it seemed to be hollowed into the earth itself, she felt a little easier when she realized that there was nothing wrong with her eyes and that she was in a dark hole without any kind of light.

The next concern on her list was getting out of there. If she herself did not know where she was, it would be hard for her friends to find her. Hence she would have to try to get out of there before her oxygen ran out. And the main problem about doing that came down to the fact that her exosuit did not seem to want to turn on.

All electronic systems, whatever their nature and purpose, have a power supply whose job is to carry electricity from the battery to wherever it may be needed. The exosuit was no exception. The only setback was that she did not have a detailed enough knowledge of the exosuits' specifications to let her know where the batteries and power supply were. She supposed that all those important parts of the suit would be in the horizontal hump at the back where she knew oxygen and other supplies were stored.

But she was clear that without light, without tools and without being able to access that area of the suit without getting out of it, it was going to be a difficult business finding out what the problem was. And she would certainly need some kind of replacement, which she did not have. The situation did not look good. She was locked up inside a useless suit, underground and with an alien whose language she could not understand a word of.

I've got to move from here, even if I have no energy, she thought.

She tried to get up, and ended up needing Shildii's help again. Despite the fact that she could not communicate with him, he seemed to be very alert to all her movements.

She thanked him in his own language. *"Vi nak."*

She stretched out her arms as much as she could and noticed that despite the lack of electronic assistance she was able to move them with some effort. Once she was on foot, moving with relative ease seemed feasible. She took a couple of steps, but she must have chosen a posture which meant that the suit's center of gravity ended up overwhelming her own weight, so that she fell on her face. Immediately Shildii helped her up again. The boy was certainly pretty strong; had it not been for him, getting back on to her feet would have involved a titanic effort.

"Thu shyi ghak wiivarublov ii li naa wodu ondo," he said.

Once again she reminded him she could not speak his language. *"Ju wok Koply."*

"Pi yopwaathi," he said resignedly.

She made a new attempt to move around, stretching her arms out in front of her, and began to take small steps, with some difficulty. The suit was not intended to be used without electricity, but she supposed that the engineers would have considered possible battery or supply failure, so that at least she could move carefully. The space they were in was not very wide, and she had hardly walked four meters when she touched the opposite wall.

She tried to move her head as well, so that she could look around. She could see very little, but she became aware that what little light there was came from a small opening above. She could not make out what it was, but it reminded her of a square whose sides emitted a faint light.

That looks like a trapdoor, she thought. *They must've thrown us in underground and then shut it.*

She waved at the trapdoor to see whether Shildii could make things clearer.

She asked if it was a door. *"Shyin am?"*

"Biif," he said: Yes.

She repeated the question, pretending to reach it and open it. *"Shyin?"*

"Ju, thii pi fash."

She took this to mean that that they could not reach the door because it was too high. But at that moment an absurd idea occurred to her. The space seemed very cramped, like the cellar of a house, too small even to hold more than one person. Perhaps if they climbed one on top of the other they would be able to reach the trapdoor. She was not very hopeful, but who knew, perhaps their captors had not realized this and the trap door might not be bolted.

She wondered which of the two possibilities might be better, but she dismissed the idea of climbing onto the boy's shoulders. It was hard enough as it was to take a few steps, and she did not even want to imagine what climbing onto someone's shoulders would involve. In any case, if the suit was well-designed she would not have to make much of an effort to bear Shildii's weight on her shoulders. All she needed to do was find a position which would let the structure of the suit itself hold his weight, which she calculated to be ninety kilos or so.

So she pointed to her own shoulders.

"Shildii, *shyin*," she said. At the same time she mimicked opening the door.

He looked closely at the trap door, assessing the chances and the risk for some time.

"*Biff, lu shii lu vif,*" he said at last.

Biff: that means he can.

Emily pressed her helmet and the back of her suit as hard as she could close to the wall, leaving a little space at the bottom to avoid toppling backwards. She also spread her legs a little apart to give herself rather more lateral stability. The entrance-gap seemed to be close to one of the walls, so if he could reach the trapdoor they might have a chance.

She twined her fingers at the level of her pelvis to provide him with a support he could use to climb onto her shoulders. Between the two of them they would add up to three meters of combined height. If only it could be enough.

Shildii put his left foot on her hands, and after making sure she could bear his weight he pushed himself up. The suit bore the extra tension caused by his weight, so that she barely needed to make an effort. Once that first step was taken he put his right foot on her left shoulder, and immediately she heard the sound of his claws brushing against something wooden, presumably the trap door. Then he gave a sigh of frustration.

Instantly she felt a stab of disappointment. *It's bolted on the outside.*

Shildii stopped making any noise, though she could feel the suit wobbling to either side. He must be studying the trapdoor from several angles. At the end of a minute which seemed to go on forever he jumped down from her shoulders.

"*Lu jiiwaad zaan,*" he said.

Emily did not understand this, but from the tone of his voice she knew he had seen something. She thought she heard him sitting down on the floor and tearing the cloth of his jerkin. After a while he was in front of her once again, urging her to link the fingers of the suit together to give him the support he needed to climb up on to her shoulders.

They repeated the process, and he scrambled up. It seemed to Emily that it took him ages to do whatever he had in mind to do, but to judge by the constant mutters of frustration he was making, carrying out his idea must be a complicated business.

Until suddenly there was a note of triumph in his voice, and she heard the metallic sound of a bolt sliding. He opened the trapdoor a crack, but even so, there was not much visible change in the light which was coming in. This could only mean it was nighttime. Shildii gathered momentum and pushed the trapdoor with all his strength. The noise of the wood slamming against the floor was like thunder in the middle of the night.

Hell, they're going to hear us.

Shildii gathered momentum again and climbed on to the edge of the hole. Wobbling a little, he vanished through the opening.

A moment later he poked his head out of the opening once again. "Emily, *pi li numma, lu li thii taa fa a pidoch juw.*"

But before she could repeat that she had not understood a word, he vanished, leaving her there alone. Although it was not long before she heard the sounds of commotion outside. There was someone else there.

They've caught him, she thought, suddenly afraid.

"Radio silence again," Robert ordered. "And stay alert, I think we're close."

The five soldiers had just left the main road to venture into what appeared to be a less busy area. They were silent, but their movements were perfectly synchronized and as stealthy as possible. Robert went in front, setting the pace and repeatedly checking the trails which appeared on his visor. Infrared vision was very useful in these circumstances, but the images were less sharp than they would have been normally. Added to which they could only see clearly a few meters ahead.

The Keplerian footsteps were considerably harder to make out than the ruts made by the wooden cart. In fact Robert lost the trail several times and they had to go back a few paces until they found it again. They were moving too slowly, and they had no idea how far the place where Emily was being held might be.

Suddenly they heard the sound of a sharp blow in the distance. Immediately Robert and the rest of the group stopped and aimed their assault rifles in the direction of the area the sound had come from. It was not repeated.

Then they heard commotion coming from the same direction. There were Keplerians, and they seemed to be shouting. Robert released one hand from his rifle and signaled to the others to move forward more quickly, but with the same stealth.

Soon they saw a hut in the distance, and Ada was able to translate what the Keplerians were arguing about.

"Get down on the ground," one of them was saying.

"Do as he says," the other one said. "Or we'll have to kill both of you."

"We haven't done anything to you," a third voice said. This one sounded a lot younger.

"Hit him with the foreigner's weapon, see if he that makes him obey," a fourth voice said.

Ada located the source of the sounds, and after taking a small detour she was able to locate the heat signals the conversation was coming from. There were also two other heat signals inside the hut, lying on what appeared to be cots. Outside were four figures, one rather smaller, with his hands raised, and three larger ones who seemed to be surrounding the first.

Robert pointed to Ferrara and another soldier and directed them both inside the hut. The two other soldiers followed him until the figure with his arms raised suddenly changed his expression. He had seen them. The other three turned around at once.

"Stop!" one of them shouted.

"Drop your weapons," Robert said grimly, thanks to Ada's translation.

Without a word one of the other two Keplerians, who looked very nervous, fired what looked like a Taser at him. Its two ends hit his suit and delivered an electric shock. With a couple of easy movements Robert lowered his rifle and with the other hand pulled the two wires out, barely flinching.

"One day remind me to explain to you all what a Faraday cage is. Now drop your spears and that little toy before one of you gets hurt."

Two of the Keplerians obeyed immediately, but the third ran away in the opposite direction. Robert signaled to one of his soldiers, who ran after him. He might have been a Keplerian, but he was no match for the power-assisted military exosuit, which was capable of reaching fifty kilometers per hour. It took him less than a minute to catch up with him and tackle him to the ground.

Robert and the other soldiers tied the hands of the two Keplerians and left them sitting against the wall. Ferrara joined the party with another two Keplerians, who seemed to have been asleep inside the hut, oblivious to all the commotion outside.

"Where's Emily, Shildii?"

"This way," the boy said as he turned to go behind the hut.

There he pointed to a small wooden trap door, which was open. Robert peered inside and finally saw her down there, leaning against the wall in the same position Shildii had left her in.

"Do you need any help, Ms. Rhodes?" he asked, relieved to see that she seemed to be in one piece.

She looked up. "Robert! You've no idea how glad I am to see you!"

He could see that she was barely moving. "Your suit's out of energy, right?"

"No, it's fried. I think they shot at me with some sort of Taser, or an electromagnetic impulse."

He nodded. "With a Taser. So you can imagine who's behind all this."

"Garth!"

"I'll go fetch a ladder to get you out of there." He disappeared through the hole, but reappeared again to add: "Don't go anywhere!"

Emily let out all the accumulated tension in a burst of laughter. The role of damsel in distress was not much to her taste, but she was glad to be able to joke again. Robert, with Shildii's help, had found a ladder, and now lowered it down the hole. Emily tried to move her suit toward it. She had some trouble climbing the rungs, but little by little she managed to leave that underground hole.

"Thank you," she sighed as she hugged him with all her might.

He peered through her helmet. If they had not been wearing those wretched suits, their bodies would have been glued to one another. "Are you all right?"

"Yeah, a little tired and I have a headache, but I'm fine. Although I think my ear implant has fried completely. There's an annoying ringing in it."

"Well, we'll have that checked at the station." He was checking her thoroughly as he spoke. "Do you have any oxygen?"

"Yeah, I was even able to drink some water and eat a little mash. The only problem I have is that I can't see anything. Without energy in the suit I haven't any infrared vision."

"Well, that I can do something about." He switched on his helmet light.

"I'm so glad to see you," she said, almost without moving away from him.

"You scared us to death."

"Yes, I know, and I'm sorry. But please let's leave the scolding for later."

He smiled. "All right, let's see what we're going to do with these guys here."

They went over to where Ferrara and the other soldiers were holding the five Keplerian kidnappers. Emily was finally able to see her captors. Two of them were in plain green military uniform, but the other three only wore plain gray breeches.

These two must have been keeping watch when Shildii opened the trapdoor while the other three were asleep, she guessed.

She checked the badge on their uniforms. It was not the same one the soldiers Khikhya had sent to fetch her and Rakesh had been wearing. On this one was a stone tower with two swords crossed in front and a shield at the back in a duller green than the cloth of the uniform itself. She supposed this must be the badge of the Khaavahki people. What she did know for sure was that these soldiers were nowhere near as fierce or well-armed as the ones who had stormed the study when they had been there with Yisht.

"Who sent you?" Robert asked.

None of them opened their mouths. They did not even look at him, perhaps because the light form the torches was hurting their eyes.

He showed them a Taser, evidently of human make. "Who gave you this?"

He got the same result, so he grabbed one by the jerkin and lifted him a few centimeters off the floor. Then he shone the helmet light into his face.

"I don't think you realize how serious this business is," he said. "You know there's nothing to stop me executing you right here, don't you?"

"We…" the poor wretch with his feet off the floor muttered, "…we were only given orders… to do we had to do."

"Who?" Robert shouted.

"A Khaavahki high command."

"What's his name?"

"I don't know. Honestly… none of us know."

Robert let go of him and turned to Emily.

"I don't think we're going to get much more information out of them, this lot are just pawns. What are we going to do with them?"

"Let them go."

"Let them go?" Ferrara exclaimed.

"Yes, let them go," she repeated. "What else do you want us to do with them? Keep them prisoner at the base? We don't have any detention area ready for holding Keplerians, and it's more than likely they won't survive in our air. And I guess all that about executing them was just a sideshow…"

"Of course," the lieutenant said. "Who do you take me for? I wouldn't be able to do a thing like that."

"I know. We have to let them go. I don't want to be responsible for unleashing some absurd escalation of violence between humans and Keplerians."

"And what do we do with Shildii?"

"He's just a kid. I'd imagine he was tricked. We'll take him home, his family'll be worried sick. Tomorrow I'll have a talk with him to try and understand what happened."

Robert turned back to the captors and untied them.

"You're free," he said. "But thank her, she didn't want to keep you."

"Thank you, ma'am," the Keplerians said. They sounded sincere.

All five of them made haste to get out of the door and were soon lost in the darkness of the night. The Earth group did the same a little later once they had searched the hut thoroughly.

"Can you manage to walk to the base without help?" Robert asked.

"How far are we?"

"Twenty kilometers or so."

"I don't think I can even manage a couple of kilometers."

"Ada, find us a clearing nearby where a transport could land."

"There's one a couple of kilometers to the west of your position," came Ada's voice.

"Pass the coordinates on to Lieutenant Balakova. Tell her to approach the extraction point in half an hour."

"Copy that."

Robert and one of the soldiers carried Emily piggyback to the area Ada had pointed out. Shortly before they reached it they heard the engines of the transport approaching. Along the way they found the trail the cart had left on its way toward the East, the one Robert had decided not to follow. Just before they reached the agreed spot they found two draft animals tethered to a wooden cart.

"Is this the cart that brought you here, Shildii?" Robert asked.

"Yes, I think so."

"What do we do with it?" Ferrara asked. "Looks as though they just left it here."

"We'll have to release the poor animals. I doubt whether they'll be able to survive like that much longer."

"Let's take them with us," Emily suggested.

"Take them with us?"

"Yeah, why not? They're called *fhores,* by the way, and relatively speaking they're quite like draft horses on Earth. I'm sure we'd find them useful at the base, and Chad'll be delighted to be able to study something that doesn't either have roots or hop from flower to flower."

"Horses?" Ferrara repeated. "I don't know what kind of horses you might have seen on Earth, but these look more like starving rhinoceroses with wigs."

"But the transport's not set up to carry animals," Robert pointed out.

"Katrin's a very good pilot. I'm sure she'll be able to fly without too much shaking."

"Okay then, let's release them."

The docile animals barely flinched when they took off their harnesses and led them to the clearing, where the transport was waiting for them. They all climbed into the hold, tethered the two *fhores* to one of the areas equipped to secure cargo and took their seats on one side of the cabin.

Emily tried to keep an eye out for Shildii's reactions, seeing that he seemed very nervous about boarding a human ship for the first time. And although her suit was still not working, Ferrara's, from where she was sitting on his other side, did the translating.

"Don't worry, Shildii," she told him. "We're taking you home, but we're going to do it by air."

Shildii nodded without a word, though he was obviously uneasy.

"You'll have a funny feeling in your stomach and also in your head," Emily warned him. "But don't worry, that's normal."

"All right," he said at last.

The pilot, who had already been warned about the cargo they were carrying in the hold and the additional stop they would need to make to leave Shildii as close as possible to his home, began the take-off maneuver with the delicacy and tact of the expert she was.

Shildii grasped his seat tightly when he felt the ship rising, but Emily could tell by his expression that it was more because of that surprising sensation than because of fear. After the first few moments he seemed to be enjoying the flight. The journey to the clearing near his cabin barely lasted five minutes. Emily decided not to accompany him to his home, not wanting to complicate things by appearing with a missing Keplerian they must surely be searching for by now.

A few minutes later they landed at the base. They brought out the *fhores* and left them tethered to a small tree nearby. There they would have rich grazing once the sun had risen again. Once they were on land, while the others got rid of their exosuits, Robert helped Emily into the facilities. With no battery to help, her suit was going to need to be coupled to its terminal to feed its servo-motors.

Robert took off his helmet and exosuit to be more comfortable, then pushed back the hood of his jumpsuit. Emily noticed that his hair, which was a little longer and more tousled than when she had first met him, had begun to curl. He went up to her and very gently helped her to take off her helmet and plug her suit into the terminal.

Immediately it began to emit an unmistakable electrical buzzing which stopped when it was completely open, freeing her from her metallic cage. Still, she did not step out of it, but stayed still with her heterochrome eyes fixed on Robert's green irises.

"Are you all right?" he asked.

"Yeah, I've never felt better."

"Oh, and why's that?"

"Because after thinking about it and going over it again and again, I've decided I'm about to kiss you…"

He looked into her eyes, and though they were both aware that they were not alone in the hall, this time neither of them looked away. Time stopped while they both nervously enjoyed the moments prior to the first kiss. They relished the short-lived feeling of that first moment, the tingling at the pits of their stomachs, the repressed desire they were about to give free rein to.

Without a word she put her arms around his body and her hands behind his athletic back. Then, on tiptoe, she kissed him at last. She felt the warmth and softness of his lips, and the moist caress of his tongue made a shiver run down her spine. Robert responded by stroking her cheeks and her hair and returning the kiss passionately.

Their bodies, fused into one, beat with the same accelerated pulse, like a symphonic orchestra in perfect harmony. The kiss, which both of them would remember to the end of their days, lasted almost a minute, but seemed a mere moment to both of them.

Then they drew back their lips very slowly.

"Thank you," Emily said.

"Thank you?"

"Yeah, for everything. For coming to my rescue, for being the way you are, for always being there."

Tenderly, he rearranged her rebellious curls, which after a long and stressful day had managed to escape from where they had been tied up.

"You can't imagine how often I've wanted to kiss you," he admitted. "Ever since that first moment when our paths crossed at the station. Although I hope this'll be the first of many."

"Done," she said, and kissed him again.

29
Gathering strength

November 1, Year 0
Magellan base, Kepler-442b

Emily went to bed that night with a broad smile on her face despite everything that had happened. Ferrara herself, who had seen the kiss, had congratulated her in the corridor.

"High time you took the step," she had told her.

It was almost noon when she woke up. They had arrived at the base in the early hours of the morning and it had been hard to get to sleep. Her mind had been on overdrive from the moment she had got into bed, going over everything that had happened, good and bad. And of course there was still that damn ringing in her left ear which was pitilessly hammering her head, which ached enough as it was.

By the time she got out of bed there was no-one left in that area of the enormous room. In the other half someone was still asleep, but she did not go in to see who it was as she was sure it would be one of the soldiers who had formed part of her rescue party the day before. She went into the mess hall and got herself a good shot of coffee. Soon Evelyn and Paula appeared. Both of them waited for her to sit down, watching her with mischievous smiles on their faces.

"And…?" Paula said.

Emily did her best to pretend. "And what?"

"Don't act dumb with us," Evelyn protested. "Ferrara told us everything that happened yesterday."

"But first of all, are you feeling all right?" Paula asked with concern. "You must've been pretty scared, right?"

"To tell the truth, I almost didn't realize what was happening."

She told them about her confinement and how she had managed to get Shildii to open the trapdoor to the cellar. Her friends listened attentively, sighing with fear and putting their hands to their heads at some moments in her story.

"Oh, yes!" She turned to Evelyn. "I need you to check my ear implant. I can hear a steady, annoying ringing and with that Taser shot it's stopped working."

"Oh, it must've melted. There's not a lot we can do here. The equipment for that kind of procedure is at the station. I'm afraid we'll have to go back there to put another one in. Can you hear properly?"

"Well, I don't really know. I can hear you, but mostly with my right ear. The ringing's so intense I couldn't really say whether I can hear anything."

"We'll check it at the surgery. It won't be anything we can't sort out."

Paula tried to lead the conversation back to where they both wanted. "On the other hand, let's not stray from the point. I'm sure a new implant will solve the problem. But what about… the other business?"

Emily looked down in embarrassment.

"Well… we kissed…"

Evelyn and Paula beamed as they watched her changing expression: hope, perhaps a trace of fear, a little excitement…

"And by the way, it was high time," Paula pointed out. "You've been going around in circles for months."

"And you make a very nice couple," Evelyn added.

"I don't know… I had my doubts…"

"Doubts? What doubts could you possibly have?" the nurse asked.

"Oh I don't know, the project, our responsibilities… I don't want it to get in the way of anything we're doing here."

"Interfere?" Paula said with a mischievous giggle. "Emily, in case you hadn't realized yet, we've got to perpetuate the species!"

Evelyn burst into laughter at this witticism.

"That's supposed to be precisely our responsibility," Paula insisted. "How do you intend to do it otherwise?"

"There are embryos and artificial wombs in the station," Evelyn reminded them.

"But that's no fun at all!" Paula pretended to look horrified. "It's better to make children the traditional way."

Emily blushed again. "Don't go so fast! All we've done so far is kissed, we haven't even spoken together again, we're nowhere near bringing children into the world."

Despite her friends' eagerness, she was grateful for the distraction. She had almost forgotten that the day before she had been taken against her will by Keplerian soldiers. But after this pleasant conversation, she had to get back to her professional duties. She had a journey to organize, and for the moment neither her ear implant nor her exosuit was working. She would have to go to the station to sort out both problems.

A transport picked her up and took her back to the Asimov. She had to use one of the non-assisted replacement suits at the base to go outside. Even so, they took her own as well so that Director Patel's engineers could take a look at it. The suit was receiving electricity when connected to its terminal, so the problem might have been in the battery, the supply or some component which regulated the suit and which might have suffered with the impact of the Taser.

Once she was back at the station Emily went first to the engineering section with her suit. Director Patel listened carefully, looking rather troubled, to her account of everything that had happened the day before. Of course he confirmed that one of his engineers would take a look at her suit at once and let her know when it was ready.

She had made an appointment with Dr. Schmidt at the infirmary to have a new implant if it turned out to be necessary.

"You've been through this before," the doctor reminded her. "It's a simple procedure and you won't even feel it. But it might take a bit longer than usual. I'd like to check the state of your ear, because since this sort of problem isn't a usual one, I want to make sure everything's in its place. I wouldn't want you to have any trouble in the future."

Through a robot arm controlled by the doctor she was given a small dose of anesthetic behind her ear.

"Right, we're going to go on with the surgery. You'll lose hearing in your left ear entirely, but don't worry, it's what normally happens."

Emily, who was lying on her right side, was aware of the probe in her ear, though she felt neither pain nor discomfort. Just as Dr. Schmidt had told her, she suddenly lost all hearing in that ear. She was almost grateful for the fact after so many hours with that annoying ringing sound accompanying her.

"The anvil is slightly damaged," the doctor said after a few moments.

"Oh dear, is that serious?"

"Luckily, not really. We can give you a replacement, although at least for the moment I'd rather keep your own, which is always better than putting in a prosthetic. It's a nano-fissure, so we'll see how it evolves over the next few weeks. If it doesn't mend by itself we'll put in a prosthetic instead."

"Okay."

After a few minutes she was able to hear through that ear again.

"I'm going to test the implant," the doctor warned her.

She heard a series of beeps which went all along the entire scale of perceptible wavelengths.

"Can you hear the beeps?"

"Yeah, I can hear them."

"Great. Well then, that's it. You can get up, carefully."

She tried to sit up on the bed, feeling a little dizzy.

"Are you all right?"

"Yeah, it was just a moment of dizziness. I must've gotten up too fast."

"It might be because you've spent several hours with your ear damaged. Neither the implant nor the problem with the anvil should cause you any dizziness as they don't affect the vestibular system of your ear, which is responsible for balance and spatial orientation. Anyway, I recommend you rest for a couple of days."

"Fine," Emily replied. She knew perfectly well that she was not going to be able to take any notice of this.

After leaving the infirmary with her new implant, she contacted Director Patel to find out about her exosuit. They had found more than one problem in it and would take a little longer to resolve it, so she decided to pay a visit to the deputy director. When all was said and done, she had just been abducted and was now preparing to make a dangerous trip to the mountains. He must be worried about her.

"How are you?" he asked her. "I didn't want to call you this morning, I guessed you'd be very tired."

"I'm fine," she assured him. "I just had another implant put in. Mine had been fried, and the engineers are working on my exosuit."

"When do you leave?"

"In two days."

"Be very careful. And I don't just mean the weather conditions, since you're going to be outside for several days. Be careful about everything, don't trust anyone. As you've seen by now, not all Keplerians are to be trusted."

"Yeah, unfortunately I had to learn that lesson the hard way."

"Who do you think was behind what happened yesterday?"

"Somehow, directly or indirectly, Captain Garth,.

"And yet you don't seem too convinced," he pointed out.

"Yeah... I can't figure out the motivation. The captain, according to Khikhya, seems to be in touch with the Khaavahki. But I don't understand what he could gain by getting involved in some kind of internal political war."

"Who knows what's going on in that sick mind? He only wants chaos to reign," David said. "Or maybe he's made a deal with the Khaavahki leader to get rid of an important ally of the Wiikhaadiiz ofiz."

"I don't know, it could be a bit of everything, but it was all pretty strange, and I can't work out what kind of strategy there is behind it."

"That's exactly why you need to be very careful. Someone seems to be taking a lot of trouble to welcome you to the planet."

"Yeah, but this time we'll be going with an escort."

"What are you expecting to find there?"

"I haven't any clear idea," Emily admitted. "On the one hand, it's a unique opportunity to get to know the Keplerians better. Rakesh is very keen to study the Gaal-El from close at hand. On the other hand, I'd like to know if they've ever had any news of the Galileo. They seem to be a religious order that's come down in the world and I have my doubts about whether they'll be able to give us any clue, beyond getting to know the history of the Keplerians."

"You'd better not build up your hopes," he advised her. "I'm very much afraid we'll never know what happened to your father. We need to move on."

"I know," Emily said. "But I have to make the most of any possibility, however slight."

"I can understand that, but I don't want you to be obsessed with it. It's not a good moment for looking back at the past."

After a light meal in the mess hall, Emily went back to the engineering area. Here Director Patel, together with a couple of engineers, was checking the electrical system of her exosuit with great interest. As it was completely open, it looked as though they had not yet found the solution.

"Hello, Emily," the director said. He looked overwhelmed. "I'm afraid we haven't got your exosuit fixed yet. We've come across one or two problems. As you know, those suits weren't built to support electric shocks, so that a lot of the system has been charred."

"That doesn't sound too good."

"It certainly doesn't," he admitted. "If we didn't have a shortage of equipment since the rebels abandoned the project, I'd tell you it'd be better if you didn't use that suit. But all in all, I think we're going to have to change almost the entire circuitry."

"I need the suit to make a trip lasting several days," she reminded them.

"I know, I know," the director said. "We're doing what we can, but I'm afraid even if we managed to fix this suit it might fail again at any moment."

"Well then, what can I do? I don't want to have to take anyone else's suit."

"Well, we could give you a new suit from the store. But there's another possibility, though I'm not sure how much you're going to like it."

"What's that?"

"It turns out we've been spending weeks, even before the rebellion, working on some prototypes. We retired a number of exosuits and installed air filters like the ones at the base. That means there's no need to load them with oxygen. Instead it's extracted from the planet's own atmosphere."

"What? But that's wonderful! It'll give us greater autonomy…"

"Yes, that was the idea, but we had one or two problems that still haven't been fully tested. We wanted to use the space occupied by the oxygen tank to add more batteries for longer life, but we haven't had time. Other urgent jobs keep adding themselves to the list."

"What chance of failure do they have?"

"Actually, at least in their current state, minimal," one of the engineers confirmed. "We haven't taken off the oxygen tank yet, so in case of problems with the filter the suit would go back to using the tank. When we add the new batteries, that's when we wouldn't have a plan B. In that case, if the filters fail, the suit would always have to be plugged in to a source of oxygen."

"I get that," she said. "But in their current state the risk is nil."

"Very, very slight," the director corrected her. "Nil is too absolute a word, and we don't like to use it here."

"Okay then, if you have it in my size I'll take it."

The following day Shildii appeared at the base again. Emily decided to act as naturally as she could, even preventing Robert from being present during the conversation. She did not want the boy to feel guilty or threatened by what had happened.

"Did you have any problems at home?" she asked when the boy had finished breakfast.

"My mother was a bit upset," he admitted. "If you weren't Khikhya's guests I'm practically sure she'd never let me come here again. At the moment she doesn't like the idea very much, but she's letting me."

"That's understandable," Emily said. "Human parents always worry about their children, and I guess it's the same for Keplerians."

"Yes, I guess so," he said with a shrug.

"Can we talk about what happened the other day?"

A shadow of guilt appeared in his gaze. "Yes."

She anticipated him. "Don't worry, it's fine. Among humans and Keplerians there are always bad people. I'm afraid that's universal. We're both well, and that's what really matters. What I need you to understand is that there are many powers at play here, things neither you nor I understand yet. And we have to be cautious about everything we do, because it might affect those around us in ways we can't even imagine."

She paused, aware that the same comment might apply to herself as well.

"Do you trust me?" she asked.

"Of course."

"And you can certainly trust me. I can assure you I don't want anything bad for you or for any other Keplerian. But maybe you shouldn't trust me, because I'm from a foreign species and I might be trying to trick you into trusting me."

Shildii looked at her in a strange way, scrutinizing her.

"I know that's not true."

"Oh, really? How can you be so sure?"

"I know," the boy assured her. "It's only the people in my family who've worried about me the way you have. I know you're not lying. Friends don't lie to each other."

Emily was surprised, though deep down very pleased, by his words.

"I just want you to be careful," she said. "I don't want anything to happen to you because you're the first Keplerian to have had contact with a human."

"I won't let myself be tricked again," he said with unusual assurance for someone of his age.

"I'm glad to hear that. But now I need to know who they were and why they wanted to do what they did."

"They came to my house a couple of days ago, they started to point at me and they called me a liar."

"A liar?"

"Yes, they said I'd made up all that stuff about humans to get to Khikhya."

"Aha, I see."

"I told them it was all true, that I'd met you long ago and you were my friend. But they didn't believe me. They told me that if it was true I had to prove it."

"And they asked you to take me to the hut."

"Yes, they asked me not to tell you anything about them so you wouldn't get scared," Shildii said, looking ashamed. "I never thought it could be a trap. I'm sorry."

She reassured him with an affectionate hug. "That's okay. But you know what? My father, who was a very wise man, when he saw I'd made a mistake he'd always ask me if I'd learned anything from it."

"Not to trust anyone?"

"Yeah. And I suppose it's a good lesson, except that you can always trust your family and friends. Did you see them coming to fetch us yesterday?"

"Yes, your friends got us out of a real mess. The one you call lieutenant was very worried about you."

Emily's heart skipped a beat.

"Yes, I guess so, but why d'you say that?"

"Because he was always thinking about you. When he realized you couldn't walk properly, you couldn't see and your ear hurt, he never left your side even for a moment."

Emily turned, aware that she was outside the base and that as always, there he was, watching from a distance, always thinking about her, always there.

"Yeah, I'm very lucky to have friends like him, right?"

"Yes." He half-closed his eyes. "Emily's very lucky."

30
The Hermit

November 3, Year 0
Magellan base, Kepler-442b

They had spent the previous day making preparations for the journey. Emily and Robert had decided to take two mules laden with supplies and oxygen, in case anything happened. They also took other kinds of supplies, such as medicines, blankets, survival kits and even vacuum-packed cake to give as a present to the leader of the Gaal-El.

They had both talked about the suitability of taking firearms and had agreed that as a precaution, seeing they knew neither their guide nor the dangers they might come up against, the most sensible thing was for the four of them to go armed.

"Remember, they have biometric control," Robert had told her to persuade her. "No-one except us will be able to use them."

Emily was going to find it hard to share this small adventure with him without even being able to touch him. The proof of that had been the long embrace they had enjoyed before they got into their suits. She had wanted to feel the warmth of his body and the strength of his arms holding her for one last time. But ahead of them were a few days when the isolation of their suits was not going to allow them any kind of human interaction.

Although the location where they were to meet the guide was on this side of the river, Robert, Emily, Ferrara and Rakesh had gone to the clearing to wait for Yisht, as she did not know how to reach the base by herself. They had to wait a few minutes before a small cart pulled by two *fhores* appeared. Yisht jumped off the back of it and greeted them. This time she was wearing different clothes, warm and comfortable, and also shoes, which was not usual among the Keplerians they had met so far. She was carrying a hefty backpack containing more warm clothes, supplies and a kind of rolled-up mat.

"Robert, Ferrara, this is Yisht," Emily said. "Yisht, this is Robert and this is Ferrara."

"Pleased to meet you," the girl said. "You're soldiers?" she asked, obviously curious.

"Yes," Robert said in, surprise, as he was not carrying weapons at that moment. "How did you know?"

"From the color of your metal shell. It's green, like the ones our soldiers wear."

He smiled. "You're right, they're green."

They went back to the base, where they had left the two mules fully laden. Yisht took the opportunity to fill a small metal canteen when they had crossed the river again. Once they had secured the loads the mules were carrying all over again, they set off.

"Where to?" Robert asked.

Yisht pointed. "Northwest. We have to follow the river until we come to the great waterfall. After that we follow the instructions Khikhya's given me."

"Don't you know the way?" Emily asked in alarm.

"No, I've never been on this side of the river. In fact very few Keplerians cross it now. It's dangerous."

"And yet the Keplerian we're looking for lives on this side, right?" Ferrara asked.

"Yes, that's right."

"What better place to live if you don't want to be found?" Robert pointed out.

"Do you know him, Yisht?" Rakesh asked.

She shook her head. "I don't even know what he looks like or why he lives on this side of the river. I don't even know how Khikhya comes to know of his existence. All I know is that his name is Haagar and that he'll take us to the Gaal-El by a route it seems he's the only one who knows."

Their progress was sometimes quite difficult, as they had to avoid vegetation and underbrush almost continuously. Even so, the south bank of the river was not as thickly-wooded as the north, so that they were able to enjoy the light of the Keplerian sun during much of the way.

"Ada," Robert asked, "have you located the waterfall?"

"I think so. Assuming it's the one Yisht means."

Yisht turned excitedly. "I didn't know Ada would be coming with us!"

"That's right, Ada's with us and helps us whenever we go anywhere," Emily said. "But this one isn't your Ada. This one has never spoken with you."

"Are there more than one?" she asked in surprise.

"Yeah, you could say we have lots of them. And they talk among themselves," she added with a smile.

"Even mine?"

"No, yours is isolated."

"Isolated? But that's terrible."

"Don't worry, Yisht," came the voice of Ada herself. "I'm not like you, I don't feel loneliness the same way, and for me time doesn't go by the way it does for you."

"Even so, I don't like the idea that my Ada's all by herself."

"When we come back from our journey we'll try to sort that out," Emily promised.

They walked on uneventfully for a couple of hours. On the way they saw birds, insects, a wide variety of plant species and even the occasional small predator that fled as soon as it caught sight of them.

"How are you doing, Yisht?" Rakesh asked. "It's our first excursion with a Keplerian, so we don't know when you have to rest or whether the pace is too fast."

"Oh, I'm fine, it's comfortable. I suppose we can stop at lunchtime, though we should almost have reached the waterfall by then."

Robert noticed that she was taking out a small device from her backpack.

"What's that?" he asked.

"This? It's a compass."

"Oh! Could I see it?"

"Of course!"

The compass was the size of the palm of a hand, and its frame was made of a beautiful dark wood. A rather scratched glass protected the interior, but symbols were visible on the circular plate inside, which held to a fixed position despite the turns Robert gave the little box.

"This is the first time I've ever held a compass," he said excitedly.

"So don't humans use compasses to orient themselves?" Yisht asked.

"We used to, long, long ago. Our ancestors used them. We have Ada, and she's the one who helps us to orient ourselves."

"Oh! I see."

He handed it back to her. "It's an instrument I'd only ever seen in museums until now."

The group followed the riverbank until a few hours later they came at last to an enormous and spectacular waterfall which must have been some eighty meters high. The noise had begun to be noticeable some time before they saw it, but it was almost deafening now they were near where the water reached the ground. The river was very full on this upper reach, with the rainfall and the meltwater from the gigantic mountain making the waterfall a spectacle in every sense. The water, instead of running down the surface of the mountain, welled out from an enormous opening which the current itself had hollowed out over the years within the stony heart of the mountain.

The abundant red vegetation gave the scenery the appearance of something more-than- natural, because though the waterfall had eroded the rock of the mountain itself, around it the forests of red-leaved trees reared without order or apparent limit, in some cases towering over the waterfall itself. They were very far from any kind of civilization. Here Nature was the sole owner of the place.

"Taro and Chad would love it here," Emily murmured.

"They certainly would," Ferrara said, open-mouthed. "Although poor old Taro's been quite depressed since those ceremonial swords of his were stolen."

"Yeah, that's true."

"Your planet is very beautiful, Yisht," Robert told her.

"Thank you!"

"I think it's a good moment to stop for a while, would you agree, Yisht?" Emily asked.

"Yes, that would be fine. To be honest, I was beginning to feel hungry."

They looked for somewhere comfortable and accessible where they could rest and get their strength back. Yisht took some Keplerian food out of the backpack she had brought with her. Her diet seemed to consist of some of that familiar grayish bread, together with dried meat and nuts. Although she looked rather tired, she had not complained once in the course of the whole journey. Now she was chewing those small strips of cured meat eagerly. For the others there was only one item on the menu: the infamous oatmeal mash they all loathed so much.

"And what about you all, how can you eat inside those metal clothes of yours?" Yisht asked curiously.

"Our suits have a tank of a sort of cereal mash that gives us the nutrients we need to last out the day," Emily explained. "But actually it doesn't taste very good."

"Oh dear, and what do you usually eat? I've tried the delicious choc-o-late? Cake," she added carefully. "Did I say that properly? What else do you eat?"

Emily smiled. "Yes, you said it very well. From what I saw in your market I think we eat very similar things. We use grain to make bread and other foods, we eat meat, fish and vegetables."

"Ah, that's interesting. And what kinds of vegetables do you have on your planet?"

"They're very different from the ones here," Rakesh said. "Here the vegetation's red, but on Earth it's nearly all green."

"That's right, I've seen your planet many times. It's very beautiful, but it seems strange to me that everything should be so green there."

After sharing a relaxed chat, gathering their strength and rehydrating in a spot which on Earth would surely be overrun with tourists, they decided to set off again.

Yisht pointed up to the sky. "We'd better move on. It looks as though it's going to rain."

Ferrara nodded. "Yes, it's getting dark very fast."

"Which direction do we need to take?" Robert asked.

"A little over four kilometers on, following the edge of the cliff by the waterfall, there should be an ancient, narrow path that starts to go uphill. Once we're on it we follow it for another five kilometers."

It was not long before it began to drizzle, and though at first they were not aware of it as they were walking under the shelter of the trees, soon great drops began to fall, soaking both the ground and them. Emily, noticing that Yisht was getting quite wet, searched in one of the mules for a waterproof jacket in military green.

"This'll keep you dry," she said as she fastened the hood, "at least the upper part of your body."

Yisht was surprised to see the drops of water sliding down the jacket and falling to the ground. "Wow, the water slides off!"

"Yes, the material's different to yours. And we're wearing these suits of ours, so none of us needs it. You can keep it."

"Oh! Thank you very much, Emily!"

Just as she had told them, they came to a narrow path which started at the level they were at and began to climb the mountainside, winding between the trees which grew thickly there. It did not seem to have been much used recently and was barely more than a thin line of compacted earth free of vegetation.

"It doesn't seem to be a major commercial route," Rakesh pointed out. "There are no cart-tracks as there are in other paths."

"How far to Haagar's cabin?" Emily asked Yisht.

"According to my instructions, about five kilometers."

"Does he know we're coming?" Robert asked.

Yisht shrugged. "I don't know. I just have to give him a message from Khikhya so that he can help us."

Robert nodded. "Right. Just in case, we'd better stop talking. We shouldn't take this hermit's hospitality for granted."

They went on along the narrow path, going uphill now. The slope was not very steep, but they noticed that Yisht's breathing was speeding up a little. The girl did not seem to be in the best condition for a trip like this. Whatever the case, she put up with the pace without complaining. The drizzle went on falling on the crowns of the trees which lined the path, but only reached their suit visors in the form of huge drops. Yisht seemed happy to be wearing the jacket.

They had walked a little over four kilometers and still had seen no sign that would lead them to believe that anyone lived in that landscape. However, just as the path turned to the right, something whistled over Robert's shoulder at enormous speed. An arrow buried itself deeply in the trunk of the tree just behind him.

"If I were you," a deep voice shouted from a long way away, "I wouldn't take a single step further. The next arrow goes straight into that metal head."

The group stopped dead, taken by surprise by that sudden threat.

"Turn around," the mysterious voice went on. "There's nothing for you here."

"We're looking for Haagar," Yisht shouted.

"Haagar doesn't want anyone looking for him. Go away before my patience runs out."

"Khikhya sent us," she called.

The voice took a few moments before it replied.

"All the more reason for you to turn around at once. Khikhya isn't welcome here any longer."

Yisht did not know what else to say. She looked hesitantly at Emily.

Emily took a step forward with her hands visible. "We need to get to the Gaal-El village."

A new arrow flew through the air and plunged mere centimeters from her feet. Robert was able to guess the place it had been shot from, but was unable to locate the marksman.

"Don't take another step, foreigner," came the voice again. "And tell those two soldiers with you to leave their weapons on the ground if they don't want me to open another breathing hole in their throats."

Emily turned to Robert and Ferrara and gestured to them to leave their weapons on the ground.

"If you want to get to the Gaal-El there are much safer ways than this," the voice went on. "Go back the way you came."

"The roads are being watched," Emily said. "We're not going to move from here until you agree to help us."

"Don't tempt your luck!" the hidden man shouted with far more energy and a touch of frustration. "Do you think I won't be able to put an arrow through your heads?"

Emily did not add anything more, but she folded her arms to make it clear that they had no intention of moving. After a few tense minutes without communication of any kind they heard a loud yell of rage which echoed through the forest. This was followed by the sound of leaves rustling and the unmistakable snap of a branch breaking, then finally they saw a figure coming toward them from fifty meters away. Behind him came two quadrupeds.

The mysterious Keplerian approached them, while his animals sniffed the area threateningly. They looked rather like the creatures Robert had come across during the mission against the Yokai several weeks before, but though these creatures looked very dangerous, they were smaller. One of them had a coat of black hair and was a little larger than the other, which was brown. Despite this, it was the brown one which was staring at them much more threateningly, showing the dense lines of teeth in its three jaws.

"Yora! Philais!" the Keplerian shouted when he reached them. "Back!"

The two creatures obeyed at once, though the smaller one went on showing its sharp teeth as it moved to stand behind its master without taking its eyes off the strangers for a moment.

Emily was looking closely at the mysterious Keplerian. He looked quite old, though he was fit and his movements were agile. His unkempt clothes consisted of an old leather vest and a large brown fur coat which covered his back from shoulders almost to knees. On his head was what had once been the jaws of some fierce animal.

"Does that damn harpy think she can go on ordering me around all my life?" he burst out as he stared them up and down. "What the hell are you lot, and what d'you want from old Haagar?"

"We're humans, we come from another planet," Emily said, aware of how strange it sounded. "And this is Yisht, Khikhya's personal assistant. She's sent us to look for Haagar because we need to get to the Gaal-El, and the Khaavahki are keeping watch on all ways into the village."

He stared at them disdainfully. "The mountain road is very dangerous. Not appropriate for city people or delicate foreigners. I suggest you reconsider what you're doing."

"We've reconsidered it already," Robert said.

"Well then, you ought to reconsider it again." He turned his head quickly and fixed his gaze on the lieutenant.

Seeing that these new arrivals had no intention of turning back the way they had come, he added: "I've warned you. I'm not going to wait for any of you, I'm not going to risk my life for any of you. And if I have to push you off a cliff to save my life, never doubt that I'll do it." Then after a pause he turned and added: "Follow me. We'll leave at dawn."

They went up a winding path until they came to a small open area. Here in a corner, well sheltered from the wind, stood an old wooden cabin. The wild old Keplerian slammed the door open and left his hunting gear to one side.

"Sit down wherever you can." He turned to one of his animals and stroked its head with his huge right hand. "We're not used to having visitors, are we, Philais?"

Haagar fetched firewood from a corner of the cabin and prepared to light a fire in the small fireplace. The place was not very big, but it was well-lit and welcoming. There was a wooden rocking chair, a bench along one side, a small rectangular table with a couple of benches and at the far end a bed with a spartan mattress stuffed with hay. There could be no doubt whatever that that this was the house of a hermit.

He pointed to their helmets. "Something tells me Keplerian food isn't right for you. But I wouldn't mind betting this young lady is hungry."

Yisht nodded shyly.

"Right then, if we mean to cross the mountain we need to build up our strength." He was getting his utensils ready for cooking. "Tomorrow's going to be a hard day."

He grasped a pot and filled it with water from a huge waterskin, then took a couple of jars from a cupboard and added a pinch of their contents. After this he chopped some reddish vegetables and a tuber covered in swellings which looked like a sweet potato when it was cut. From a row of hooks beside the door he took a piece of game, already skinned, cut it into small pieces with the massive knife he carried in a sheath at his belt and added everything to the pot. Then he hung this from the metal frame over the fire.

When he sat down to wait for his dinner to be ready, Yisht handed him a sealed letter from Khikhya. Haagar took it in his calloused hands and opened it delicately. Emily noticed that the letter had a special emotional charge for the old hermit. He read it carefully, then bowed his head in thought. And then he screwed the letter and envelope into a ball and threw them into the fire. For a few minutes no-one said a word. The old Keplerian watched sadly as the fire, in a mere few moments, destroyed what until then had contained an important message. Emily feared that it might have troubled him enough to make him refuse to help them, but suddenly the hermit's expression returned to normal.

"Right," he said, stirring the contents of the pot with a wooden spoon as he spoke. "This won't take long now."

"How come you know Khikhya?" Yisht asked, to break the ice.

He turned round abruptly to reproach her. "That's none of your business!"

However, he had second thoughts when he realized that she meant well.

"I'm sorry, I... I guess I'm not used to having any more company than my animals." He was watching the simmering pot. "We grew up together… but it's been so long, all that seems to have been in another life."

They were all aware of the pain Haagar still harbored deep inside him. There was no doubt that he had had a relationship with Khikhya, but perhaps her state as tribal leader made her unsuited to forming a family. The old man must have loved her dearly in the past, because otherwise what could explain his willingness to take on a task like this?

Dinner was soon ready. Haagar took pains to offer Yisht a calorific feast to combat the more-than-likely freezing temperatures they would have to put up with the following day. He served the food in a couple of bowls with a wooden ladle and offered her a spoon. She took a couple of chunks of bread out of her backpack and offered one to him, and he was obviously grateful to be able to sample some civilized food.

The Keplerians sat down at the table and Haagar began to dig into the stew heartily. All the same, Yisht sat there without taking a mouthful. She looked uncomfortable seeing her three companions sitting there watching them both.

"What's the matter, little one?" he asked her. "Don't you like *vod* stew?"

"No, it's not that." She indicated the rest of the group.

"Oh, by all the thunder!" Haagar exclaimed. "Excuse my manners. What can I do for you?"

"Don't worry," Emily said, "we're eating too."

Rakesh was licking his lips. "To tell you the truth, I wouldn't mind trying that stew. It looks good."

"I'll give you a plateful," Haagar said immediately.

"Oh, no, no! Don't worry, we can't eat your food... we can't even breathe your air."

"Well, well, so that's why the humans don't take off that armor of theirs," he said to himself. "Well, that's a real shame, because this is delicious." He belched loudly. "Isn't it, child?"

"Yes, it's very good," Yisht said truthfully, as well as rather more decorously.

Haagar had two more helpings, but, in spite of his insistence he could not manage to make Yisht accept any more. As soon as the meal was over he gave the remains of the *vod* to his two animals, which gulped them down.

"Now then, I think we ought to rest," said a much more amiable Haagar once his appetite had been satisfied. "We have two days of hard travel ahead of us."

"Two?" Emily asked. "We thought we'd only need one."

"Not unless you can fly. We'll spend a night on the way to the village."

Emily made the appropriate calculations. If she had not been wearing the prototype suit, they would have had problems with oxygen.

"I only have the one cot," he said sadly. "I'll sleep on the floor. The young lady had better have the bed, she'll need a good rest."

"We'll sleep on the floor beside the fire," Emily said.

Robert brought one of the mules into the cabin, and the four connected their suits to the supplies. In Emily's case all she needed were water, food and electricity. They lay down on the floor beside the embers of the fire. Though the suits had a thermal system, it was always better to save some energy in these circumstances. Emily and Robert huddled together.

"Rest well," Haagar said. "We set off at first light."
Robert stroked her helmet lovingly. "Good night, Emily."
"Good night, Robert."

31
Trip to the mountains

November 4, Year 0
On the way to the Gaal-El village, Kepler-442b

When Emily woke at first light, her whole body felt stiff. The suit was not comfortable enough to sleep inside. She became aware that her neck, back and shoulders were cramped and aching. She tried to stretch as best she could.

I'll have to ask Director Patel to get them to improve the ergonomics of this suit, she thought.

Robert, Ferrara and Rakesh were already up.

"Good morning, Emily" Rakesh whispered.

Emily realized that Yisht was still asleep. She could hear her rhythmic breathing from the bed.

"Good morning, Rakesh." She looked again at how placidly Khikhya's young assistant was sleeping. "She seems to have been tired."

Rakesh nodded. "Yeah, and if I weren't in this tin can I guess I'd be even more tired than she is."

"Where are the others?"

"Outside. Haagar asked them to help him move something. I guess he'll have wanted to finish whatever he was doing before we interrupted him."

A few minutes later they appeared at the door, and Haagar shut it with such a bang that the noise woke Yisht.

"Good morning," she said, sleepy-eyed. "Is it morning already?"

"It is, young lady," Haagar said. "And we need to have a good breakfast, it's going to be a long hard day."

He prepared a dish of dried meat, berries and something that resembled cheese. And although Emily did not remember seeing any animals capable of giving milk nearby, it seemed that the hermit was able to provide almost everything he needed for himself. Yisht ate avidly, though she seemed a little uncomfortable because no-one else was eating beside her.

"Aren't you eating?" she asked their host.

"I ate a long time ago. Old men like me only need a few hours of rest."

"We need to get going," Robert said. "The suits are charged and the mules are ready."

As soon as Yisht had finished her breakfast Haagar fetched his enormous bag, a waterskin, his weapons and a small backpack of warm clothes, and urged them to set off.

"We'll be going round the mountain during the first part of the day," he explained. "This is the easiest part, so keep your strength in reserve. Afterwards we'll be going through the mountain."

"Through the mountain?" Rakesh repeated.

"Yes, we'll be going through the old mines. And yes, before you ask, that'll be the most dangerous part of the journey."

"Are you leaving your animals here?"

He nodded. "The mines are too dangerous to bring animals with you."

"Well, that certainly is reassuring," Rakesh muttered to himself.

They began the climb, this time without following any kind of path or road. The day seemed to be peaceful; the fine drizzle of the previous day had given way to shy rays of light peering through the clouds and the enormous crowns of the forest trees. The animals that lived there were expressing their gratitude for this pleasant interlude with an endless chorus of varied sounds.

"What did they get out of these mines?" Emily asked.

"Several kinds of ore," Haagar said, "but so many generations ago no-one remembers."

"Are they as old as that?"

"They certainly are. This area must have been a lot more heavily-populated in the past. In some places you can still come across remains of ancient Keplerian settlements."

"What put an end to them?"

"It's hard to be sure. Keplerians' memory is very short. The Gaal-El might know what happened. The only thing I can tell you for sure is that this area isn't safe."

"Why is that?"

"Inside the mines there are night stalkers."

"What?" Emily and Robert exclaimed simultaneously.

The hermit smiled. "To judge by your reaction, I'd say you've come across them already."

"Yes, we have," Robert said. "And it wasn't the happiest experience."

"True. Those bastards are capable of tearing your guts out with one swipe of a claw."

The hermit opened his leather vest and showed them three large scars which ran along the lower part of his belly.

"Did a night stalker really do that to you?" Yisht asked in horror.

"That's right, young lady."

"And we're going to go into a cave full of them?" Rakesh asked nervously.

"That's what I said. And we'll even be spending the night in there. You can't claim I didn't warn you the route was going to be a dangerous one."

Emily and Robert looked at one another incredulously. This hermit friend of Khikhya's must be either very brave or very stupid. They had spent weeks convinced that the only Yokai in existence lived to the east of the area where the accident to the Icarus had happened, but they had just found out that there were more settlements scattered across the continent.

The path went on for some time without any further incident, but this discovery made silence into another companion on the journey. And so, almost without exchanging a word, they went up the mountain, going around it in the opposite direction to the one they had taken the day before, but climbing all the time. Haagar decided to stop for a rest beside a small clearing where the vegetation was lower.

"This is a good place to have something to eat and get our strength back."

A small stream of crystal water wound through the vegetation. Both Haagar and Yisht, who followed the hermit's example, drank what was left in their canteens and refilled them with fresh water.

A little later they went on with the ascent, crossing a rocky ridge without much vegetation except for a few dry, isolated bushes, but when they were about to reach the top the four humans of the expedition were left open-mouthed at what they could catch a glimpse of through the highest foliage of the trees, barely fifty meters ahead.

"Dear God!" Emily muttered.

"There's more than one of them," said Ferrara.

Despite the obvious height of the trees, above their crowns there rose the tip of an obelisk, similar in size and proportions to the one they had seen in the planet's other continent several weeks before. It was the same dark color and had the same nozzles at the top, and everything indicated that these too were the sources of the famous molecules Chad and Taro were studying.

"What's that, Haagar?" Emily asked.

"They're primeval artifacts. They were here long before any of us. No-one knows what they're for, all we know is that to the Gaal-El they're sacred."

"Did their gods build them?" Rakesh asked.

He shrugged. "I haven't the slightest idea, and nor do I care. But they certainly worship them as that."

"Are there more like this one?" Robert asked.

"Yes, I've seen three different ones. But I've heard there are many more, beyond the areas I know."

"Ada," said Emily, "save this location. And analyze all the satellite images of the planet. I want to know where the others are."

"Copy that."

The group did not approach the obelisk, but went around it at a distance. The route Haagar had traced did not pass it, so Emily said no more about it. After all, they had seen one before.

"In just over a kilometer we'll start to see the first entrances to the ancient mines," Haagar said very seriously. "I need you to do exactly what I tell you to at every moment, whatever happens. Is that understood?"

"All right, then," Emily said, a little taken aback by his tone of voice.

In the course of the route they could see a remarkable change in the appearance of the forest. There were more and more rocky areas and less vegetation. It was beginning to be harder to find any shade, as the huge trees had given way to small red bushes and underbrush.

They reached an area where even the stones on the ground had a darker tone. Fifty meters ahead they saw a huge gap which must be the entrance to the mountain. They had come to one of the main points of access to the ancient mines.

"Wait here," Haagar ordered them. "Don't move. Don't do anything. Whatever happens, stay here."

"All right," Emily said, not knowing the reason for so much mystery.

Haagar went up a steep hill between the rocks until he had disappeared into the distance.

"Where could he have gone?" Ferrara asked after a few minutes.

Robert shook his head. "No idea. But all this seems very strange to me. Something tells me we shouldn't be here."

Emily bent down to check a rather odd-looking stone.

"It's a bone!" she exclaimed. "We're surrounded by bones!"

They were all alarmed to realize that many of those dark stones were the bones of innumerable strange creatures scattered across the mountainside. Suddenly, and before they could be genuinely afraid, they began to feel the earth shaking. A murmur of sound was approaching from somewhere nearby.

"What's that noise?" Emily asked.

Robert grasped his rifle and moved to stand between his friends and the source of the din. "It sounds like a stampede."

They heard a few deeply worrying brays. Suddenly a huge animal appeared from nowhere and fixed its dark eyes on them. It was the size of an elephant, with huge spiral horns on its head and a body covered with long black hair. Its snout was long, showing sharp teeth every time it brayed. It was coming toward them at top speed. And behind it came a dozen smaller animals which resembled it, striving to follow the leader of their pack.

"Stay behind!" Robert shouted as he aimed his rifle at the creature.

The animal and its braying followers, far from slowing down, came on toward them at the same speed. Robert pulled the trigger. The shot echoed like thunder, and though it hit its target it only served to spur the creature on even more. He and Ferrara opened fire again, but there seemed to be no way of stopping that kind of mastodon.

Suddenly a figure leapt from a high rock, with an intimidating yell. Haagar had hurled himself on the creature, brandishing his axe, and buried it deeply in its neck. The creature, seriously wounded, changed its course slightly as the tremendous impact made its way toward the opposite side. The huge animal ended up toppling to the ground, taken unawares by the violent attack. Haagar drew back his double-edged axe in a swift movement and with another tremendous blow to the same part of its neck managed to subdue the creature. Blood flowed freely from the monstrous animal's neck, darkening the stones and bones scattered around.

Haagar got up quickly and turned to face the remaining the creatures. He raised his arms and gestured at them with a series of threatening yells. The rest of the pack, now leaderless, stopped and after a few moments of hesitation fled back the way they had come.

"I told you not to do anything!" he complained bad-temperedly as he shoved Robert's rifle away.

"I… the creatures were coming straight at us, I just tried to defend the group."

Haagar gave a sarcastic laugh. "I can see how efficient human weapons are. But what you don't know is that it's useless to attack a *ghup* head-on. Or that the *ghup's* neck is the only place the skin's thin enough to bury an axe in, which is why you have to take them by surprise from the flanks. Or that the rest of the pack runs away the moment they're left leaderless." He pulled the huge axe out of the creature's neck. "Now the whole mountain knows we're here."

After wiping the blade of the axe and putting it on his back very carefully, he added: "Quick, we've got to move before nightfall."

"But what about the creature?" asked Rakesh, who was obviously still frightened. "Are we going to leave it here?"

"Yes."

"But why?"

"It's the offering you pay for crossing the mines," Haagar said. "And now let's leave the questions for some other time. We've got to get to the other entrance before it gets dark."

Time seemed to be pressing the experienced Keplerian, so they obeyed without putting up any objections. After all, he seemed to know perfectly well what he was doing. They went on walking until they reached an area that was far more exposed to the weather. The temperature had dropped drastically since they had left the cabin, and Yisht had been forced to cover herself with one of her furs to keep warm.

The four humans, on the other hand, were not aware of much difference, partly because their suits were perfectly insulated and partly because Ada was controlling the thermal system and always kept them at a pleasant nineteen degrees Centigrade inside their suits.

At last, after another long stage in their journey, they came to the opening Haagar had mentioned. It was slightly smaller than the one before.

"It's here," the Keplerian said. "From this point on there's no light and we're going to have to move silently. But above all, check where you put your feet. If you have any questions, now's the moment to ask."

"How far do we have to go?" Yisht asked.

"Quite a few kilometers. The galleries of the mines are a real labyrinth. Don't stray from the group, because even I wouldn't be able to find you."

They went into the cave and finally left behind the light of the sun, which was already beginning to be hidden. In the space of just a few meters Ada had to activate the infrared vision of their suits.

We have no coms now, she thought after she had checked her visor.

The gallery they were moving along seemed reasonably wide, at least for the time being. The place seemed ancient, the humidity was beginning to be more than obvious and the temperature had dropped another couple of degrees. Soon they came to a fork, where Haagar did not hesitate even for a moment. Every now and then they saw stretches of the cave which were propped up with very old lengths of wood, which seemed to have been there for several thousand years and which at any moment might rot away altogether and bring the whole gallery down.

They passed a number of forks, vaults, intersections and roads, and Emily had soon completely lost any idea of where they were or which direction they were taking at each crossing. Luckily Ada, even though she still had no connection to the station, was able to record every movement of their suits.

Rakesh, who was in front of Emily, suddenly gave a start which put half the group on the alert. In one of the galleries were piles of bones, forming a small, macabre ossuary which had given the anthropologist a fright.

The deeper they went into the mine, the more sunken galleries they came across. What was obvious was that the mine had been used over many generations of Keplerians, who had hollowed out the mountain with thousands of these galleries which crisscrossed to make the most complex possible labyrinth. Here it would be all too easy to get disoriented and lose any sense of time.

Suddenly something happened to interrupt their progress. As they passed the intersection of four galleries, they heard guttural growls from one of them which sounded horribly familiar.

"It's nighttime now," Haagar whispered almost inaudibly. "We need to get a move on if we want to get to the safe area."

They did this, until they reached a new intersection and he stopped dead in his tracks.

"What is it?" Emily asked.

"We have a problem. This gallery has caved in."

"And what does that mean?" Robert asked.

"It means we'll have to risk taking another of the intersections."

"Do you know where the other galleries lead to?" Emily asked.

"No."

"In that case we certainly do have a problem," said Rakesh.

"Isn't there anything else we could do?" Robert asked.

"No. We'll have to take this other intersection and try to find an exit. And let's hope we don't come across them."

They all swallowed. They were going to have to take the risk, not only of getting lost in that complex labyrinth of corridors and galleries, but also of coming across the Yokai in a confined space, perhaps with their rearguard compromised.

"Whatever we do, we'd better do it now," Emily said.

They took the other possible intersection, which went deeper into the mountain. From it, unfortunately, they could hear muffled growls.

"It smells terrible," Yisht complained.

"It's the stench of death," Haagar said darkly.

He was the one who made the decisions at every moment, leading them by the galleries which were most likely to lead them to wherever it was the hermit intended to come out of the mountain. It was some time after they had left the sunken gallery behind that he stopped again. But this time it was not because of a cave-in but because of the unmistakable sound of water. A natural gallery crossed their route, and through it, deep within the mountain, ran a small river.

"So what do we do now?" Emily asked.

"We're too high up and too far into the mountain for this to end in the great waterfall," Haagar said thoughtfully. "I don't know where this river ends, but we have to cross it."

He began to take off his clothes.

"What are you doing?" Yisht asked.

"It's meltwater. If you don't want to die of hypothermia, we have to cross without clothes so that when we get to the other side we have dry clothes to put on."

Emily weighed up the odds. It did not look very deep, but the force of the flow might be enough to drag them away.

"Wait," she said. "I'll go first."

She brought one of the mules forward and roped it to the other. The first one moved forward into the water. It had to correct the angle it was leaning at to keep its stability the moment it reached the point where the current was stronger and could cause it problems. Luckily it was neither as deep nor as strong as they had feared. But of course a single misstep could easily be fatal for any one of them.

Once on the other side, both mules arranged their legs so that they could exert more strength and tensed the rope to make the crossing easier for the others.

"Here I go," Emily said.

"Be careful," Robert said anxiously.

The rope was very tight. Emily clutched it and went into the water: first up to her feet, then to her knees and lastly to her waist. The current was powerful, but with the assistance of the suit she was able to cross almost without effort.

"I think I've got to the deepest part," she said when the water had reached her chest.

Then she put her foot on a rock which made her slip and almost lose her balance, but she managed to keep hold of the rope.

"Be careful," she called once she had finally reached the other side. "There are one or two slippery rocks."

"I'll go next," Haagar said. He rolled his warm clothes into a large bundle and threw it to the other side of the river, along with his other belongings.

The intrepid Keplerian grasped the rope firmly and began to cross to the other side very carefully. He managed it without any trouble, but by the time he got to the other side he was shivering with cold. He took a blanket from his bundle and dried himself vigorously.

Then came the turn of Rakesh, who crossed very carefully and without incident.

"Yisht, your turn now," Robert said.

The girl took off her clothes and put them in her backpack. She asked Ferrara to throw it to the other side for her because she did not think she could manage to cover the distance, then began to cross.

"It's freezing!" she said the moment she put her feet into the water.

"Come on, Yisht!" Emily called from the other side.

The girl gripped the rope tightly and began to get deeper and deeper into the water. She tried to go faster, but seeing how unstable the riverbed was she decided to take her time despite the cold which had begun to take over her body.

As soon as she was near enough, Emily gave her a hand and pulled her out of the water. She was shivering violently and her teeth were chattering rhythmically. Emily helped her to get dry and put on her clothes again.

"Get close to Haagar," she said. "You two are the only sources of heat we've got."

They hugged one another, while Ferrara reached the other side and Robert and the other mule set off.

"The best way to get warm is to move," Haagar said.

They went on, with poor Yisht still shivering. Haagar went on carefully selecting the galleries which would form their route until they came to a natural grotto which must have been used by the ancient miners as either a store or somewhere to pile up the ore before it was taken outside the mine. And yet there was something different there.

"Be very careful," Haagar whispered. "I don't think we're alone."

One by one, in absolute silence and pressed against the wall all the time, they crossed the open space toward the right. On the other side, barely a few meters from them, there was someone. Dozens, perhaps hundreds of creatures were moving their heads rapidly from side to side. There was no doubt that they were Yokais.

And yet none of those creatures seemed particularly troubled by their presence. All they could hear were a few slight growls and shrill moans which were far from threatening. As they went on Emily realized the truth: *they're the female Yokai with their cubs*! she thought.

She imagined that although they were following their progress curiously they did not feel threatened by them and hence were letting them pass. If the males had been there, the situation might have been different.

They crossed this natural cavern and went on their way, following Haagar's indications. Although he had never been this way, he seemed to be able to orient himself there reasonably well. The temperature went down again as they went on.

"We're near the outside," he said.

"How can you tell?" Rakesh asked.

"The air's less stale here."

It was not long before they found a way out. Outside, though there was no trace of light, they felt snow and heard the blizzard which they suspected would make the rest of their journey even more difficult.

"We'll spend the night here," Haagar announced.

"What?" Ferrara said in surprise. "Here? Aren't we too near the Yokai?"

"Yes, but I don't suppose they'll come near with this storm."

"It doesn't look as if we have much choice," said Emily.

"Do you know where we are, at least?" Rakesh asked.

"I'm not sure. We'll have to find out tomorrow, once there's some light and the storm dies down. It's too dangerous to go out now."

They improvised a small camp in a corner of the gallery, near the exit but sheltered from the cold outside. Robert arranged the mules to form a barrier in case of an attack from the Yokai, while Emily helped Yisht to prepare a bed which was as warm as possible, although the young Keplerian did not seem to be getting much warmer.

"Can we make a fire here?" Emily asked.

"It wouldn't be very advisable," said Haagar. "The stalkers have a pretty sensitive sense of smell. The fire would disturb them, and in no time we'd have a little welcome committee here."

"I see. That's out, then."

Haagar offered Yisht some dried meat and she shared what little bread she had left with him. They all ate almost without exchanging a word. Over and above the cold and the tension of that intense day, exhaustion had begun to take its toll. Even though she was wearing her suit, Emily realized that she was worn out. Hence, after covering themselves as best they could with all the blankets the mules were carrying, they huddled together to stop the cold from getting into their bodies and got ready to sleep. And although Haagar promised to be alert, Ada took charge of waking them up if she detected any unexpected sound or movement.

32
The snow-covered pass

November 5, Year 0
On the way to the Gaal-El village, Kepler-442b

Emily spent the night in an uncomfortable half-sleep. Though she was very tired, the tension of the moment and the whistling of the wind outside made her wake up every now and then. When she opened her eyes that morning, only Haagar was awake.

"Good morning," she greeted the Keplerian.

"Good morning. Did you manage to sleep at all?"

"Off and on. Any signs of the Yokai?"

"I'd say they went back to the rest of their brood a couple of hours ago," he told her in a whisper. "Since then there's been less activity."

Once they were all awake they had a light breakfast. Very soon they would have to get going. The first rays of light were already coming in through the way out of the labyrinth and everything outside seemed to be calm.

"How far is it from here to the Gaal-El village?" Rakesh asked Haagar.

"I'm not sure. This exit isn't the usual one. I need to find my bearings when I go outside, but I'd say we're too high up. You're starting to notice the lack of air."

Emily checked the altimeter in her suit: four thousand and eighty-two meters. She did not mention it because she understood that this was a piece of information which would not interest Haagar. After all, without any kind of instrument at his disposal, it was clear that he was guided by his instincts.

"Right then, on we go again," he said once they were all ready.

Outside they found a cloudy day. A beautiful white cloak covered the sloping surface in front of them. The terrain was rather irregular, and they were worried about walking on without knowing what was under the snow.

One misstep and they would roll hundreds of meters down the mountainside.

Haagar looked around in all directions, then up. He also leaned out carefully to see what was below. Luckily there was no mist and they could make out the tiny trees many meters further down.

"We have to go back," he said, and pointed. "We should've come out by that area down below."

He searched in his bag, took out a pair of snowshoes made of wood and cord and put one on each foot.

"I understand you haven't brought snowshoes with you, right?"

"No, we don't have any," Emily said.

His voice turned to a grumble. "All right then, in that case it'll mean slow progress. I'll go ahead to check the terrain."

They walked on very warily, with some difficulty. Every time they took a step they had no idea how deep their feet were going to sink.

Robert led the way with short, careful steps. "Step where I step," he called.

After a while Haagar came back.

"I think I know exactly the point we need to go on from," he explained to Robert. "We need to go down to that little hillock over there, then turn to the other side to go on to the snowy pass of Dipyaa."

Robert nodded. "Right."

The way down soon became long and arduous. There were moments when they sank as far as their hips, which made it difficult to make any progress, even though Robert was opening up a small path for them with his body. Emily was very worried about Yisht. She had not stopped shivering since they had left the cave. She could see that despite the quantity of clothes she was wearing, the cold still had its grip on her body. She gave her one of the silver thermal blankets they were carrying on the mule to see whether they would help her retain some warmth.

"Do you feel all right?" she asked with some concern.

"I'm very cold," Yisht said, still shivering, "But I'm all right. We have to go on."

It took them longer than they had anticipated to reach the hillock where they had to change direction. The terrain was irregular, and if they failed to take great care they might even cause an avalanche which would mean an abrupt end to their progress. The two mules brought up the rear. At least they were not affected by the cold and snow. They went on at their own pace, analyzing every step they took and securing their footing thanks to their thousands of sensors.

At last they reached the point where Haagar had originally planned to come out of that labyrinth of galleries which made up the mines.

"From here, in normal conditions, we'd be four hours from the Gaal-

El village," he announced. "But at the pace we're managing it'll take us more than double that."

Emily calculated. "That would mean we'll get there when it's almost nightfall."

Halfway through the morning they stopped in a gully in the mountain, where they found some shelter and where luckily there was no snow. They needed to get their strength back and have something to eat. Yisht was able to get a little warmth back, but Emily realized that she was very weak. She turned to Haagar.

"Can we make a fire here?"

"What with?" he asked. "There's no wood for kilometers, and even if there were it'd be green and wet."

"We don't need wood. I'm asking whether it's safe to light a fire."

The hermit shrugged. "Yes, it's safe. I don't suppose any of the Khaavahki you're trying to avoid will be keeping an eye on the mountains."

Emily rummaged through the equipment they were carrying in one of the mules. After a few moments she opened a waterproof bag and took out a rectangular block which looked like compressed wood, fifty centimeters or so across. She separated a few strips from this and arranged them on the ground to make a small pyramid. Then she separated a final strip and broke it in two. At the two newly-snapped ends there appeared two flames of orange fire. Haagar almost fell back from the shock.

"By my grandfather's horns! How did you do that?"

Emily burst out laughing at his reaction. "This is human technology. These strips have a high calorific content. A fire like this can give heat for an hour. Inside there's a bar made of a pyrophoric compound which bursts into flame spontaneously when it comes into contact with the oxygen in the air."

She placed the two strips she had just split, which were now giving out a generous flame, under the pyramid she had just made on the ground with the remaining strips. In a few seconds they had a fire which was giving out a pleasant warmth.

"Young lady," Haagar said, "I have to acknowledge that very few things surprise this old Keplerian by now, but this human technology for making fire has managed to."

Emily took the waterproof bag and offered it to him.

"Keep it. You can use it as wood, or to light real wood by breaking a strip in the middle. I know it's not a fair payment for the risks you've had to take, but take it as a goodwill gift."

"Oh!" he said, sounding a little uncomfortable. "I… I didn't mean… But thank you. Thank you very much. It's a great gift."

At last Yisht seemed to be feeling a little warmer. She sat down with her feet and hands close to the improvised fire.

"Thank you, Emily," she said. "I'm getting warmer now."

"What are you hoping to find from the Gaal-El?" Haagar nerved himself to ask. "If I can ask, of course…"

"Answers," Emily said. "We've lost some of our own people, and they might know what happened to them."

"I'm sorry to hear that. And I'm even sorrier to be pessimistic, but I very much doubt whether you'll get any answers from the Gaal-El. They're no longer the wise, respected people they were years ago. The Keplerians stopped believing in their nonsense long ago. Their leader Waafdiv is just a poor devil who spends his days drowning his sorrows in the bottom of a jug of tree-mead."

"Even if he is, we need to try."

Once Yisht began to give signs that she was feeling better, they went on. Once again Robert took leadership of the group and set the path for the others while Haagar inspected the route a few meters ahead. The two mules brought up the rear, as usual. This time they were able to go a little faster, as coming down to a lower altitude was now allowing them to move through an area with less snow. Even so, the steepness of the terrain made things very difficult.

"We're coming to the Dipyaa pass," Haagar informed them in one of his many comings and goings. "We're going to have to be very careful, it's quite a narrow pass, not suitable for those who suffer from vertigo. And the wind there is usually very strong. I calculate that we'll get there in half an hour."

Emily and the others noticed that the slope of the mountain was becoming steeper and steeper. By the time they reached the Dipyaa pass, what they had on their left was a vertical wall of rock.

"You'd better not look down," Rakesh suggested. He was regretting having looked out over the abyss.

"Or up," Haagar added.

Emily, unable to contain her curiosity, looked up. The snow which had fallen during the previous few days, together with the permanent ice of the area, had created something like the bill of a white cap which jutted out thirty meters above their heads. If any fragment of it were to break off, there would be no escape-route.

"The pass goes on for a kilometer, more or less," Haagar warned them. "Further on it widens a little, but here we have a stretch where we can only go in single file. Be careful where you step, because if one bit of rock were to work loose it might mean the end for us."

He led the way and the others followed in a line: Robert, Yisht, Rakesh, Ferrara, Emily and finally the two mules. The first steps were slow for fear of taking a wrong step. At the same time the wind was blowing strongly, and every now and then an intense gust would give them trouble.

Emily was keeping an eye on the mules, because though they could manage well on almost any kind of terrain, their legs were far enough apart to mean that the narrowness of the pass was a problem for them. Despite this, they seemed to be doing quite well. In fact they themselves had decided to lean the cargo toward the left-hand wall to modify their center of gravity and leave them ready for anything.

They had crossed almost half the pass when they came to a narrow turn which Haagar recommended them to negotiate sideways. He took off his backpack, pressed his back against the stone of the wall and began to walk sideways, stepping with all the care in the world along the small ledge cut into the rock which acted as a path.

Robert, who was carrying nothing but his rifle, let it hang loose to keep his balance better and reached the end with no problem. Yisht was unsure how to manage it. She was carrying a hefty backpack full of blankets and coats. Robert turned back and stretched out his arm to her.

"Give it to me," he said.

Yisht took off the backpack and took a step forward, holding it out to him with her left arm. A few tense moments followed when it seemed that the weight and size of the backpack might unbalance her and make her plunge into the abyss. However, he was able to grab the pack and make room for her to keep going. Emily gave a loud gasp of relief when she saw that Yisht had passed that narrow stretch safely.

Rakesh, whose tension was obvious, began to take small but sure steps. It took him longer than expected because he scarcely dared to look down to avoid losing his balance. Next came Ferrara, and like Robert she simply had to loosen her grip on her rifle to be able to cross safely.

Now came Emily's turn. Like the others, she decided to flatten herself against the wall behind her.

Step by step, she told herself.

First she secured her body with her left foot, then once she had a grip she moved her right foot to join it.

And again, she said to encourage herself.

She realized that she was dragging her feet along the narrow ledge, so to avoid stumbling she decided to raise them a little higher. The suit reacted with precision and in no time at all she found herself on the other side. Now only the mules were left.

The first was the survivor from the Copernicus. Emily saw its legs come together almost on the edge of the cornice, then with small, steady steps it moved on along the edge of the corner. It hesitated a couple of times when it came to what it felt were weaker areas, so here it chose to take one or two longer steps. And although it seemed impossible because of the narrowness of the ledge, it reached the other side.

"Wow," Haagar said, sounding impressed. "This is the second time human technology has surprised me today."

"In that case you should see what vacuum cleaners are capable of," Rakesh joked.

The other mule followed its predecessor's example. Everything was going well, except that in this case the mule did not make a correct assessment of the risk of stepping on particular stretches of the edge. It went on taking small steps until it was unlucky enough to step on an unstable area, losing the support of its front legs when part of the ledge beneath it caved in. And although with a rapid movement it moved its legs together, it could not gain enough traction to avoid the fall.

Haagar was horrified by what he was seeing.

"Run!" he yelled as loudly as he could. "Quick! We've got to get to the other end!"

Shocked into action by the hermit's alert, they broke into a run without really understanding why. The crash as the mule hit the ground dozens of meters below took a while to be heard. But a little later they heard a deep, heavy crack from the impact. The snow which had accumulated on the lower part of the cornice fractured, causing a large block of ice to be undermined and collapse. Other sizeable blocks of snow which it had supported began to fall one after the other, causing a chain reaction which in a very short time reached the jutting ledges above their heads. They all ran as if the devil were after them, not stopping to consider the narrowness of the stretch they were running through.

Emily was unable to turn around or look up until the vertical wall on her left almost vanished completely and became a wider and safer area. A deafening noise hit the narrow corridor they had just passed along. The jutting ledges of ice had fallen on the pass and almost certainly caused part of the rock to collapse with the impact.

"If we hadn't reacted so quickly, we'd be dead now," Rakesh muttered with his heart in his throat.

"I withdraw what I said," Haagar said. "Your gadgets don't impress me that much."

"Yeah, same here," Robert agreed.

"What was on the mule?" Rakesh asked.

Emily was still getting her breath back. "Food, water, oxygen…"

"So what are we going to do now?" he asked uneasily.

"We've got some of all that on the other one. Except that I'm afraid it won't be enough for the journey back."

"Well, I'd say there's no way back through here," Ferrara said. "We'll have to find some other way of getting back to the base."

"We'll worry about that later," Robert said. "We'd better get moving. I don't want to be here if there's another avalanche."

They followed the route Haagar was leading them by. Luckily, by now they seemed to have left all the dangerous points of the journey behind.

"From now on it'll all be downhill," he said reassuringly.

"That's exactly what scares me most," said Rakesh.

Very soon the snow became thinner until it had almost disappeared completely. Once again they went into a wooded area and even found a small path which according to Haagar led to the Gaal-El village.

They reached it from the west. It was much smaller than Wiikhaadiiz ofiz and was in a worse condition. On all sides they saw ancient wooden houses abandoned and destroyed by the passage of time. The avenues were choked with undergrowth. It was obviously somewhere which had known better times.

The sun was giving its last rays of light, and in the dense vegetation of this forest the light began to grow dimmer. In addition the village was hemmed in by huge stone cliffs, which made everything even darker.

In the avenues they did not see a single soul, so that it looked like a ghost town. Barely so much as an old Keplerian resting in the porch of his rickety home, smoking and making the most of the last bright minutes of the day.

"Wow," Ferrara said, "this place looks as if it's in real decay."

"The population of the Gaal-El has shrunk drastically over the last few hundred years," Haagar explained. "There are barely any priests left, and the younger inhabitants are drawn away by the other, more developed villages. Here they're doomed to poverty. I don't think there are more than a thousand inhabitants, and I'm pretty sure most of them are old."

They walked along avenues of majestic trees which must have been thousands of Keplerian years old. Emily felt sure that at another time this place must have been worth seeing. Now, on the other hand, everything was derelict and overgrown with vegetation, which made it hard to build new structures to replace the old ones, which were falling to pieces.

"I don't understand how they can live in these conditions," Ferrara said.

Haagar shook his head. "Most of them have never known anything else."

They came to a crossroads. To judge by the height of the trees, the more cared-for look of the houses and the absence of vegetation, this must be the heart of the village. It was a very long way from offering the good impression Yisht's village had given them the first time they had seen it, and though the wooden buildings were better-kept, and they could even see a couple several floors high, made of stone, they could not be compared with those of Wiikhaadiiz ofiz.

A youngish Keplerian wearing a tattered gray robe came over to them. He seemed rather nervous and uneasy

"Greetings, foreigners," he said. "My name is Liikmi, and I have been sent by the high priest Waafdiv."

"Greetings, Liikmi. My name is Dr. Emily Rhodes, and these are my companions, Lieutenant Robert Beaufort, Private Ferrara and Dr. Rakesh Kumar. And these are our friends Yisht and Haagar."

The young Keplerian greeted them with a nod and led them to one of the buildings nearby, one that seemed to be in relatively good condition even though it was made of wood. In the small stone fireplace inside, the flames of a generous fire crackled cheerfully. A few tables and a small wooden counter made it plain that this had been some kind of inn in another time. But like the rest of the village, its appearance suggested that it had known better times. Now, without the customers to be expected in a busy place, it had fallen into abandon. Perhaps even its former owners had grown old and passed on to a better life.

"The high priest has ordered me to accommodate you in the village so that you can spend the night here and rest. I would imagine that your journey must have been a long and hard one."

"It certainly has," Emily replied. "Thank you."

"Are you hungry? I can bring you something to eat, if you so wish."

Emily looked at Yisht, in whose eyes she could see gratitude for the offer.

"Yes, please, but only for these two. And I think they'd be grateful for something hot."

"Of course. Please wait here, I'll be back shortly."

He left the cabin and crossed the avenue in the direction of another building. Yisht took off her backpack and went to the fireside to get warm. Haagar, Ferrara and Rakesh, exhausted, sat down at one of the tables.

"Do you think this place is safe?" Emily asked Robert.

"I haven't seen any military presence. And as Haagar says, the population is very old. I don't suppose we'll have any problems here. Were you expecting something like this?"

She shook her head. "Not really. Yisht's village is impressive compared to this. It looks like the ruins of an ancient civilization. We'll see what happens tomorrow."

Liikmi came back together with a girl wearing a gray dress. Between the two of them they were carrying a small cauldron and a couple of wooden plates, two spoons and two large jars of drink.

"We didn't know whether you wanted only water to drink," Liikmi said, "so we've also brought a jug with the fermented sap of some of the trees of this area. It's from the cellar of the high priest himself."

Haagar was grateful to have something to drink after two days of travel, and Yisht, who declined the fermented drink, very nearly gulped down generous helpings of the stew the Keplerian girl had given them.

"I have to admit, this high priest knows what he's doing," Haagar said, very pleased with his jugful.

"I think I've eaten too quickly," Yisht muttered. She had put her hands to her stomach now that she had finished her plateful.

The Keplerian girl cleared the table and left them with Liikmi.

"If you like," he said, "I can take you to the rooms where you're to spend the night."

Rakesh nodded. "All right, it feels like time to go to bed."

They went up a wooden staircase to the upper floor, where he opened a couple of locked doors with a huge metal key and invited them to go in. He pointed to either side.

"This one for the gentlemen, and this one for the ladies."

His eyes opened wide when he saw the mule climbing the stairs and going into the room which had been set aside for Emily, Yisht and Ferrara.

Emily smiled at his expression. "Don't worry, it's a female, and it's coming with us."

"There are several beds here," he said. "Tomorrow I'll come and fetch you as soon as the first rays of sunlight appear in the sky. And then we'll go up to the monastery, where the high priest is expecting you."

"Thank you, Liikmi," Yisht said.

The young man gave a slight bow, and they heard him go downstairs and close the door of the building after him.

"Will you all be all right?" Robert asked. "We could all sleep together, it's all the same to us if we have to use the floor."

"It's fine," Emily said. "I'd rather give Yisht some privacy for one night."

"Okay, then. Ferrara's arranged a drone to keep watch on the area and Ada will warn us. And if there's any problem, we have the radio."

"Oh yes, and you can take the mule. I don't need oxygen, and Ferrara can charge her battery and her tank tomorrow while we go up to the monastery."

"Okay."

She came closer to him. "It's a shame we can't take our suits off. Even if it was just for a moment."

Robert put his arms around her, and although it was a very pleasant sensation it was very far from feeling like a real embrace.

"True," he said. "It's a real shame."

33
The cult of the Gaal-El

November 6, Year 0
Gaal-El village, Kepler-442b

She was more tired than ever, but even so she could hear Yisht muttering in her dreams all night, having constant nightmares and waking uneasily from time to time. That, added to Ferrara's snoring and the discomfort of the suit, made her wake up every now and then.

But as soon as the first timid rays of light came in through the small window of the room they were sharing, she heard the creaking of the wooden floor in the next room. She knew that one or other of the men must be awake now and that it was time to get up.

"Yisht?" she called.

"Good morning," came the reply.

"Were you able to get some rest?"

"I think so. Although I had a lot of nightmares."

"Do Keplerians dream too?"

"Yes, but not always of nice things, I'm afraid."

"We have a lot of things in common. Since I've been here I keep realizing that both our species are quite like each other. We might not look very much alike physically, but the ways our bodies work are similar, and so are our societies."

Yisht shrugged. "Yes, it's curious."

"It makes you think."

"What do you mean?"

"That despite the fact that we have technology that's advanced enough to let us cross the universe from one end to the other," Emily explained, "we human beings, I guess just like the Keplerians, know very little about our origins. In ancient times we had cults like that of the Gaal-El, and in them we fantasized that either one or several gods had created Earth and human beings. Many of those creeds fell into oblivion, but later on others emerged, though it's still true that we don't know our own past.

"There were even pseudo-religions which held that humans had really been created or modified by other intelligent beings from another planet to populate ours, but in the end they were dismissed as superstitions. I've never believed any of that sort of thing, I suppose I've always preferred to believe we're all the result of a marvelous coincidence of genetic mutations and constant evolution which have made us as we really are.

"But ever since we came here and got to know your civilization, I'll admit that I'm beginning to have doubts about whether there really is some superior race that's been experimenting with us in different places."

"Do you think the gods the Gaal-El pray to created humans too?" Yisht asked in disbelief.

"It sounds like total madness. But by this point nothing would surprise me."

Ferrara was still snoring placidly on the floor. They woke her up, and all three went downstairs, where the rest of the team was waiting for them.

"Good morning!" Emily said. "Did you both sleep well?"

"I did," Rakesh said. "I was so tired I didn't even notice how uncomfortable this suit is to sleep in."

Liikmi appeared suddenly in the cabin. He was carrying a tray of fruit, dried meat and something which resembled cheese. He greeted them courteously.

"Good morning. I brought this for your breakfast."

"Thank you, Liikmi," Yisht said.

"Is there anything I can do… well, for you?" he asked the four humans.

"No, thank you," Emily said. "We have our own food."

He nodded, and hesitated for a moment over whether to stay there waiting for them to have their breakfast, but in the end went out and left them to themselves.

"He seems very kind," Robert said.

Yisht nodded, "Yes, all the Gaal-El are like that."

Emily's attention had been caught by the fruit of various sizes and colors which the high priest's assistant had left in a small basket. "Actually, that Keplerian fruit looks really good."

"Anything looks good compared with this damn mash," Ferrara said resignedly as she sucked her breakfast.

Once Haagar and Yisht had finished eating, the ever-attentive Liikmi appeared again and cleared the table.

"Will it be it all right if we leave as soon as I've dealt with all this?" he asked.

Robert nodded. "Whenever you want."

And so the six traveling companions added a seventh to cover the last stage of their trip: the climb to the Gaal-El monastery. The path, which set off from one of the main arteries of the village, was paved and looked both long and steep. From below they could get an idea of how it wound along the mountainside and climbed a couple of kilometers higher along the fifteen or so which separated village from monastery. At first dense trees escorted their progress, but as soon as they turned the first two tight corners, first to the right and then to the left a few meters later, the trees began to disappear.

A small, ancient stone wall bordered the route, and at every corner there was an ancient statue. These seemed to be depictions of leading members of ancient Gaal-El society. Emily supposed they must be the high priest's ancestors, or else respected figures who had contributed to the cause. But most of them were in such a deplorable state that their features could only be made out with difficulty. Even the inscriptions at their feet were illegible thanks to the natural erosion of the stone. The stone wall too had also collapsed here and there. That climb was a faithful reflection of the decadence of what had once been the proud village of the Keplerian leaders.

As they climbed along the paved road, and now with no further impediments in their way, they could contemplate the impressive views revealed by the stony hillside. That day there was not a single cloud in the sky, and the red of the trees was especially intense at that time of year.

"What marvelous views," Yisht murmured.

"Impressive indeed," Rakesh agreed.

After several hours and many bends in both directions, they came to an expanse of stone. At its entrance two huge, much-eroded statues, which had certainly seen better times, welcomed the visitors. On both sides of that flat area a multitude of small stone buildings seemed to act as storehouses and places of worship for the believers. A mere fifty meters away there rose an impressive flight of marble steps, decorated with columns and busts of another plethora of illustrious figures. And at the far end, rising above the stairs, they saw the façade of the monastery at last, carved directly into the rock of the mountain. It rose majestically, despite the years which had passed over it.

On it was a series of columns ornamented with geometric designs and reliefs of animals which seemed to come to life as the sunlight filtered between them. In the upper part was an enormous arch covered with mysterious inscriptions which welcomed them to the imposing temple of the Gaal-El.

There was little activity there, barely a couple of people in their gray robes carrying gardening tools. They went up the stairs, admiring the amazing details of each of the marble busts which escorted them. Somehow the material which had been used to build this place had withstood the passage of time far better than the rest of the village.

"This is magnificent!" Yisht exclaimed.

"And the detail on these busts is exquisite," Rakesh added.

"They represent the ancient high priests of the cult," Liikmi explained proudly. "Unfortunately our people have lost the grandeur of those ancient times, and we find it difficult even to keep what we have here standing."

Once they came to the temple entrance they were able to get a true idea of the size and detail of the monastery façade. The stone was somewhat worn by time, but despite this they could get an idea of the amount of detail in the friezes and images of typical Keplerian life.

"If you come with me, Dr. Emily Rhodes," Liikmi said, "I'll take you to the high priest."

"Of course."

They crossed the threshold of the temple. Emily was awed by the fine detail on the sheet of red metal which covered the two huge wooden doors. In each of them there were five landscapes, one above another, showing the beliefs and customs of the Gaal-El. And though she could not stop to look at them closely, she could at least get an idea of the talent of the artist who had engraved them in that reddish metal.

Inside the temple it was dark, and she had to turn on the infrared vision of her suit to see anything. What she saw left her impressed. What seemed to be the entrance to a temple built by the Keplerians was in reality a cavern, both enormous and impressive, which must have been taken over by the ancestors of the Gaal-El as a temple to pray in.

On the ceiling of the cavern itself there were vividly-colored frescoes, which despite their poor state of conservation gave the impression that in another epoch they might have rivaled those of the Sistine Chapel.

Liikmi asked to be excused for a moment and went to one of the sides of the cavern. There he fetched a small clay jug and filled it with water from a basin. When it was full he came back to where Emily was waiting.

"Follow me this way. The high priest, as is usual, will be at the altar."

She had trouble making anything out further than a few meters away, but she managed to catch a glimpse of a kind of reredos at the front of that cavern which had been converted into a religious temple. There, just as Liikmi had said, was a beautiful altar of solid white marble. Lying on the floor with an empty jug in his hand they found a middle-aged Keplerian dressed in a worn, stained robe. Although had it not been in this deplorable state it might have been as fine and luxurious as that of Khikhya herself.

Without saying a word to the Keplerian, who appeared to be snoring placidly in an impossible position, Liikmi poured the contents of the basin on to his head.

The Keplerian woke up abruptly. "By all the gods!" he yelled. "What's happening?"

"Illustrious one, the foreigners are here."

The high priest gave a start and leapt to his feet.

"Oh! I see now. Why wasn't I informed the moment they arrived?" he asked with feigned indignation. He turned to them. "Welcome to our humble abode," he added, and made a clumsy bow which almost made him trip over.

Emily was not quite sure what to do in this situation. She had already been warned that this Keplerian passed his time drinking. She was beginning to doubt whether he was going to be able to help them with anything, particularly seeing that he could barely stay on his feet.

"Liikmi, tell the other brothers. What kind of welcome are we offering our guests?"

His young assistant sighed, bowed and withdrew to follow the high priest's orders. The leader of the Gaal-El, still only half-awake, seemed to search for something around him. He soon found it on the floor on the far side of the altar. It was an elegant staff of gray wood with a metal pommel, which he picked up and used as a support to keep himself upright. Emily did not even want to imagine how that Keplerian must stink of alcohol.

"Allow me to show you our temple," he began. "It was built using the cave where our ancestors hid from the threat of the Khol. All this you can see now was for centuries the main shelter of the Keplerians in very distant times, far earlier than the Great Revolt. This temple is the only thing we have left which is earlier than that fateful date. In the frescoes above is written the prophecy which gives meaning to our cult.

"The Gaal-El were a proud people. My ancestors were loved and respected by all Keplerians. They led our civilization wisely and with respect for tradition, awaiting the coming of the Keplerian gods who would free us from the tyranny of the Khol.

"However, time went by, and the Keplerians stopped waiting for the ancient prophecies to come true. They became conformists, and in a way lost the hope of freedom. Nowadays the duty of the high priest of the Gaal-El is reduced to keeping memories of that ancient wisdom alive, the echoes of a past era in which the Keplerian people still had hope."

Despite the high priest's obvious lack of dignity and hygiene, quite apart from another set of obvious problems, Emily detected a great melancholy in his way of speaking. He himself was a faithful reflection of the current state of his cult, forgotten by the other Keplerians and without any clear purpose. His only duty was that of preserving a legacy which was falling apart and now ran the risk of dwindling into a mere memory. Who would not feel a great sorrow in his situation? At once she felt an enormous compassion toward that scruffy Keplerian.

"Ever since I entered the order and was selected by my predecessor I have had the honor of preserving the work others built before me. But time has the power of undermining all hope, and one may reach a point where one begins to wonder whether this path really has any meaning.

"When Khikhya visited us a few days ago, I suppose something of that young, cheerful novice awoke inside me. A race of foreigners who had just come to our planet. To tell you the truth it was not really what we were expecting, or at least not what my ancestors passed on to me. But what if in the end our sacred texts were not to be interpreted literally? What if they were only preparing us to make the right decisions when the opportunity presented itself? Wouldn't that be something wonderful, something worth fighting for?"

Emily saw a spark of hope in his eyes which made her heart sink. When she spoke, she chose her words with extreme care.

"I'm sorry to tell you we humans haven't come to help the Keplerian people against the threat of the Khol. In fact we didn't even know of the existence of the Keplerians until we came here."

"Perhaps even you do not know your true destiny. A few days ago I was only a poor drunkard who had given his life away to apathy and despair, and now I find myself talking to a foreigner who in some way might represent what all my ancestors, from the last of them to the first of them all, were waiting for during their whole lives until death took them."

Emily did not want to take away the high priest's hope, but she needed to resolve the doubts which had gone with her on that journey.

"Waafdiv, I'll be honest with you. If we agreed to come all the way here, it was because Khikhya assured us that you have a great deal of knowledge about Keplerian history. Our people set off from our planet in two different ships. Our own arrived safely, but we've found no trace of the other. We need to know whether at any moment in Keplerian history your ancestors came across humans like us."

The Keplerian was thoughtful.

"An event of that kind would have been deeply important to my predecessors," he said confidently. "I'm convinced that something like that would be mentioned in one of the thousands of historical texts we have at our disposal. I'm sorry to tell you that I've never heard anything about the human people, nor about any other people. Apart from the Khol, obviously."

Emily's hopes of finding the fate of the Galileo evaporated like smoke. Her disappointment must have been so obvious that the high priest made an effort to be less definite.

"However, we can always go over the history of our people to see if we can find anything that could help you find your fellow-humans."

"You're very kind," she said, but without much enthusiasm.

"Don't thank me. I'm not seeking to trick you, we have an interest in this as well. I'd also like to show you something of our history to see how you may be able to help us. In fact I'm the one who should be thanking you. You've made me regain hope."

Emily thanked him for his honest kindness. He had said this sincerely, without evasion. She understood the situation this Keplerian found himself in very well. And it was no less true that if humans intended to stay on this planet, then sooner or later they would have to face the Khol. Which meant that perhaps their creeds were not so crazy after all and the true purpose of the humans on this planet was that of saving the Keplerians from their captors, or at least of doing their best to, considering they had no arsenal at their disposal.

"But wait a moment," the high priest said suddenly. "I thought several of your people were going to come with you."

"Oh yes. They have. One of Khikhya's assistants and a Keplerian guide came with us too. They're waiting outside the temple."

"Oh, that wretched Liikmi! What kind of hosts are you going to think we are? Let's go and see them."

Both of them went back to the open area outside the entrance, where the remainder of the group were waiting patiently. Emily saw that Liikmi had gathered together a large group of followers who were waiting patiently beside her friends.

The sun was at its zenith, and on a clear day like this even its light could be troublesome for someone who had just come out of somewhere as dark as the Gaal-El temple. Emily beckoned her friends with a wave and introduced them one by one to the high priest.

Suddenly something attracted his attention, and he turned to stare at something moving behind Robert. Four robot legs appeared behind the lieutenant's back. The high priest's expression changed completely, his dark eyes stared and his mouth twisted into a grimace of astonishment and fear.

He turned to Emily with the expression of one who has had a true epiphany. "By all the gods! You are the ones! You are the gods of copper! You!" He pointed to Emily. "You are the chosen one!"

At once his knees bent to touch the floor and he stretched his arms out toward her in a deep bow. Without stopping to think for a moment Liikmi himself, together with the other followers who had assembled there followed his example and bowed before Emily and her friends.

"What are we missing?" Ferrara whispered at the sight of this surreal situation.

Emily, feeling rather flustered, was not at all sure how they had reached this point. "I think he believes I'm a kind of savior, or something like that."

"So what did you tell him?" Robert asked.

"Nothing. In fact I tried to explain that we're not here because of them."

Ferrara gave her an ironic smile. "Well, that seems to have been a great success."

The cultists began to intone a series of psalms in Emily's honor.

"Hail, Woman of Metal! Savior of the Keplerians!"

The adventure continues in the next book:

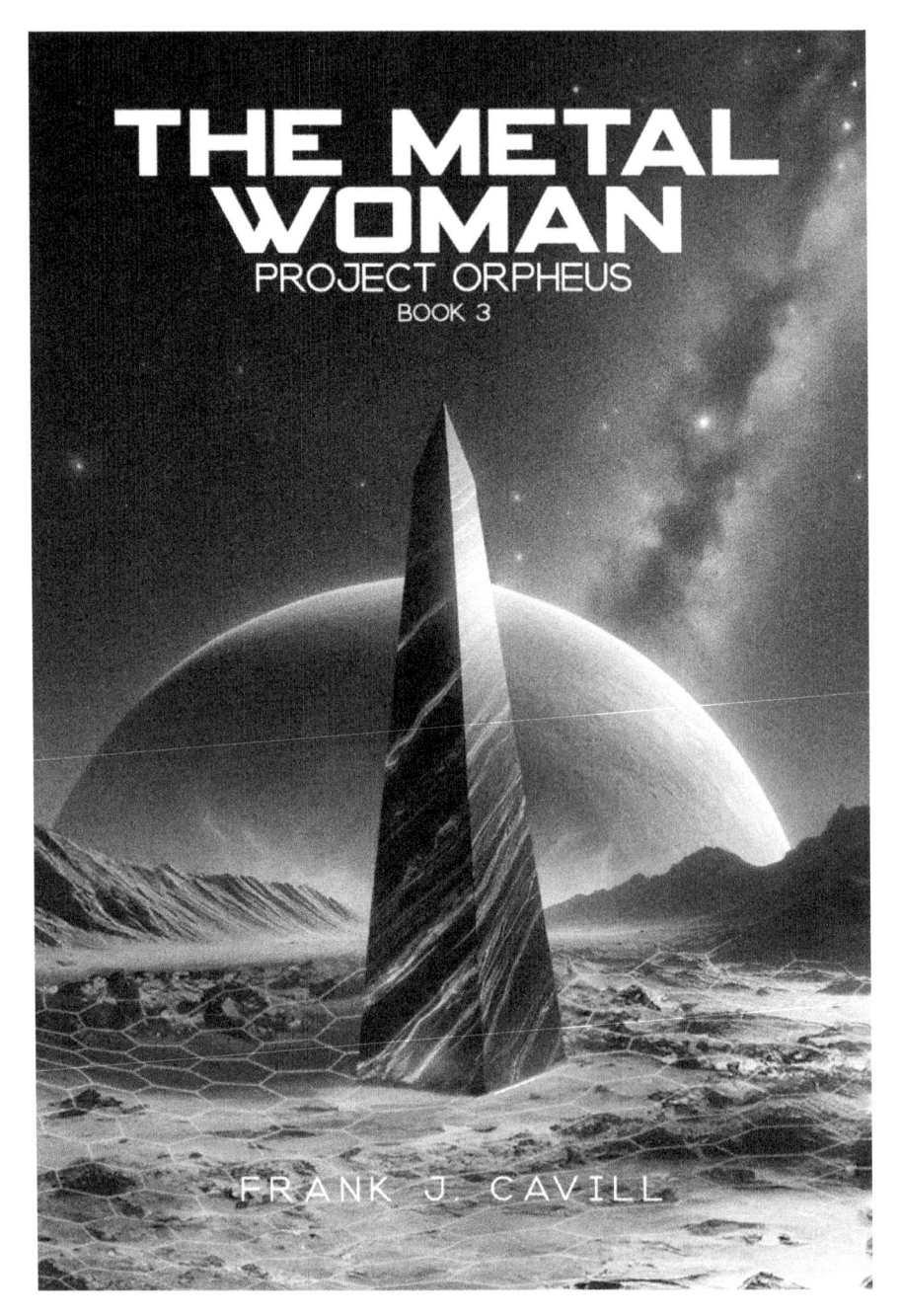

The Metal Woman (Project Orpheus, Book 3)

THE METAL WOMAN
PROJECT ORPHEUS
BOOK 3

FRANK J. CAVILL

Acknowledgements

I would like to thank everyone who made this book possible. It's very hard to condense into a few lines what all the support and good advice I've been given since embarking on this journey have meant to me. And even at the risk of not doing it justice, I'll give it a try:

To my great friend and mentor, Pedro Urvi. You showed me the way and helped me walk it. All of this has been possible thanks to you. A thousand thanks.

To the entire Peterson Publishing team. Especially to Mon, Luis, and Kenneth for pushing me to follow the yellow brick road. None of this would have made sense without you. Many, many thanks.

To Ana C., Miguel G., Andrea E., and Nuria M. for being the best alpha readers anyone could hope for. Your advice, corrections, and ideas have been vital to bringing this project to completion. Thank you so much!

To David C., with whom I embarked on this adventure. None of this would have happened without you. I hope our paths continue to run parallel and that we can enjoy the journey together. See you at the end of the road!

To Susana R. L., if Pedro is the father of this book, you're the mother. Your advice and corrections have allowed me to get this far. I treasure your teachings. I hope to be a worthy student of the best teacher possible. Thank you so much!

To Pilar García, for designing the covers that allow this drop of water to stand out in the ocean. Thanks for everything!

To Tanya, Christy and Peter, for being the guardians of language, the sentinels of perfection. None of this would be the same without your skills. A million thanks!

To Aitor C., for your explanations and ideas on orbital mechanics and astrodynamics. Thanks to you, everything is much more realistic. Truly, thank you!

To my parents, whose efforts made me who I am. I hope you're proud of what I've achieved. Thank you for giving me everything.

To my sisters, for always being there when needed, encouraging my crazy ideas, and supporting me every step of the way. A thousand thanks!

To the rest of my family—nieces, nephews, uncles, cousins, brothers-in-law, and everyone else—thank you so much!

To all my friends, for always being there. A little piece of this novel is yours too. Thank you!

To you, the reader, for choosing my books. I hope you've enjoyed the journey and that you'll join me for the adventures ahead. Once again, I'd like to ask you to leave a positive review so others can enjoy this wonderful world we've created. Thank you from the bottom of my heart.

And finally, to Yuvi, the light that guides my steps, my inspiration. The only person capable of putting up with my nonsense. All this is for you.

Thank you very much, and with warmest regards.

Frank J. Cavill.

Note from the author:

I really hope you enjoyed my book. If you did, I would appreciate it if you could write a quick review. It helps me tremendously as it is one of the main factors readers consider when buying a book. As an Indie author I really need of your support.

Just go to Amazon and enter a review.

Thank you so very much.

Frank J. Cavill

Author

Frank J. Cavill

I would love to hear from you.
You can find me at:

All my books: relinks.me/FrankJCavill
Web: frankjcavill.com
X: @FrankJCavill
Facebook: facebook.com/frankjcavill
Threads: @frankjcavill
Instagram: @frankjcavill
Tiktok: @frankjcavill
Bluesky: @frankjcavill

Mail: frankjcavill@gmail.com

FRANK J. CAVILL

Copyright ©2024 Frank J. Cavill
All rights reserved.

Thank you for reading my books!

See you in:

The Metal Woman (Project Orpheus, Book 3)

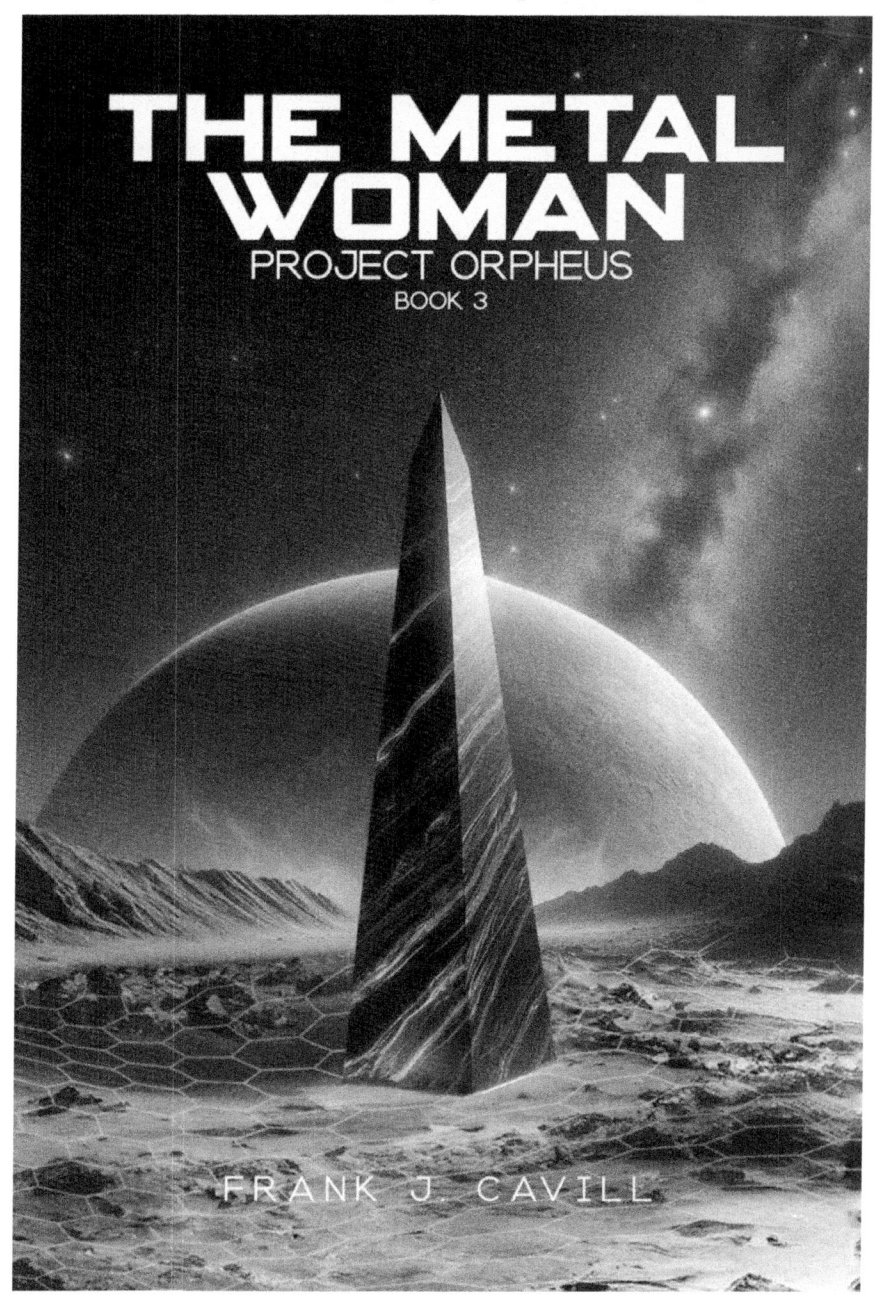

Printed in Great Britain
by Amazon